D1329861

Hope Harbor

Center Point
Large Print

Also by Irene Hannon and available from
Center Point Large Print:

Private Justice series:
   Trapped
   Deceived

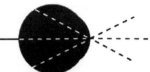

Hope Harbor

IRENE HANNON

CENTER POINT LARGE PRINT
THORNDIKE, MAINE

This Center Point Large Print edition is published in the year 2015 by arrangement with Revell, a division of Baker Publishing Group.

This book is a work of fiction. Names, characters, places, and incidents are the products of the author's imagination or are used fictitiously. Any resemblance to actual events, locales, or persons, living or dead, is coincidental.

The text of this Large Print edition is unabridged. In other aspects, this book may vary from the original edition. Printed in the United States of America on permanent paper. Set in 16-point Times New Roman type.

ISBN: 978-1-62899-654-8

Library of Congress Cataloging-in-Publication Data

Hannon, Irene.
Hope Harbor / Irene Hannon. — Center Point Large Print edition.
pages cm
Summary: "When vacationing nonprofit CEO Michael Hunter accidentally knocks cranberry farmer Tracy Campbell off her bicycle, a friendship blossoms—and soon Tracy recruits him to save a town charity. They make a great team, but they agree romance is not on the agenda. But in Hope Harbor, Oregon, love and hope bloom—and hearts heal"—Provided by publisher.
ISBN 978-1-62899-654-8 (library binding : alk. paper)
1. Farm life—Fiction. 2. Large type books. I. Title.
PS3558.A4793H67 2015b
813'.54—dc23
2015015448

To Margaret and Tony Breslin of Ireland.

Thank you for the generosity, kindness,
and hospitality you've shown to
Tom and me through the years.
Whenever we visit my dad's birthplace,
you make us feel as if we're coming home.
You are cousins extraordinaire!

May God always hold you
in the palm of his hand.

1

Closed until June 13

Michael Hunter stared at the hand-lettered sign on the Gull Motel office, expelled a breath, and raked his fingers through his hair.

Not the welcome he'd been expecting after a mind-numbing thirty-six-hour cross-country drive to the Oregon coast.

And where was he supposed to stay for the next three weeks, until the place opened again?

Reining in the urge to kick the door, he leaned close to the glass and peered into the dim, deserted office. Rattled the rigid knob. Scanned the small, empty parking lot.

The sign hadn't lied. This place was out of commission.

He swiveled toward the marina down the hill, where boats bobbed in the gentle swells. The motel might be a bust, but at least Hope Harbor was as picturesque as promised. Planters overflowing with colorful flowers served as a buffer between the sidewalk and the sloping pile of boulders that led to the water. Across the wide street from the marina, quaint storefronts faced the sea. A white gazebo occupied a small park where the two-block-long, crescent-shaped frontage road dead-ended at a river. More shops lined the next street back, many adorned with bright awnings and flower boxes.

The town was exactly what he'd expected.

But with the only motel closed, it didn't appear he'd be calling it home during his stay in the area.

A prick of anger penetrated his fatigue. Why had the clerk let him book a room if the motel was going to shut down for several weeks? And why hadn't someone corrected the mistake in the thirty days since he'd put down his deposit?

If shoddy business practices like this were indicative of the much-touted laid-back Pacific Northwest lifestyle, the locals could have it—especially since such sloppiness meant he was now going to have to find another place to rest his very weary head.

He reached for the phone on his belt, frowning when his fingers met air. Oh, right. He'd taken it off as he'd rolled out of Chicago two days ago—a very deliberate strategy to make a clean break from work. Wasn't that the point of a leave of absence, after all?

But the cell was close at hand.

Back at his car, he opened the trunk, rooted around in the smaller of his two bags, and pulled it out.

Three messages popped up once he powered on, all from the Gull Motel.

He played the first one back, from a woman

named Madeline who identified herself as the manager.

"Mr. Hunter, I'm afraid we've had an electrical fire and will be closing for about three weeks for repairs. Please call me at your earliest convenience so we can help you find other lodging." She recited her number.

The second and third messages were similar.

So the shutdown had been unexpected, and someone *had* tried to call him.

Slowly he inhaled a lungful of the fresh sea air, forcing the taut muscles in his shoulders to relax. Driving for fifteen hours two days in a row and getting up at the crack of dawn this morning to finish the trip must have done a number on his tolerance. Giving people the benefit of the doubt was much more his style. Besides, he was used to operating on the fly, finding creative solutions to problems. Glitches never phased him. His ability to roll with the punches was one of the things Julie had loved about him.

Julie.

His view of the harbor blurred around the edges, and he clenched his teeth.

Let it go, Hunter. Self-pity won't change a thing. Move on. Get your life back.

It was the same advice he'd been giving himself for months—and he intended to follow it.

As soon as he figured out how.

Fighting off a wave of melancholy, he tapped in

the number the woman had provided, his index finger less than steady on the keypad. For a moment he examined the tremors, then shoved his hand in his pocket. He was tired, that's all. He needed food and sleep, in that order. The sooner the better. Things would seem brighter tomorrow.

They had to.

If this trip didn't help him sort out his life, he was out of options.

While the phone rang, he looked toward the harbor again, past the long jetty on the left and the pair of rocky islands on the right that tamed the turbulent waves and protected the boats in the marina. His gaze skimmed across the placid surface of the sea, moving all the way to the horizon where cobalt water met deep blue sky. From his perch on the hill, the scene appeared to be picture perfect.

But it wasn't. Nothing was. Not up close. That was the illusion of distance. It softened edges, masked flaws, obscured messy detail.

It also changed perspective.

If he was lucky, this trip would do all those things for him—and more.

"Mr. Hunter? This is Madeline King. I've been trying to reach you."

He shifted away from the peaceful panorama and adjusted the phone against his ear. "I've been traveling cross-country and my cell was off.

I'm at the motel now. What can you suggest as an alternative?"

"Unfortunately, there aren't many options in Hope Harbor. But there are a number of very nice places in Coos Bay or Bandon."

As she began to rattle off the names of hotels, he stifled a sigh. He hadn't driven all the way out here to stay in either of those towns. He'd come to spend time in Hope Harbor.

"Isn't there anything closer?"

At his abrupt interruption, the woman stopped speaking. "Um . . . not anything I'd recommend. I could probably find you a B&B that's closer, but those are on the pricey side. Most people book them for a night or two at most, and I believe you intended to stay for several weeks. Plus, B&Bs tend to be geared to couples."

Good point. A cozy inn would only remind him how alone he was.

"Okay . . . why don't you line me up with someplace for a few nights while I decide what I want to do. Bandon would be my preference, since it's closer."

"I'll get right on it."

"Don't rush." He inspected the two-block-long business district, such as it was. "I'm going to wander around town for a while and grab a bite to eat."

"Sounds like a plan. And again, I'm sorry for the inconvenience."

Once they said their good-byes, he grabbed a jacket from the backseat and locked the car. The midday sun was warm, but the breeze was cool —by his standards, anyway. Perhaps a slight nip in the air was normal for Oregon in the third week of May, though.

Stomach growling, he started down the hill. If he weren't famished, he'd head the opposite direction and check out the big, empty beach at the base of the bluffs on the outskirts of town that he'd spotted as he drove in. A walk on the sand past the sea stacks arrayed offshore would be far more enjoyable than wandering along—he glanced at the street sign as he arrived at the bottom of the hill—Dockside Drive.

The two-block waterfront street didn't take long to traverse, and by the time he was halfway down the second block it was clear his food options were limited to a bakery and a bait-and-tackle shop with a sign advertising takeout sandwiches for the fishing crowd.

All the real restaurants must be in the business district, one street removed from the marina.

Just as he was about to retrace his steps, a spicy, appetizing scent wafted his way. He squinted toward the end of the block, where a white truck with a serving window on one side was perched at the edge of the tiny waterside park with the gazebo. Charley's, according to the colorful lettering above the window where a couple of people were giving orders to a guy with a weathered face and long gray hair pulled back in a ponytail.

Another whiff of an enticing aroma set off a loud clamor in his stomach.

Sold. Whatever they were cooking, he was eating.

With a quick change of direction, he stepped off the sidewalk to cross the street.

"Hey! Watch it!"

At the frantic female voice, he swung around . . . and jumped back just in time to avoid a collision with the bicycle heading directly toward him.

The cyclist, however, wasn't as fortunate.

She swerved away from him. Tottered a few more yards. Crashed to the pavement in a tangle of arms, legs, groceries, and wheel spokes.

It took him no more than a few seconds to recover enough to go to her aid, but by then she was already scrambling to her feet.

"Are you okay?"

She glared at him with vivid green eyes, rubbing her hip with one hand and shoving back the golden-brown hair that had escaped from her ponytail with the other.

"I'll live—but next time you might look before you charge into traffic."

"I'm sorry." Lame—but what else could he say? "Let me help you with your bike." He reached for it, but she beat him to it.

"I've got it." She set it on its wheels and gave it a quick once-over.

"If there's any damage, I'll be happy to pay for it."

She lowered the kickstand. "It's in better shape than my groceries." Expression peeved, she surveyed the broken eggs on the pavement, then began gathering up the canned goods that had rolled a few yards away.

While she corralled the wayward tins, he picked up a package of ground beef and a semi-mashed loaf of bread. He also retrieved a crinkled white bakery bag. Through the gap in the top he spied a crushed cinnamon roll.

An instant later the bag was snatched from his grasp. "I can take it from here." She held out her hand for the bread and meat too.

His stomach bottomed out at the blood oozing from a nasty scrape on the fleshy part of her palm, below her thumb. "You're hurt."

She gave the abrasion a quick inspection as she plucked the meat and bread from his grasp. "It's not bad. I'll deal with it after I get home." She turned her back and continued to repack her plastic grocery bags.

"Look . . . let me replace the damaged food at least."

"Don't worry about it." She tucked the bags into the baskets on either side of her back fender and swung one long, jeans-clad leg over the bar on the bike. "Just look before you leap next time, okay?"

With that, she pushed off, did a U-turn, and pedaled back down the street.

Michael followed her progress until she disappeared around the corner, then shoved his hands into his pockets.

What else could go wrong today?

Appetite evaporating, he detoured to one of the benches spaced along the waterfront. Nice of the town to provide a spot for residents and visitors to chill out and let their cares melt away.

Except his didn't.

Instead, the familiar emptiness and dark despair that had been his steady companions for the past eighteen months crept over him, casting a pall nothing could overcome—not the bright sunlight, not the two thousand miles he'd put between himself and his memories, not the upbeat name of this town that had beckoned him, holding out the promise of a better tomorrow.

Hope Harbor?

He rested his elbows on his knees and dropped his head in his hands, snuffing out the idyllic view.

As far as he was concerned, whoever named this place had goofed.

Anna Williams handed her money to Charley Lopez as he passed her order through the window of the food truck, then sniffed the to-go bag. "Smells delicious. What's the secret ingredient today?"

Charley's smile revealed two rows of gleaming white teeth in his latte-colored face. "Nothing special. A fish taco is a fish taco."

"Not when you make them. What kind of fish did you use?"

"You planning to give me some competition?"

She snorted. "I'm sixty-nine. My professional cooking days are over."

He rested his elbows on the counter, looked left and right, and lowered his voice. "Halibut—with a touch of cilantro. The rest"—he winked and snapped his fingers—"is magic." Leaning sideways, he snagged another parchment-wrapped bundle and held it out to her. "Would you mind giving this to that guy on the bench as you pass? He seems like he could use a pick-me-up."

Anna shifted sideways. The man's back was to her, but it didn't take Oprah-level empathy to recognize his posture of defeat. "Any idea who he is or what's wrong?"

"Not a clue."

Nor would their local taco expert attempt to find out. The man didn't miss a thing that went on in town, yet he never asked questions. Never gossiped. Never passed judgment.

Maybe that's why they got along.

"I guess I could give it to him." She took the extra order. "You want me to pass along a message too?"

"Yeah." Charley grabbed a slip of paper, scribbled a few words, and folded it in half. Resting an elbow on the counter, he leaned across and tucked it in a fold of the parchment paper. "I'd take the tacos over myself, but I've got more customers on the way." He gestured behind her as several guys in hard hats crossed the street, heading their way. "That repaving on 101 might be annoying for drivers, but it's been a boon for my business."

"Will you be cooking tomorrow?" Anna eased away from the window as the road crew approached.

"Depends on the weather and the catch of the day and my mood." Flashing her one more grin, he turned to greet the new arrivals.

Juggling her bag and the extra order of fish tacos, Anna started toward the man on the bench. Only Charley could have persuaded her to approach a stranger. Why, she hardly talked to people she'd known most of her life. What was the point? No one cared about you except family, and once they were gone . . . well, it was best to make your peace with being alone.

Her step faltered, and she pivoted back toward the food truck. There was a line now, and Charley was bustling around inside. If he wasn't so busy, she'd march back there and tell him to deliver his own freebie.

On the other hand, he'd never asked a favor of her before—and it was hard to fault a kind gesture.

Resigned, she continued toward the bench, giving the man a once-over. He was still sitting with his head in his hands, a few flecks of silver glinting in his dark brown hair. Not one of the vagrants who occasionally passed through town, though. His jeans might be worn enough to put him in that category, but his shoes were polished leather. She shook her head. The way people dressed these days. This guy could be a yuppie—or whatever they called those upwardly mobile younger folks who liked to defy convention and do things their way. For all she knew, he was some Silicon Valley start-up executive who'd taken a road trip up the coast to bemoan the loss of a million-dollar deal.

No reason to feel sorry for someone like that.

Straightening her shoulders, she cleared her throat to get his attention. "Excuse me."

The man didn't respond.

"Sir? Excuse me."

At her more forceful tone, he lowered his hands and twisted around to face her.

Instantly the air whooshed out of her lungs.

Was that . . . ?

She dropped the extra order of tacos on the

seat of the bench and groped for the back to steady herself.

"Ma'am?" The man rose, concern creasing his brow. "Are you all right? Would you like to sit down?"

She focused on his eyes. Blue, not brown.

It wasn't John.

Of course it wasn't.

John hadn't set foot in this town for almost twenty years—nor was he likely to ever again.

But if, by chance, their paths ever did cross, she'd recognize him, thanks to today's wired world. And except for the eyes, this stranger could be his double. Same color hair, same build, same mid- to late-thirties age, same six-foot-twoish height.

What a bizarre coincidence.

"Ma'am?"

She sucked in a shaky breath. "I'm fine. You just . . . you remind me of someone I haven't seen in quite a while."

"Why don't you sit for a minute?" He picked up the order of tacos she'd dropped, making room on the bench.

Easing back, she started to shake her head. She'd be fine as soon as her heart stopped pounding. There was no reason to linger.

Yet looking at this man . . . The resemblance was uncanny. It would be easy to pretend he *was* John.

A powerful yearning crashed over her, stalling

her lungs again—but she quashed it at once. Wishing wouldn't change a thing. It was too late for such nonsense. What was done was done.

Still . . . what harm could there be in indulging her little fantasy for a few minutes?

"I believe I will." She lowered herself to the bench, perching on the edge.

The man retook his seat and held out the order of tacos.

She waved it aside. "Those are for you. Compliments of the chef." She hooked a thumb toward the food truck.

Surprise flattened his features, and he turned toward Charley, who touched the brim of his Oregon Ducks baseball cap in salute.

"Why?" Her bench partner examined the package.

"He put a message inside . . . there." Anna flicked the corner of the folded piece of paper.

The man removed it, read the words, and sent Charley a speculative look. Then he tucked the small slip of paper in his shirt pocket without offering to share the message.

Despite her curiosity, Anna curbed the urge to ask him about it. Sticking your nose in other people's business only led to trouble.

When the silence lengthened, she opened her bag, pulled out her own parchment-wrapped bundle, and pointed to his. "Go ahead, dive in. Best fish tacos on the West Coast." As long as she was sitting here, why not eat her own while they were hot and fresh instead of lugging them home, as usual?

Besides, eating would give her an excuse to extend their encounter.

Slowly the man unwrapped the paper. "They smell great."

"Charley's got a magic touch."

The man bit into a taco, the tension fading from his features as he chewed. "This is amazing." He wolfed down two while she worked on her first, slowing only as he picked up the last one.

"You must have been hungry." She swiped up a glob of sauce that had dropped onto the parchment in her lap. Why did good things always have to be messy?

"More than I realized. I've been on the road for two and a half very long days and didn't stop too often for food."

"Where are you from?"

"Chicago."

"That *is* a long drive. You just passing through?"

A shadow passed over his face. "I might be now. I'd intended to stay for a few weeks, but the motel is closed. They're trying to line up another place in Bandon or Coos Bay, but Hope Harbor was my destination. It won't be the same if I stay some-where else."

I, I, I. No mention of a wife, though he wore a ring.

Interesting.

"You've been here before?"

His eyes shuttered and he went back to eating. "No."

In the sudden silence, his "back off" message came through loud and clear.

Fine. People had a right to privacy, especially about painful subjects. They didn't need to be poked and prodded and questioned by nosy strangers . . . or by well-meaning friends. And pain radiated from this man's pores—pain that was somehow related to Hope Harbor.

He finished his last taco, wadded up the paper, and tossed it in the small trash receptacle beside the bench. "Thank you for delivering my lunch. I'll stop by and give my compliments to the chef too. If I end up staying around, he's got himself a new . . ." He stopped, pulled his phone off his belt, and checked the screen. "The manager from the Gull Motel. I guess they found me a place to stay. Excuse me."

As he angled away on the seat, Anna finished her second taco and tuned in to his side of the conversation.

"Are you sure there wasn't anything in Bandon? . . . When does it end? . . . But that would mean packing up again Monday . . . Yeah, I suppose." He sighed and dug through his pockets for a pen and paper. "Go ahead and give me the details."

While he took notes, Anna rewrapped her third taco for an evening snack. Madeline must have told him about the antique car rally in Bandon this weekend. The way that annual event had grown, every hotel room was probably booked. Her bench mate was going to end up in Coos Bay—much farther away from Hope Harbor than he'd planned.

Unless . . .

The idea that popped into her mind was so startling—and out of character—she stopped breathing. Where on earth had that preposterous notion come from? Was she crazy? This man was a stranger. He might be a criminal. Or a dead-beat. Or one of those con men who cozied up to unsuspecting seniors, then took advantage of them.

No. Scratch that last item. She'd approached him, not vice versa.

Nevertheless . . . why would she even consider making such an offer?

Because he looks like John.

Her fingers crimped the edges of the package in her lap, the parchment crackling in protest. What a stupid reason to get all Good Samaritanish. Let him stay in Coos Bay and commute. The drive wasn't that . . .

"It appears I have a room." The man slid his phone back onto his belt and stood, his weary smile tinged with a soul-deep fatigue. "I'd better be on my way. Thank you again." He extended his hand.

Say good-bye and good luck, Anna.

Still clutching her taco and the empty bag, she rose. "I live in town. I might be able to offer you a place to stay." Her words came out stilted. Choppy.

His eyes widened slightly and he lowered his hand. "I beg your pardon?"

The man couldn't be any more shocked than she was. That was *not* what she'd intended to say.

Yet for some strange reason, the offer felt right.

And in truth, what harm could there be? It wasn't as if he'd be sharing her living space.

Letting her instincts guide her, she slid her taco into the bag and rolled down the top as she spoke. "I have a small annex on my house, with its own entrance and a kitchenette. I used to rent it to tourists, but they came and went so quickly the whole thing was more trouble than it was worth. If you're planning to stay for an extended time, though, I'd consider letting you use it. It would be far more economical than a motel." She quoted him her old weekly price.

He was still staring at her as if she'd invited him to join her for a rocket ride to the moon. "But . . . you don't even know my name."

As the idea began to take hold, her usual cut-to-the-chase manner returned. "That's easy to fix. I'll start. Anna Williams. I've lived here since I came as a bride more than forty years ago. Worked in the high school kitchen most of my life. These days I cook for Father Murphy and Reverend Baker. Feel free to talk with them if you want references. Their churches are at opposite ends of town, but I expect they're on the golf course today if they're following their usual Thursday after-noon routine. You can also stop in at the police department and talk to the chief. I used to babysit her. And you are?"

"Michael Hunter."

"Are you a wanted man?"

He blinked. "No. I, uh, took a leave of absence from my job in Chicago for . . . personal reasons."

"Nothing related to alcohol or drugs, I hope." She gave him the same stern look she'd used to intimidate the high school boys who tried to pilfer an extra cookie in the lunch line.

"No." A glint of amusement sparked in his eyes, bringing them to life for a fleeting second. "You could have your sheriff check me out too, if you like."

"I may do that." She set her purse and taco on the seat of the bench, pulled out a notebook, and wrote down her address. "You can stop by in a couple of hours if you'd like to see the place. It'll take me that long to put things in order." She ripped out the sheet and handed it to him. "Are you interested? I don't want to waste my afternoon cleaning if you're not."

He studied her, slowly nodding. "Yeah. I think so." He dug around in his pocket and pulled out a business card. "Here's a little more information about me for your sheriff to work with."

She adjusted her glasses as he handed it over. Michael P. Hunter, chief executive officer of St. Joseph Center—"dedicated to dignity, self-sufficiency, and independence," according to the tagline. Must be some sort of Christian-based charitable endeavor that helped get people on their feet and lead productive lives.

Impressive—assuming he was legit.

And her intuition told her he was.

She tucked the card in the pocket of her sweater and stuck out her hand. "It's a pleasure to meet you, Mr. Hunter."

His grip was warm and steady. "Likewise." After a firm squeeze, he tipped his head toward the taco stand. "I'll pay my respects to the chef. See you later this afternoon."

With that, he strolled over to the truck and waited off to the side while Charley finished with a customer.

Anna walked the other direction, pausing at the corner. Charley was leaning on the counter, talking to Michael, and an echo of laughter drifted her way. Huh. The taco-stand owner had managed to inject some humor into her sober bench mate. Well, good for him. The man from Chicago seemed as if he could use a laugh.

Then again, who couldn't?

The two men disappeared from view as she turned the corner . . . along with some of her confidence. For all she knew, the card Michael had given her was a fake. St. Joseph Center might not even exist—though that would be simple to verify on the net. Still—picking a man up off the street . . .

If he was having as many second thoughts as she was, however, he might not bother to show up. And that could be for the best.

But you'll be disappointed.

Snuffing out the annoying little voice that was the bane of her existence, she picked up her pace. Fine. Maybe she did hope he'd follow through—but his resemblance to John had nothing to do with how she felt. The uncanny similarity might have drawn her to him at first, but the emptiness in his eyes had sucked her in. That young man had come here seeking relief from his pain. Searching for answers, perhaps, or resolution, or solutions. Why not help him if she could?

And if fate was kind, he might succeed far better than she had.

Because Hope Harbor had offered her none of those things for twenty long years.

2

Tracy Campbell turned into the drive for Harbor Point Cranberries, wincing as she bounced on the narrow bike seat. Who knew there were so many ruts and grooves on her two-mile route from town . . . or that she'd hit every one? And how could she only have noticed them today, after making this trip thousands of times?

Then again, she'd never been nursing a black and blue hip or a raw palm—all thanks to an oblivious pedestrian who didn't have enough sense to stay out of traffic.

She huffed out a breath and tried to shift her anatomy into a more comfortable position.

Unfortunately, there wasn't one.

At least she'd almost reached her destination.

Keeping one eye on the bumps in the gravel entry road, she surveyed the dike-enclosed cranberry beds on either side, the plants lush with new growth, their pale pink flowers creating a sea of color. Gorgeous. Her favorite season on the farm. Or it would be until fall, when dark red cranberries bobbed to the surface of the flooded beds, creating floating scarlet islands against the brilliant blue sky.

Truth be told, every season here had a beauty all its own.

For you, anyway.

As the stomach-knotting caveat echoed in her mind, she squeezed the handlebars. This wasn't the time to dwell on the past. Not when she was about to share some news with Uncle Bud that had serious ramifications for their future.

She spotted him in the bed closest to the house she'd called home for most of her life. It had been sweet of her uncle and his new wife to invite her to move back after they married, but they hadn't put up too much of a protest after she'd teased them that the small bungalow wasn't big enough for her and a couple of honeymooners. Her small rented guest cottage at the edge of town was fine until she had the funds to build her own place here, on this land that had been worked by three generations of Sheldons.

If the land was still theirs by then.

As the kink in her stomach tightened, she raised a hand in response to her uncle's wave. He walked over to join her while she stood her bike near one of the wild rhododendron bushes that dotted the farm.

"I didn't expect to see you this afternoon—but unexpected pleasures are the best kind." He pulled off his work gloves and gave her a hearty squeeze.

Sucking in a breath, she wiggled free.

"What?" He backed off to scrutinize her. "You don't like your uncle's hugs anymore?"

"I love them—but I had a close encounter with

the pavement after dodging a pedestrian this morning while I was riding my bike home from the grocery store. It left me with assorted colorful souvenirs." She patted her hip and held up her bandaged palm.

A shock of gray-streaked brown hair fell across his forehead as he cocooned her fingers between his work-roughened hands, lines of worry creasing his forehead. "You sure you're okay? You didn't hit your head, did you?"

Tenderness welled up inside her. From the day he and Aunt Carol had taken her in twenty-two years ago, they'd treated her like their own daughter. Her birth parents couldn't have loved her more. "No. I'm fine."

"The other victim anyone we know?"

"Nope. Some guy I'd never seen before. A tourist, probably. And he wasn't a victim. He jumped back after I yelled at him and emerged unscathed—which is more than I can say for my eggs."

"Hmm. I was going to ask if you wanted to help me with an insecticide application, but in light of your injuries, I'll let you off the hook. The fire-worms thank you." He gave her a mock bow, his clear blue irises twinkling. "You going up to the house to see Nancy? I smelled some sweet treat baking at lunch that ought to be cooling by now."

"I might do that . . . but I need to talk to you first."

He gave her a keen look, his weathered face testament to the half century he'd spent tending these beds day in and day out, no matter the whims of Mother Nature. "We're in serious trouble, aren't we?"

At his quiet comment, she squinted at him. "How did you know what the topic was?"

The corners of his mouth lifted, but his eyes were sad. "I've never been a numbers guy, but I read the industry news. I may not know the exact dollar amount of our bottom line on a day-to-day basis—that's your department—but I've seen the trend. The price of cranberries keeps falling, and costs keep going up. It doesn't take Einstein to figure out that's a big problem. More and more family-run cranberry farms like ours are disappearing every year." He tightened his grip on his gloves. "How bad is it?"

She gestured to the dike. "Why don't we sit?"

"That bad, huh?"

"Let's just say I want to indulge my aching hip. Besides, I brought some financial statements. They're in my bike basket."

"We could go to the house if you'd rather."

"No. Let's stay here." She gazed out over the terraced beds, the faint, droning buzz of the pollinating bees as familiar and comforting as the sea stacks off the beach and the smell of fish tacos at Charley's. All constants in her life for as long as she could remember. None of them ever changed.

Too bad other things did.

"Here is fine by me." He took a seat on the dike.

Refocusing on the present, she retrieved the folder and dropped down beside him.

He eyed the stuffed file. "Before you open that, go ahead and give me the bad news straight up. Then we can go into the details."

Typical Uncle Bud, wanting to deal with the hard stuff upfront. He might love this place, but he was a realist. As he'd always told her, sticking your head in the sand to escape problems only worked if you were a sand crab.

"Even with both of us taking on extra part-time work to supplement our income, plus cutting operating costs to the bone, the farm has been losing ground for the past five years. If that trend continues, we'll barely break even this year—and next year we'll be in the red." She rubbed her forehead. "I love this place as much as you do, but I don't know how we can continue to operate on these margins."

"Are you thinking we should sell out to a bigger grower who's all about economies of scale and mechanization?" His tone remained conversational, but his nostrils flared.

She tugged at a renegade runner from one of the plants. "That's one option. But I'd like to keep it as a last resort."

"I won't argue with that. These seventy acres are

my life." He scanned the fields around them. "I can't imagine letting some big, faceless operation take over. Your grandfather and grandmother sweated blood sixty years ago to plant their first eight beds—and the next four weren't any easier. All I ever knew growing up was cranberries. Even as kids, your father and I weeded in the spring and summer and harvested in the fall. You did the same." He shook his head. "It'd be a shame to let that legacy die."

"I agree." She smoothed a finger along the dog-eared edge of the file she'd been working on late into the night for the past few days. "But the numbers don't lie and there's nowhere to cut. We already run a bare-bones operation, and our equipment is getting old."

"Aren't we all. Much as I hate to admit it, the work seems harder with every new growing season." Uncle Bud sighed and surveyed the blossoming beds around them. "You know, maybe we *should* let this place go. I don't want to saddle you with a losing proposition—plus a boatload of debt. You're young and smart and well educated. There's a whole world out there that could offer you an easier, better life."

She shook her head. "I've sampled that world. It might be easier financially, but it's not better. This is where I belong, Uncle Bud. My heart is here. It always has been and it always will be. There has to be a solution."

"I could pick up some more hours at the golf course. They'd be glad to have me, with the shortage of reliable workers around here for groundskeeping work."

"I don't doubt that, but I hate the thought of your already long days getting longer." She yanked at a tenacious dandelion.

"I've never been afraid of hard work, honey. And Nancy was saying the other night that much as she loves me"—he paused to wink—"she misses the gals she worked with at the café. I believe she was hinting that she wouldn't mind going back for two or three shifts a week."

That wouldn't add a whole lot to their coffers . . . but every contribution helped.

She squeezed the weed in her hand, then tossed it aside. "There are a few new businesses in town. I could pay them a visit, see if they need the services of a CPA."

"How much outside income would we have to generate this season to not only break even but build a little cushion?"

She opened the file, did some quick mental calculations, and gave him a number.

"With all of us taking on some extra work, we should be able to hit that, don't you think?"

"Yeah. This year."

"Then let's go with that plan. We can regroup in the fall and decide on next steps. No sense worrying about it all summer. Let's do our best and leave the outcome to God." He rose. "Now you go on up to the house and get yourself a treat. Nancy would love the company."

"Why don't you join us?" She stood too, trying not to wince.

"I may do that—after I take care of a few things out here."

That meant it would be just her and Nancy sharing coffee and dessert. Some chore would distract her uncle, as usual, and he'd end up staying in the beds until dinner.

But perhaps today he also needed some breathing space to absorb her bad news—and try to come to grips with it.

"Okay. I'll see you soon." She gave him a cautious hug.

"You take care of those bumps and scrapes."

"Will do." With a wave, she returned to the road, tucked the file in the basket, and pedaled toward the house.

When she looked back, he was already in the middle of the cranberry plants, bending down to examine a blossom, immersed in the only world he'd ever known. A world they both loved and would do anything to preserve.

But as she guided her bike down the gravel road, she had a sinking feeling that no matter how hard they all worked, they were merely pushing off the inevitable.

The truth was, it would take a miracle to save Harbor Point Cranberries.

And miracles were few and far between.

This was crazy.

Frowning, Michael slowed his car as he turned onto Anna Williams's street.

Why in the world would he consider accepting an offer of housing from a stranger whose references he hadn't bothered to check? Back home, his decision-making routine always included thorough research and analysis.

But Hope Harbor wasn't Chicago. Nor was it the quiet, peaceful destination he'd expected to find at the end of his long journey. Instead, he'd been greeted with an unwelcome surprise at the motel, a near calamity with a bicyclist, a free lunch from a philanthropic taco maker, and a lodging proposition from a stranger.

No wonder he was feeling off balance.

He dug in his shirt pocket for the slip of paper with Anna's street number but pulled out the cryptic message from Charley instead. Easing to the side of the road, he flipped it open with one hand and reread the Bible citation.

Job 14:7–9.

Strange. The man hadn't struck him as the religious type during their chat.

Curiosity piqued, he pulled out his phone. Might be interesting to see what that passage was all about while he dithered over Anna Williams's offer.

Once the chapter opened, he scrolled down and read the verses Charley had called out.

"For a tree there is hope; if it is cut down, it will sprout again, its tender shoots will not cease. Even though its root grow old in the earth and its stump die in the dust, yet at the first whiff of water it sprouts and puts forth branches like a young plant."

Michael skimmed the unfamiliar passage again, his grip tightening on his cell. How had the taco man discerned that a stranger on a bench was nursing a withered heart and spirit?

And how had he known the perfect passage to offer? It was far more uplifting than the oft-quoted verses from Psalms or Matthew that were typically cited when words of consolation or hope were needed.

Weird.

If every day in Hope Harbor was this unnerving, it might be best to move on after all.

He tucked the slip of paper back in his pocket, pulled out the one Anna had given him, and tapped it against the steering wheel. Maybe he ought to chuck this whole thing and head for the place the woman from the Gull Motel had found for him.

No. It would be rude to stand up a kind stranger who'd spent the past couple of hours cleaning.

But he wasn't obliged to rent the place. If he got any more strange vibes, he could—and would—walk away.

Accelerating again, he continued down the street until he spotted the white-frame Cape Cod that matched the address she'd given him, the promised annex on the right side. Roses bloomed beside the columns supporting the small front porch, and the property was surrounded by a weathered picket fence. The street was quiet, and the place was tidy, well maintained, and within walking distance of the harbor.

So far, so good.

He set the parking brake, and as he slid from behind the wheel, a movement inside the front window caught his eye. Anna—or the husband indicated by the wedding ring she'd worn, no doubt wondering what had possessed his wife to recruit a lodger from a park bench. In her spouse's place, he'd certainly be on his guard.

Michael pushed through the gate and arrived at the porch in a few long strides.

Anna answered on the first ring—but only opened the door halfway. "I wasn't sure you'd show."

"I did have a few second thoughts." Candor deserved candor.

"Join the club." She waved a hand toward the side of the house. "I'll meet you by the entrance to the annex. It's in the back." She shut the door in his face. A moment later, the lock clicked.

Huh.

The woman was as cautious as he was about this arrangement.

Some of the tension in his shoulders slackened. If she was wary about *him*—a reasonable reaction by an honest, law-abiding citizen—she wasn't some nutcase. And in this small seaside town where bicyclists injured in accidents didn't threaten to sue and taco makers doled out free food along with a healthy helping of hope, an offer of hospitality from a kind but guarded stranger suddenly didn't seem so odd.

He turned, descended the steps, and circled the house.

At the edge of the annex, he paused. The back of the Cape Cod was as well kept as the front. Grass neatly clipped, a table and solitary chair centered on an uncluttered patio, pruned bushes spaced around the yard.

If the accommodations were as meticulous as the exterior of the house, he might just quash his big-city caution and go for it.

Anna pushed open the sliding door at the back of the house, exited, and met him at the annex. After fitting a key in the lock, she opened the door and waved him in. "Take your time. When you make a decision, knock on the back door."

With that, she retraced her steps and disappeared into the house.

One thing he wouldn't have to worry about if he stayed was a talkative landlady—a strong selling point, since he hadn't come here to meet people or make new friends or socialize.

Snap decisions might not be his usual forte, but once he crossed the threshold of the annex, he was 95 percent certain this was the spot for him. The room was spacious, with a queen-sized bed in the rear separated from a couch and easy chair in the front by a folding screen. To the right was a tiny kitchenette equipped with a fridge, micro-wave, and two-burner stove, along with a café table for two. The cabinets were stocked with more dishes and pots and kitchen utensils than he'd use in two years, let alone two months. The bath had all the basics, and a shower was more his style than a Jacuzzi, anyway. Overall the place was far bigger than any motel room. It was also spotless.

Sold.

He exited, crossed to the sliding glass door that led from the patio to the main house, and knocked.

When Anna pulled the door open, a mouth-watering, warm-from-the-oven scent wafted out, tickling his taste buds.

"I'll take it." Michael pulled his checkbook out of his jacket. "This is much nicer than a motel."

The subtle tension in her features eased. "Okay. Good." She wiped her flour-dusted hands on the towel draped over her shoulder and joined him on the patio. "You can write your check at that table."

Still no invitation to come inside, even though he'd be living on her premises for weeks. Wary as she was, she'd surely had her friend the police chief run some basic information—and knew he wasn't some reprobate. Yet she didn't want him in her house.

Curious.

He moved to the chair, sat, and flipped open the cover of the checkbook. "How much would you like upfront? I'm planning to stay about six weeks, give or take a few days."

"Let's go two weeks out—in case one of us changes our mind."

A sensible suggestion . . . but he doubted any change of heart would be on his end.

"Fair enough." He wrote in the amount, signed the check, and handed it over. "Is it all right if I bring my stuff in before I run to the grocery store?"

"Of course. You can park on the right side of the driveway while you're here. Just leave room for me to get my car in and out of the garage. Oh . . . the rental also includes weekly housecleaning. On Saturday afternoons, unless that day is a problem."

An unexpected bonus. With most longer-term rentals, you were on your own for cleaning.

"Saturday is fine."

She tucked the check in the pocket of her apron. "If you need anything while you're

41

here, knock on the back door. I also left my cell number in the left kitchen drawer in case I'm not home. Otherwise, I'll respect your privacy."

No mention of a husband.

She must be divorced or widowed.

"Thank you."

With a dip of her head, she took a step back. "I hope you have a beneficial stay."

He cocked his head. An interesting choice of word. Most people would have said enjoyable.

Did everyone in this town have some sort of ESP?

"Thanks." He edged toward the side of the house. "I'll let you get back to your baking while I bring my bags in."

She was gone when he returned with his paraphernalia, and he didn't linger outside. Great as those tacos had been, lunch was long past. Stocking up on some basic food supplies and scrambling a few eggs were his priorities tonight.

Eggs.

He pushed through the door, eyes narrowing as an image of the slender woman on the bike flashed through his mind. She'd taken a hard fall. The scrape on her hand had been nasty—and what other less-visible trauma had she suffered? Was she still hurting?

That notion didn't sit well.

Too bad he didn't know who she was. At the very least, a note of apology seemed in order.

He set his two cases beside the bed. Might his landlady be able to identify her from a description? Hope Harbor wasn't all that big—three, four thousand people at the most—and Anna had lived here for decades. Maybe he'd ask her if the opportunity arose.

But when he returned from his shopping expedition an hour later, she was nowhere to be seen—and knocking on her door the very first night might not be wise. If he made a pest of himself, she might throw him out after the two-week test run.

Juggling his grocery sacks, he unlocked the door, nudged it open with his shoulder—and froze. The scent that had wafted out from Anna's house earlier now filled the annex—and it took him no more than a second to spot the source.

A plate of fresh-baked cookies rested in the center of the small café table.

After dumping his groceries on the counter, he made a beeline for the treat . . . but pulled up short when he reached the table. They looked—and smelled—like his favorite soft ginger cookies.

The ones Julie used to bake.

He picked one up, the warmth from the oven seeping into his cold fingers as he took a careful bite and chewed.

No.

These weren't exactly like Julie's. There was a subtle flavor difference.

But the taste was close enough to send a tiny quiver down his spine. It was almost as if his wife were welcoming him to the town she'd loved.

Cookie cooling in his hand, Michael shook his head. Ridiculous. Signs . . . symbols . . . omens . . . they were all mumbo jumbo. A last resort for desperate people seeking reassurance or answers —and he wasn't that desperate.

Yet as he finished the cookie, it was hard to pass off all that had happened today as mere coincidence. Julie certainly wouldn't have. She'd always seen God's hand in everything. Like that day they'd gotten a flat tire in the middle of a torrential downpour during a long-overdue outing to the country for a picnic. To make matters worse, she'd left her cell phone at home and his had died. The icing on the cake? Their spare tire had been low on air.

While he'd griped and grumbled, she'd patted his arm and reassured him it wasn't the end of the world. The rain would stop eventually, and meanwhile, why not turn on the emergency flashers and enjoy their picnic in the car?

She'd finally coaxed him back into a better humor, and as they'd started on dessert, the rain did taper off. A passing motorist stopped to see if they needed help, then called a road service for them.

"This may have been your lucky day." The older man had pocketed his phone as he spoke.

Michael hadn't tried to hide his skepticism. "I can't see how a flat tire qualifies as lucky."

"Well, I don't know where you folks were going, but there's a bad accident about twelve, fourteen miles up the road. Real bad." He grimaced, shaking his head the direction he'd come from. The way they were heading. "Multicar. It looked to me like there were fatalities. If nothing else, the flat kept you out of that traffic snarl—but it might also have kept you out of the accident."

Julie hadn't said a word, but in the silence that fell while they waited for the road service truck to arrive, he'd known she was thanking God for keeping them safe—and praying for those in the accident who hadn't fared as well.

And as he moved to the cabinets in Anna's annex and began putting away his groceries, Michael knew exactly what she'd say to him if she were here now.

"I'm sorry your visit has gotten off to a rough start, but give the place a chance. Everything happens for a reason. Trust in God and go with the flow."

He slid the eggs into the refrigerator, not certain the woman on the bike would agree with that sentiment as she nursed her bruises and scrapes.

But for now, he was going to do his best to chill out, take this visit a day at a time—and give Hope Harbor a chance to live up to its name.

3

As the congregation launched into the refrain of the final song, Michael gave up any pretense of singing and stuck his hymnal in the slot on the pew in front of him.

He didn't belong here.

Just because he'd spotted this small church while exploring the town over the past two days—and just because this was where he'd have been if Julie were with him—didn't mean he should have come alone. Sunday services hadn't been part of his life for the past eighteen months . . . nor had they been on his itinerary for this trip.

The last resounding chords of the organ died away, and he fell in with the crowd exiting the pews. A few people gave him a polite nod and smile, but no one said more than a simple hello. Not a problem. He hadn't come to church today to socialize. Nor, in all honesty, had he come to commune with God. He was only here because this was where Julie would have wanted him to be on his first Sunday in Hope Harbor.

But without her by his side, the experience had been as flat as a glass of soda that had lost its fizz. The songs had been pleasant, the Scripture readings familiar, the sermon well organized and well delivered . . . but he felt emptier now than he had when he'd walked through the door.

Because attending church was supposed to uplift, not depress.

Next Sunday he was sleeping in.

Shuffling along with the crowd, he emerged into a day as gray as his mood. The coy Oregon sun might poke through at any moment and dispel the gloom, as it had yesterday, but nothing would brighten his world.

Spirits plummeting, he stepped out of the line of people waiting to greet the minister and zipped up his windbreaker. Small talk was even lower on his agenda than attending church.

A lot of the congregants were surging toward a table on the lawn, where coffee and donuts were being served, but he'd downed his morning allotment of caffeine while he shaved—and the thought of ingesting a sugar-coated lump of fried dough turned his stomach.

A walk on the beach sounded much more appealing.

As he prepared to make his escape, he glanced toward another table a few feet away from the coffee and bakery treats. The milling congregants blocked most of his view, but it must be the sign-up booth the minister had mentioned for some sort of charitable endeavor the church supported. Smart marketing, to put it close to the free donuts and . . .

The crowd parted for an instant, and he froze as he caught a quick glimpse of wavy, golden-brown hair.

The same color as the bicyclist's.

Could that be her?

Although he leaned sideways to get a better view, the crowd didn't cooperate.

Tucking his hands in the pockets of his jacket, he edged closer. If he was patient, a line of sight would eventually open up.

Less than thirty seconds later, he had the answer to his question.

Yes, it was the same woman.

She looked different today, though, with her hair falling in soft waves around her shoulders, her subtle makeup drawing attention to her large eyes and soft lips, her crisp green blouse and slim khaki slacks flattering her slender figure.

And if he'd had any lingering doubts about her identity, her bandaged hand—not to mention her slight wince when the other woman behind the table bumped her as she leaned across to retrieve some sort of brochure—chased them away.

Maybe his church attendance this morning hadn't been a total loss after all. Now he could issue a better apology than the one he'd offered on the fly in the street on Thursday. Plus, he wouldn't have to bother his reclusive landlady for an ID of the victim. All he had to do was stick around until the crowd thinned, then approach the woman.

While he waited for his opportunity, he leaned against a tree trunk and busied himself with his cell to discourage unwanted conversation.

Ten minutes later, as the churchgoers began to disperse, he made his move.

The woman was alone behind the table now, crouched down as she stowed some material in a box at her feet, most of her body hidden by the "Lend a Hand to Helping Hands" banner that hung in front of the table.

"Excuse me."

Her chin jerked up, and as recognition dawned in her eyes, she tottered. An instant later she plopped onto the ground with a gasp, a flash of pain whipping across her face.

So much for making a better impression the second time around.

"I'm sorry—again. I didn't mean to startle you. I actually came over to apologize for my first faux pas. Let me help you up."

He started to circle the table, but she clambered to her feet and held up her damaged palm. "I think it's safer if you keep your distance."

Given the nature of their encounters to date, he couldn't fault her caution.

"Okay." He returned to his position across the table from her. "But I'd still like to apologize."

"Accepted." She steadied herself on the table, her fingers long and slender as they splayed in a graceful curve. Nice. But her short, unpolished nails were a disconnect. He would have pegged her as the type who went for manicures and—

"Did you need something else?"

At her pointed question, he yanked his focus back to her face. "Um . . . no. I just wish there was some way I could make more concrete amends for Thursday."

She tipped her head, her expression speculative. "Are you a tourist?"

It took him a second to recover from the non sequitur. "Sort of—but on a longer-term basis."

"How long?"

"I plan to be here for a few weeks." Now it was his turn to be curious. "Why?"

"You could volunteer for Helping Hands." She tapped the sign-up sheet on the table. "As you can see, we haven't had a lot of takers."

He skimmed the form. Too bad his mind had wandered while the minister talked about the organization.

"I, uh, don't really know anything about it."

"Then I'll give you our spiel. Helping Hands is an all-volunteer organization that does what the name says—we offer a helping hand to anyone in the community who has a need. You name it, we do it—or we line up someone who can. It's a joint effort between Grace Christian"—she indicated the steepled structure behind him—"and St. Francis on the other side of town. Both churches were doing similar community outreach, so about five years ago they combined resources. Any skill you have, we can use—even on a short-term basis." She picked up the pen and held it out to him. "Can I recruit you?"

He eyed the writing implement. No way. This trip was about searching for answers and finding direction. It was *not* about making a commitment of any kind—especially one that would clutter up his mind with other people's problems.

That's what had gotten him into trouble in the first place.

Before he could formulate a diplomatic refusal, the woman retracted her hand, folded her arms, and skewered him with a shrewd look. "You're trying to think of a polite way to say forget it, aren't you?"

He shifted his weight. "It's just that I don't think I could do a whole lot in the short time I'll be here. Besides, I don't have any talents to offer." He skimmed the sheet on the table, where volunteers had listed their expertise. "I have no skill at plumbing or carpentry or painting, I don't have any medical training, no one would want to eat any meal I cooked . . ." He extended his hands, palms up.

"What do you do for a living?"

The lady was either obtuse or very tenacious.

Based on her intelligent green eyes, his money was on the latter.

He should have kept on walking after church and gone directly to the beach.

"Nothing at the moment. I'm on a leave of absence."

"What *did* you do?"

An ache began to throb in his temples. "Look, I didn't come over here to get the third degree. All I wanted to do was apologize." Irritation sharpened his voice despite his attempt to rein it in.

His annoyance didn't daunt the woman across from him one iota. "You also said you wished there was some way you could make amends for Thursday. I'm offering you one."

"I was thinking more along the lines of replacing your damaged groceries or . . . or taking you out to lunch."

She blinked at him, clearly as surprised by the out-of-the-blue invitation as he was.

Posture stiffening, she bent her head and gathered up the papers on the table. "Neither of those is necessary." As she leaned down to tuck the items in a tote bag at her feet, her hair fell forward, hiding her face.

But her wedding ring was on full display as she gripped the table.

Michael stifled a groan. Great. She probably thought he was trying to pick her up—and a churchgoer like her wouldn't be too enamored with a cad who asked a married woman for a date.

He needed to fix that misperception. Fast.

"For the record, I didn't notice your ring until now. I wouldn't have mentioned lunch if I'd seen it sooner."

Straightening up, she sent him a puzzled look. "What?"

"Your ring." He motioned toward her left hand.

She glanced down. "Oh. No, that wasn't . . ." She stopped. Rubbed her uninjured palm down her slacks. "Listen, I'm sorry I put you on the spot about Helping Hands. The need is great, and we don't have enough volunteers to handle the volume, but you don't even live here. Forget I asked."

As she slung her tote bag over her shoulder and began removing the tape that held the banner to the front of the table, a niggle of guilt tugged at his conscience.

"It's not that I'm unsympathetic." He moved to the opposite end of the table and pulled off some tape too. "It sounds like a very worthwhile endeavor."

"It is. I've been involved for two years as a volunteer, but joining the board last year was eye-opening. Even though Reverend Baker and Father Kevin—Father Murphy—do their best to provide oversight and coordination, they have a lot of other responsibilities and rely on the lay board to handle most of the day-to-day operation. Frankly, with the requests accelerating, I think we're in over our heads. None of us can give the organization more than a few hours a week, and that's not cutting it."

They met at the middle of the table. She removed the last piece of tape, lifted her chin . . . and his heart stammered.

Her green eyes might be troubled, but they were also gorgeous.

Another tug of guilt yanked at his conscience, the source entirely different than the first one. He hadn't traveled two thousand miles to admire another woman, no matter how attractive she was. Nor ask her to lunch. There was no room in his heart for anyone except Julie. Merely *noticing* another woman felt wrong.

Dipping her chin, she retreated a few steps. "If you'll hold your end, I'll roll this up."

"Sure." His response came out scratchy and not quite steady.

He remained where he was, feeding her the banner in silence.

"Thanks." She tapped the edge of the roll against the table, secured it with a rubber band, and turned back to him, leaving a gap between them. "I hope you have a pleasant stay here. Hope Harbor has a lot to offer."

Without giving him a chance to respond . . . or introduce himself . . . or apologize again . . . she did a one-eighty and crossed to the minister. Within seconds they were deep in conversation.

Get out of here, Hunter.

Turning on his heel, he headed the other direction, toward the beach that had already become part of his daily routine. If he was lucky, he'd have the long stretch of sand to himself again today while he strolled, the sea stacks silent sentinels as he stopped to examine an agate or a chunk of driftwood or a piece of kelp. It was a perfect place to relax . . . think . . . clear his mind.

Except this morning he had a feeling his mind would be occupied with thoughts of the nameless woman from the bicycle incident. The nameless *married* woman who would be off-limits even if he was interested in getting to know her better . . . which he wasn't.

It would be best to forget about her. He'd offered an apology, and she'd accepted it. That should be sufficient to put the matter to rest, even if he'd rather make more tangible amends.

You still can—by volunteering for Helping Hands.

Picking up his pace, he ignored the prod from his conscience. Not happening. That was the very kind of thing he'd come out here to avoid.

It doesn't have to be a huge commitment. Helping with one small task for a few hours might alleviate your guilt about the accident— and erase some of the worry from those green eyes.

He started up the hill that led to the bluff overlooking the beach, trying to eradicate that suggestion from his brain.

It refused to budge.

Expelling a breath, he increased his speed. Why had he been born with a conscience that cut him no slack—especially one that always gave him sound guidance? He could ignore it, as he'd done on occasion . . . but that usually left him with regrets.

And he had enough of those to last a lifetime.

The alternative was to do as the woman had asked and pitch in with Helping Hands.

But that didn't feel comfortable, either.

Why not think about it today, sleep on it tonight? Hope Harbor appeared to be a town filled with surprises. Nothing had gone as expected so far. Who knew what tomorrow might hold?

Perhaps even a reprieve from Helping Hands.

Uncle Bud made one final adjustment to the mower and straightened up. "She should be ready to roll. I tuned her up over the weekend. You sure you're up to this?"

Tracy pulled on her baseball cap. With her sore hip, jolting around on the mower over the tops of the dikes wouldn't be her first choice of chores on this Monday morning, but the grass needed cutting and her uncle was a lot faster at insecticide application than she was. Nevertheless, they'd both be hard at it until sundown.

"I'm fine." She pulled a pair of work gloves out of the back pocket of her jeans and tugged them on. "By the way, I talked to the golf course. No problem on the extra hours, starting later this week. And the café was more than happy to put Nancy back on the schedule."

Tracy sent him a dismayed look. "I feel like a slacker. A Helping Hands issue came up on Friday, so I didn't get a chance to contact the new businesses in town about accounting work. I'll give it top priority tomorrow."

Her uncle cocked his head. "Let me guess. Eleanor Cooper ran out of milk or eggs or butter again, then talked your ear off when you delivered whatever she needed."

"What can I say?" She gave him a sheepish shrug. "The woman's eighty-seven and mostly housebound. She gets lonely. And no one else on the volunteer list was available."

"Or willing to give up a chunk of their day."

She dismissed his comment with a wave. "They're all good people. They were just busy."

"You are too." Uncle Bud propped his fists on his lean hips. "You know I admire your commitment to that group, but I also worry you're stretched too thin. Your charitable work and this farm can take over your life if you let them."

"So?" She gave him a teasing nudge with her shoulder. "I can't think of any better way to spend my days."

"I can. Or one that's at least as satisfying."

Uh-oh. She knew where this was heading.

Somehow she managed to hold on to her smile. "You've become quite the romantic since you met Nancy."

"Romance is good for the soul."

She leaned over and gave him a quick peck on the cheek. "It can be—and I'm very happy for you. Nancy's a wonderful woman, and you deserve another chance at love. I, however, am content with my current status. Cross my heart." She drew an *X* on her chest. "So I vote we table this discussion. Besides, I have grass to cut." She climbed onto the mower.

"I know you think you're happy, but—"

She started the engine, shutting him out with a grin.

He narrowed his eyes and crossed his arms. His lips moved, but she couldn't hear a word he said.

Perfect.

Pointing to her ear, she hiked up her shoulders, put the mower in gear, and rumbled away.

When she risked a peek back, Uncle Bud was still watching her—and his determined stance told her this topic would come up again.

Drat.

Keeping one hand on the wheel, she swatted at

an annoying bee. He meant well, of course. Her whole life, he'd always had her best interest at heart. But he was off base with this crusade. Marriage wasn't in her game plan.

Besides, there weren't a whole lot of single men in her age bracket in Hope Harbor, anyway. Even the guy who was responsible for the throbbing bruise on her hip had worn a ring. Odd that he'd been alone both times she'd seen him, though—and he'd always said *I,* not *we,* while discussing his visit and his plans. Plus, he'd asked her out to lunch. None of that jibed with the ring.

Still, what did it matter? On the slim chance he was available, she wasn't interested.

As for that annoying tingle in her nerve endings when she pictured his deep blue eyes, strong jaw, and trim, athletic physique . . . well, any woman would notice—and appreciate—a handsome man. That was normal.

But it would go no further.

Flicking away another troublesome bee, she revved up the engine and started down the first dike.

Uncle Bud might think she deserved a second chance at romance, but he was wrong.

Craig was proof of that.

A tsunami of guilt crashed over her, the harsh memories stealing her breath, the regret and angst more intense than they had been in months.

Clenching the wheel, she gritted her teeth.

Reliving the past was an exercise in futility. She couldn't change what had happened. All she could do was move on—and never forget the painful truth she'd learned from that traumatic experience.

Tracy Sheldon Campbell wasn't wife material.

4

Had his landlady disappeared off the face of the earth?

Empty cookie plate in hand, Michael surveyed the sliding door that led from her house to her patio, the vertical blinds closed tight. In fact, all the blinds and shades in the house were closed. Did she ever let the sunlight in? Or come out to enjoy the well-groomed yard or patio? The small table with the single chair hadn't been occupied once in the four days he'd been here. Nor had he caught so much as a glimpse of Anna Williams.

Yet if the woman was as reclusive as she seemed, why had she offered him a place to stay?

Baffled, he started back toward the annex. Stopped at the sound of an electric garage door opening.

Anna was either coming or going.

Picking up his pace, he circled around to the front of the Cape Cod . . . just in time to watch her car disappear into the garage. The door began to descend almost before her rear bumper cleared the safety beam, closing her into the shuttered house that shouted "keep out."

He juggled the plate in his hands. If he left it on the table in his room with a thank-you note, she'd find it Saturday when she cleaned.

But after wrestling with his conscience most of the night over Helping Hands and finally conceding the battle, he needed the bicyclist's name. He could track down the minister at her church and explain the whole thing—but if Anna knew who she was, that would be a whole lot easier. In view of his hostess's reticence, she wasn't likely to give him the third degree about why he needed that information, as the minister might.

Halfway to the front porch, however, he paused. She'd told him to knock on the back door if he needed to talk with her, and it might be prudent to abide by the rules if he wanted his unofficial lease renewed after his two-week trial period was up.

Altering his route, he circled back to her patio and rapped on the sliding door.

Thirty seconds passed.

Forty-five.

A minute.

Just when he'd decided she was going to ignore him, the slats on the vertical blinds pivoted and slid to the left. Anna stepped into view, flipped the lock, and opened the door a mere twelve inches.

He gave her his friendliest smile. "Sorry to bother you, but I wanted to return this and say thank you. The cookies were great."

She took the plate he held out, lips flat. "Father Murphy is partial to that recipe. I bake him some every week, and I didn't think he'd miss a few." She reached for the door to slide it shut.

No invitation for further conversation.

He might have to ask the minister for the bicyclist's name after all.

"Well, if he does, tell him they went to a worthy cause." He tried once more, ramping his smile up a notch.

Didn't work.

The woman's sour demeanor seemed set in stone.

"He won't notice. Counting cookies isn't—"

A sudden crash from inside the house cut her off.

She swung around, hand still on the door.

In the murky depths behind her, Michael detected a movement on the floor. Peered into the shadows.

"Is that a . . . rabbit?"

She looked down. "Oh, for goodness' sake. I must not have latched the cage properly."

Leaving the door cracked, she crossed to the small, quivering cottontail. But as she approached, it hopped out of her reach.

She tried again, with the same result.

"Why don't we try tag teaming this?" Michael opened the door another few inches, squeezed through, and approached the rabbit from the other side.

The little critter cowered . . . then lunged for the open slider.

Michael dropped down to one knee. "Not so fast, Thumper."

The rabbit veered behind an end table as he grabbed for it, tangling itself in a cord. The lamp on the table rocked, and Michael grasped it with one hand. Somehow he managed to capture the rabbit with the other—but he lost his grip on the fur ball as he lifted it. The lamp steadied, but while he fumbled the squirming rabbit, a framed photo fell off the table. Glass shattered . . . and the little guy wriggled free.

Michael dove after it and finally snagged the nimble creature.

Quiet descended.

After taking a moment to catch his breath, he rose from his prone position, keeping a firm but gentle hold on the bunny. "What this guy lacks in size he makes up for in speed."

Anna moved behind him, closed the door, and reached for the rabbit. He released his hold, and she cradled the quivering mass of fur against her chest. "There, there, you're okay." She stroked the frightened bunny, her voice soft and comforting. "You'll feel much better after you see the treat I got you at the grocery store."

Michael stared at the woman. The stern planes of her face, the hard line of her mouth, her no-nonsense manner were gone, replaced with softness, warmth, and affection.

Was this the woman she'd once been?

And if so, what had happened to steal all the joy and tenderness from her life?

"I appreciate your help." She transferred her attention from the rabbit to him, and while some of the usual aloofness was back in her tone, a touch of warmth lingered. Enough for him to broach the subject of the bicyclist?

"No problem." The rabbit began to squirm again, and he tipped his head toward it. "He might be happier in his cage until he calms down."

"Yes." She hesitated. "I'll be back in a minute."

While she was gone, he straightened the lamp, untangled the cord, and carefully collected the broken glass. Holding the shards in his palm, he picked up the frame, intending to set it back on the table.

Instead, he did a slow blink.

The young man in the photo could have been him twenty years ago.

"He's back in his cage, and I locked the . . ."

As Anna spoke, he turned.

Her gaze dropped from his face to the photo in his hand, and her voice trailed off.

He waited for her to continue. To explain. Surely she'd noticed the uncanny resemblance, would comment on it.

Yet the silence between them lengthened.

At last he set the frame back on the table and held up his handful of broken glass. "Is there somewhere I can get rid of this?"

"The trash can . . . in the kitchen." She twisted her hands in front of her, then angled toward the door behind her, giving him access.

He edged past her, into a clean but dated room with Formica countertops and avocado appliances.

"It's on the right, over there." She led him to a plastic trash can beside the counter.

As he deposited the glass, he took a quick inventory of what had once been a breakfast room. Now it was filled with assorted cages and boxes for birds and animals. In addition to Thumper, who was now watching the proceedings from behind bars, Anna's menagerie included a small bird and a baby raccoon.

All at once, a bright red splotch dropped onto the tile floor by his shoe.

"You must have cut yourself." Anna leaned closer to examine his hand.

Despite his caution, one of the pieces of glass had managed to slice his index finger.

"It's no big deal. A small bandage will take care of it."

"I have plenty of those."

Before he could protest, she opened a floor-to-ceiling cabinet beside him. In addition to peel-and-stick bandages for humans, it contained assorted varieties of birdseed, eye droppers, heavy gloves, rolls of gauze, water bowls of different sizes—everything she'd need to care for injured or abandoned animals.

"You can wash it off in the sink." She motioned behind him.

He did as instructed, drying the cut on a paper towel she provided.

"This is an antibiotic cream." She squeezed some onto a bandage, then secured the sterile covering around his finger. "Sorry you got dragged into this. I've never had an animal escape."

"I hope he didn't do too much damage, other than the broken glass in the picture frame."

She ignored the opening he gave her to talk about the young man in the photo.

"Nothing that mattered. I had some flowers on my hearth, but the vase had no sentimental value. Nothing else broke."

Except the picture frame.

An off-limits topic, it seemed.

"You have quite a collection here." He gestured to the animal hospital.

She shrugged. "It's hard to ignore a creature in need—especially the babies. All of these were abandoned in the woods where I walk every day." She gave each of her three nonhuman tenants a brief glance. "I take them in until they're old enough to survive on their own. I have plenty of room. It's a big house for one person."

"Have you lived here alone for a long time?" Short of asking her directly if she was a widow, he didn't know how else to get that information— or why it mattered. Except he was curious about this taciturn, reserved woman who had let her guard down for a few brief moments with the rabbit. What lay under the aloof façade she presented to the world?

"A lifetime." The words quivered, and she turned away to close the supply cabinet. When she spoke again, her voice had regained its usual no-nonsense timbre. "Almost twenty years, to be more precise. Thank you again for your help with the rabbit."

He was being dismissed—and he hadn't yet broached the subject that had brought him over here in the first place.

"Glad to be of assistance." He walked through the small den to the sliding glass door, where he stopped. Better spit out his question. Who knew when he'd see her again? "I did have another reason for stopping by. I know you've lived in Hope Harbor for decades, and I thought you might be able to give me the name of a woman I need to contact here. I spoke with her after church on Sunday. She volunteers with an organization called Helping Hands."

"I know all about that group—but they have dozens of volunteers. What does she look like?"

He described her. "She also said she was on the board."

"That would have to be Tracy Sheldon . . . no, Campbell now. Most of the other female board members are much older."

"Do you know how I could get in touch with her?"

"She moved into town a couple of years ago, but she spends most of her time out at the farm."

"Farm?"

"Harbor Point Cranberries, about two miles south of town. There's a sign on the highway. It's a family business—for now, anyway." She sent a pointed glance toward the clock on the wall. "I need to make a batch of cookies for Reverend Baker."

No subtleties about this woman—but no need for him to linger, either. He had the information he needed.

"I have things to do too." Like take a drive to a certain cranberry farm. He crossed the threshold but stopped on the other side to flash her a grin. "What kind of cookies does the reverend like?"

Her lips gave a slight twitch, as if they wanted to turn up but had forgotten how. "Pecan chocolate chip—and he doesn't count his cookies, either, if you'd like a few."

"I never say no to cookies."

With a dip of her head, she shut the door, locked it, and closed the vertical blinds, once more insulating herself from the world.

But as Michael returned to his room, pocketed his keys, and grabbed his jacket, he had a feeling her self-imposed isolation had nothing to do with animosity toward her fellow man and everything to do with some deep-seated hurt that had robbed the joy from her world.

And while their lives might be very different in every other respect, that was one thing he and his landlady had in common.

Tracy pulled the mower into its spot in the equipment shed, shut off the motor, and swiped her forehead on the sleeve of her T-shirt. Busy morning. She'd finished the tops of the dikes around all the beds, trimmed the grass growing in the center of the gravel road, and mowed around the equipment sheds and pump houses.

Not bad for four hours' work.

Now came the fun part.

She wrinkled her nose and took a swig from her water bottle.

Swinging the weed eater back and forth on the sides of the dikes might not be on her top-ten list of favorite farm chores, but every bed she and Uncle Bud did themselves saved money—even if they only paid the teenagers they hired from the high school minimum wage.

She stretched, took another guzzle of water, and recapped the bottle. In an hour or so she'd hunt down Uncle Bud and go see what Nancy had on the menu for lunch. First, however, she needed to weed whack.

Picking up the weed eater, she weighed it in her hand. It wasn't all that heavy, and once she got into the swinging rhythm she'd be able to cover a lot of ground—but there was no way to avoid the sore muscles she'd be nursing tomorrow thanks to her first grass gig of the season.

After hoisting the tool over her shoulder, she exited the equipment shed and trekked toward the first bed, letting the soothing drone of the bees and the occasional call of a bird lull her. Could any place on earth be more peaceful?

Or it *was* peaceful until the faint crunch of tires on gravel intruded on the serenity, followed by barks from Shep and Ziggy as they abandoned their bog-rat pursuit to investigate the intruder.

She lifted her hand to shade her eyes against the midday sun. Unless Nancy was expecting a guest no one had mentioned, it was probably some tourist who'd seen their sign, thought Harbor Point Cranberries sounded quaint, and turned in hoping to see bright red berries floating in the bog and a homespun stand selling cranberry products.

Her mouth twitched. This could be entertaining. The surprise on people's faces when they realized the beds were dry most of the year and that this was a working farm with no tourist trappings was always comical.

A dark gray Focus came into view, traveling slowly on the gravel road, and she continued toward it. Better to head the visitors off at the pass.

The two large border collies bounded up beside her, still barking, and the car stopped.

She reached down to give the dogs a pat. Her canine companions might sound and look intimidating, but only critters intent on pillaging the cranberry beds needed to fear them.

She moved closer to the driver's window, stopping a few feet away. Shep and Ziggy would probably come to her defense if she was threatened, but why put that theory to the test?

The window rolled down—and despite the sunglasses that hid his blue eyes, she had no trouble identifying the driver as the man who'd caused her bicycle accident.

Was the guy stalking her or what?

"What are you doing here?" She raised her voice to be heard above the barking dogs.

"Looking for you. I come bearing gifts—consider them a peace offering." He lifted a Styrofoam cup in one hand and a white bakery bag in the other. "Will I be risking life and limb if I get out of the car?" He eyed her yapping bookends.

"Maybe." She squinted at him. "How did you know where to find me?"

"I have my sources. Aren't you curious about what's in here?" He swung the bag back and forth.

"No."

He studied her for a couple of seconds, sized up the dogs, and pushed the car door open.

She took a step back.

The two collies closed in on him, sniffed around, then muzzled their barks and plopped on their haunches while he gave them a pat.

So much for her security shield.

But there was no reason to be nervous. Uncle Bud was within shouting range, and she'd be willing to bet she could outrun this guy in his fancy leather shoes in spite of his longer legs. Besides, she also had a weed eater over her shoulder, and she could give it a pretty lethal swing if she had to.

She lowered the piece of equipment, positioned it in front of her, and gripped it in both hands like a spear.

Twin grooves creasing his forehead, the man set the cup on the hood of his car and removed his dark glasses. "I think I need to apologize again. I didn't mean to scare you."

She lifted her chin. "You didn't." *Liar, liar!* "We just don't get many visitors out here."

"Actually, I'm here in the category of volunteer."

She furrowed her brow. "You want to work on the farm?"

"No. I was talking about Helping Hands. After further consideration, I decided I'd offer my assistance for at least a few hours. Between that and this"—he held up the bag again—"I'm hoping I can finally make amends for last Thursday."

She loosened her grip on the weed eater and lowered it a hair. If the man was serious about volunteering, it would behoove her to be a bit more welcoming.

"Why did you change your mind?" The question came out conversational rather than confrontational. Good.

"It seemed like the right thing to do—not that I have many handy skills. But if you can find one you can use, I'm willing to sign up for a few hours." He held out the bag. "We could talk about it while you eat this."

She lowered the weed eater to the ground, propped it against her hip, and took the peace offering. The dogs nosed in, but she nudged them back with her leg as she peeked in the bag.

A cinnamon roll from Sweet Dreams Bakery— her favorite indulgence.

"A replacement for the one that got crushed on Thursday." He leaned back against his car. "I felt bad about the bread and the eggs too, but destroying your dessert—that definitely needed to be rectified."

No reason to tell him she'd eaten the smashed roll anyway.

"Thanks."

He picked up the cup of coffee and held it out. "In case you want to eat it while we talk about Helping Hands."

Shep and Ziggy wandered back toward the cranberry beds, obviously more interested in chasing four-legged interlopers than listening to a human conversation.

"I don't even know your name."

He transferred the cup to his left hand and extended his right. "Michael Hunter, from Chicago. I'm staying in town with Anna Williams. I understand she cooks for your pastor."

She did a double take.

This guy was staying with Anna Williams?!

"How on earth did you manage that? She hasn't rented out her annex in years."

"I have no idea. I was sitting on a park bench on the wharf, and she joined me. The offer of a place to stay came out of the blue."

Uh-uh. Not computing. The man might have charisma—not to mention a killer smile—but Anna wouldn't be susceptible to either. Nor would she invite a stranger home.

He lowered his hand. "You could call her if you want to check my story."

Warmth crept across her cheeks. Was she that easy to read?

"I don't blame you for being skeptical. I would be too, in your place. Anna's not the most . . .

gregarious person I've ever met. I'll admit I was more than a little suspicious about her offer at first. In hindsight, however, I think it was providential." Once more he offered his hand. "Shall we try again?"

She wiped her palm on her jeans and took it. "Tracy Campbell."

His larger hand swallowed her fingers, his grip firm, warm—and somehow reassuring.

"Is there somewhere we could sit while we talk about Helping Hands?" He glanced around.

"The dike's my usual spot." She gestured to the earthen wall around the nearest bed and inspected his spotless jeans and crisp cotton shirt. "But you're not dressed for sitting on the ground."

"Dirt washes out." Without waiting for her to respond, he walked over to the earthen bank she'd indicated and sat.

Nice to know the man wasn't worried about getting his clothes—or his hands—dirty.

She gave him another discreet perusal as she joined him. He appeared to be in excellent physical condition . . . a perfect candidate to reattach Eleanor Cooper's guttering, which had been on the Helping Hands to-do list way too long. The sag in the front was more pronounced every time she stopped by with some grocery item or prescription the woman needed. It didn't take a lot of skill to tackle a job like that. She'd do it herself if she had a spare minute—and didn't hate ladders.

After dropping down beside him, she opened the bag again. The aroma of cinnamon wafted up, setting off a rumble in her stomach, and she slowly inhaled. Nirvana. She'd ruin her appetite for the lunch Nancy was preparing if she ate the whole thing, but a few bites couldn't hurt.

"I can hold the coffee while you tackle that." Michael inspected the huge cinnamon roll as she pulled it out and set it on the bag. "I hope it's still warm. I had them heat it up."

She tore off a piece. "It is. Would you like to share?" She scooted the bag across her lap, closer to him.

"No thanks. I couldn't resist getting one for myself while I was there . . . and I ate the whole thing. You can keep what you don't finish for later."

She didn't argue. Sweet Dreams cinnamon rolls were a special treat. "Did you have any specific ideas about how you wanted to contribute to Helping Hands?" It might be more polite to give him a chance to offer suggestions before she threw the gutter job at him.

"I can do simple home repairs. Very simple."

Perfect.

She bit into the warm roll, letting the icing dissolve on her tongue. "How do you feel about gutters?"

He cocked his head. "As in . . . ?"

"Reattaching. We have an elderly woman on

our list who could use a hand with the one on the front of her house." She reached for the coffee and took a swig.

"I think I could handle that."

"Good. That will repay in full any debt you think you owe me. And Eleanor Cooper, who owns the sagging gutter, will also be grateful."

She handed back the coffee and tore off another piece of the roll, giving him a surreptitious appraisal. Hmm. Maybe she'd been too hasty in assigning him a job. Michael Hunter came across more as the white-collar type, and they had plenty of need for that kind of help too. If he happened to be an attorney or computer expert, Eleanor's gutters might have to wait.

"You know, you never did tell me what you do for a living. We have people who need professional help too, if that's more your forte."

When he didn't respond, she stopped chewing and looked over at him.

Uh-oh.

His shuttered face told her she'd overstepped —the same reaction she'd gotten after inquiring about his background yesterday. But what was the big deal? It wasn't as if she'd asked him his age or weight . . . or why he was here without his wife.

Better try to lighten the atmosphere. "Whoops. You must have some sort of clandestine job— like CIA operative or undercover FBI agent. Forget I asked."

A few silent seconds passed.

Then he slowly dug into his pocket, extracted a card, and held it out.

After wiping her hands on one of the napkins in the bottom of the bag, she took it and read the information.

Michael Hunter was the CEO of a charitable organization?

Not at all what she'd expected.

And why would he be gun-shy about mentioning such an admirable job?

She fingered the card. There was a story here, and even though his personal history was none of her business, she wanted to know more.

But unless she handled this with a whole lot of delicacy and discretion, she had a feeling the man beside her would be out of here in a heartbeat, taking both his story and his offer of help with him.

5

He should have prepared for this contingency.

As Tracy scanned his card, then sent him a curious look, Michael's gut clenched. She'd asked about his background yesterday; it had been foolish to assume he could preempt further questions by offering to do some simple home repair.

She lifted the card. "Is this anything like Helping Hands?"

Based on her tentative tone and body language, she'd picked up his signals that this wasn't a topic he wanted to discuss in detail. Good. Perhaps a few pertinent facts would suffice.

"Not exactly. We try to help people struggling with a variety of issues—homelessness, addiction, family violence—get their act together and achieve independence. The operating philosophy is based on the old saying that if you give people a fish you feed them for a day, but if you teach them to fish you feed them for a lifetime."

"Sounds very worthwhile." The comment was casual—but her eyes continued to probe.

"It can also be all-consuming."

Whoa!

Where had *that* come from? He was supposed to be sidestepping questions, not generating them.

"I can understand how there could be a high burnout factor in a job like that if you didn't pace yourself." She watched him—and he had a feeling she was seeing a lot more than he wanted to reveal. "Is that why you took a leave of absence?"

Closing his fist over a clump of grass, he stared out over the fields. In addition to her many other assets, the lady had solid instincts. "Partly."

He braced for another query . . . but none came.

Had she finally gotten his butt-out message?

He looked toward her, and she shifted her attention to the cinnamon roll, tearing off another section she played with but didn't eat.

His cryptic reply had accomplished his goal and deflected further queries—but based on her blush, he'd also made her feel like an annoying busybody.

This visit wasn't going anywhere near as well as he'd hoped.

Time for some damage control.

"Look . . . I didn't come to Oregon to talk about my life in Chicago, okay? The whole point was to leave everything behind. But yes, I burned out in my job—and I also lost my wife eighteen months ago."

Her head jerked toward him, her eyes wide and filled with shock.

Michael blinked. He rarely spoke about that heartbreak even with family or friends. Why had he shared it with this stranger?

None of this was making sense.

"I'm so sorry."

At her hushed, caring comment, his emotions swelled—followed at once by a sweeping sense of panic. How had this woman managed to free feelings he'd kept on a tight leash for months?

The answer eluded him—and until he found it, he needed to put some distance between them.

"Thank you." He stood, juggling her coffee. "My cell number is on the card. Let me know when you'd like me to take care of that gutter." He held out the cup.

She took it, rising as he began to turn away.

"Listen, I don't want to push . . . but would you be willing to consider a different kind of assignment?"

Hesitating, he angled back to her. "Such as?"

"I mentioned yesterday that our volunteer board is in over its head. We could benefit from a professional appraisal and some recommendations to improve our effectiveness. With your experience running a large nonprofit organization, an evaluation from you would be a lot more valuable to us than a gutter repair." Her words came out in a breathless, nervous rush.

A bee buzzed his ear, and he lifted his hand to shoo it away.

Too bad he couldn't shoo away her request as easily.

Unfortunately, she was right. Even with a paid staff and significant budget, St. Joseph Center had faced its share of challenges. Running an all-volunteer organization with limited funding had to be very tough. If he reviewed the Helping Hands structure and operational system, he might be able to offer some constructive ideas— and a big-picture review shouldn't take all that long.

Best of all, most of it could be done in the privacy of his room.

"I guess I could do that." His acquiescence came out more grudging than he intended.

Nevertheless, her face lit up. "Thank you. Let me talk to our board members, solicit their ideas, and establish some clear goals for the review before we pull you into it. I don't want to waste your time."

"Sounds reasonable. You have my number."

A bee began to buzz around the cinnamon roll in her hand, undeterred by her evasive maneuvers.

He moved back toward her and waved it off while he relieved her of her coffee cup. "You better put what's left in the bag unless you're going to eat it now."

"I'll save the rest for later." It took her a couple of tries to slide the sticky bun back in—and the tremors running through her fingers weren't helping.

Had he caused them?

Could be.

He hadn't exactly been Mr. Congeniality for much of their conversation.

"I can take that back now." She reached for the coffee.

He passed the cup to her, trying to find some neutral topic that would put her at ease and conclude today's encounter on a more relaxed, upbeat note. "This is quite a layout. How many acres do you have?"

"Seventy—sixteen planted in cranberries. Our

twelve beds range in size from one to two acres and are spread out over the land to take advantage of the terrain for terracing." She surveyed the property, pride shining in her eyes. "This farm has been in my family for three generations."

"On your father's or mother's side?"

"Father."

"So you and your husband inherited the business?"

Her shoulders stiffened. "I work the land with my uncle. My husband is—he died two years ago."

Michael's lungs stalled. The vibrant young woman beside him was a widow?

He grappled with that bombshell for a few moments, then sucked in a breath. Apparently he wasn't the only one with some serious grief in his recent past.

"Now it's my turn to say I'm sorry."

She dipped her chin in acknowledgment. "I'll give you a call once I meet with the board. And thank you for this." Lifting the cup and the bag with the half-eaten cinnamon roll, she took a step back.

Their conversation was over.

Five minutes ago, he'd have welcomed the chance to escape. Yet all at once he didn't want to leave. He wanted to stay and comfort this woman who seemed so alone and in need of a sympathetic ear.

Or was he projecting his own needs on her?

Hard to say—and based on her rigid stance, this wasn't the time to try to find out.

He pulled out his keys. "You're welcome."

He returned to his car, slid behind the wheel, and started the engine. The dogs came running as he maneuvered the Focus around and aimed it toward 101, and Tracy called out to them, shooing the two collies out of his path as he guided the car down the road.

For an instant as he drove past, their gazes met. He lifted his hand. She hefted her coffee.

Then she disappeared behind him.

He continued toward the highway, taking one final look in his rearview mirror as he approached a curve that would hide the scene behind him from view. She'd set the coffee down on a rock and was bending over to pet the dogs, holding the white bag aloft as they lifted their noses toward it and no doubt sent a silent plea with those big brown eyes.

With a twist of the wheel, he pulled onto 101 and accelerated back to town on the much smoother, paved road. If she was as kind and generous as he suspected, her afternoon snack was already gone.

And despite the tiny alarm bell that began to jangle in his mind, he suddenly found himself looking forward to seeing her again . . . and wondering if he could ferret out any more information about her from his tight-lipped, reclusive landlady in the meantime.

Taking care not to leave any smudges, Anna fitted the new piece of glass into the picture frame, set the photo on top, and slid the back into position. Then she turned it over and studied the smiling young man.

John Phillip Williams.

Her son.

Frame in hand, she lowered herself into the chair at the café table tucked against the kitchen wall, next to the animal rehab center occupying the space that had once held the dinette set where she and George and John had shared so many meals. Getting rid of the big family table had been harder than she'd expected—but why keep it when it would never be needed again? When sitting at it only hammered home the loneliness of her solitary life? Far better to use the space for a productive purpose.

The chickadee let out a soft whistle—long, short, short—and she glanced over at the bird she'd nursed to adulthood. Soon she'd have to set her feathered friend free.

Anna sighed. Letting go was always difficult; all the creatures that found refuge in her house had their charms and unique, endearing personalities. But once they were ready to test their wings— literally or figuratively—all you could do was set them free and hope for the best.

She refocused on the photo, the image misting

as she inventoried John's features. From George he'd inherited the supple lips that smiled often and merry, sparkling eyes. Her contribution had been the too-thin nose and firm—no, make that stubborn—chin. How often had the two of them clashed because of that shared trait?

Too many times to count.

Yet George, with his kind, gentle manner, had always been able to tease them out of their mulishness if they dug in their heels over some issue that wasn't important in the big scheme of things.

She traced a finger over John's square jaw. Would the two of them have fared better if George had been alive when the crisis arose that drove the divisive wedge between them? An issue so acrimonious neither had ever attempted to resolve it?

Maybe.

In fact, mediator that he was, George would no doubt have found a way to avert the final scene that had led to ultimatums and accusations and words said in anger that could never be retracted . . . or forgotten.

Instead, their clash had escalated—and she'd lost both husband and son in the space of six months.

If only it was possible to . . .

Anna ruthlessly quashed that thought and swiped a hand across her eyes. What was done was done. It was foolish to get weepy over events that had happened almost two decades ago. Even if a reconciliation had been possible in the beginning, it was too late now to change anything.

Straightening her shoulders, she returned to the den, crossed the dim room, and replaced the photo on the end table.

As she set it down, the faint sound of a door opening and closing came through the far wall, and she paused. Her tenant was either coming or going.

Taking a quick detour to the vertical blinds, she tilted one to peek out. No sign of anyone. Hard to say if he was . . .

All at once, the sound of running water came from the annex.

Question answered. Her boarder was here.

Releasing the blind, she swiveled back toward the picture. Michael had noticed the resemblance yesterday, after he'd chased the rabbit. He might not have voiced the question in his eyes, but his curiosity had been piqued. Finding a photo of someone who could be your twin brother had to be disconcerting.

Too bad.

John wasn't a subject she intended to discuss with anyone. What had happened all those years ago was no one's . . .

All at once, faint music seeped through the wall, and she strained her ears. Was that . . . *Rhapsody in Blue*? The piece John had played so masterfully at his last piano recital before he went away to college and his focus shifted from music to more practical pursuits?

Yes.

How proud they'd been of him that night—and the well-deserved accolades he'd received.

But encouraging a professional interest in music would have done him a disservice, as both she and George had agreed. To his credit, John had accepted the reality that music wasn't the most lucrative or stable career and majored in business instead.

And he had done well at it.

Very well.

Anna swiveled toward the computer on the far wall, the screen caught in a shaft of sunlight streaming through the slat in the blind that hadn't fully closed. No reason to do a Google search on her son today; unless he'd been promoted again since January, there wouldn't be anything new.

Still . . . seeing his photo on the screen would be comforting, even if the connection was ephemeral —and one way.

She clenched her fingers, struggling to summon up the self-discipline that confined her to a twice-a-year net search on him. Doing it more often would be self-indulgent.

Yet what harm would there be in giving herself this small treat before she dropped off Reverend

Baker's cookies and swung by the St. Francis rectory to take an inventory of the kitchen and compile her weekly shopping list?

With the beam of sunlight pointing the way and the driving beat of *Rhapsody in Blue* urging her forward, she gave up the fight.

It would be nice to see if there was anything new in John's life—and pretend for a few minutes she was still part of it.

"For someone who's been hard at it since the crack of dawn, you don't have much of an appetite."

At Uncle Bud's comment, Tracy looked up from her barely touched plate to find him and Nancy watching her.

"Are you feeling okay, honey? You always scarf down my pot roast."

"I'm fine. And it's great, Nancy." She forked a piece of carrot. Eating too much of the cinnamon roll Michael Hunter had brought her an hour ago was no excuse for skimping on the meal Nancy had worked hard to prepare. "I just have a lot of things on my mind today."

Uncle Bud took a roll from the basket beside him and began buttering it. "Is that young man you were talking with earlier one of them?"

She smothered a groan. "I didn't see you around while he was here." She chewed the carrot and cut a piece of meat, giving the food her full attention.

"I was having some trouble with the copper spray and had to duck into the equipment shed. I saw you in the distance."

"Mmm." She speared the meat with the tines of her fork, trying to come up with a way to frame the encounter that would keep her uncle from charging full-tilt into matchmaking mode. "Did you get the spray issue worked out?"

"Yes." His eyes began to twinkle. "So who was that young man? You two appeared to be having a very intense discussion. And what were you eating?"

She squinted at him. "How did you see all that from the equipment shed?"

Now it was his turn to busy himself with the food on his plate. "I started to come over to talk to you, but once I got close I decided it might be better not to interrupt."

Nancy looked back and forth between them. "I seem to have missed out on some very interesting activity happening right under my nose. Tell me more."

"You know as much as I do." Uncle Bud swirled a piece of meat in the rich gravy with his fork. "Tracy will have to fill us in on the rest."

She gathered her carrots into a nice, neat pile, thinking fast. The best plan might be to give them the basics and try to play down the whole thing.

"His name is Michael Hunter, and he's the man

to blame for this." She held up her healing palm. "He stopped by to apologize."

"Very thoughtful—but how did he find you?" Uncle Bud poured himself another glass of iced tea.

"I think Anna Williams told him who I was. He's staying in her annex."

Nancy's eyes widened. "You're kidding."

"Nope. He says she found him sitting on a bench by the wharf and offered him lodging."

Nancy set her fork down. "In the five years I've lived in this town, Anna has never so much as said hello to me. I always smile and greet her when our paths cross, but the most I get is a stiff nod."

"That's all anyone gets. I don't know what's going on, either—and apparently, neither does Michael." Tracy took a sip of her water.

"Very intriguing." Uncle Bud rested his elbows on the table, his own meal forgotten. "The man must be quite a charmer if he can win over Anna Williams."

By sheer force of will, Tracy kept her blush in check. "He's very pleasant."

"Did you find out why he's in town?" Nancy went back to eating.

She gave them a brief overview of his background. Very brief.

As she finished, Uncle Bud took another slice of pot roast. "Sounds like a very upstanding man. You don't pursue a career in the nonprofit arena unless you have a heart for helping people."

"I suppose that's true. Anyway, to make amends for the mishap on Thursday, he agreed to give us some assistance with Helping Hands."

"How old is he?" This from Nancy.

When Tracy hesitated, her uncle stepped in. "Mid-to-late thirties. One of those men you and your lady friends would call a hunk."

Her eyebrows rose. "Really? Too bad I didn't get a gander at him. Is he married?"

Tracy squirmed in her seat as they both looked at her. "He's a widower."

Sympathy flashed across both their faces, but she didn't miss the subtle gleam in her uncle's blue irises.

Wonderful.

Balling her napkin in her lap, she sent him a warning scowl. "Don't get any ideas, Uncle Bud."

"About what?" He winked and slid an amused glance toward Nancy.

"Look, he's only passing through." She emphasized each word. "At most, he'll be here a few weeks."

"A lot can happen in a few weeks. Pass the rolls again, would you, Nance?" Her uncle held out his hand for the basket, keeping one eye on his niece.

Debate the point or let it go?

Let it go. Remember the line in Shakespeare about protesting too much.

Right.

Besides, it wasn't likely she'd see Michael all that much. Perhaps a meeting or two about Helping Hands, one of which would involve all the board members. Their interactions would be professional and straightforward. And once he offered his recommendations and analysis, he'd go back to doing whatever he came out here to do and leave her in peace to come up with a plan to keep Harbor Point Cranberries afloat.

Until then, she needed to make certain her uncle stayed focused on the work at hand, not the stranger in town.

"Have all the fertilizers come in? I took a quick inventory over the weekend, and the potash hadn't shown up yet. Should I call the supplier again?" She finished off her potatoes, doing her best to maintain a neutral expression.

Since his eyes continued to twinkle, she suspected he'd already figured out her strategy—but he gave her a reprieve on personal topics and moved on to business issues for the remainder of lunch.

By the time the meal ended and they headed back to work in the beds until the dipping sun forced them to call it a day, Tracy was beginning to think she might have convinced her uncle and his wife that her earlier encounter with Hope Harbor's Chicago visitor was inconsequential.

But Uncle Bud's comment as they parted at the equipment shed deflated those hopes.

"You never did tell me what you were eating while the two of you talked."

She grabbed the weed eater, her aching shoulder sending out a loud protest. "A cinnamon roll. The one I bought at the bakery last Thursday got squashed in the bike incident."

"A sweet treat delivered by a handsome man." He waggled his eyebrows. "No wonder you weren't too hungry at lunch."

With that, he ambled off, insecticide in hand.

Tracy watched him leave, letting out a sigh. Uncle Bud didn't miss much, the old softie.

However, even if Michael Hunter was handsome enough to not only drive all thoughts of food from her mind but also activate long-dormant hormones, their relationship would never progress beyond casual acquaintances.

She wouldn't let it.

Because no matter how hard Uncle Bud pushed, she had no intention of falling for anyone ever again.

End of story.

6

Michael paused in the doorway of the annex to shake the sand from his shoes, eyeing the patio table with the solitary chair. Nice spot to sit and soak up some of the sun that had peeked out as he finished his daily walk on the beach—and far more appealing than the annex for reading the next few chapters of his mystery novel.

He slid his feet back into his deck shoes and inspected Anna's side of the house. Closed up tight as the sea anemones that coiled into a protective tuck if he got too close during his beach walks. She hadn't said his rent included use of the patio—but why would she mind? As far as he could tell, she never came into the back-yard. The lawn service that had been here yesterday saw to the maintenance.

Decision made, he grabbed his book and a soft drink and crossed the yard to the table and chair. He'd stay for an hour or until the capricious sun disappeared, whichever came first.

Thirty minutes later, he heard the sliding door open behind him.

Uh-oh.

Psyching himself up to be reprimanded and banished to the four hundred square feet he'd rented, he removed his sunglasses, stood, and faced the house.

Instead of scolding him, however, Anna walked over and set a plate of plastic-wrap-covered cookies on the table. Pecan chocolate chip, as best he could tell—the ones she'd pilfered from Reverend Baker's batch?

"I've had these sitting on my counter for you since last night. I tried knocking a few times, but you were out."

"Thank you. They look great." He motioned to the table and chair. "I hope you don't mind me using your patio. It's a nice, quiet spot to enjoy the sun and a good book—but I don't want to infringe on your privacy."

"You aren't." She scanned the yard, a hint of melancholy whispering at the edges of her voice. "I used to sit out here quite often, but it got to be *too* quiet." Her words hitched, and she turned away. "You're welcome to use the patio anytime."

"I'm sure you have a lot to do, but would you like to share a cookie or two with me first?" The spontaneous invitation spewed out before he could stop it.

Weird.

Why would he want to hang out with his unsociable landlady?

Yet he *had* been hoping for an opportunity to ask her more about Tracy—and he was almost as intrigued by this mystery woman as he was by the appealing cranberry farmer . . . for very different reasons.

No matter his motivation, however, it didn't appear his curiosity was going to be satisfied today. She fiddled with her apron and withdrew a few steps. "Why?"

Not the response he'd expected.

"Why what?"

"Why do you want to spend time with me?"

"Well . . ." His mind raced, trying to come up

with a plausible but vague answer. "Eating by yourself is lonely. And it *is* pretty quiet out here, as you said."

She flicked a hand toward his book as she continued to edge toward the house. "You have that to keep you company."

He ran his thumb across the page, a sudden pang of sadness welling up from deep inside him. "To tell you the truth, it's more distraction than company. Sometimes it's easier to put off thinking about the hard stuff."

As his admission hung in the air between them, he frowned. What had prompted *that* revealing comment?

Nevertheless, it halted her retreat.

"I read a lot too."

He studied her guarded face. Was that an overture for more discussion—or merely a polite reply?

Only one way to find out.

"Getting lost in someone else's story can be a great escape." He closed the book. Perhaps a few more candid disclosures would draw her out. "My own story hasn't been too upbeat these past few months. I lost my wife eighteen months ago—and I'm still dealing with a lot of regrets."

A shadow passed over her eyes. "Regrets have a habit of lingering, sometimes a lot longer than eighteen months. Especially if they involve people we love."

Did her regrets involve the young man in that picture frame he'd knocked over? Her husband? Both?

"I expect that's true. If you have any advice about how to deal with them, I'm open to suggestions."

She gave a short, mirthless laugh. "You're asking the wrong person. Maybe Tracy Campbell can offer you some guidance."

What was that supposed to mean?

"I met with her yesterday, but . . . I'm not sure I understand your suggestion."

Anna shrugged. "I expect she has a few regrets . . . yet she seems to be carrying on fine. She must know a secret we don't."

"What kind of regrets?"

Anna's shoulders stiffened, and dismay tightened her features. "That's for her to share, if she chooses. I've said too much already. I'm not one to talk about other people's troubles behind their backs. I can't imagine what's gotten into me." She clasped her hands in a tight knot in front of her.

Michael hesitated. Curious as he was, if he pressed her about Tracy, she'd shut down. Better for the moment to focus on the mystery of the woman standing a few feet away.

"I can tell you're the kind of person who respects other people's privacy—and values your own. I admire that." He searched for a benign topic to keep the conversation going. "Um . . . how's the rabbit doing?"

Her posture relaxed a bit. "None the worse for wear."

"Glad to hear it—though the same can't be said of your picture frame." He did his best to maintain a casual tone. "I'd be happy to replace the glass, since I broke it while in hot pursuit of our furry friend."

"I already took care of it." She smoothed her palms down her apron. Picked off a dried crumb. "In case you were wondering, that's my son's senior picture from high school. I'm sure you noticed he looks a lot like you."

"Yes." If she was willing to talk about the photo, they must be making progress. "The resemblance is uncanny. Does he live in the area?"

"No. Seattle."

"At least he's not too far away. Do you get to see him often?"

Her face contorted. "No. We haven't spoken in twenty years."

She and her son had been estranged for two decades?

No wonder she wore such a heavy cloak of sadness.

"I'm very sorry to hear that."

She angled away from him, toward the shuttered house, her manner once more brisk and impersonal. "It's ancient history now. Life goes on. Enjoy the cookies."

Before he could respond, she hurried back inside and closed the door.

Slowly Michael retook his seat and regarded the treat she'd given him. Anna might not have accepted his offer to share the cookies, but what she *had* shared was much more substantive.

What could have caused such a terrible rift between a son and a mother who obviously still loved him?

And her comment about Tracy was just as perplexing. What sort of regrets might the young widow harbor? Could they be anything like his?

No.

He picked up his soda. Took a long swallow. Tracy seemed like the kind of person who would have her priorities straight. Who would always put the people she loved first.

Perhaps her regrets had more to do with Anna's earlier comment, about Harbor Point Cranberries being a family business—for now. Was the farm in financial trouble? Had Tracy made some operational mistakes that had put it in jeopardy, along with her and her uncle's livelihood? That could certainly cause regrets.

Yet somehow he had a feeling hers were far more personal.

Could they be related to her deceased husband?

So many questions . . . so few answers.

Michael took another swig of soda, picked up

his mystery novel again, and opened it to the page he'd been reading when Anna came out.

But even though the book had been lauded as riveting and spellbinding by prestigious reviewers, he couldn't lose himself in it again.

Because the mysteries much closer to home were far more intriguing.

"May I interrupt—or will I be eating burned meat loaf if I do?"

Turning, Anna found Reverend Baker hovering on the threshold of the kitchen.

Hmm.

The minister rarely bothered her during her visits to prepare his dinners for the week and stock his fridge. Like all the other Hope Harbor residents, he'd long ago gotten the message she didn't like chitchat and preferred to be left alone.

He must have a serious matter to discuss.

"You aren't interrupting anything important. I'm in the cleanup phase." She wiped her hands on her apron.

He strolled in. "Don't let me delay you—I can talk while you wrap things up. I'll even help, if you like."

"No, thanks. I have a system."

The man chuckled and slid onto a stool at the island. "You sound like my Esther, God rest her soul. She had the sweetest disposition of any woman I've ever met, but in the kitchen she was the commander in chief—and pity the poor soul who got in her way. Now and then she'd let me help with the dishes, but in general I tried to stay out of her way."

Anna rested a hip against the countertop. "I have a feeling I would have liked her."

"Everyone did. It's hard to believe she's been gone for eight years." He pulled a grape off the bunch she'd deposited in the fruit basket earlier. "Moving here after she died, to a new town and a new church, was a wise choice, though. A change of scene can help put the past to rest and force you to forge ahead with life."

The minister was certainly in a talkative mood today.

Kind of like she'd been earlier, with Michael on the patio—a lapse she didn't intend to repeat twice in one day.

"I suppose that can be true." She swiped up a speck of tomato sauce from the counter. "But there's a lot to be said for staying in one place too—especially if it's been your home for most of your life. Familiar territory has its pluses."

"Also true. Leaving behind happy memories would be hard."

Yes, it would.

As for the unhappy ones—not hard at all.

But those would have followed her wherever she went, anyway.

"So what did you need to talk with me about?"

She kept scrubbing the counter. If she stayed busy, she could listen to what he had to say without a lot of eye contact or engagement.

"Not talk so much as say thank you."

She stopped and glanced over at him. "For what?"

"For giving Michael Hunter a place to stay. Did you know he was the CEO of a charitable organization?"

"Yes." She resumed scrubbing. "He gave me one of his cards the day we met."

"Well, Tracy Campbell convinced him to review Helping Hands while he's here and offer some recommendations—which we desperately need. Father Kevin and I had the best of intentions when we created the organization, but neither of us had a clue it would end up being so consuming. We've been at our wits' end about how to deal with the demands. Now, thanks to your generosity, help has arrived. Without your kind gesture, our path might never have crossed Michael Hunter's during his stay. It's a gift from God—and the answer to a lot of prayers."

She dismissed her role in the affair with a flip of her hand. It had nothing to do with generosity. The whole thing had started with his uncanny resemblance to John.

"You should thank Charley instead of me. If he hadn't asked me to take a complimentary order of tacos over to the bench, I'd have walked right by. Besides, Michael was looking for Tracy anyway for some reason."

"Yes. He caused her to have a slight bicycle accident and wanted to apologize." The minister's expression grew thoughtful. "You know, when you consider all the pieces that had to fit together to bring this about, the whole thing is remarkable. God does amazing work, doesn't he?"

Anna sent him a skeptical look. He knew better than to dump a bunch of God talk on her. She and the Almighty had parted ways years ago—a fact she'd shared with Reverend Baker the first time he'd brought up the subject.

"Still holding out, I see." The man chomped into the grape, his demeanor amused rather than reproving.

"You know where I stand, Reverend."

"Yes. You were very clear about that early on— and I've respected your wishes. I must admit, though, I've always wondered what happened. I know you and your family were once active members of this church." He held up a hand as she started to speak. "That was a comment, not a question. However, if you decide at some point you'd like to talk about it, my door's always open. We'd love to have you back in the congregation."

She swiped a final speck off the counter and twisted on the faucet to clean the pots too bulky to fit in the dishwasher. "I appreciate the thought, but I'm content with my life as it is."

"Are you certain?"

She began banging the pots. "Yes."

The stool scraped across the floor. "In case that changes, my invitation stands. And whether you choose to accept it or not, I believe your generosity was part of God's plan. So my thank-you stands too."

Footsteps sounded. Faded. Silence fell.

She washed two pots before casting a surreptitious peek over her shoulder.

The minister was gone—along with his God talk. Good.

She plunged the brownie pan into the water, working on the crusty edges of batter stuck in the corners. She should have washed it earlier, before the batter hardened. It was always much easier to clean up messes when they were fresh.

A principle as applicable to relationships as to pots and pans.

Her hands stilled, and she drew in a long, slow breath. Too bad she hadn't realized that years ago. Before it was too late. Before the chasm between her and John was so wide only God himself could bridge it.

But at this point, why should he? The Bible was full of verses that condemned hardness of heart, and her heart had hardened long ago—like the remnants of these brownies.

She scraped at a particularly stubborn piece of crust.

Stubborn.

That's what she was. What she'd always been.

And it was a bad way to be.

Reverend Baker might think of her as a lost soul, but she knew her Bible. Knew what it said about hardened hearts, stiff-necked people, and pride . . . as well as judgment and forgiveness.

Knew also that on every single score, she'd failed—and that her failures had cost her her son.

Were still costing her her son.

Because even after all these years, she couldn't bring herself to admit that maybe . . . just maybe . . . she'd been a little harsh. Not that she'd been wrong to condemn what John had done. No. Sin was sin, and he'd admitted his guilt.

Yet he'd done nothing to make amends.

Steam rose from the water, and Anna lifted her arm to wipe a bead of sweat off her forehead.

It wasn't as if she'd cut him off cold, though. Hadn't she hoped and prayed he'd have a change of heart, that he'd call and tell her he was not only sorry for what he'd done but willing to try to make things right?

Yet days went by. Weeks. Months. Years. And not a word from her son.

Was it possible he'd been waiting for *her* to apologize?

She shook her head. Why did life have to be so complicated?

The final piece of hard crust came loose at last,

and she moved the pan under the running water to rinse it. Jerked back when the hot liquid burned her hand.

Twisting the faucet to cold, she slid the pan onto the counter and stuck her stinging hand under the cool stream. Better—but that red spot would be there for a day or two.

Getting burned was a hazard for cooks . . . and mothers.

While the water sluiced over her fingers, she watched through the window as two seagulls waged a turf battle with strident cries.

Again, like her and John.

With an exasperated sigh, she leaned over and turned off the water. It was time to leave all these unsettling thoughts behind and go home.

Except they followed her to the gas station, hovering in the air while she filled up her tank, and continued with her down Dockside Drive to Charley's.

"Perfect timing, Anna. I was about to close up for the day." Charley wiped his hands on a towel and gave her one of his genial grins. "Having a late lunch?"

Was she? It was past lunchtime . . . but she wasn't hungry.

So why had she ended up here?

Too late to retreat now, though, with Charley leaning on the counter waiting for her order.

"I guess I am."

"Coming right up." He began cooking—but kept talking. "How are things working out with your tenant?"

"How did you know I had a tenant?"

"Michael asked about you when he came over to thank me for the tacos the other day. He said you'd offered to rent him the annex. I gave you a glowing recommendation." His white teeth flashed.

"Yes, but how did you know he'd decided to accept?"

The man lifted his shoulders. "It was meant to be. Providence."

She narrowed her eyes. "Don't start with that. I just heard the same story from Reverend Baker."

"Smart man." He put a generous dollop of sauce onto each taco.

"That's ridiculous." Irritation sharpened her voice. "Everything that's happened is nothing more than coincidence."

"Ah." As usual, Charley took no offense at a customer's bad humor. Instead, his smile broadened. "You know what they say about coincidence—it's God's way of remaining anonymous."

She remained silent as she studied the back wall of Charley's kitchen, which was papered with layers of drawings Hope Harbor children had given him through the years. *Was* God's hand in this?

Perhaps.

The admission was grudging, but there'd been too many coincidences to assume they were all random—especially Michael's resemblance to John.

"Is your new tenant enjoying Hope Harbor?"

Anna pulled a ten-dollar bill out of her wallet. "I have no idea. We don't talk much."

"No? A pity. You two are very simpatico."

The Hope Harbor taco chef was full of surprises today. "I hardly know the man, Charley."

He wrapped up her lunch, slid it in a bag, and handed it through the window, along with her change. "I have a feeling you and he will get to know each other much better."

"Maybe I don't want to get to know him."

"What we want and what God sends our way are often two different things—but he always has our best interest at heart. Remember that, sí? And now I'm closing up shop for the day."

Without waiting for her to respond, he rolled down the aluminum window.

Anna stood for a moment, inspecting the bench she and Michael had shared five days ago, when her world was steady and her state of mind resigned, as they'd been for almost two decades.

Now . . . now there was a subtle tension in the air. A disconcerting sense that things were about to change. That the quiet, isolated life she'd grown accustomed to was poised to undergo a radical transformation.

All of which was nonsense, of course. She'd given Charley's fanciful comments far too much credence. What did he know about her, anyway? Or Michael, either. Certainly not enough to jump to the kind of conclusions he'd shared with her.

Yet as she slid behind the wheel of her car, the spicy aroma of the tacos tickling her nose, she had the oddest feeling that the spice in her life wasn't going to be confined to Charley's cooking any-more.

And while she pulled away from the taco stand with a tingle of apprehension thrumming through her nerve endings, a healthy dose of anticipation seasoned the trepidation—along with an emotion she hadn't experienced in a very long time.

Hope.

7

Michael Hunter was fast—and good.

Leaning back from her laptop, Tracy tapped a finger on the kitchen table and reread the final paragraph of the Helping Hands comments he'd attached to his email.

Insightful, concise, thoughtful—and his pre-liminary ideas, along with his questions, were smart and practical.

Plus, he'd managed to put this analysis together in a day and a half—far less time than it had taken her to get the board together for a special session to discuss their goals for his review.

She scanned his questions again. Some would require board input, preferably with him present —but why not tackle the ones she could handle right now? Uncle Bud wasn't likely to bend his no-work-on-Sundays-except-during-harvest rule, and the two second-quarter tax estimates she needed to complete for clients could wait until after dinner.

Besides, it would be nice to hear Michael's voice.

A twinge of guilt tugged at her conscience—but hiding from the truth, much as she was tempted to do so, wouldn't change it. The fact was, she liked Hope Harbor's newest temporary resident. He was considerate, kind, compassionate, handsome . . . and single.

That last item was the problem.

She shouldn't want to hang around *any* man, especially one who was unattached and much too appealing. It could only lead to trouble. She didn't need—or want—romance in her life. She might have failed Craig in a lot of ways, but she could at least be true to his memory.

Rising, she shoved her fingers into the pockets of her jeans and wandered over to the window that framed the sea. Fog swirled about, reducing visibility and obscuring most of the view—but the relentless, restless waves were out there, surging against the sea stacks . . . just as guilt and grief surged against her conscience.

More so since Michael Hunter had entered her life.

A shiver rippled through her, and she freed her hands to rub her arms. She was letting the gray weather stir up unhappy memories. Unnerve her.

And that was foolish.

She straightened her shoulders. Michael didn't have to be a problem. Her contact with him wasn't personal, after all. It was business. As long as she remembered that, there was no need to worry.

Suppressing a niggle of doubt about that conclusion, she returned to the table, double-checked his email for the phone number he'd provided, and tapped it into her cell.

He answered on the second ring, though his voice was faint.

"Michael? It's Tracy Campbell." Much to her relief, her greeting came out composed and professional, despite the tremor in her fingers. "I've read your initial report and wanted to try to answer some of the questions you raised. Is this a convenient time?"

"Yes. I was planning to . . ." The next words were garbled. " . . . if that's all right with you. It shouldn't . . ." His voice faded out.

"Michael?" She pressed the phone closer to her ear. "I can't hear half of what you're saying."

"Sorry. My reception . . . and spotty here. I'm in town, so . . . in person?"

She missed a lot of his words—but she got the gist.

He wanted to get together.

Her pulse took a slight uptick. Not the best idea.

On the other hand, the man was doing them a favor—and given his phone issues, it would be easier to communicate face-to-face.

She'd just have to deal with it.

"That's fine. Where would you like to meet?"

"Why don't I drop by your place?"

That comment came through loud and clear.

Her hand tightened on the phone. Michael Hunter here, in her cottage? That could be a problem.

Say no, Tracy.

"Um . . . okay."

What in the . . . ?

"I've got my pen in hand. Go ahead and give me your address."

Her heart began to hammer. Trying to back out now would be embarrassing. And what excuse could she use? *I find you attractive, and that scares me?*

Right.

Better to let things ride and focus on keeping their meeting impersonal and efficient.

She recited the address and gave him directions. "It's at the south edge of town, on the bluff.

I'm in the guest cottage behind the main house."

"Got it. I'll be there in less than ten minutes."
The line went dead.

For a long moment she remained unmoving, phone in hand.

A visit from a handsome man was so not in her Sunday plans.

She scanned the cottage. Her bedroom might be on the messy side, but the main living room/ kitchen space was tidy.

The same couldn't be said of her, however. She inspected the worn jeans and faded T-shirt she'd changed into after church. It was attire much more suited to working on the farm than entertaining a handsome man.

You're not entertaining him, Tracy. You're consulting with him.

Check.

She stood. Tucked in her T-shirt. Smoothed her palms down her jeans. This outfit was fine. It suited her much more than the nicer clothes she wore for church and client meetings. You only primped for someone you were trying to impress.

And she wasn't trying to impress Michael Hunter.

She wandered down the hall to the bathroom and surveyed her image in the mirror over the sink. Hair tangled from her earlier walk on the windy beach, face wiped clean of makeup by the mist hovering over the landscape, faint lines of weariness at the corners of her eyes thanks to her long hours at the farm yesterday.

Not a very attractive picture.

But again—it was her. If Uncle Bud and Nancy were stopping by, it wouldn't even occur to her to primp.

The sound of crunching gravel came through the open window . . . and all at once one hand reached for the brush and the other groped in the drawer for her makeup bag.

Okay. Fine.

She'd smooth out her hair, put on a touch of lipstick and mascara, make herself a bit more presentable.

But she was absolutely not going to let their get-together run any longer than necessary or become anything more than a straightforward business meeting.

No matter what kind of tricks her heart might play on her.

The guest cottage behind the high-end, bluff-hugging vacation house was pleasant, if small—but why didn't Tracy live on the cranberry farm she loved?

One more missing piece in the puzzle that was Tracy Campbell.

Michael maneuvered his car into a spot next to an older model Civic, picked up the bag beside him, and walked to the front door. If fate was kind, maybe he'd discover a few of those AWOL pieces today.

She answered his knock at once, cheeks slightly flushed. Had she been waiting on the other side, anxious to greet him?

Not that he cared, of course. He hadn't come to Hope Harbor looking for attention from anyone, least of all an eligible woman.

Besides, someone with Tracy's many attributes would have suitors lined up at the door if she was in the market—which she wasn't, based on her distressed demeanor when she'd mentioned her deceased husband a few days ago.

At least they shared that much in common.

"Welcome. Did you have any problem finding the place?"

"No. Your directions were perfect."

"Glad to hear it. I've gotten my uncle lost so many times I've been fired as his navigator. He claims I was born without the directional gene." She flashed him a . . . nervous? . . . smile. "Come on in." She backed up to give him access.

He edged past her, into a room about the size of Anna's annex but with a more spacious feel, thanks to the vaulted ceiling and skylights above the open floor plan. "Nice."

"I was lucky to find it." She shut the door and joined him in the center of the room. "In exchange for keeping an eye on things for the owners, I get low rent and a great view."

"Sounds like a deal—although I'm surprised you don't live at the farm." It couldn't hurt to try to get a few of his questions answered. Worst case, she'd brush him off.

Instead, she offered a lot more information than he expected.

"I used to. My mom and dad and I lived there until they were killed in a small plane crash when I was ten. After that, my uncle and aunt moved in and took over the job of raising me. Since they didn't have any children, it worked out well all around. But I moved out a couple of years ago after . . ." She stopped. Sucked in a breath. Cleared her throat. "When my uncle got serious about Nancy. Two's company and all that."

"You must miss it."

She lifted one shoulder. "I do. But someday, God willing, I'll build my own place out there. I have a good friend from college who's an architect in LA and would do a super job with the design. Best of all, BJ is planning to move here soon." This time there was no restraint in her smile.

Michael's antennas went up. Tracy had a male friend who was willing to trade big city architecture jobs for small Hope Harbor projects? There was only one reason he could think of for a decision like that . . . and it didn't sit well.

He did his best to adopt a casual tone. "That will be quite a change. He'll have some serious adjustments to make while he transitions from LA to small-town life."

Her mouth twitched. "BJ is a woman—though she's used to people making the assumption you did." Then her humor vanished. "But she has her reasons for wanting to move. Good ones." When she continued, her tone was brisk. "Why don't we sit at the dinette table? I've got your email open on my laptop."

That was all he was going to learn about her friend.

And it was enough, now that he knew her gender—for reasons he didn't intend to dwell on.

Michael took a chair at a right angle to her and set the brown bag on the table. "I come bearing gifts."

She surveyed his offering. "Based on that delectable aroma, I'm guessing you visited Charley's."

"I'm becoming a regular there. His tacos are now a staple of my diet. Since it's almost dinnertime, I thought we could eat while we talk. Unless you have other meal plans."

"Nope. My dinner was going to consist of leftover chicken from last night at the farm. Nancy's a wonderful cook, but nothing compares to Charley's fish tacos. They're one of my splurges whenever I have some extra cash on hand. What would you like to drink?"

"Water or a soda would be fine."

As she rose to get their beverages, Michael studied her. The fish tacos weren't inexpensive, but even on his modest nonprofit salary, they hardly qualified as a splurge.

Things must be very tight on the farm.

"I hope Diet Sprite is acceptable." Tracy slid back into her chair.

"Fine." He popped the tab, letting the carbonation hiss while she took a drink of her water and reached for her laptop. "Why don't we eat before we tackle business?"

She hesitated—but capitulated. "Not a bad idea. The tacos are great but messy. Do we need some extra napkins?"

"Nope. I'm a veteran of Charley's by now. I brought plenty." He dug them out of the bag, then divvied up the two wrapped bundles.

"Would you like a plate?" She started to rise again.

"This is fine. I'm used to eating on one of the benches at the wharf. A plate would feel too fancy and ruin some of the ambiance."

"I agree. Some things are best enjoyed unadorned." She began unwrapping her tacos.

He did a quick sweep of his lovely companion's casual attire, simple hairstyle, minimal makeup.

Yep. Unadorned was just fine.

"Charley's quite a character." Forcing himself to switch gears, he peeled the paper back on his dinner too. "Some days when I stop by, the place is shut up tight. And no hours are posted. How can he make a living with such a haphazard schedule?"

"He doesn't." She bit into a taco. Closed her eyes. Chewed slowly. "Mmm." Only after she swallowed did she resume the conversation. "Charley makes tacos for fun. Always has, as far back as I can remember. His stand is a town fixture, grandfathered in when the wharf was rezoned and spruced up a few years ago. He's looked the same my whole life too. The man never seems to age. He makes most of his income from painting."

"Houses?"

Amusement glinted in her green irises. "Hardly. He's a very successful artist. Several prestigious galleries around the country sell his work. Charley says the taco stand lets him express his creativity in a different way, takes him back to his roots in Mexico where his grandmother taught him to cook, and gives him the social interaction he needs . . . plus the chance to dispense philosophy along with fish."

Michael chuckled. "Like I said, quite a character. In fact, this town is full of them."

"You think? Who else interesting have you met?" She gathered up a piece of green pepper and some shredded cabbage that had escaped from the tortilla.

"My landlady, for one."

"Ah. Yes, Anna is . . . interesting. Have you had much opportunity to talk with her?"

"She's not a talker."

"No kidding. Still, you must have found a way to get her to open up. It would take some serious charm to wrangle an invitation to stay at the annex."

"I doubt charm had anything to do with it. She approached *me*. I think it had more to do with my resemblance to her son."

She stopped unwrapping her second taco. "You know about her son?"

"Only that she has one."

"How did you find out that much?"

"I knocked over his photo while I was helping her catch one of the critters that escaped from her menagerie."

Tracy's eyes widened. "She let you in her house?"

"Not exactly. I was standing in the doorway when a rabbit got loose, and I invited myself in. It took two of us to catch the frisky little guy."

"I'd heard she kept animals, but I don't know of any eyewitnesses other than you. No one's been in her house in years."

"Then how did you hear about the animals?"

She lifted one shoulder. "Hope Harbor is a very small town—meaning privacy is in short supply. There are very few secrets here."

Hmm. If Anna's background was common

knowledge, maybe he could ask a few questions without sounding too nosy.

"So tell me about her son. It's kind of weird to find a photo in a stranger's house that could be you in your younger days."

"I imagine it would be." She took another bite of her taco, silent as she chewed. "I guess I lied about there being no secrets here. No one knows what happened with her son. He'd be close to forty now, I think. He was ahead of me in school, so I never knew him—but from the stories I've heard, he was a nice guy. As far as anyone knew, the Williamses were a normal, happy family. Then her son, John, went away to college, her husband died . . . and a few months later John stopped coming home."

Michael cocked his head. "That's weird."

"Tell me about it." She dived into her third taco. "After that, Anna began closing up. She still went to work every day as a cook at the high school until she retired, but she stopped going to church, cut out all social activities, and became sort of a hermit. An unfriendly one, at that. Trust me, her inviting you to stay in the annex is the talk of the town." She inspected him. "Do you really think it's because you remind her of her son?"

"I can't think of any other reason." He started on his last taco too.

"Interesting. A mystery in Hope Harbor."

"More than one."

Whoops.

Dumb comment.

"What do you mean?" She took a big bite of her taco and watched him while she chewed.

Since he couldn't very well tell her she was the other one, he blurted out the first thing that came to mind. "Well, the way you all have managed to keep an organization like Helping Hands running on a volunteer basis in spite of the accelerating demand for services is pretty mystifying."

"True. Which is why the board and our two clergy directors all asked me to express their deepest appreciation for your help." She finished off her taco, wiped her hands on a napkin, and pulled her laptop closer. "Shall we move on to that topic while you finish?"

No. I'd rather ask some questions about you first.

Stifling that inappropriate response, he offered the only possible alternative. "Sure."

For the next thirty minutes, she answered as many of the questions that had come up during his review as she could, deferring a few to board discussion. But in contrast to a lot of the boards he'd dealt with during his nonprofit career, where members liked to see their names on the roster but never wanted to get their hands dirty dealing with "clients," Tracy came across as a hands-on person. She knew the administrative side of the

123

organization in exceptional detail—but she also knew the people side.

And if he'd had any doubts about the latter, the phone call that interrupted them as they were winding down—from a client Tracy identified as a Helping Hands regular—confirmed it.

"Do you mind if I take this?" She looked up from caller ID. "I should be able to deal with the issue fast."

"No problem. I have no agenda for the rest of the day."

Phone in hand, she stood and walked a few paces away—but he had no difficulty hearing the conversation.

"Hello, Eleanor. How are you today? . . . Oh, I'm sorry to hear that . . . Yes, it has been, but the weather around here is always fickle . . . Yes, I know you do . . . Uh-huh . . . uh-huh . . . No, it's no bother at all. I can have it to you within the hour . . . No, no, don't worry about it. You're close by. I'll see you soon."

When Tracy turned back, Michael arched an eyebrow. "Why are Helping Hands calls coming directly to you? According to the documents I reviewed, the organization has a hotline."

She retook her seat and picked up a stray bite of fish from her last taco. "Eleanor is a special case. I answered her first call for help last year, and she sort of latched on to me. She's eighty-seven and mostly housebound with fading eyesight and bad knees, so whenever she gets lonesome she finds excuses to call. Tonight she ran out of milk, and since the doctor told her to drink three glasses every day . . ." Tracy gave him a sheepish shrug.

In other words, the woman across from him was a sucker for a sob story . . . and people took advantage of that.

But it was hard to fault a tender, caring heart.

All at once, the name and age of the caller clicked. "Is this the same woman who has the sagging gutter?"

"Yes. I'm working on that problem too. One of the new volunteers from our drive at church last week is a carpenter. I already called on him for an emergency ceiling repair this week, but I'm going to tap him again in a couple of days for Eleanor's job. We try not to overdo requests for help, though. It burns people out."

"Eleanor hasn't burned *you* out."

"The truth? There are days my patience wears a little thin . . . but I try to put myself in her place—and be grateful for youth and health."

Michael finished the last bite of his taco, debating. All he had waiting for him at the annex was his mystery book and a landlady who was probably barricaded in her closed-up house. He might have come to Hope Harbor to be by himself, but an evening alone suddenly held zero appeal.

"I'll tell you what. Why don't I follow you over there and take care of the problem?"

She blinked. "But you've done enough already. Your review is far more valuable to us than a gutter repair."

"Well, two good deeds have to be better than one—and as I said, my evening is free."

"Are you certain?"

"Yes." He gathered up the remnants of their meal. "We're about finished with that, aren't we?" He nodded toward her laptop.

"Yes. The rest of the questions will have to be dealt with at a board meeting, which we'll arrange to suit your schedule."

"Then let's go fix a gutter." He stood, trash in hand. "Where do you want—"

Rap, rap, rap.

At the interruption, he angled toward the back door.

"Ignore that. It's just Floyd, looking for a hand-out."

The knocking continued as Tracy rose and picked up their glasses.

Michael frowned. Some homeless person—whom she knew by name—needed food . . . and she didn't care?

Major disconnect.

Tracy was a kind, caring woman who gave above and beyond to Helping Hands. Who ran errands that didn't come close to qualifying as

126

emergencies for old ladies on a Sunday evening.

Why wouldn't she respond to this need at her own back door?

Unless . . . could this be another Helping Hands regular who'd made a pest of himself and worn out his welcome? Perhaps taken too much of a personal interest in a certain volunteer?

The guy might even be dangerous.

A spurt of adrenaline surged through Michael.

"Do you want me to get rid of him?" He raised his voice to be heard above the persistent tapping.

"No need. He'll go away on his own eventually if I don't answer."

He frowned. "If you want to discourage him, it might not hurt for a guy to show up at your back door to chase him off."

She gave him a blank look . . . and then one corner of her mouth twitched. "I don't think the gender of the chaser-offer will matter."

Strange. She didn't appear to be in the least annoyed by the rude intrusion, let alone nervous.

Maybe he was making too big of a deal out of this.

"Your call, of course—but I could give it a try if you'd like."

"Sure. Have at it." She propped a hip against the counter and folded her arms.

The remains of their taco dinner still in hand, he crossed to the back door, unlocked it, and pulled it open.

No one was there.

He sent Tracy a puzzled glance over his shoulder.

Smiling full out now, she pointed to his feet.

He dipped his chin. A seagull was standing on her stoop, inches from his shoes, beak tipped up. All at once it let out a raucous squawk.

"Michael, meet Floyd, who I made the huge mistake of feeding the first few evenings I was here. He has now declared himself my BFF and comes calling every night about this time. As you can see, he's very persistent if I don't answer."

Floyd screeched and flapped his wings.

"You might want to see if there's a bite or two left in those wrappings. Floyd isn't picky."

Michael edged back from the shrieking bird. "Won't he keep coming if I feed him?"

"He'll come anyway—and it's okay. I think he's lonely. In the beginning he brought his wife, but he's been coming by himself for the past four months. I guess something happened to her."

A husband-and-wife seagull pair.

Tickled by that fanciful notion, Michael dug out a few stray pieces of taco filling and tossed them to Floyd, who scarfed down the treat. "Maybe he'll get married again."

"He might, down the road . . . but gulls mate for life, and this one's still in mourning. On the plus side, though, he eats more than he used to." She wandered over, stopping near his shoulder, a faint, pleasing scent wafting his way. "At first after he started showing up alone, he wouldn't eat at all, no matter what I offered. I think he just wanted to be in a familiar place, was trying to stick to his normal routine. Not a bad grief plan, actually."

Some nuance in her inflection told him she wasn't only talking about seagulls anymore. That she and her friend Floyd had gone through similar trauma.

He could relate.

Holding on to the door with one hand, he turned toward her. She was inches away, a faint sprinkling of freckles arching over her nose, her green eyes filled with pain and loneliness and . . . was that a touch of longing? . . . as their gazes locked.

Several charged beats of silence ticked by.

At last, she swallowed and took an abrupt step back. "You can c-close the door now. He'll either leave or hunker down on the stoop for a while. And we have places to go."

Yeah, they did.

But as they headed out to their respective cars, as he followed her first to the market in town to get milk and then to Eleanor's house, he couldn't help wondering what else he and Tracy might have in common besides a trauma in their pasts.

And where those commonalities might lead if either of them happened to be open to romance.

8

"I can't thank you both enough. Are you sure I can't tempt you with another glass of lemonade and some more fudge cake? I have plenty—and I know you're partial to chocolate, Tracy."

She gave Eleanor a hug. "No, thank you, but it was delicious."

"I'll second that." Michael moved forward.

Tracy exchanged places with him, watching as he took the older woman's hand between his. The man was obviously accustomed to dealing with the elderly. He'd raised his volume as soon as he realized Eleanor's hearing aids didn't always pick up everything, and his gentle touch now suggested he understood that older people's fragile skin bruised easily.

She had a feeling he was very good at his job.

"You can bring your young man back anytime, Tracy." The older woman gave Michael a once-over, then winked at her, the sparkle in her eyes undimmed by age. "He's a keeper."

Tracy smothered a groan. This was the third "your young man" her Helping Hands client had used, and no amount of correcting had dissuaded her.

"He's only visiting for a few weeks, Eleanor."

"But I'll do my best to stop by and see you again." Michael picked up the hammer from the bannister. "I put your ladder back in the storage shed."

"Thank you." The woman eased closer to him, leaning heavily on her cane, and inclined her head toward Tracy. Though she dropped her voice, her words carried in the quiet evening air. "Don't you give up on her, you hear? She might think she's done with men, but she'll come around with the right kind of wooing. And she's worth the effort, trust me. Kindhearted, thoughtful, pretty as a picture, smart—she's a CPA, you know."

Oh, for pity's sake.

Tracy grabbed Michael's arm and tugged him toward the porch steps. "I'll talk to you soon, Eleanor. Call if you need anything."

"I'll do that, sweet child—but don't worry about me. You focus on keeping that man of yours happy."

They were out of here.

She half dragged Michael down the walk, not stopping until they reached their cars.

After pulling out her keys, she gripped them tight in her fist and forced herself to meet his gaze. "Sorry about that. I don't know what came over Eleanor. I had no idea she would jump to such starry-eyed conclusions."

"Don't worry about it." Michael seemed more amused than annoyed as he handed her back the hammer he'd borrowed from the guest cottage's meager supply of tools. "She strikes me as a very nice lady."

"She is . . . and she's usually far more discreet."

"I guess at that age people feel free to call 'em like they see 'em."

What was that supposed to mean?

Tracy searched his face, but the setting sun behind him shadowed his features.

If he was suggesting there was romantic potential between them, however, she needed to set the record straight.

Now.

"Look, Michael . . ." She angled away from Eleanor's house to block the octogenarian's view if she happened to be watching the scene playing out at her curb. "In case you're thinking that I . . . that we might . . . that our relationship could . . ." She stopped. Exhaled. "Sorry. I'm not very adept at this kind of . . . interpersonal stuff."

The amusement faded from his demeanor. "No worries. I get your drift. And just to set the record straight, I still love my wife. Eleanor's match-making attempt was entertaining, but I'm not in the market for romance, either. The road I see ahead for myself is a solo one." He shoved his hands into the pockets of jeans that fit him oh-so-nicely. "I hope that takes the pressure off."

"Yes." And something more, though she couldn't put her finger on what had suddenly vanished, leaving a barren spot in its place. "I appreciate your candor."

A ribbon of mist swirled between them, and Michael nodded toward the sea. "I have a feeling we're about to get socked in. I better get back to Anna's while I can still see the road. Let me know when the board is ready to meet to discuss the rest of the questions I raised. I can have final recommendations to you within a day or two after that."

"That would be great. Thank you again for the treat from Charley's—plus the gutter job."

His smile didn't reach his eyes. "I'm always glad to lend a hand if help is needed."

"An admirable trait."

His mouth flattened. "Not always."

What did that mean?

But he was striding toward his car before she could figure out a diplomatic way to phrase that question.

Thirty seconds later, he pulled past her with a wave and disappeared into the mist, leaving her to puzzle over his odd comment.

How could helping others ever be a less-than-admirable trait?

As she slowly slid behind the wheel of her car and fitted the key in the ignition, their earlier conversation about mysteries flitted through her mind. Anna's uncharacteristic behavior—as well as the story behind her son's disappearance—were big ones.

But so was the woman's new tenant.

However, given his comments minutes ago, Tracy had a feeling her curiosity about his background—and his enigmatic statement— wasn't likely to be satisfied. Those kinds of confidences were only shared with very close, trusted friends . . . or a romantic interest . . . and he'd been very clear that wasn't where their relationship was headed.

The exact conclusion she'd already come to herself.

How lucky was that? Now she wouldn't have to worry about things getting messy or complicated.

Straightening her shoulders, she put the car in gear and pulled away from Eleanor's curb.

Yet as the house receded along with the older woman's romanticism . . . why did she suddenly feel bereft instead of relieved?

Helping Hands board meeting set for Thursday at 7 PM. Please advise if this is acceptable.

Michael skimmed the email message from Tracy again. It was professional. Businesslike. To the point.

And as lukewarm as the cooling cup of coffee he'd picked up in town while grocery shopping.

But what else should he expect after their

strained parting at Eleanor's two days ago?

Sighing, he put his coffee in the microwave to rewarm, typed in his assent, and punched send.

Perhaps he should have been a bit more diplomatic in his response to her stammering rejection on Sunday.

Wait.

Rejection was too strong a word.

She'd simply been trying to clarify that despite Eleanor's insinuations, she had no interest in romance with anyone. It hadn't been personal. And he was of the same mind-set. Romance wasn't on his agenda, either.

So why had he felt miffed when she'd set clear boundaries for their relationship?

And why had he overreacted by setting those boundaries in concrete with his I'm-a-solo-act-from-now-on speech?

He propped a hip against the counter as the turntable in the microwave continued to rotate. Rehashing their exchange was nuts. He'd be out of here in a few weeks, Hope Harbor and its quirky residents left far behind. Her sudden aloofness didn't matter in the big scheme of things.

Except she'd looked sort of sucker-punched after his little tirade.

He closed his eyes, trying to erase the image of her pinched face.

It refused to budge.

Get over it, Hunter. You'll never see her again once you go back to Chicago. In fact, you might never see her again after Thursday's board meeting.

True.

So why didn't that make him feel any better?

The microwave pinged, and he removed the cup. Took a sip. Waited for the caffeine to perk him up.

It didn't.

Instead, the weariness and desolation he'd hoped to leave behind in Chicago seeped more deeply into his bones. How could he trek two thousand miles in search of answers only to end up with more questions?

The coffee sloshed, and he discovered his hands were trembling—concrete evidence his trip to Hope Harbor was a bust.

Beating back another wave of melancholy, Michael grabbed his book. Maybe if he lost himself in his mystery for an hour or so, his mind would clear and he could untangle his muddled thoughts.

Book in one hand, coffee in the other, he shouldered through the back door and started across the lawn.

Halfway to the patio, he stopped.

When had that second chair been added to the table?

He frowned. It hadn't been there yesterday,

when he'd come out to read for an hour. And it hadn't been there this morning when he'd left for his walk on the beach, he was certain of it.

Could Anna be expecting company?

No. That didn't fit with the image he—and everyone else in Hope Harbor—had of her.

But what else could it mean?

No matter. She'd told him he could use the patio. Why not claim one of the chairs until he was asked to vacate?

Less than five minutes later, just as he was beginning to escape into the sinister world of espionage and an epic, world-threatening plot, the sliding door rumbled open behind him.

So much for his reprieve from reality.

Stifling his disappointment, he closed the book, picked up his coffee, and turned.

Anna approached with a plate of what appeared to be brownies, a mug, and a handful of napkins. "No need to get up."

He hesitated, halfway out of his chair. "Are you certain? I don't want to infringe on your privacy."

"I have plenty of privacy in there." She tipped her head toward the house as she set the plate on the table and placed the napkins beside it, keeping her face averted as she fussed with them. "I thought I might sit out here awhile, if you don't mind. We could share some of my marble brownies."

She was asking him to sit with her? Reciprocating the invitation he'd given her a few days ago?

Amazing.

He sank back into his chair, trying to hide his astonishment. "I'd like that."

With a dip of her chin, she claimed the second chair. "Help yourself."

He took a brownie and bit into it while she picked up one for herself.

"These are great." He tried to identify the subtle yet distinctive taste tickling his tongue. Failed.

"Thank you. I've had the recipe for years. It's one of the few I make from the old days. John was very fond of them—and they were always a hit at the church potluck suppers, along with my scalloped potatoes."

"They have a unique flavor." Michael inspected what was left of his brownie. "It tastes like almonds . . . but the nuts look like pecans or walnuts."

"They're walnuts. The flavor is amaretto."

Amaretto?

Who'd have guessed his straitlaced landlady kept liquor in the house, let alone used it in cooking?

"The brownies are spiked?"

"Don't worry. They won't make you tipsy." A wry thread wove through her words. "There are just two tablespoons in the whole pan. Inebriation is only a problem for the cook, if she decides to take a few nips while she bakes—which I never do."

Michael squinted at her. Was that a touch of . . . humor . . . in her eyes?

Could be.

"I don't care what's in them—they're the best brownies I ever ate. May I?" He gestured toward the plate as he finished off his first square.

"That's why I brought them out."

They chewed in silence as Michael tried to think of conversational topics that might engage the woman, draw her out—but she saved him the trouble.

"So tell me what you've been doing with yourself since you arrived in Hope Harbor."

No-nonsense Anna wanted to chitchat?

This day was full of surprises.

Following her lead, he gave her a rundown on his activities—his visit to the cranberry farm, his work with Helping Hands, daily walks on the beach, his frequent stops at Charley's.

"You've done a lot in less than two weeks."

"More than I expected, to be honest."

"Yes." She gave him an appraising scan. "I was under the impression you wanted privacy and downtime."

"I did." He took a sip of his coffee. "It's odd how life rarely turns out the way we plan, isn't it? I tend to grumble about the unexpected twists and turns, but my wife always called it divine Providence."

"So did my George." She broke off a piece of her brownie. "Strange you'd bring up that subject. I had a similar discussion the other day with both Reverend Baker and Charley." She pressed her fingers against a few loose crumbs on the table and deposited them in a neat pile on her napkin. "By the way, Charley thinks we were meant to be friends."

Michael mulled that over as he finished his second brownie. "He could be right. Charley strikes me as a very perceptive soul. In fact, he gave me a Bible citation the day I arrived, though how he knew I needed those words is a mystery." Another one in a growing list—but he kept that to himself.

"What was it?"

"It was from Job." He set down his coffee, pulled the verse up on his phone, and handed it over.

She read it in silence. Scrolled through it again. Held the phone out to him. "I'm not familiar with that passage—but I'd like to think it's true."

"I would too. And I guess as long as people are alive, a new beginning is always possible. Only death can rob you of that opportunity." His voice choked, and he wrapped his fingers around his mug as he stared into the dark depths.

A moment later, a hand with arthritic knuckles

touched his forearm. "I'm not a churchgoer anymore, Michael. God and I aren't on the best of terms." Anna used the gentle tone she reserved for her rescued animals. "But I'm beginning to believe he brought you into my life for a reason, and that good will come of it for both of us." With a pat on his shoulder, she stood. "I'll leave you to your book now. Take the rest of the brownies back to the annex. And I want you to know that even though I haven't prayed in a long while, I'll be asking God to help you find whatever you're seeking in Hope Harbor."

He remained where he was while she walked back to the house, struggling to process this strange turn of events.

Anna Williams, the antisocial widow who spoke to as few people as possible and isolated herself from both God and the community, was going to pray for him.

And whether or not his own journey gave him the answers he sought, his trip had yielded at least this one small miracle.

"I think she's dead, Tracy." Uncle Bud stood and looked at her across the ailing tractor. "The transmission finally went belly-up—and considering old Bessie's age and other ailments, it wouldn't make sense to fork out thousands of dollars for a new part."

Doing the mental math, Tracy fought back a

wave of panic. They didn't have enough idle money lying around in the farm account to replace Bessie even with a used model.

"Nancy and I can help out with the expense from our personal stash, honey."

Pressure built behind her eyes. That was so like her uncle—always putting the farm first and his own needs last. The man didn't have a selfish bone in his body.

"I don't want you to raid your retirement fund. That magic sixty-five you've been targeting isn't far down the road." Tracy tried to remain calm, but a quiver ran through her voice.

"So I work an extra year or two. No big deal. Truth be told, I'm not certain retirement is all it's cracked up to be. Besides, I'm not keen on leaving you saddled with this place by yourself. It's too much for one person."

Hard to argue with that—and there wasn't much budget to hire any part-time help, either.

Make that no budget after this catastrophe.

But it wasn't fair to ask Uncle Bud to lengthen his work life, either. He deserved some carefree years for the fishing and travel he'd always back-burnered—not to mention for his new wife.

"If we can get this place on its feet, I'll be able to manage with some seasonal help—and that's my top priority. I want you to have your retirement." She nudged the recalcitrant tractor with her toe. "As for old Bessie, I guess we can't complain too much. She's served us well far beyond her normal life expectancy, thanks to your magic touch with all things mechanical. But I was hoping we could get through this season, buy ourselves a few months to come up with an idea that would bail us out."

"How much do we have in the farm account?"

She gave him the paltry total. "I also have some second-quarter billings out. That money should be coming in over the next couple of weeks. If we pool all our resources, we can survive this. And I did round up a new customer. That will help down the road—but this will wipe out our current reserves. If any other unexpected expense comes up . . ." She rubbed her temple, where a dull ache was beginning to throb.

"Let's not look for trouble, okay?" Uncle Bud circled the tractor and put his arm around her, his grip strong and steady and comforting, as always. "We said we'd leave things in God's hands this year. I vote we stick with that plan."

"He doesn't seem to be helping us out much at the moment."

"Second-guessing the big man, huh?" He gave her a reassuring squeeze.

"Don't you sometimes wonder why bad things happen?" She searched his kindly, weathered eyes, the crinkles at the corners due as much to his ready smile as to his life in the fields.

143

"Of course. I'm human. But at the end of the day, I give it back to God. Trying to understand his ways is an exercise in futility. All we can do is our best and then trust that whatever happens, he's present and in charge."

That had been her philosophy too, once upon a time—before tragedy and grief and guilt had undermined her confidence in the Almighty.

She leaned into him, finding comfort in his solid, lean strength. "Well, let's get the current crisis taken care of and pray the rest of the season is smooth sailing."

"Amen to that." Uncle Bud gave her shoulder a final squeeze and moved over to his workbench. "Since Bessie's out of commission, you want to spot-spray weeds? I can join you as soon as I unclog a couple of sprinkler heads. We'll have to water tomorrow if it doesn't rain."

"Sure." She grabbed her work gloves and walked over to the shelf holding their two five-gallon backpack sprayers. "I'll make some calls to our neighbors tonight and see if anyone has an older model tractor they're willing to sell. If that doesn't pan out, I'll do some digging online."

"I bet we'll find one nearby, with the economy what it is and more farms going belly-up every day." He started to turn away. Stopped. "Almost forgot. Nancy wanted me to ask you to dinner tomorrow night."

"Tell her thanks, but we have a special board meeting for Helping Hands. I'll barely have a chance to squeeze in a quick shower after we finish here."

"What's up?"

She pulled one of the sprayers off the shelf. "Michael Hunter's going to come by for some discussion before he prepares his final report. He had a number of questions I couldn't answer."

Uncle Bud stopped fiddling with whatever had occupied him on the workbench and gave her his full attention. "So you've talked to him since that day he came by here?"

She busied herself with the herbicide prep. "Once. Most of our communication has been by email and very businesslike." No need to tell him they'd shared an impromptu taco dinner in her cottage.

"He might be worth getting to know better. Sounds like a nice man."

"Forget it, Uncle Bud. He made it very clear he has no interest in romance."

"Is that right?" He folded his arms and propped a hip against the workbench. "Seems to me like you two must have talked about a lot more than business."

She'd walked headfirst into that one.

Backpedal, Tracy.

Feigning nonchalance, she lifted one shoulder. "He mentioned his wife, whom he still loves very much. End of story." She slipped her arms through the straps on the backpack, shrugged it into place, and walked toward the door.

"I loved your aunt very much too, but meeting Nancy made me realize that sometimes God offers us unexpected second chances."

Her step slowed. At the doorway, she paused and pivoted slowly back. "I think it's possible to move on from grief. Guilt is a different story. It never goes away." Her words hitched, and she swallowed. She'd never admitted that to anyone, but based on the compassion that softened her uncle's eyes, he already knew about the burden weighing her down.

"It can . . . if it's misplaced."

"Mine isn't."

"Maybe it would help if you—"

"I need to get busy or I'll be at this till dark." She might have finally admitted her feelings of guilt, but she wasn't ready for discussion. Or platitudes. Or advice. "I'll see you later."

He let her go without another word.

Once in the fresh air, she blinked to clear her vision and hurried toward the tranquil fields that had always offered her solace, focusing on the somnolent drone of the bees. The cheery call of the chickadees. The faint echo of Shep and Ziggy's distant, playful barks. All the normal, everyday sounds that never failed to calm and comfort her.

Yet today she couldn't shake the nervous energy coursing through her.

Why, oh why, had she spoken of her feelings to Uncle Bud and opened that whole can of worms? Keeping them inside was best. Had always been best. Now her uncle would take her side and reassure her she wasn't at fault—and it would be so very easy to accept that. To let him convince her she was blameless.

But she knew better.

As did God.

And no amount of talking would change that . . . even if a certain Chicago nonprofit executive made her wish it could.

9

Stupid, stupid, stupid!

Swallowing past her disgust, Anna glared across the kitchen floor at Thumper—as Michael had dubbed him—who was regarding her at eye level from several feet away.

"This is . . . all . . . your fault . . . you know."

He responded with a twitch of his whiskers, almost like he was holding in a laugh.

"And it's . . . not funny."

But neither was the accident her furry friend's fault. She should never have lunged for him when he'd attempted a second escape. In fact, she should have released him days ago. He was more than ready to fend for himself.

Now look at the pickle she was in—flat on her back on the floor, her shoulder screaming in pain with every breath she stingily metered out.

A bone must be broken.

Beads of sweat broke out on her forehead, and her heart began to hammer.

She needed help.

Fast.

Trying to keep her body as still as possible, she slowly turned her head and scanned the kitchen for her cell phone. It wasn't on the counter . . . next to her purse . . . in the charger . . . there! It was on the café table.

Ten feet away and out of reach.

Thumper hopped over. Close enough for her fingers to brush his soft fur. He must sense there was no chance she'd snatch him up and relegate him back to his cage. Had he come to offer comfort?

She stroked his haunch. He was a friendly little guy. Companionable.

Too bad he couldn't retrieve the phone for her.

And too bad she couldn't just stay where she was, wait for someone to come home and find her.

Except no one came home to this house anymore but her. Nor did anyone call, other than charities soliciting donations and mechanical voices promising to reduce her credit card debt.

Father Murphy and Reverend Baker would notice if she didn't show up to cook, and after a few days Charley would wonder why she wasn't stopping by for tacos—but she couldn't wait for one of them to realize there was a problem.

She had to summon help herself.

Focusing on the cell, she assessed the situation. At least the phone was on the edge of the table. Within grasping distance if she could manage to sit up and scoot over there. Once she had it in hand, it would be a simple matter of calling 911.

She could do this.

She *had* to do this.

Bracing for the pain, she rolled to her right side.

A moan erupted from deep inside her as knives stabbed her shoulder, sucking the air from her lungs. Her whole body grew clammy, and she began to shake. Badly.

This wasn't going to work. She'd never make it to the table before she passed out.

But what other choice did she have?

A tear trickled out of the corner of her eye, and she swiped it away with trembling fingers. It was her own fault no one cared about her. Hadn't she made it clear for years she was self-sufficient? Didn't need anyone? Wanted to be left alone?

Well, she was alone now.

That isn't true. I am with you always.

She stopped breathing.

Why had that promise from Scripture echoed in

her mind? Was the comforting reminder coming from . . . God?

No. Not much chance of that. Why would he talk to a stiff-necked woman who had snubbed him for almost two decades?

Yet . . . if God *was* with her, might he give her the strength to get to that phone?

She surveyed the ten-foot chasm separating her from the cell, the distance as formidable as a ten-mile trek. She'd definitely need a source of strength beyond her own to make that trip.

And since no one else was going to come to her aid, why not put it in his hands and hope for the best?

"Michael, on behalf of myself, Father Kevin, and the entire board, thank you again for spending the past hour and a half with us, for all the analysis you've already done, and for the recommendations you'll be putting together. You've been the answer to our prayers."

As Reverend Baker wrapped up the meeting and the board members applauded, Michael's neck warmed. "I haven't done that much. Besides, based on everything I've learned, you may not be too happy with my suggestions. I'll offer several options, but given your finite resources, the most practical one might be to simply scale back."

"We've toyed with doing that in the past, but it's difficult to say no to people who ask you for help." Father Kevin folded his hands on the church's conference room table and leaned forward, his expression troubled.

"I understand your dilemma." Far better than they knew. "But operating within more limited parameters and helping some people is preferable to closing up shop and helping no one. I know some of your board members are already stretched to the limit with Helping Hands demands." He scanned the group seated around the table, his gaze lingering for a moment on Tracy.

She dipped her chin and gathered up the papers spread in front of her.

"That's true." Reverend Baker nodded. "And it may be easier to make that kind of hard decision if the recommendation comes from a seasoned nonprofit professional like you." He stood and indicated a table to the side, where several cakes and beverages were displayed. "I hope you'll stay a few minutes to enjoy some hospitality and give our members a chance to thank you personally."

"I'd be happy to." Michael rose too.

As the meeting broke up and several people came over to chat with him, the minister put his phone to his ear and withdrew slightly from the group.

By the time he'd been plied with cake and coffee, the cleric was ending the call and motioning to Father Kevin and Tracy. While

Michael continued to converse with the other board members, he kept an eye on the trio in the corner. From their frowns and serious discussion, he had a feeling another Helping Hands case had been dropped in their laps.

So much for trying to wrangle a few words with Tracy.

Perhaps that was best, though. What would he say? He'd taken personal discussions off the table during their last conversation at Eleanor's, and his business with Helping Hands was concluding. There was no other reason for a one-on-one chat.

Except he liked being around her.

That was the truth, no matter how guilt-inducing—and dangerous—it was.

And he hadn't a clue how to deal with it.

He ran out of cake and conversation with the board before the two clergymen and Tracy wrapped up, and with no further excuse to linger, he deposited his disposable cup and empty plate in the trash, retrieved his Helping Hands file and notepad from the table, and exited the meeting room.

Mist had moved in since he'd arrived, and he turned up the collar of his coat as he stepped outside. His decision to drive tonight instead of walk had been a smart one.

After setting the meeting material on the seat beside him, he started the engine, put the car in gear, and . . .

Squinting, he peered through the windshield. Was that bike leaning against the side of the church Tracy's?

He gave it a more thorough inspection. It looked like the Schwinn she'd been riding the day of the accident. Hard to be certain in the dim light, though. Yet she *had* rushed into the meeting at the last minute, flushed and out of breath—as if she'd pedaled hard and fast to get there on time.

Frowning, he tapped a finger against the steering wheel. The trip home, up the hill to the cottage on the bluff outside of town, would be taxing—not to mention dangerous, with the darkness and mist reducing visibility.

He didn't like the whole notion.

His engine continued to idle while the remainder of the board members filed out. Father Kevin crossed the lawn to the rectory. Reverend Baker hurried toward his car.

Still he waited.

Several more minutes passed, and he cracked his window as the glass began to fog. This really wasn't any of his business. He ought to go home.

But he didn't.

Instead, he shut off the engine.

Ten minutes later, Tracy appeared. She pulled the door of the building shut behind her, tested it, and hurried toward her bike.

"Tracy!" He slid out from behind the wheel.

She halted and swiveled toward him. Though

her exit had triggered a security light, her face remained in shadows. The surprise in her inflection, however, was clear. "Michael?"

"Yes." He walked toward her. Too bad he hadn't worked on a game plan while he was waiting. Now he'd have to wing it. "I, uh, thought this was your bike. It's not the best night for cycling." He stopped a few feet from her, near enough to see the pulse hammering in the hollow of her throat. Had he startled her . . . or was she happy he'd waited?

He tamped down the foolish flush of pleasure triggered by the latter possibility.

"I'm used to this kind of weather."

"You'll be cold and wet halfway home, despite that." He motioned toward her slicker.

She positioned her Helping Hands folder in front of her, like a shield. "I'm fine. And I have to go. A situation came up that I need to work on ASAP."

"I noticed you and the two clerics huddled in the corner. A Helping Hands issue?"

"Yes. A complicated one."

"Want to talk about it?"

She hesitated. "It's too damp to stand out here and chat, and I locked the church hall behind me."

"We could sit in my car." Maybe if he could get her that far, she'd agree to let him drive her home. She could always retrieve her bike in the morning.

"Thanks, but there's not much to talk about. A

call came in on the hotline from a mother who just learned her sixteen-year-old daughter is pregnant. She's a basket case, her husband is ranting, and the daughter is threatening to run away. She's trying to find a neutral place for her daughter to stay until everyone calms down and they figure out how to deal with this."

"Messy."

"Yeah. The girl's locked herself in her room and is holding off on her threat until she sees what kind of options we can offer."

"What are you supposed to do?"

"Go through the Helping Hands resource list and see if I can come up with someone willing to take her in for a couple of weeks."

"Doesn't this family have any relatives?"

"Not in the area—they're recent transplants. Besides, they don't want to broadcast the news." Tracy massaged her temple. "I really need to go. I have payroll to do for one of my clients tonight too."

Payroll? Eleanor had said Tracy was a CPA, but . . .

"I thought you worked on the cranberry farm."

"Accounting is a side job. It helps pay the bills." The mist grew heavier, and she edged away. "Thanks again for the offer of a ride. The board will look forward to getting your recommendations."

With a lift of her hand, she hurried toward the

bike, stowed her files in a saddlebag, and took off down the street. Within seconds, her headlamp disappeared in the mist.

So much for his powers of persuasion.

A raindrop bounced off his nose, compelling him to pick up his pace as he returned to his car. If this soup morphed into a downpour, she'd be soaked to the skin within minutes, slicker or no slicker.

Fortunately, the rain remained light during his short drive back to Anna's. And Tracy didn't have all that far to go. Less than a mile. If she pedaled hard, she might beat the—

He hit the brakes as he swung onto Anna's street and flashing lights strobed across his windshield. Despite the heavy mist, he could pick out a police car and an ambulance.

Both were parked in front of Anna's house.

Stomach clenching, he sped down the street, whipped into the driveway, and jogged toward the open front door—just in time to meet two EMTs trundling out a stretcher.

Anna, her face gray and scored with new lines, was lying on it.

"What happened?" He addressed his question to the EMT in the lead.

"Are you a relative?"

"No. He's my guest." Anna glared at the man. "I already told you I don't have any relatives. My body may be hurt, but my mind's working fine."

The EMT grinned. "The morphine must be kicking in."

"So what happened?" Michael tried again.

Anna transferred her attention to him. "I fell and hurt my shoulder."

"Where are they taking you?"

"Coos Bay." This from the EMT in the rear as he passed.

He fell in beside the stretcher, next to Anna. "Do you want me to call anyone?"

"We already asked that." The lead EMT threw that over his shoulder as they approached the ambulance.

"No. There's . . . no one to call." Her voice was more subdued now.

"Are you sure?" He touched her ice-cold hand.

Her eyelids flickered closed, and she swallowed. "Yes."

"We need to load her up, buddy."

He hesitated. A trip to Coos Bay wasn't in his plans for nine-thirty on this Thursday night—but who else did Anna have?

"I'll follow you."

"Michael . . . no. Too much trouble." Her words faded as she disappeared into the ambulance.

"Give me the hospital information." Michael filed it away in his memory as one of the EMTs reeled it off and shut the door. A few moments later, the vehicle rolled down the street toward 101.

"If you want to take off, I'll lock the place up." A police officer emerged from the shadows, radio in hand.

"Thanks. I'd appreciate that."

Michael returned to his car, tapped the name of the hospital into his GPS—and tried to psyche himself up for a slow drive north through swirling mist on a winding road.

He couldn't muster much enthusiasm.

Hands gripping the wheel, he hesitated. Anna had told him not to follow her . . . and he'd much prefer to spend what was left of his evening with a cup of coffee, one of her amaretto brownies, and the novel he couldn't seem to make much head-way on. That held far more appeal than a sterile, antiseptic-smelling ER.

Yet she had no one else—or no one she was willing to contact. And she'd reached out to him. Offered to pray on his behalf.

He had to go.

Sighing, he pressed on the gas and pointed the car toward the highway.

How in the world had he managed to get himself so enmeshed in this small community in a mere two weeks, anyway?

It didn't make sense.

But once Anna was safely home, once he handed over his recommendations for Helping Hands, he was going to focus on his reason for coming to Hope Harbor in the first place. He'd spend time alone. Walk the beach more. Think. Plan. Perhaps even pray a little himself. This trip was about evaluating his life and discerning his future, and there would be no more detours.

It might not be easy to forget about Anna and her estranged son, the problem-plagued Helping Hands organization, or a cranberry farmer who right now was getting ready to burn the midnight oil as she struggled to help a family in crisis while juggling two jobs.

But he was going to give it his best shot. The last thing he needed in his life was more complications.

As the rain intensified, reducing visibility further, he increased the speed of the wipers. A mileage sign for Coos Bay was caught in his headlights for an instant as he passed, then receded into the blackness behind him.

Funny.

Two weeks ago, desperate to stay in Hope Harbor, he'd turned down a perfectly nice hotel in Coos Bay. Anna's invitation had seemed like a godsend.

Now . . . he wasn't so sure.

Because if staying in this town continued to distract him from his real purpose for being here, maybe her generosity hadn't been such a blessing after all.

10

"I think she's coming back to us."

As the unfamiliar female voice spoke, Anna struggled to lift her eyelids—a gargantuan task.

Once she managed to prop them open, the world was a blur. She squinted at the two figures hovering over her—a woman she didn't know and . . . her heart stumbled. Could that be . . . ?

"John?" She reached toward him.

He took her hand in a warm clasp. "No, Anna. It's Michael. Your tenant."

Michael.

Of course.

John hadn't been part of her life for a very long time.

Swallowing, she blinked away the fuzziness and gave her surroundings a once-over. Was this a . . . hospital?

Yes.

The memories flooded back. The fall in her kitchen. The excruciating pain in her shoulder as she'd scooted inch by painful inch over to the table and called 911. The ambulance ride in a haze. The prick of an IV needle. Blessed relief . . . then nothing until now.

She glanced down at her left arm, which was

supported by a pillow and captured in a sling—but it wasn't in a cast.

That was a positive sign . . . wasn't it?

"I didn't break it?" She tipped her head toward the injured appendage.

"No. You dislocated your shoulder." The scrub-attired nurse finished fiddling with the IV and walked toward the door. "I'll let the doctor know you're awake. She'll want to talk with you before she signs the release order."

Release order.

What sweet, sweet words!

Anna closed her eyes. She could go home to her house and her critters and her normal life.

Thank you, God. For this blessing . . . and for giving me the strength I needed to get to the phone.

The silent words came unbidden—but they were deserved. It was only right to give credit where it was due. No way would she have been able to drag herself across the room through the agonizing pain without divine intervention.

"How are you feeling?"

She raised her eyelids as Michael took the nurse's place beside the bed, scrutinizing him. He looked exhausted—and he needed a shave.

"Why did you come? I told you not to." Her response came out sharper than she intended.

He lifted one shoulder, his demeanor still friendly despite her rudeness. "I figured you'd

161

need a ride home if they let you leave—and it would be a long taxi trip to Hope Harbor."

A pang of shame washed over her. This man owed her nothing, yet he'd gone out of his way to be a good Samaritan. At the very least, he deserved a heartfelt thank-you—and an apology for her bad temper.

"I'm sorry." The words came out stiff, like a window that hadn't been raised in years and had to be forced open, protesting loudly all the way. "That wasn't very gracious of me. I appreciate your kindness. What time is it?"

He lifted his arm and twisted his wrist. "Seven-thirty."

She frowned up at him. "How can that be? I didn't call 911 until close to nine."

"Seven-thirty a.m."

She blinked. "I've been here all night?"

"Yeah. The ER had a busy evening. A car accident on 101 in the fog, with multiple injuries far more serious than yours. You got bumped down in the queue once they evaluated your damage. But they kept your IV loaded with pain meds until they could take care of the dislocation."

His explanation registered at some peripheral level, but she was too busy grappling with the implication to pay much attention.

Michael had kept vigil in this hospital all night. For her.

Her vision misted, and she groped for his hand. "You must be dead on your feet."

His tired smile as he gave her a gentle squeeze was more telling than his evasive response. "I've put in longer nights with my job on occasion. I can catch up on sleep once we get you home."

The door opened again, and a woman in a white coat swept in carrying a clipboard. "Mrs. Williams, I'm Dr. Stevens. How does the shoulder feel?"

"Much better than last night."

"I'm not surprised. Dislocations can be very painful, but in general once we get the ball back into the socket, the severe pain diminishes almost at once. Not to get too technical, but you had what we call an anterior dislocation. It's a common injury in falls—especially when you try to break the fall by stretching out your hand. Is that what happened?"

"Yes."

"Well, the good news is you don't have any apparent soft tissue damage—the ligaments, tendons, and muscles all appear to be fine. As a result, you should see fairly rapid improvement."

"How rapid?"

"I'd estimate three to four weeks in the sling."

"That long?" How was she supposed to drive and cook for her clergy clients and keep up the house and her animals one-handed?

"You don't want to rush back into full use too soon. If you do, you could injure the shoulder joint or even dislocate it again."

Anna bunched the sheet in her hand. "But I have obligations. And what about simple things, like cooking meals and getting dressed and . . ." Her voice trailed off as a wave of panic washed over her.

"Is there anyone you can call on for short-term help?"

"No."

The doctor flipped through the papers on the clipboard. "Then you may want to retain the services of a home health aide for the first couple of weeks. We can give you some information on providers." She signed the top paper and handed the clipboard to the nurse behind her. "Any questions?"

Anna's mind was spinning too fast to form a coherent thought. "No."

"I'd suggest you see your primary care doctor in the next few days. He or she can recommend a physical therapist. Once the pain and any swelling diminish, shoulder exercises will help you regain muscle strength. In the meantime, over-the-counter pain meds should take care of any discomfort, but I've written a prescription for something stronger in case you need it. We'll give you all that paperwork. I hope you have a speedy recovery." She finished her rapid-fire download with a quick smile and whooshed out the door toward the next patient.

"I have most of your paperwork right here." The nurse moved in closer to the bed. "There are a few things for you to sign, then I'll help you get dressed."

Michael had stayed in the background during the doctor's briefing, but now he stepped forward. "I'll wait outside while you finish up in here. Once you're ready to leave, I'll bring the car around to the door."

"We won't be long." The nurse was already elevating the head of the bed and preparing to remove the IV. "Stay close."

"I'll do that." He transferred his attention to her. "Hang in, Anna. You'll get through this. It's just a matter of logistics at the house. Nothing that can't be handled with a few phone calls."

She locked gazes with him, this man who somehow seemed able to see into her heart and grasp her worry. Who was doing what a son should do in an emergency. What *her* son would have done if she hadn't been so stubborn.

But Michael was a fine substitute in her moment of need.

Another blessing she didn't deserve.

She swiped a hand across her eyes and managed to choke out a thank-you.

Michael winked and slipped out the door.

Once he left, she signed paper after paper, trying

to process everything the nurse was telling her. But her mind kept drifting to the logistics Michael had referenced. She supposed she'd have to consider some home health care—but strangers in her house? A shudder rippled through her. Perhaps there was some other solution.

However, as the nurse began to help her dress and the difficulty of that simple task even *with* another pair of hands began to register, Anna faced the truth.

Like it or not, she was going to need some assistance.

And since John was lost to her and she had no real friends in town, her only option would be to pay a stranger to do tasks a friend or family member would have done out of love.

Michael wiped a weary hand down his face, exited the ER, and drew in a cleansing lungful of the crisp morning air.

Hospitals were the pits—and ERs were worse. They were suffocating, anxiety-ridden hellholes.

With fingers that weren't quite steady, he unscrewed the cap on the bottle of OJ the nurse in the intake area had offered him and took a swig. Coffee would be better, but the sweet juice did help chase away some of the bitter taste on his tongue.

Too bad it couldn't chase away the bitter memories as well.

Recapping the bottle, he slowly exhaled.

Leave the past in the past, Hunter. Focus on today. On the positives.

Right.

Today's big positive was that Anna's injuries weren't serious, and once they healed she could resume her normal life.

Until she reached that point, however, she would need help.

He uncapped the bottle and took another drink, leaning back against the wall of the building as the evaporating mist began to offer glimpses of clear blue sky. His resolution to get back on course with his own quest might have to be put on hold for a day or two while he helped Anna line up a service that would . . .

He froze.

Wait.

Might there be another option?

Slowly the seed of an idea took root in his mind. Grew. Blossomed.

It was an ideal solution.

Except he doubted Anna would agree.

Still, it was preferable to hiring some stranger who would invade her home and rob her of the privacy she cherished—though convincing her of that might take every ounce of his persuasive powers.

If the option was even available at this point.

But that was easy enough to check.

He finished off his juice in three long gulps, tossed the empty container into the trash bin near the ER entrance, and pulled out his cell.

It was too early for phone calls.

Bleary-eyed, Tracy peered at her bedside clock. Almost eight?

Maybe it wasn't too early . . . unless you'd been up until two in the morning working on a Helping Hands crisis, finishing the payroll for a client, and trying to round up a used tractor to replace old Bessie.

Another few minutes of sleep would have been nice before she cycled out to the farm for a full day of manual labor.

Sighing, she grabbed her phone off the nightstand and croaked out a greeting.

"Tracy?"

At the familiar baritone voice, the fog vanished from her mind. "Michael?"

"Yes. You sound a little hoarse." He paused. "I'm sorry, did I wake you?"

"Um . . . I was getting up anyway. I had kind of a late night." She swung her feet to the floor and stood. He probably thought she was a lazy slug, still in bed on a workday at this hour. Not an impression she wanted to leave—for reasons she didn't care to analyze. "On top of the Helping Hands crisis and that payroll project I mentioned, I was scouring the net for a used tractor. Ours died this week. Since I succeeded on two of the three, the late hours paid off. What's up with you?"

"Two out of three . . . does that mean you haven't found anyone to take the teen yet?"

"No, but I only managed to connect with six of the ten candidates I culled off the master volunteer list." She wandered into the bathroom. Looked in the mirror. Grimaced. She needed a caffeine infusion—bad. "I'll try the others this morning. I'd take her in myself except her parents are adamant she have supervision, and my long days at the farm wouldn't allow me to monitor her activities." She padded down the hall toward the kitchen.

"Well, I think I may have a candidate for you."

She jerked to a stop at the counter, her big toe connecting with the kick plate underneath. "Ouch!"

"What's wrong?"

She balanced on one foot and inspected the injury. "I stubbed my toe. What did you just say?"

"I think I found someone to take the girl. Anna Williams."

She lowered her foot to the floor. "You're kidding."

"No. Let me tell you the story."

She listened as he recounted the events of the previous evening and his all-night vigil.

"Are you still at the hospital?"

"Yes."

And she thought she'd had a tough evening.

"You must be exhausted."

"I'll catch up on sleep later. Here's the thing—the girl needs a place to stay with supervision from a responsible adult. Anna certainly qualifies . . . and she's going to need some help with daily chores for the next two weeks. However, she isn't keen about some stranger from a home health service invading her space."

Tracy lifted her foot again and massaged her throbbing toe. "She doesn't know this girl, either—or her parents."

"But the girl wouldn't be paid help. They'd be doing each other a favor. I think that would sit better with Anna."

"Have you mentioned it to her yet?"

"No. I wanted to make sure the job hadn't been filled."

"It hasn't—but I need to find someone fast or throw in the towel so the family can seek help elsewhere."

"I'll talk to Anna on the drive back and call you within the hour. We're about to leave the hospital. Can you wait that long?"

"Yes—but I'm not holding my breath." Tracy lowered her foot to the floor and dumped some coffee into a filter . . . though she hardly needed the caffeine infusion now. Her brain was percolating at full strength. "Home health care people come and go; they don't live at your house.

Anna doesn't even invite anyone over for coffee, let alone an overnight stay."

"It can't hurt to give it a shot."

"I suppose not."

"Do you know any details about this girl's situation? I expect Anna will ask."

"Yes." She shoved the filter into the coffee-maker and poured water in the top while she talked. "Reverend Baker got the whole story from the mother—or her perspective on it, anyway. They relocated to the area about six months ago from the Midwest. Job transfer. Grace—that's the daughter—hated having to leave in the middle of high school, and she had difficulty breaking into the established cliques here."

"A lonely teen plus a bunch of unruly hormones. Not a great combination."

"That about sums up the problem. The parents' names are Ellen and Ken Lewis, if Anna asks."

"Does the girl have any other issues? Drugs, alcohol, smoking?"

"Not according to her parents."

"Got it. I'll call you back within an hour."

"I'll keep my phone handy." The soothing aroma of coffee began to fill the cottage, and she inhaled a lungful. "And thank you for trying, no matter the outcome."

"Let's hope it's positive—for everyone. Talk to you soon."

Clapping her hand over a lingering yawn, Tracy

set the phone on the counter and pulled out a box of cereal.

Talk about a strange turn of events. Wouldn't it be amazing if the town hermit agreed to end her self-imposed isolation?

And Michael's kindness to the unsociable woman who'd offered him lodging was just as extraordinary.

Kindness, however, seemed to be part of his DNA. Making amends with cinnamon rolls, plying her with tacos, fixing Eleanor's gutter, lending his expertise to Helping Hands, a sleepless night in the ER . . . and now stepping in to offer a potential solution to the current crisis with the teen and her family.

The word *remarkable* hardly did him justice.

But remarkable as he was, and persuasive as he might be, Tracy had a feeling that getting Anna to agree to house-sit a pregnant teen in exchange for assistance with daily chores was going to be one very tough sell.

11

"Absolutely not. I won't have a girl like that in my house." Anna narrowed her eyes at Michael as she juggled the remains of her fast-food meal in her lap. "Is that why you bought me breakfast? To butter me up?"

Her chauffeur kept his attention on the road, his expression neutral, his tone mild. "No. We both needed to eat. I'm sure you were hungry, and I was starving."

She winced. Of course he was. The man had spent a sleepless night in the ER. She should have bought breakfast for *him,* not the other way around.

"Sorry."

"No problem. I'd be out of sorts too if I'd spent a night hooked up to an IV. What did you mean by 'a girl like that'?"

Her hackles rose again, despite his conversational manner. "Isn't it obvious? A good girl wouldn't get herself pregnant at sixteen. She must be the loose type."

"From what I gathered, she was more lonely than loose."

Anna sent him a disapproving scowl. "Are you condoning her behavior?"

"No. But I guess I've gotten more tolerant of mistakes as I've grown older and made plenty of my own. It seems to me it's better to treat people in the midst of a crisis with compassion than censure or criticism. I try to leave judgment in God's hands these days."

"Hmph." She looked out the window, one shoulder stiff, the other aching as the sting of his words echoed in her heart. Not that they'd been directed at her past, of course. Michael didn't know her history. No one in Hope Harbor did.

Yet what he'd just said . . . it was the sort of comment George might have made if he'd been on hand when she and John reached their moment of crisis.

And it was the sort of comment this family needed to hear.

But Michael was a far better candidate to share such a message than she was.

She leaned back against the headrest and closed her eyes. Nothing but the lulling hum of tires on asphalt broke the silence as one mile passed. Two. Three.

She peeked at him. Was he waiting for her to say more? To capitulate, perhaps?

Well, let him wait. She wasn't budging on this. The last thing she needed in her home was a pregnant teen with questionable morals. What if the girl tried to sneak her boyfriend into the house in the middle of the night? A stunt like that would put her smack in the middle of this mess, and she was through with messes. Had been for almost two decades. Walking a wide circle around trouble was a far safer route to follow.

"Anna . . ." Michael's gentle voice broke the silence at last. "This is an ideal solution. You need help for a couple of weeks, preferably of the live-in variety. If this girl is willing to abide by the rules you and her parents set, wouldn't it be better to have her in your house than a variety of strangers who come and go every day?"

He wasn't giving up.

Well, neither was she.

"There's no place for her to sleep." She kept her focus on the road ahead, chin elevated, back ramrod straight. "George turned the third bedroom into an office."

"What about the second bedroom?"

"It's John's."

"Could she use it?"

"No."

He didn't press that point.

Smart man.

"Is there a sleeper sofa?"

She fidgeted, the empty food wrapper in her lap crinkling in protest as she balled it in her fist. "Yes, but it's not very comfortable—or private."

"I don't think this girl cares. She just wants to be away from her parents until everyone's emotions simmer down—and it would be better for her than living on the street as a runaway."

Anna frowned. Would the girl really run away— or was that an idle threat? The stories she'd read in the paper about runaways were chilling. If this Grace did happen to be basically a good girl who'd made one big mistake, she wouldn't be sweet and innocent for long if she ended up on the street.

But why was that her problem?

She squeezed the crumpled wrapper tighter, until her fingers began to ache. "What does the baby's father have to say about all this? He and his family should assume some responsibility for the girl. It takes two to tango, after all. No doubt there's fault on both sides."

"She hasn't identified him yet. She's afraid her father might punch out the kid—or the kid's dad."

Anna sniffed. "Hard to blame him if he did."

"Maybe not, but it wouldn't solve anything. Don't you think there are more productive solutions?"

She cradled her arm against her body, trying to keep her shoulder as stationary as possible in the moving car. Like what? The teens were both underage, far too young for marriage. Nor were they old enough to raise a baby. They were practically children themselves.

"I don't know. I suppose they could discuss the situation with the boy's parents. In fact, all six of them could talk this thing out and come up with a plan everyone can live with."

"A reasonable suggestion. Still, it doesn't solve the problem at hand."

True.

Another mile of silence passed while she stared out the window, blind to the scenery as she tried to find ways to punch more holes in Michael's proposal.

At last he spoke again, his tone measured and without a trace of censure. "It's your decision . . . but this family needs help, Anna. If this thing gets out of control, it could cause fractures that will never heal."

Like the ones in your own family.

He didn't have to say the words for the parallel to come through loud and clear.

And whether or not he knew it, it was the most effective argument he could have used. It might be too late to salvage her relationship with her son, but this family hadn't yet crossed the point of no return.

Hard as she tried to cling to her objections, they began to crumble.

Besides . . . there were practical reasons to think about the arrangement he'd suggested, as he'd noted—and in the end, the girl and her family might not go for it anyway.

She loosened her grip on the crumpled paper and let the wadded ball drop into her lap. "I would only consider your idea after meeting with the family. Could that be arranged?"

It was faint, but she picked up his soft exhale. "I'll talk to Tracy. She's coordinating this hot potato. I think your request is very reasonable." He cast her a warm smile. "You won't regret this, Anna."

She didn't respond.

But as the miles flew by and Hope Harbor grew

closer, as doubt began to peck away at her decision, she hoped he was right.

"You're kidding." Tracy rested a hand on the half-filled fiberglass tub of fertilizer in the equipment shed. "How did you manage to convince her?"

"I could attribute it to charm—but I think practicality had a lot to do with her decision. However, she wants to meet the family before she commits."

"I can set that up. When would be a convenient time?"

"The sooner the better, for both parties' sakes. Fortunately, Anna's right-handed, but it was apparent in the few minutes I spent with her in her house after we got back that she's not going to be able to do a lot of everyday tasks by herself."

"I'll ask Reverend Baker to arrange a meeting. He's done some additional checking on the family through the references they provided. They appear to be solid. He also knows Anna, so I'm confident he'll give her a fine recommendation. I hope this works out."

"I do too. I'll let Anna know the reverend will be in touch—and then I'm going to crash."

"Sounds like a plan. And Michael, thank you again for stepping in on this. I was worried we'd have to turn this family down. My last four prospects were iffy."

"Glad to help." A yawn came over the line. "Sorry."

"Get some sleep. I'll give you an update later." She ended the call, started to dial Reverend Baker's number—and discovered Uncle Bud watching her from the doorway.

"For a man and a woman who have no interest in each other, you two talk an awful lot."

She pressed the end button again. Her call could wait a few minutes.

"Good morning to you too." She shoved the phone in the pocket of her jeans and began filling the fertilizer tub on the spreader again, trying for nonchalance. "And for your information, that was a business call. A situation with Helping Hands."

"Uh-huh." He entered the shed and trudged over to the fungicide sprayer, resting a hand on the homemade machine he'd crafted a dozen years ago. "Sounded pretty friendly to me." His voice rasped.

Tracy looked over her shoulder. "You okay?"

"Yep." He fiddled with the sprayer, angling away from her.

She went back to work, bracing for his next comment or question about Michael.

It never came.

Maintaining an air of busyness, she cast a surreptitious peek his way, watching as he went about the fungicide prep.

Hmm. Usually, Uncle Bud's actions were quick

and precise and efficient. Today he was slow and stiff, moving as if he hurt.

She squinted at him. Was he a bit flushed too? And where was the mischievous sparkle in his eyes that always accompanied his teasing comments?

He started to cough, the hacking sound coming from deep within his lungs.

And he kept coughing.

Stomach knotting, Tracy crossed to him.

Up close, he appeared even worse. His cheeks were sunken, and the hand she placed against his forehead came away hot.

Too hot.

"You're sick."

"I'll be fine."

"Uncle Bud." She grabbed his arm to keep him from walking away. "You have a fever."

"A degree or two. It'll pass." Another fit of coughing slammed through him, and he sagged against the sprayer.

"Okay . . . enough of this I'll-muscle-through stuff. You have a fever—of more than one or two degrees. You're coughing. I'm guessing by your stiff movements that your whole body aches. What have I missed?"

He felt behind him for the seat on the sprayer and sank down. "Headache, sore throat, fatigue."

"You have the flu."

"Nobody gets the flu in June."

"I guess you're special. Does Nancy know?"

"No. I got up early and came outside. Can't afford to be sick. There's too much to do."

"I'll admit it's not ideal timing, but let's be glad it isn't harvest season." She tried to sound as upbeat as possible—but he was right. She might have found them a new tractor at a reasonable price, but that purchase would leave them zero budget for emergency help.

Meaning her long days had just gotten a whole lot longer for the next couple of weeks. The mowing, fungicide and fertilizer application, spot-spraying weeds, watering, a few fence repairs would all be on her shoulders—unless she could find a way to earn some extra cash pronto that would allow her to hire a high school kid for ten or fifteen hours a week. And somewhere in there she had to take care of her accounting clients too.

"I can hear those gears grinding at warp speed in your brain." Uncle Bud pushed himself to his feet. "I might not be able to stand on the fertilizer spreader for hours, but I can sit on the sprayer and get the fungicide application done."

"Forget it." She put her arm around his shoulder and guided him to the door. "I'm walking you back to the house and turning you over to Nancy."

"I can get there on my own."

"Nope. I don't trust you. You'll sneak off to work on one of those fence breaks." She kept walking.

His shoulders drooped. "You want the truth? That wouldn't happen. I hardly have the energy to get back to the house."

He plodded along beside her, none of the usual spring in his step. He stopped once to cough, the warmth of his skin singeing her fingers through the sleeve of his T-shirt.

Nancy came out on the porch to meet them as they drew close, twin creases embedded in her forehead. "I saw you two from the window. What's wrong?"

"Our fearless leader has the flu." Tracy gave her uncle's arm a squeeze, then released him to Nancy as Shep and Ziggy raced up.

His new wife helped him up the steps, did the hand-on-the-forehead test, and shook her head. "Bud Sheldon, what were you thinking, going out in the fields in this condition?"

The dogs nuzzled his fingers, and he gave them each a pat. "I was thinking cranberries."

"Well, you're going to be thinking chicken soup for the next few days." Nancy propelled him toward the door.

"Good luck keeping him in bed. He hates being sick even worse than he hates fireworms and bog rats." Tracy rested one foot on the bottom step and pulled her baseball cap more firmly over her hair.

"Don't you worry about that. I know how to deal with problem patients." Nancy winked over her shoulder. "If you hold down the fort, I'll hold down your uncle."

"Deal."

The two disappeared into the house, and Shep and Ziggy trotted over to her. After a quick pat, they raced off, leaving her alone.

Very alone.

Taking a deep breath, Tracy slowly retraced her steps to the equipment shed, trying to psyche herself up for the marathon to come.

A cloud scurried over the sun, casting a shadow on the earth. Appropriate. This whole season had been filled with shadows. Bad news on the balance sheet. The loss of old Bessie. Uncle Bud being felled by the flu. And no rescue in sight for their longer-term financial problem.

She paused and looked up at the sky, now more gray than blue.

Are all these minor catastrophes a message, Lord? Are you telling us it's time to let the farm go? To give up the place our family has loved and nurtured and worked for three generations? Are you trying to tell us we're just postponing the inevitable?

She waited, watching the clouds. The bees continued to drone. The dogs continued to bark. The birds continued to chirp.

God remained silent.

No surprise there. Booming commands from above only happened in the Bible.

But how were you supposed to follow his guidance and discern his will if you couldn't hear his voice?

Let's do our best and leave the outcome to God.

Uncle Bud's advice echoed in her mind—and it was sound.

Besides, what other choice did she have?

So she straightened her shoulders. Picked up her pace. And prepared to do her best.

The tension in the air was as thick as it had been the day John walked out the front door with two packed suitcases and never came back.

Anna surveyed the group assembled in her living room. Ellen and Ken Lewis were sitting on the sofa across from her, close to each other but not touching. The mother's eyes were distraught and confused, her face etched with concern, her hands clenched in her lap. Beside her, the father's dark irises smoldered, and his posture was taut as a rubber band about to snap. He sat on the edge of the seat, as if prepared to jump to his feet at the slightest provocation, chin set, shoulders rigid, fingers flexing. Like he was itching for a fight.

Grace had claimed a chair on the far side of the room—part of the group but sufficiently removed to make a statement. A bulging backpack rested at her feet, in case they all agreed she would stay. The teen's long brownish hair was pulled back into a ponytail, the harsh style accentuating her narrow face. She had her mother's soft lips and her father's strong chin, but her eyes were all hers—hazel and filled with defiance . . . though fear lurked in their depths.

Reverend Baker, who'd collected and delivered the family to her doorstep, was in the kitchen with a cup of coffee, at her request. She wanted him nearby in case things got out of hand, but she was the one taking in a stranger. This was her show to run.

"Are you certain none of you would like a beverage? I know Reverend Baker would be happy to get you one."

"No, thank you." Ellen managed the hint of a smile. Her husband shook his head. Grace didn't respond.

"Very well." Anna shifted, cradling her arm as she tried to find a more comfortable position. "Reverend Baker has explained my situation to you. I'm told you're all seeking a safe, neutral place for Grace to stay, which I may be able to provide." She directed her next comment to the teen. "I need assistance with routine chores— dressing and other personal tasks, light cleaning, caring for my animals, some simple cooking. I would expect you to be available and willing to help during daytime hours. Are we clear on that?"

"Yes, ma'am."

The girl had some manners.

One positive in her column.

"Do you have any questions?"

"No, ma'am."

Anna refocused on the parents. "From my end, this arrangement would need to last for a minimum of two weeks. Are you comfortable with that?"

"Yes."

"I don't know."

The parents spoke simultaneously.

Ellen touched her husband's arm. "Ken, we talked about this before we came over."

"I know we did." He shot to his feet and began to pace. "But waiting isn't going to change anything. We need to get the name of that boy and deal with this." He stopped and planted his fists on his hips as he glowered at his daughter. "You know I can get that information from your cell log."

Grace rose too, and faced off against him, the color leeching from her complexion. "That's an invasion of privacy!"

"I pay the phone bill and you're underage. Once you stop acting responsibly, you forfeit any right to privacy."

"Ken." The mother stood and rested her fingers on his arm. "We promised Grace we'd wait until we all calmed down before taking any action."

"Yeah, well . . . I'm having some second thoughts."

Grace picked up her bag. "Then I'm out of here."

She sounded just like John had the day he'd stalked out without a backward glance.

"Honey . . . wait. Please." Ellen took a step toward her daughter, her tone placating, one hand still resting on her husband's arm. "Running away isn't going to solve anything. We need to stay calm and think this through. Ken . . ." She turned back to her husband and nodded toward the couch. "We agreed this was the best plan. Let's stick with it, okay?"

He hesitated, shoulders stiff, poised to say things Anna knew he might regret. So like her nearly twenty years ago.

But at his wife's urging, he retook his seat.

So did Grace.

All thanks to Ellen's intervention. The voice of reason . . . as George would have been on that long-ago day.

Perhaps with the mother's peacekeeping efforts and some outside help, this family would survive.

And she could provide that help.

"I'm sorry." Ellen sent her an apologetic look. "Emotions are running high all around, as you can see."

"That's understandable." Anna cradled her injured arm to take some of the pressure from the sling off her neck. "It's a difficult situation."

"To put it mildly." Anger flashed in Ken's eyes.

"But we'll figure out a way to deal with it, once we're all thinking more clearly." Ellen stroked his arm and spoke across the coffee table. "That's why we thought a short separation might be beneficial. If you're willing to take Grace."

From the moment Michael had broached the idea until the family walked in her door, Anna had been nervous about the whole notion. Yet all at once a gentle calm infused her—and the choice seemed obvious.

"I'll be happy to, as long as she promises to stick close and follow whatever rules you've set."

"The rules are simple. No computer or cell phone, no talking to this boy while she's here, and no running away." Her father sent Grace a don't-mess-with-me look.

She glared back. "I'll follow those rules if you promise not to check my cell records and cause trouble."

"I'm not the one causing trouble."

"I think we can all agree to those rules." Ellen glanced from her husband to her daughter.

"And I don't want you guys calling here constantly, either." Grace lowered her chin and picked at some peeling polish on her thumbnail. "I need some time to think too."

Ken started to speak, but Anna intervened.

"I think that's a wise suggestion. Distance can help restore perspective. However, I'll be happy to call you every day to let you know how things are going."

"That would be perfect." Gratitude softened Ellen's features.

"Then I guess there's nothing else to discuss."

Anna spoke again to Grace. "Would you let Reverend Baker know we're wrapping up in here?"

The girl rose without a word and disappeared down the hall.

"We can't thank you enough for offering your hospitality, Mrs. Williams." Ellen stood and came around the coffee table, hand extended. "Things have been so volatile . . . this is new territory for us. Grace has always been such a good girl."

Ken pushed to his feet too. "That's why I want to get my hands on the punk who did this to her—and lock her in her room until she's eighteen."

"And you wonder why I threatened to run away?" Grace stormed back into the room, the minister on her heels. "He didn't do anything to me I didn't fully cooperate with. Was it a mistake? Yes. Am I sorry about it? Yes. But it's done—and if we can't find a solution we can all live with, I'm outta here."

"Grace, you're only sixteen. Where would you go? Besides, we're a family. We stick together." Ellen moved toward her.

She backed away from her mother. "I just want to be left alone right now, okay? I'll stay here. We'll all think. Maybe we can work this out." The last word caught on a sob.

Reverend Baker scanned the group. "Does that mean you're taking Grace in, Anna?"

"Yes."

"Splendid. A sound plan all around, I'd say.

We'll leave the two of you to work out your living arrangements."

Daughter and parents faced each other across the room, Grace's shoulders taut, Ellen's eyes shimmering, and Ken's jaw still chiseled in granite.

Finally he took his wife's arm and they followed Reverend Baker out.

Once the door clicked shut behind them, Anna turned to her new houseguest. "Would you please lock the front door, Grace? There's a flip lock and a bolt."

The girl complied in silence, disappearing down the hall in the wake of her parents.

And as the click sounded in the quiet house with an ominous ring of finality, Anna hoped this limb she'd stepped out on wasn't going to crack under the weight of conflict and send her tumbling into disaster.

12

Was that Tracy?

Michael stopped, adjusted his sunglasses against the brilliant glare of the late morning sun, and squinted into the distance. The woman sitting on the sand, leaning against a rock, looked like her—but he walked this beach every day, and they'd never run into each other.

He started forward again. It was probably some tourist. Maybe the wife of that guy at the water's edge who was searching for agates or petrified wood or other flotsam. Or she might be part of that picnicking family group a bit farther down.

Maintaining an ambling pace, he glanced around. The beach was a lot more crowded than usual—if two dozen people could be called a crowd—but it was Sunday, after all. A day of rest and relaxation.

For some, anyway.

He toed a piece of beached kelp, the blades as twisted as his emotions, the bulbous, balloon-like bladders that kept the plant afloat as bloated and ready to pop as his taut nerves.

This was crazy.

Why should he be more stressed now than when he'd arrived? The beginning of his trip might not have been quite as smooth as he'd expected, but he'd finished his Helping Hands report yesterday, Anna had a live-in helper and didn't need his assistance, and he was now free to devote himself to the solitude and escape he'd craved when he'd left Chicago.

Yet the ability to dial things down, to sit on the beach in total relaxation like that woman by the rock, eluded him.

He cast another glance at her as he prepared to pass.

Froze.

It *was* Tracy.

He gave her a quick sweep. Her head was tipped back against the boulder, as if she was enjoying the parade of clouds across the blue sky, her eyes masked by sunglasses. Not an unusual sight on the beach. But the black slacks, crisp green blouse, and blazer draped over her shoulders were more suited to Sunday services than sand.

Why was she here, all dressed up like that?

He hesitated. Should he interrupt her solitary respite and try to find out or keep walking?

Keep walking, Hunter.

His jacket whipped around him as he debated . . . and all at once a gust of wind caught the Frisbee being tossed by the family group and sent it sailing directly toward Tracy.

Letting his reflexes take over, he ran toward the soaring disc, leaped, and grabbed it midflight.

"Sorry about that!" One of the kids jogged toward him.

"No problem." He threw it back, and the youngster caught it.

Given the shouted exchange, he expected to find Tracy watching him once he turned back.

She wasn't.

In fact, she hadn't moved a muscle.

Weird.

He walked closer . . . and her even breathing and slack hands explained her lack of response.

She was sound asleep—her purse beside her a tempting target for a fleet-footed thief.

Michael did another scan of the beach. Hope Harbor might be a small town, but bad stuff happened everywhere. He couldn't walk away and leave her vulnerable . . . could he?

Ignoring the voice in his head that reminded him she was a native and would understand better than him the risks—if any—of falling asleep with an unattended purse on the beach, he strode across the sand and dropped down to rouse her.

But up close and in repose, her features relaxed, Tracy Campbell short-circuited his lungs. The slender arch of her throat, her soft lips, and the gentle curve of her jaw . . . lovely.

And much too appealing.

He needed to get out of here before . . .

She stirred, and from his position beside her he could see her eyelids flutter open behind the dark glasses.

No chance of escape now.

Better warn her she had company before she discovered him watching her.

Using the first excuse that came to mind for invading her turf, he grabbed her purse and dangled it in front of her.

With a soft gasp, she sat up straighter and twisted toward him.

"I could have walked off with this."

"Michael." She said his name in a voice husky with sleep that stirred his long-dormant libido.

The red alert warning in his mind began to flash with more urgency.

He set the purse back down and eased away as a cloud covered the sun, dimming the glare. "You might want to tuck this somewhere safer."

With a wry smile, she relaxed back against the rock. "A purse snatcher would be disappointed if he took that. My wallet is in my other bag. Not that he or she would get much even if it *was* in there." A shadow passed over her face that had nothing to do with the cloud activity above—followed by a yawn. "Sorry. To tell you the truth, I've never passed out on the beach like this before. Instead of detouring here after church, I should have caught a quick nap at home before I tackle my to-do list at the farm."

"You work on Sundays too?"

"Not when Uncle Bud is in charge. But what he doesn't know while he's down with the flu won't hurt him. Besides, there isn't much choice. The work has to get done, and if your crew is cut in half . . ." She shrugged.

Frowning, he lowered himself to the sand beside her and took off his sunglasses. "Are you telling me you and your uncle run that whole farm by yourselves?"

She removed her glasses too, revealing faint shadows under her lower lashes that hadn't been there in their previous encounters. "Sixteen acres of beds can be handled by *one* person most of the year, but since we both have outside jobs too, the farm really needs the two of us. And during harvest we hire a couple of part-time people."

"You mean you're doing everything out there yourself, plus your accounting work and the Helping Hands stuff?"

"I'm trying to. Whether I'll keep all the balls in the air remains to be seen. How are things going with Anna?"

He had to forcibly switch gears at her abrupt change of subject. "Fine, as far as I can tell. I stopped by yesterday and met Grace, who was very polite and seems conscientious. Anna said it's working out fine so far."

"At least that's one crisis I can cross off my list." She checked her watch, let out a small groan, and reached for her purse. "I need to get going. I only meant to sit here and rest for five minutes. Somehow that morphed into half an hour. But the sun felt good."

"It's gone now, though." He scrutinized the sky. The clouds that had been on the horizon were fast covering up the expanse of blue. "I haven't yet gotten used to the rapid weather changes out here. One minute it's sunny, the next it's gray and gloomy and depressing. I have to admit I much prefer the sun."

She slipped her sunglasses back on, snatched

her purse and shoes, and stood—all in the space of a few heartbeats.

It took him a second to recover from her sudden move, and by the time he rose, she'd slung her purse over her shoulders and backed off.

Bad vibes wafted his way.

"Is something wrong?"

"No."

Her denial was definitive, but her taut posture and pinched features said otherwise.

"Tracy, I . . ."

She retreated a few more paces. "I need to go. I'll see you around."

Shoulders stiff, she swiveled around and hurried toward the steps that led from the beach to the bluff road above.

He propped his hands on his hips and followed her progress. What was with that prickly reaction? Could she be mad because he'd startled her?

No. She'd been amiable as she'd answered his questions about the farm.

After that, they'd talked about Anna and . . . what?

Another gust of wind kicked up some sand at his feet. Weather. The last thing he'd said had been some innocuous comment about the changeable weather.

Why would *that* tick her off?

Mystified, he watched as she stopped at the base

of the stairs, slipped on her shoes, and began to ascend. Was she annoyed out of some misplaced sense of civic pride, interpreting his comment as an insult to her hometown?

That was a stretch.

Maybe she was just tired. Fatigue often left people touchy and out of sorts. He certainly hadn't been in top form after his all-nighter at the ER, and sleep seemed to be a luxury in Tracy's life at the moment. Plus, she was under a lot of pressure.

Yet as she disappeared over the top of the bluff, never once looking back, he had a feeling there was more behind her reaction than lack of shut-eye or stress.

A lot more.

Might it be connected to Anna's suggestion early on, that he should ask Tracy for advice about how to deal with regrets?

Possibly.

But given her miffed attitude just now—not to mention a brutal work schedule that wasn't liable to put their paths on a collision course in the near future—there wasn't much chance he'd have an opportunity to say hello, let alone ask her for advice.

Unless he could think of some way to *make* their paths intersect.

Not a smart idea, buddy. It's safer to stay away.

Right.

Shoving his hands into his pockets, he resumed his walk.

Yet even as he acknowledged the soundness of that advice, his mind was already working through scenarios that might give him a chance to spend more time in the company of a lovely cranberry farmer.

Pausing in the middle of the bed to swipe her forehead on the sleeve of her T-shirt, Tracy surveyed her progress.

Not bad.

Assuming the weather held, at this rate she'd have the fungicide done by noon tomorrow. Then she'd finish the fertilizer application. Also on the plus side, the evening rains were eliminating watering from her list of chores for now.

But man . . . She assessed the lush growth around the beds. The grass on the dikes and roads was getting out of hand. Mowing would have to wait, though. Fungicide and fertilizer were a much higher priority—

She blinked as a blue-jeans-clad man appeared on top of the dike, spotted her, and lifted his hand.

Michael?

Why would he be here after her rude departure earlier on the beach?

The man must be a glutton for punishment.

She shut off the engine and stood, wiping her

palms down the denim on her thighs. *Stay cool, Tracy. He has no idea why he touched a nerve this morning—or why you've spent the past few hours down in the dumps.*

But *she* did—and the implication wasn't sitting well. An innocuous remark about the weather should only have an impact if she was attracted to the man who'd made it.

And she wasn't.

She wouldn't let herself be.

Especially after that remark.

Straightening her shoulders, she crossed the bed, climbed the dike to stand beside him, and summoned up a smile. "I didn't expect to see you again today."

"I don't have any plans for the afternoon, and I thought you might be able to use a hand."

She furrowed her brow. "With what?"

"This." He swept his arm in an arc. "It sounds like you have a long list of chores to do."

She tried to digest his offer. "You want to work on the farm?"

"Yeah." He exhaled. "I think I offended you this morning. I have no idea why, but I apologize. I hoped we might be able to mend our fences if I backed up that apology with some sweat."

She folded her arms. "You don't have to do that—and no apology is necessary. It was my fault. I'm just . . . a little tired. I'm sure you have better things to do on a Sunday than work on a farm."

"As a matter of fact, I don't. And I need some exercise beyond my casual strolls on the beach. In Chicago, I tried to get to the gym two or three times a week. Here, I've been more or less a couch potato—and my body is telling me to get moving before everything atrophies."

Atrophy? No danger of that as far as she could see, with those lean hips and the muscles bulging below the sleeves of his T-shirt.

"I can't let you spend your Sunday doing manual labor."

"You are."

"I own this place."

"And I'm bored." He gave her a cajoling wink. "I promise to try my best not to do any damage, if you're worried about that."

The man had some serious charisma.

"No. Cranberry farming isn't rocket science."

"Then put me to work. What can I do that doesn't require a lot of training?"

Tracy eyed the overgrown dikes around them. If he was sincere . . .

She tucked her fingers into the front pockets of her jeans. "How are you with a weed eater?"

"I know how to use one." He cocked his head. "But isn't there a more substantive way I can contribute?"

"Keeping the grass on the dikes and road under control is a huge task. It's not hard, but it's labor-intensive and difficult to stay on top of this time of year, even with both Uncle Bud and me working. If I had some help with that, I could focus on the fungicide and fertilizer applications without the grass chore hanging over my head."

"In that case, weed eating it is. Point me in the right direction and I'll let you get back to your . . ." He regarded the sprayer in the middle of the bed. "Whatever you were doing."

"Fungicide." She gestured toward the equipment shed, the peak of its roof visible through the trees. "The weed eater's hanging on the wall in that building. It's ready to go. There are work gloves and goggles in there too. You could start with this bed. The sides of the dikes are a mess."

"What about the top?" He inspected the grass beneath their feet.

"We have a riding mower for that. If you get tired of weed eating, you can switch."

"Got it. I'll find what I need."

He started to turn away, but when she touched his arm, he froze and looked over his shoulder.

"This is above and beyond, you know. Manual labor couldn't have been on your agenda for Hope Harbor."

"I've done a lot of things since I've been here that weren't on my agenda." His focus shifted to her hand on his arm, and she yanked it back as he slipped his sunglasses on, masking his eyes. "And this one's a win-win—you get some help, and I get some exercise."

"Way more than you probably need—or want."

"If I get tuckered out, I'll let you know."

Before she could respond, he retraced his steps across the dike.

She watched him for a few moments, then slowly returned to the sprayer and revved up the motor again.

Talk about a strange turn of events.

Maybe Michael did want an activity to replace his gym visits back home—but there were plenty of opportunities for exercise in Hope Harbor that didn't involve dirt and bees and calluses.

So what was the real reason the Chicago non-profit executive had volunteered for such scruffy duty?

Was it possible he just liked her company, despite what he'd said about following a solo road?

She guided the machine down the length of the bed, trying to squelch the little trill that possibility sparked. What silliness. She was reading far too much into this simple gesture of kindness. Michael Hunter wasn't the type to walk away from someone in need, and that's all his offer of help was—an example of his caring, generous nature. Reading anything more into it was foolish.

Yet once he returned and began cutting the grass with measured, methodical sweeps of the weed eater, biceps bulging, broad shoulders flexing, she found her gaze straying to him far too often.

And more than once, she found him looking her direction too.

Which did nothing to tamp down her heightened sense of awareness—or tame her misbehaving heart.

So she finished the bed as fast as she could and moved to the next one, several hundred yards away.

Unfortunately, the physical separation didn't help a whole lot. She could still hear the weed eater, still picture the easy swinging rhythm he'd established.

And for a fleeting moment, she could almost pretend that her old dreams about having the companionship of a special man in the fields on a regular basis had come true. A man who relished the farm she loved as much as she did.

This was how it should be.

How she'd always wanted it to be.

A sudden wave of yearning swept over her, so strong she almost lost control of the sprayer.

Clamping down on the wheel—and her foolishness—she managed to keep herself on course. Dreams were fine, as long as they were grounded in reality. As long as you pursued them with your eyes wide open and understood the risks. As long as you didn't let wishing and hoping and rose-colored glasses blind you to reality.

Michael Hunter was a nice man. In another time, another place . . . who knew what might have happened?

But he was a nonprofit executive, not a cranberry farmer. He was going back to his life in Chicago soon. He was still in love with his wife. And he wasn't crazy about cloudy weather.

None of which would bode well for a future with him if she *did* happen to be interested.

So she'd be grateful their paths had crossed for these few brief weeks, and for all the help he'd given her—but when the time came, she'd say good-bye and do her best to forget about him.

Because this was her home . . . and unless she could find a way to mitigate her grief and guilt, unless someone came along who could embrace Hope Harbor and love the cranberry farm as much as she did, she'd go it alone.

13

This was hard work.

Shoulder-straining, backbreaking work.

The kind of work Tracy did every day.

Michael propped his foot on the slanted edge of the dike, resting the weed eater on his thigh while he gave his screaming biceps a break. So much for all those weights he'd lifted in Chicago.

No wonder Tracy was lean and fit to the extreme.

Hard work aside, however, it wasn't too difficult to understand why she loved the farm. Taxing the body instead of the brain was a refreshing change of pace. So was filling your lungs with fresh air and enjoying the sun on your shoulders and petting the dogs when they trotted by.

If it wasn't for the pesky bees swarming all over the place, the farm would be idyllic.

As if on cue, another one buzzed around his ear. How many had he swatted away since arriving three hours ago?

Too many to count.

Just as he prepared to resume trimming the dikes, a slender woman with short, gray-streaked hair appeared at the end of the bed. The uncle's new wife?

When she motioned him to join her, he shut off the weed eater, laid it on the grass, and walked across the top of the dike.

As he drew near, she held out her hand and confirmed his guess. "You must be Michael. I'm Nancy Sheldon, Tracy's aunt. I called Tracy's cell to let her know I had an afternoon snack ready, and she mentioned you'd volunteered to help. She doesn't want to stop, but I'm hoping you can convince her to take a break. That girl would work till she drops if someone didn't rein her in."

He removed his safety goggles and gave the woman's hand a firm shake. Tracy wasn't in sight, but based on the faint thrum of the sprayer's motor, she wasn't far away. "I can try, but she strikes me as a woman who knows her own mind."

"That she does—and more's the pity some-times." Leaving that enigmatic statement hanging in the air, Nancy indicated the direction from which she'd come. "I put some drinks and a snack on the bench under the willow tree. She can show you where it is. And if you can't convince her to join you, sit for a while yourself. With Bud out of commission, we're very grateful for your assistance. We may not be able to pay you, but we can feed you."

"I'll enjoy the treat. Thanks."

"My pleasure. Well . . ." The woman looked him up and down with a smile he couldn't interpret. "I best get back to the invalid. Tracy warned me he'd be a difficult patient, and she was right. Keeping that man horizontal is a challenge." With a flutter of fingers, she retraced her steps.

Michael turned the other direction and followed the pattern of dikes that enclosed the terraced beds until he spotted Tracy. She was intent on her work, moving at a steady clip, maneuvering the sprayer like the pro she was.

He observed her for a couple of minutes, analyzing her pattern. She appeared to be finishing up this bed, traveling his direction. No need to interrupt her until she was done. Whatever treat Nancy had delivered could wait.

For now, enjoying the sight of Tracy was treat enough.

Dropping down to sit on the dike, he watched

her execute a turn at the end of the bed, in total control of the odd-looking machine with narrow wheels and a boom on both sides that extended about twelve feet. Either the contraption wasn't as unwieldy as it seemed, or she was just making the whole thing look easy.

He had a feeling it was the latter.

As she reached the far end of the bed, she glanced over her shoulder to check something behind her and caught sight of him.

The sprayer veered slightly off course, but her quick jerk on the wheel pulled it back in line. Keeping one hand on the helm, she held up a single finger and maintained a steady course.

Three minutes later, after finishing the bed, she pulled to the edge and shut off the motor—but stayed in the seat.

Maybe he'd be taking his break alone after all.

"I didn't want to interrupt until you were at a stopping place." He drew up his feet and rested his forearms on his knees.

"Stopping places are hard to find." She shaded her eyes as she tipped her chin up toward him. "Are your shoulders giving out?"

"Not quite—but I'm feeling them."

"Wait until tomorrow." Her tone was wry, her expression sympathetic. "After my first weed-eating session of the season, I can hardly move them for a few days."

"Thanks for the encouragement."

"You could switch to the riding mower—or call it a day, if you want."

"I still have a few swings left in me. But I wouldn't object to a break, and your aunt tempted me with a snack. She said it's under the willow."

Two parallel dents appeared above her nose. "Nancy came out to find you?"

"Yes." He cocked his head. "Is that surprising?"

"Yeah. She usually stays close to the house until the bees are gone."

"You mean they leave? As in . . . migrate?"

"No. We have a rental agreement with a beekeeper who brings in two or three hives per acre in May to pollinate the cranberries. He takes them back in July."

He swatted at one buzzing his ear. "I can't say I'm sorry to hear that. They're a nuisance."

"Actually, they're quite calm. These are European honeybees, and in general they won't bother you if you don't bother them. Yellow jackets and hornets . . . different story. The honeybees do like those dandelions you're sitting next to, though."

He shifted away from the clump of weeds. "Since your aunt braved the bees to track me down, why not take a break with me? Besides, I could use a guide to the willow."

She shifted in her seat. "It's not hard to find. From the equipment shed, you can see the house.

Walk toward it, and you'll find the willow along the way. There's a bench underneath."

Not the response he'd hoped for.

"Does that mean you're not coming?"

She hesitated, and for a moment he thought she was going to change her mind.

But she didn't. "I can't stop. There's too much to do and not enough daylight hours."

"Will fifteen minutes make that much difference?"

Again, she hesitated.

"Come on, Tracy." He gave her his most persuasive smile. "It's no fun to eat alone."

She caught her lower lip between her teeth. Rubbed a palm on the denim covering her thigh. Jiggled her foot.

He waited her out.

But in the end, she held fast. "I'm sorry. I need to keep going. I'm getting a lot done, and I don't want to slow the momentum. Plus, I had a big lunch—as Nancy knows, since she provided it. But you should go see what she left. She's a great cook."

His powers of persuasion must be getting rusty.

Using one hand for leverage, he pushed himself to his feet, ignoring the protest from his shoulder. "Well, at least I can tell her I tried."

Despite the twelve feet separating them, he could hear her huff. "She sent you after me?"

Must be a touchy subject for some reason—but he couldn't lie. "She suggested I try to persuade you."

Tracy's shoulders stiffened and she yanked her baseball cap farther down over her forehead. "Enjoy your treat."

With that, she started the motor again and rolled away.

For a full sixty seconds, Michael remained where he was, wrestling down his disappointment—even though her decision to continue working was probably for the best. Neither of them wanted things to heat up.

Besides, if Tracy ever got involved with anyone again, she should pick a man she could count on to be there for her—and his track record on that score was dismal.

She grew smaller as the sprayer moved further away, and he shoved his hands in his pockets, shoulders drooping. Tracy was a sensible woman, and she was following the prudent course by keeping him at arm's length. Why would she want to share a snack under the willow with a man who'd gone out of his way to make it clear he still loved his wife?

He hadn't lied about that, either. Julie's place in his heart was secure.

But might there be room for someone else too?

Someone like Tracy?

He toyed with that notion, approaching it with

caution—and came to a tentative conclusion.

Maybe.

Assuming he could overcome the problem that had plagued his marriage.

And assuming Tracy didn't shut him out even more once she learned his story.

Two very big assumptions—and the odds weren't in his favor.

Losing interest in the snack, he headed back to the weed eater . . . until a sudden growl in his stomach reminded him the energy provided by the can of soup he'd eaten at lunch was long expended. He did need food—and a little companionship under that willow would have been welcome.

Tracy continued to move away, however, her back toward him.

But if she *had* agreed to sit with him in this peaceful place that was so much a part of her, and if the opportunity had presented itself, perhaps he could have dug deep and found the courage to reveal what had prompted his two-thousand-mile trek west. To test the waters and find out sooner rather than later whether his history was a deal breaker.

The two dogs bounded up, and he gave them a distracted pat as he pivoted toward the equipment shed and they fell in beside him. He'd find whatever Nancy had left, scarf it down, and get back to work.

No reason to linger in the shade of a willow with only Shep and Ziggy for company.

Was this her day for being rude, or what?

Tracy peeked over her shoulder in time to catch Michael disappearing over the dike toward the equipment shed, the collies bounding along at his heels. In light of all his kindnesses, would a fifteen- or twenty-minute delay really have held up her progress that much?

No.

Then again, her refusal hadn't been about the farm.

It had been about fear.

Fingers gripped on the wheel, she exhaled. That was the truth of it, and trying to pretend otherwise was foolish.

Letting the motor idle, she pulled off her cap and rubbed her forehead. It would be easy to attribute the dull ache to sun or engine noise or fatigue or a dozen other things—but none of them was the culprit.

That honor belonged to Michael Hunter.

Because in spite of her renewed resolve this morning to keep her distance, she wanted to spend more time with him.

A lot more.

Not going to happen, though. She wouldn't let it. Being in the man's presence for extended periods wouldn't be wise.

On the other hand . . . what harm would there be in a few minutes under the willow tree? She could have a quick drink, eat a few bites of whatever Nancy had left, and make certain he understood how much she appreciated his help today. The man had given up a large part of his Sunday; agreeing to sit with him while he had a snack was the least she could do to express her gratitude.

Turning off the sprayer, she swung her feet to the ground, marched toward the willow, and tried to convince herself the churning in her stomach and the quiver in her nerve endings were due to hours on the vibrating sprayer and not the man she was about to join.

Her lame theory disintegrated, however, when both intensified after he rose to greet her with a smile that seemed to boost the air temperature several degrees.

"I decided I did need a break." Her words came out breathless—but it *was* a bit of a hike from the beds.

"Great. I was just getting started." He hefted a half-eaten dollar-roll sandwich. "Your aunt said snack, but this is more like lunch." He nodded to the bench, where the sandwiches, a plate of cheese and crackers, and dessert were arrayed.

"That would be Nancy. She knows we expend a lot of calories out here." Tracy moved to the other side of the bench, leaving the food between them, and sat.

"I'm not usually a big chicken salad fan, but this is great." He took another bite of his sandwich.

"She adds green grapes and almonds." Tracy popped the top on a soda from the small cooler at their feet, angling away from the house less than a hundred feet behind her. Considering how the master bedroom upstairs offered a perfect view of the bench and that Nancy had never served an afternoon snack here before, she figured her aunt and uncle were probably up there now, watching them.

On the plus side, they weren't within hearing range.

Michael helped himself to a cracker and some cheese. "If you don't dive in fast, I might finish all this stuff off before you get your share."

"I had a big lunch. I'm more thirsty than hungry." She picked up a piece of cheese and nibbled on it.

They ate in silence while Michael put a sizeable dent in the sandwiches and cheese, then moved on to the loaf cake.

"This is good too." He inspected the slice. "Sort of like fruitcake but better. Much better."

"It's cranberry nut cake, an old family recipe my grandmother created after they started the farm here. Nancy's the keeper of it, since I don't have much chance to cook. She always has some on hand." She took a piece too.

"It has . . . zip." He went back for seconds.

"That would be the bourbon."

He arched an eyebrow, trying not to smile.

"It's not like we drink it or anything. And I think there's only a fourth of a cup in the whole loaf. But thanks to the alcohol, it keeps for months. In fact, it gets better with age—up to a point."

"I'll bet." He took a third slice.

"You must be really hungry."

"Weed eating is hard work. Isn't there any easier—and faster—way to trim the dikes?"

"A sidearm mower would be great. Also expensive. It's cheaper to pay a high school kid to do the work—when money's available. The timing on old Bessie going belly-up wasn't ideal." She finished off the cake she no longer wanted and downed it with a few swallows of soda.

"Sounds like things are tough in the cranberry business."

His comment was gentle. Cautious, almost. Like he was afraid she might get her dander up—again—and stalk off, as she had this morning.

That wasn't going to happen—but how best to respond?

She looked down, playing with the edge of her napkin. His tactful phrasing would allow her to blow off the implied question without being rude—but could she be honest about their dire straits? Michael wasn't the type to tell tales, and most of the locals had probably already guessed that Harbor Point Cranberries wasn't on the best financial footing. None of the farms were.

Besides, this man reeked integrity. She might not know him well, but her instincts told her he could be trusted with this confidence—and perhaps other secrets, if she ever found the courage to share them.

She picked up a cranberry that had fallen onto her napkin and took the plunge. "They are— especially for smaller operations. The price per pound has fallen a lot in the past few years, and more and more of the family farms are dis- appearing. It was always hard for smaller growers to make a living, but it's impossible now. All of us have other jobs. Even with that, it's hard to survive." She took a deep breath and gave voice to her greatest fear. "The truth is, unless we figure out a way to bump up revenues, we're not going to last until next season." The last few words rasped out.

His hand reached over the food and rested on her arm, the warmth of his strong fingers seeping into her skin . . . and her heart. "I'm sorry to hear that. I had no idea the situation was that dire."

"I appreciate the empathy." Pressure built behind her eyes, and she squeezed the cranberry between her fingers. "But I haven't given up hope. Who knows? We could get a lucky break." Not likely— but dwelling on negatives wasn't productive.

She bit into the cranberry and shifted the focus to him. "You must have financial challenges in your job too. It can't be easy to keep a nonprofit solvent, either."

"No." He retracted his hand, and she missed the contact at once. "Fund-raising is a big part of what I do, but I've always been the hands-on type too. I like to deal with the people we try to help as well as the numbers." He paused. "That's how I met my wife, in fact."

She studied his profile. Was that disclosure, tacked on almost as an afterthought, an invitation to ask more? Or would he shut down if she probed?

Only one way to find out.

"Sounds like an interesting story." She held her breath, bracing for a rebuff.

Instead, he opened up. "It is. Before I took the job with St. Joseph Center, I worked for a food outreach organization in Kansas City. In addition to a pantry, we had a soup kitchen that provided a hot meal every day. I coordinated the volunteer servers, and Julie was one of them. I never had much of a chance to talk with her until one Thanksgiving. We were always overloaded with volunteers on holidays, and there wasn't a lot for either of us to do. We ended up sharing some turkey . . . discovered we had a lot in common . . . and six months later we got married."

"That sounds like a plot from a romance novel."

"Yeah. All but the happy ending."

At his hoarse reply, she was tempted to reciprocate his caring gesture, to reach out and touch him. But they were talking about his dead wife now, not a family farm. A much more heartbreaking loss.

Better not to overstep.

"How long were you married?"

"Four years. We still had two pieces of our wedding cake in the freezer, waiting for our fifth anniversary." His Adam's apple bobbed. "One morning she went to work at the grade school where she taught and never came home. It was an aneurysm."

As the tragic tale lay heavy between them, Tracy's stomach twisted.

"I can't even find the words to express how sorry I am." She managed to choke out the trite platitude, wishing she could offer deeper consolation.

"It's okay. Words don't help, anyway. Nothing does. I tried burying myself more deeply in my work, hoping that might keep the grief at bay, but I only succeeded in burning out—and running halfway across the country searching for answers." He scrutinized her, as if he was trying to deter-mine whether to say more. At last he spoke again. "I was also trying to escape the guilt."

The desolation in his eyes tore at her heart as

she struggled to make sense of his words. "I don't understand. An aneurysm isn't a condition you can predict—or control."

"No, it isn't. That was God's doing, and I'm still angry at him about it—which is one of the reasons I don't often attend church. But I'm also angry at myself for not being there for Julie during our marriage."

Once more, his self-recrimination didn't compute. "That's hard to believe. Everything you've done since you've been here tells me you're kind and caring and generous—almost to a fault."

"Not almost. *To* a fault." His shoulders drooped, and he wiped a hand down his face. "My nonprofit work has always consumed my life—to the point I end up neglecting other important things . . . and people. Julie rarely complained when I was called away on evenings or weekends or holidays, and she was even willing to accept an abbreviated honeymoon so I could be back for the launch of a new program for homeless veterans. But she deserved better." Slowly he exhaled. "All she ever asked me to do was carve out a week to take a vacation with her to a place she'd loved as a child."

"Hope Harbor." The answer at last to the *why* behind his visit.

"Yes. We had it planned once, but I ended up canceling after another work issue arose. I promised to reschedule—but two months later, she was dead." He closed his eyes, and a muscle ticced in his cheek. "And I wasn't there for her then, either."

Tracy's stomach knotted. Could this story get any worse?

She braced as he continued.

"The hospital called me, but I had my phone on silent while I sat in on a crisis counseling session with a battered wife who'd come to us for help." His voice hoarsened. "By the time I got the message and arrived at the hospital, she was gone."

In the silence that followed, Tracy tried to process all Michael had told her—but her overloaded brain was in a muddle. Only one thing was clear. He'd come to Hope Harbor in search of answers . . . solace . . . forgiveness . . . absolution . . . whatever he needed to close that painful chapter in his life and move on. Yet based on the tautness in his shoulders and the hollowness in his eyes, his battle with guilt and self-reproach was far from over.

They had that much in common—except unlike him, her failure hadn't stemmed from an overabundance of unselfishness and empathy. Just the opposite. Michael's feelings of guilt were far less warranted.

Could she convince him of that without revealing the shame in her own past?

Following her instincts, she reached out to him, scooting as close as the plates between them allowed, resting her hand on the taut fingers he'd wrapped around the edge of the rustic wooden bench. "You were trying to help people who had urgent needs. I'm sure many of the situations you dealt with were emergencies that couldn't wait. Besides, doesn't all the good you did mitigate the blame?"

"I tried to use that justification too—and sometimes I almost convinced myself that neglecting her and our marriage was defensible. Deep down, though, I knew it wasn't. But since she didn't often complain, I took the easy way out and told myself I'd do better down the road, that I had plenty of time to make it up to her. And then one day, time ran out."

As Tracy tried to put together a coherent, caring response, Michael spoke again, his expression bleak.

"I have one other confession. I'd like to think I've learned my lesson about priorities—but the truth is, given the nature of my work, I'm afraid I could be sucked back into that black hole of conflicting responsibilities if I was ever in another relationship."

Of all the words he'd said, the last two stuck in her mind.

Another relationship.

This from the man who'd told her he expected the road ahead to be a solo one?

She searched his face. Was he suggesting he

might be open to romance after all? With *her?* Was that why he'd shared his dark story—in the interest of full disclosure . . . and as a warning?

So many questions . . . so few answers.

But did she even want the answers, if they forced her to do a whole lot of soul searching of her own? To dredge up all the pain she'd tucked away in a dark corner of her soul?

Mind spinning, Tracy slowly retracted her hand. She wasn't ready for this—but she had to respond.

"You could always find a different kind of job, if you think that's a serious danger."

As she spewed out a left-brain response that sidestepped issues of the heart, some emotion—disappointment . . . resignation . . . sorrow?—deadened his eyes.

"Yeah." He focused on the depleted plates between them, shifting his tone into neutral. "Shall I help you gather up the remains of our snack?"

"I can take care of it."

Without arguing, he rose and put his sunglasses back on. "The weed eater calls. See you later."

He was striding away before she could respond.

Shep and Ziggy raced up to him, and he gave each a pat without slowing his pace, removing himself from her presence as quickly as possible.

And who could blame him? The man had opened his heart to her, shared his deepest pain, and all she'd said was she was sorry and maybe he could find another job?

Cringing, Tracy stood and slowly began to gather up the plates. She'd blown it. Big time.

So now what?

As far as she could see, there were two possible outcomes. He'd either realize he'd dumped a lot on her at once and cut her some slack while she absorbed it, or he'd pull back and she'd see very little of him during the remainder of his stay.

Who knew which result was better?

But she did know *one* thing with absolute certainty.

If she wanted to take this relationship to a deeper level, the next move was up to her.

14

"Are you sure you want to let him go?" Cradling Thumper in her arms, Grace nudged the sliding door open with her shoulder.

Anna moved past the teen, onto the patio. "Yes. He's old enough to survive on his own. I should have set him free a week ago, but I got pretty attached to him, despite all the mischief he caused." She stroked his soft fur as Grace drew up beside her. "Love can survive setbacks, you know."

It was a gamble to introduce such a sensitive

subject—but the girl needed to talk to *someone*. Burying her nose in a book in the corner of the living room, as she'd done for the past three days, wasn't going to solve her problems.

Ignoring the overture, Grace nestled the rabbit closer. "Where do you want me to put him?"

"At the end of the yard. He'll find some friends in the woods beyond, I expect. I'll walk back with you . . . but let's take it slow. I don't want to fall again." Anna shortened her steps to buy the two of them a few extra minutes together. Once they got back inside the house, the taciturn girl would no doubt retreat to her book until summoned for another chore.

After several attempts to engage her in conversation produced monosyllable responses, Anna fell silent until they reached the end of the yard. "You can set him down over there." She pointed to a bush at the end of the property. "We'll wait here until he gets acclimated."

Grace did as instructed, then returned to her side.

A full minute of silence ticked by while the rabbit remained motionless.

"Why isn't he moving?" Grace picked at her peeling nail polish.

"I expect he's scared. This is strange, new territory for him."

"Yeah." She sighed. "New stuff can be scary."

Anna peeked at the teen. Her face was

scrunched up, like she was trying not to cry.

Half a minute later, Thumper lifted his nose, surveyed his surroundings, and took a tentative hop.

"That's a positive sign." Anna cupped her elbow, taking some of the weight of the sling off her neck. "Once he gets a feel for his surroundings and knows what to expect, he'll be fine."

He took another hop. Another. Finally he squeezed through the fence and scampered off into the woods without a backward glance.

"Well, that's that." Anna watched him disappear. "I'll miss that little guy, though."

"Then why didn't you keep him?" Grace turned, the only evidence of her almost-meltdown a faint shimmer in her eyes.

"You can't nurture and protect little creatures forever. At some point, you have to set them free and hope they don't get into trouble." A principle as applicable to children as animals . . . and perhaps Grace would pick up her double meaning.

The teen fell in beside her as she walked back toward the house, but the girl didn't speak until they were nearing the patio. "How come you haven't asked me anything about . . . anything?"

Anna stopped at the table and motioned to the chairs. "Let's sit a minute."

The girl's shoulders stiffened. "Are you going to lecture me like my mom and dad did?"

"No." Anna claimed one of the chairs. "I want to enjoy this sunshine and rest a bit."

Grace gave her a wary look. "You aren't going to ask me about . . . about what happened?"

"No—but if you want to talk about it, I'd be happy to listen."

She lowered herself onto the edge of the other chair. "You already heard the story."

"Not from you."

"My point of view doesn't seem to matter." Instead of anger or defiance, her choked response held a world of hurt and sadness.

Despite the girl's bad choices, Anna's heart contracted. What a predicament to be in at that age, no matter the reason. "It does to me."

The girl slumped forward and fiddled with one of the cords on her hoodie. "I'm not a bad person, no matter what my mom and dad think." Tears mottled her words.

"Did they say you were?"

"They didn't have to. I could see it in their faces when I broke the news. I knew they'd be upset, but Mom . . . she looked like someone had died. And Dad was . . ." She swallowed. "He went ballistic. He started ranting and raving and pacing around the room, and he kept looking at me like he couldn't believe I was his daughter. I felt so a-ashamed." Her voice quavered, and she scrubbed at her eyes. "I mean, I always tried to make them proud of me, you know? Back home,

I got good grades and was on the debate team and worked as a junior lifeguard—and now one stupid mistake has ruined everything. Nothing will ever be the s-same again."

That was true . . . but it didn't mean the Lewises couldn't still be a family.

"Grace . . ." Anna waited until the teen met her gaze. "You're right. What happened will change your family forever—but it doesn't have to destroy it. As long as the three of you stick together, you can survive this. Of course your mom and dad are upset. Any parent would be. But that doesn't mean they don't love you. If they didn't care, they wouldn't be trying so hard to keep things from getting out of hand. They understand that once that happens, there's no going back." Or the mother did, anyway—and sometimes a single voice of reason was enough to avert disaster.

A tear hovered on the edge of the girl's lash. "I don't really want to run away."

"What *do* you want to do?"

"I'm not sure—but I don't want to have an abortion."

Anna frowned. "Did someone suggest that?"

"My boyfriend. But two wrongs don't make a right, you know? Even though that would be the easiest solution."

"Did you tell this to your parents?"

"No. We were all yelling. No one was listening to anybody."

Anna sighed. Been there, done that. And when no one listened, things could degenerate quickly. "So what would you like to do with the baby?"

More lip biting. "I'm not ready to be a mother. I was hoping maybe someone could adopt it."

"A reputable agency wouldn't have any difficulty finding your baby a loving home. There are many fine couples out there desperate to create a family."

"That's what I thought, but . . ." Fear flickered in her eyes. "What am I supposed to do until the baby's born? I can't live at home the way things are."

Anna cradled her arm, holding it close to her body. "You'll need the support of people who love you during the next few months. Your decision to carry the baby is a courageous one and I admire you for it, but there will be repercussions. Some people will judge you, others may snub you. There could be issues at school too—and you'll still have to deal with the father. Your parents are best equipped to be your support system."

Grace shook her head. "No. I'll be an embarrassment to them. Maybe I could . . . I could go away somewhere until afterward."

Not the best idea. Running away wouldn't change the facts, and the physical distance between her and her parents could lead to an emotional distance they might never be able to bridge.

But now wasn't the time to bring that up. It would be better if Grace and her parents arrived at that conclusion themselves.

Anna opened and closed the fingers of her left hand, stiff from inactivity. "I'll tell you what . . . let's think about this for a few days. Between the two of us, we might come up with some ideas. How does that sound?"

"Okay, I guess." She twisted her hands in her lap. "And . . . thank you for not treating me like a . . . a slut. I know what I did was wrong, but I was lonely, and he understood, and . . . and we got carried away." She drew in a shuddering breath. "Anyway, it helps to be around someone who's calm."

"It's easier to be calm if you don't have any personal involvement." Far easier. "Why don't we sit here for a few minutes, then we'll run down to Charley's and get some tacos for dinner. You have your driver's license, don't you?"

Grace's eyes widened. "You mean you'd trust me to drive your car?"

Not really. But this girl could use a shot of confidence.

"If you passed the test, you must be capable."

"I am. I took driver's ed, and even Dad said he was impressed with how well I handle the car. I'll be real careful too." The tension in her features eased a few notches.

"I'm sure you will. Now let's soak up this sun

for a few minutes before we go to Charley's."

She let her eyelids drop, and the girl beside her fell silent. The sun did feel pleasant—but the solar heat wasn't responsible for the new warmth in her heart.

For once in her life, she'd tamed her tendency to not only pass judgment but vocalize it. Grace might have used poor judgment and made irresponsible choices, but the girl was also hurting and afraid, her initial bravado no more than an act. It was amazing how she'd opened up once she'd found someone who was willing to listen without condemning her.

Anna filled her lungs with the fresh air. Slowly let it out. Too bad she hadn't applied that tactic with John. How different the outcome might have been if she'd kept her opinion to herself and listened to him with an open mind.

But if she couldn't go back and change her past, perhaps she could do her part to give this family a future.

There would be no book reading on the patio for a while.

Michael propped his shoulder against the back window in the annex. Anna and Grace were still sitting at the table, an intent discussion in progress.

Interesting.

What had happened since yesterday, when Anna

had told him Grace spent her free time reading rather than talking, to convince the girl to open up? Breaching the barrier the teen had erected between them would have required finesse and diplomacy . . . two traits he wouldn't have attributed to his landlady.

The woman was full of surprises.

He wandered back to the table and picked up his soda, wincing at the twinge in his shoulder. His full afternoon of weed eating yesterday had taken a toll, as Tracy had predicted. At least he was giving his sore muscles a rest today. She, by contrast, had probably been hard at it on the farm since sunup.

After taking a swig from the can, he opened his laptop and checked his email. A note from his dad. One from his sister. He owed them both an update, based on his sister's "Earth to Michael" subject line. Several Helping Hands board members had responded to the final recommendations he'd sent yesterday too, including both clergy-men.

No note from Tracy on his report . . . though given her crazy schedule, it was possible she hadn't had a chance to turn on her computer in the past twenty-four hours.

Either that or she was brushing him off—like she had yesterday.

He finished off his soda in a few long gulps and crushed the thin aluminum in his hand. Telling her about his mistakes with Julie had been a gamble—but it had been the honest thing to do. Especially after he'd begun toying with the possibility of acting on the electricity that sparked to life whenever he was in her presence.

The likelihood of that happening now, however, appeared to be remote. Tracy might not have exhibited any visible disgust at his negligence toward Julie and his marriage, but neither had she said a single word that suggested she understood or could forgive him. The hand she'd retracted hadn't been the only thing she'd withdrawn. Her next comment about changing jobs, offered in a casual, impersonal tone, had confirmed that.

And who could blame her? Assuming she, too, might be persuaded to give romance another try, why would she want to get involved with a guy who couldn't keep his priorities straight? Who'd given faceless strangers precedence over the woman he'd loved? Who was way too obsessive about his work, to the detriment of every other aspect of his life?

She was smart to ditch him. He didn't deserve her empathy or consideration.

A knock sounded on his door, and he tossed the mangled can into the recycle bin as he passed.

When he pulled it open, Grace stood on the other side. Michael scanned the yard over her shoulder, but the patio was empty now.

"Hi." She gave him a shy smile. "Mrs. Williams

told me it was your idea for me to stay with her, and I wanted to say thank you. I don't know what I would have done otherwise. She's been really great."

Despite his own funk, he managed to coax up the corners of his lips. "I'm glad it worked out. How are you settling in?"

"Fine. In fact, she just told me I could move my stuff into her son's room so I can have more privacy. I need to get back and haul it all in there before she changes her mind. But thanks again. She's a cool lady, even if she *is* old."

As Grace hurried across the patio toward the sliding door, Michael stared after her. His suggestion that Grace use her son's room had gone over like a lead balloon—yet the teen had softened her heart.

Shutting the door, he shook his head. How about that? The town curmudgeon had a new friend.

Except she wasn't the grouch her reputation had led everyone to believe. Not anymore, at any rate.

Things seemed to be on the upswing for both Anna and her new helper.

Must be nice.

He picked up the high-stakes, high-action novel and paged through it. He had . . . what? Another fifty pages to read? The most exciting part of the book, based on all the reviews.

But who cared how fictional characters resolved

their difficulties when real life held much more compelling drama?

He tossed the book onto the table and paced around the annex, doing his best to ignore the prods from his conscience as he thought about Tracy out at the farm, trying to keep all her balls in the air. Harbor Point Cranberries wasn't his problem, after all. There was no reason to feel obligated to help just because he had strong arms and plenty of time on his hands while she spent her days racing against the clock. Hadn't one of his reasons for coming out here been to try to get his overactive guilt complex under control? To regain some perspective and accept that no matter how hard he tried, he couldn't fix everyone's problems?

Yes and yes.

He grabbed his jacket. A relaxing, early-evening walk on the beach, that's what he needed.

And he would *not* think about Tracy. He'd focus on his future.

Yet as he slipped through the door and locked it behind him, he had a feeling it was going to be difficult to think about his future *without* thinking of Tracy.

Someone was knocking on her door.

Bleary-eyed, Tracy looked up from her laptop. The room was dark now, except for the glow from her screen. No surprise, considering she'd eked out every last watt of fading daylight at the farm before calling it a night and heading home.

Another knock sounded, and she peered at the time on the bottom of the screen.

Who would come calling at nine o'clock?

Using the kitchen table for leverage, she pushed herself to her feet, padded across the cottage floor in her socks, and peeked through the peephole.

Her heart stumbled.

Michael?

She took a rapid step back. Based on his cordial but cool parting yesterday at the farm, the ball for any further contact had appeared to be in her court. Not that she intended to lob it back. The peace-offering loaf of cranberry nut cake sitting on her kitchen table was only there on the unlikely chance she decided to reach out to him.

A third knock sounded, and she jerked.

Apparently the decision had been taken out of her hands.

Fingers trembling, she flipped the lock and opened the door.

"Hi." One side of Michael's mouth lifted. "Am I interrupting anything?"

"No. I was, uh, reading over your Helping Hands recommendations. This is the first chance I had to get to it."

"Hard day at the farm?"

"Busy, anyway."

A few seconds passed while she tried to think of

something else to say, the silence broken only by the distant crash of the surf at the base of the bluff.

He saved her the trouble. "I was taking an evening stroll on the beach. With the full moon there was plenty of light, and the tide's out. I thought it might be relaxing before I turned in—although I slept like a log last night."

"Fresh air and manual labor are a great cure for insomnia."

"Then you must never have a problem falling asleep."

She managed to hold on to her smile. "Bees aside, working on the farm does have its benefits."

If he noticed her evasive response, he gave no indication. "I got a feel for that yesterday. In any case, I decided to take the shortcut back to town over the bluff, and since I was passing by I thought I'd stop in and say hello." He offered her another smile, this one more tentative. As if he, too, was questioning the wisdom of further contact and was second-guessing his decision.

But now that he was inches away, her own analytical powers deserted her. How could she think straight when the light beside the front door was casting a golden glow over his strong-boned face, accentuating the end-of-day stubble on his firm jaw and deepening the blue of his irises to cobalt? Add in those worn but well-fitting jeans and hair tousled from the wind . . . whew. The man radiated an almost illegal amount of testosterone.

Tracy gripped the edge of the door to steady herself. She ought to send this two-legged temptation on his way . . . except this was her chance to make up for her pathetic response to his story yesterday. And she owed him that.

She'd just have to ignore the little tingles buzzing through her nerve endings.

"Would you like to, uh, come in for a few minutes? I have soda or coffee. I brewed a fresh pot not long ago."

He twisted his wrist and raised an eyebrow. "A new pot of coffee at nine o'clock?"

"I'll be up awhile yet. I've got a lot of work to do."

He hesitated. "I should keep moving, then. I don't want to delay your bedtime any longer than necessary."

"Actually, I wouldn't mind some company. Other than a quick bite with Nancy at lunch and a few visits from Shep and Ziggy, I've been by myself all day. I love those collies, but our conversations tend to be one-sided. Besides, as long as you're here, I'd, uh, like to talk through a few of your Helping Hands recommendations."

After studying her, he nodded. "Okay. For a few minutes."

He followed her to the kitchen table, and she ushered him into the seat he'd occupied on his last visit. "Coffee or soda?"

"Decaf anything is fine." He shrugged out of

his windbreaker and tossed it on an empty chair.

"Not coffee, then." She rummaged around in her refrigerator and found him a Sprite. "My brew is always the high-octane stuff." She rejoined him at the table and slid the soda toward him.

"Thanks." He popped the top. "So what would you like to discuss?"

My dismal response yesterday to all the confidences you shared.

Better to start with Helping Hands, however, and hope there'd be a natural opening to introduce more personal topics.

She scrolled through the document he'd sent until she came to the recommendations section, scrambling to come up with questions. Since all of his suggestions were straightforward, there wasn't a whole lot of ambiguity that needed clarifying.

"These ideas all have merit." *Think, Tracy, think!* "So, um, if you were the one making the decision, which direction would you go?"

He played with his soda can. "I wouldn't want to prejudice a decision by offering my opinion. The board members are the ones who know the group and its dynamics best, and they're also the ones who will have to implement any changes. It should be a full-board decision."

"I agree—but I'd still value your opinion. You have a lot more experience than all of us combined."

He tapped a finger on the table, then folded his hands. "As I noted in the report, Helping Hands is a victim of its own success. The growing demand is forcing you to stretch resources too thin. That will eventually lead to burnout and loss of volunteers—which will exacerbate the problem. The best way to maintain the level of service is to have a point person who can not only devote a lot more time to running the organization than any of the current board members can but also develop and coordinate a broader network of resources. That would be my choice."

"You're talking about a paid staff member."

"Yes."

"You saw our budget. There's no money for that."

"There could be, if fund-raising was also part of this person's job. An initial commitment of dollars for salary would be required upfront, but if you got the right person, the position should pay for itself after that."

"Coming up with the seed money for the position is the issue. We could solicit from the two congregations, but it's much easier for people to volunteer services than cash. Times are tough for a lot of us. And I doubt we could recruit anyone for the job without guaranteeing salary for a year, at minimum."

"True. That's why I included a number of other suggestions." He finished off his soda.

Tracy skimmed them again. Most involved

restricting the scope of services and/or the populations served or simply turning away requests when the organization became overwhelmed. He'd also included a list of fund-raising ideas, since the Helping Hands coffers were always running on fumes.

"None of these other ideas will get us where we want to be, though. Like Father Kevin said in the board meeting, how do you say no to people who ask for your help?"

His empty soda can crinkled. "If I knew the answer to that, I wouldn't be in Hope Harbor."

The perfect opening for her apology. And perhaps he'd be receptive. Didn't his impromptu visit suggest he wasn't holding her lack of empathy yesterday against her?

Fingers wrapped around her coffee mug, Tracy took a sip of the potent brew and sent a silent appeal heavenward.

Lord, help me find the words that will comfort and heal without misleading him about my interest.

Taking a deep breath, she slowly set the cup down and laid her hand over the fist he'd clenched beside the crushed can.

His gaze flicked from her fingers to her face, his expression wary.

She swallowed. "As long as we're on that subject, can we revisit our discussion under the willow?"

"I don't have a whole lot more to say."

"But I do." A skitter of nerves tempted her to remove her hand, as she'd done yesterday, but she wrestled them into submission. There would be no overt signs of rejection today. "First of all, I want to thank you for sharing your story with me. That can't have been easy."

"No. It wasn't. In fact, while I'm close to my parents and sister, even they aren't privy to the skeletons in my closet with Julie."

Yet he'd shared them with her.

So much for keeping things impersonal.

He continued as if he hadn't expected a response. "Everyone thought I was an ideal husband—which goes to show how deceiving looks can be. Things that appear rosy on the surface aren't always as perfect as they seem."

A burning arrow of pain pierced her heart, extinguishing any lurking romantic fancies, and her hand jerked.

Michael narrowed his eyes. "Are you okay?"

No.

How could she be, when those words could have been spoken about the sham of *her* perfect marriage?

"Tracy?"

She tried to smile, grasping at the first excuse that came to mind. "Sorry. You're not the only one with overused muscles, I guess." She rolled her shoulders and rotated her neck. "I did some weed eating myself for the last couple of hours today."

"I know just where you're hurting, then."

Before she realized his intent, he was on his feet and standing behind her, his lean, firm fingers on her shoulders.

Her heart began to bang against her rib cage. "W-what are you doing?"

"Trying to help those sore muscles." He began to gently knead. "Better?"

Better? With the heat from his hands seeping through her T-shirt?

Ha.

"I can feel the tension. Try to relax." His fingers continued to work her taut muscles.

How could she relax—or think straight—with all that blood rushing to her head?

But she had to focus on her goals for this conversation: empathize with his guilt about his wife, try to convince him he was being too hard on himself, and sympathize with his fear that he might repeat that mistake in a future relation-ship—all the while sidestepping his hint that a relationship with *her* might be on his radar screen, if she was interested.

Good thing she wasn't hooked up to a heart monitor or the latter objective would be toast.

"Um . . . Michael?"

"Yes?"

"Thank you for not holding my insensitive

reaction yesterday against me. I was just . . . overwhelmed."

"Understandable. I dumped a lot on you." His hands continued their steady ministrations. "To be honest, your reaction was what I expected—and deserved. Any caring person would be shocked by my story."

"Actually, I was more shocked by the tragedy of your wife's sudden death than your problem with priorities. It's easy to see how someone in a career like yours could be caught between a rock and a hard place trying to balance personal and job commitments. But after what happened, I'm sure you'd be much more careful in the future about overextending yourself on the job front."

"I wish I had your confidence."

"You should. Any smart person learns from an experience like that, and you're smart. You're also kind and caring and conscientious. The truth is, I . . . admire you a lot. Your story didn't change that."

Mission accomplished . . . and *admire* had been an inspired word to use. Complimentary but not overly personal—and safe. It was perfect.

She waited for Michael to respond.

Instead, after an infinitesimal hesitation, he kept working on her shoulders in silence.

Uh-oh.

Maybe her word choice hadn't been so perfect. Maybe it had been *too* impersonal.

Say something else, Tracy!

"If . . . if it makes you feel any better, you aren't the only one with regrets—or the only one who's made mistakes in a relationship." As the words tumbled out, a wave of horror swept over her.

That was *not* a subject she wanted to discuss.

Again, Michael's hands stilled . . . then picked up the rhythm again. "I think some regret is normal when a spouse dies young. No relationship is perfect, and there are things all of us would change given a second chance. But I'm willing to bet you had your priorities straight."

She gritted her teeth, fighting against the sudden pressure behind her eyes and in her throat.

Don't cry! Don't cry! Don't cry!

Tracy repeated that mantra over and over and over—but it didn't help. A tear spilled out. Another followed. And another. She swiped them away as surreptitiously as she could, choking back the sob threatening to erupt, trying to keep her shoulders from heaving, willing herself to—

"Tracy?" Michael's hands froze, and she turned her head slightly.

Wonderful.

There was a damp splotch on the back of one of his fingers.

A wave of panic rocked her as he began to circle around to the front of the chair. Before he could get a glimpse of her face, she jumped to her feet and bolted for the safety of the bathroom.

"I'll be back in a m-minute." She tossed the

ragged words over her shoulder, locked the door behind her—and rested her forehead against the smooth wood.

What a disaster!

The tears continued to flow, and she fumbled for the hand towel. It had been months since she'd broken down over Craig. She'd accepted her culpability and moved on with her life. What else could she do? Tears didn't change anything . . . and she'd already cried two lifetimes' worth.

Yet one comment from Michael, and wham! The spigot was wide open again.

It didn't make sense.

Unless . . .

Sniffling, she stared at her red-rimmed eyes in the mirror and faced the truth.

Unless she was falling for a temporary visitor from Chicago who carried plenty of his own baggage and didn't like cloudy weather.

No!

She couldn't let that happen!

Because even if he happened to feel the same and they could work through all of his issues, she wasn't wife material. He might think *he* was carrying a boatload of guilt, but she had enough to fill the *Titanic*. She'd failed Craig far worse than he'd failed Julie.

No way would a kind, caring man like him be able to overlook her past.

But if he is as kind and caring as he seems,

maybe he could. And this time, you might be a better wife. Didn't you just tell him that people can learn from their mistakes?

Tracy bit her lip. Was that little voice in her head spouting wishful thinking . . . or speaking the truth?

The former, surely.

Yet despite her best efforts to contain it, a tiny ember of hope flickered to life in her heart.

"Tracy?" Michael's muffled, single word was taut with worry.

She gripped the edge of the vanity. "I'll be out in a minute."

After a few moments, his footsteps retreated.

Slowly she released the breath she'd been holding. At the most, she could hide in here another few minutes. Meaning she needed to pull herself together. Fast.

She also needed to make a potentially life-changing decision.

Yesterday, Michael had taken a risk by sharing the heartaches and regrets from his marriage. It had been an honest and courageous confession that spoke to his integrity—and his feelings for her. He wanted no secrets between them if romance entered the picture.

If she felt the same, she owed him no less.

But did she have the courage to reciprocate?

And if she did, would her tiny spark of hope glow more brightly—or be snuffed out forever?

15

Michael prowled around Tracy's cottage, casting frequent glances toward the closed bathroom door.

What was going on?

Her out-of-character tears—and flight—didn't fit. She was a strong woman who dealt with the difficulties life handed her straight up. It would take a lot to make her cry or run away.

Conclusion? The mistakes and regrets she'd alluded to were devastating.

But if she could accept and forgive his faults, he could surely return the favor—assuming she trusted him enough to share them.

The handle of the bathroom door rattled, and a moment later she emerged. Her eyes were still red and puffy, but the tears were gone.

"Sorry about that." She hovered close to the door, as if poised to dash back inside at the slightest provocation. "I haven't fallen apart like that in more than a year."

"Grief has a way of sneaking up on you—and sometimes it's hard to pinpoint the reason."

The shallow and rapid rise and fall of her chest spelled stress in capital letters as she crossed her arms, fingers clenching her elbows. "I know exactly why it happened."

He kept his stance open and receptive. "Do you want to tell me?"

"No—but I think I need to. Unless you'd rather not deal with a lot of unpleasant emotional junk."

"I deal with unpleasant emotional junk in my job every day. If I can do that for strangers, I can definitely do it for you."

The sheen returned to her eyes, but she blinked it away and gave a jerky nod. "Do you need . . . would you like another soda?"

"No. Let's just sit." He gestured to the couch in the living room. "That might be more comfortable."

Instead of responding, she turned off all the kitchen lights except the one over the stove, grabbed her coffee, and claimed the far end of the couch.

It didn't take a genius to figure out her strategy. Shadows masked expressions and emotions. She didn't want him to have a clear view of her face —and perhaps she was afraid to see his. Fearful, as he had been, of finding rejection.

But she wouldn't. He couldn't imagine anything she might say that would undercut his high opinion of her.

Circling around the couch, he sat beside her, leaving a healthy amount of personal space between them.

She took a sip of coffee, clutching the mug with

both hands. "Have you heard any stories about my husband since you've been here?"

Not the opening he'd expected.

"Only what you told me—that he died two years ago."

"I'm surprised. There aren't many secrets in Hope Harbor."

"I guess visitors aren't privy to the grapevine. The only people I've spoken with at any length besides you are Charley and Anna—and neither of them are gossips." No need to mention his landlady's suggestion that he ask Tracy for advice about how to deal with regrets.

"Then I'll start with some history." She set her coffee down and picked up one of the throw pillows, hugging it against her chest. "Even though I've always loved the cranberry farm and was convinced that's where I wanted to spend my life, Uncle Bud and Aunt Carol thought it was important for me to get a first-class education. They wanted me to have a career to fall back on if things ever went south with the business. Seems prophetic now . . ." Her voice trailed off, and she swallowed.

Michael fought the temptation to twine his fingers with hers. Not appropriate. At least not yet.

After a few moments, she resumed the story. "So I went to business school at the University of Oregon in Eugene. During those years, Uncle

Bud hired out when he needed an extra pair of hands, but I came home most weekends during the busy season to help too. My original post-college plan was to do what I'm doing now—work on the farm and take on some accounting clients. But my aunt and uncle also wanted me to experience a world beyond Hope Harbor. To know what I was giving up if I decided to stay here. When I got a great job offer in Phoenix during my senior year, they urged me to take it."

"You left Hope Harbor?" It was hard to imagine Tracy anywhere but here, in this place that suited her so well.

"Yes—but only after they pushed. As it turns out, in some ways it was a positive move. I earned an excellent salary, and the money came in handy after falling cranberry prices began to eat into the farm's bottom line. It also proved to me that Hope Harbor was where I wanted to be."

"How long were you in Arizona?"

Tracy picked at the cording on the pillow. "Seven years—far longer than I'd planned. The farm needed the money . . . and I met my husband, who was a Phoenix native. He knew I eventually wanted to come back here, though, and he was fine with that. So three years ago, after our accountant retired to Florida and money was too tight to hire farm help on a regular basis, we relocated. Craig was the regional manager for a chain of restaurants, and he was able to arrange a transfer to the Coos Bay office."

Until now, Tracy had relayed her story in a straightforward tone. But when she picked up her coffee again, the quivers in her hand were a better barometer of her emotional state. And after she took a sip using a two-handed grip, then set it carefully back down, her voice was less steady.

He braced.

The tough part was coming.

"Life was busy after we moved here. I was reacclimating to the farm and getting up to speed on the books, and Uncle Bud and I were gearing up for the new growing season. Craig was on the road more than usual, familiarizing himself with his new territory. We had the house on the farm to ourselves when he was home, though. Uncle Bud insisted on getting an apartment in town. He said we needed some space to settle in. Except we never did. Less than a year after we relocated, Craig was gone."

She paused to fish a tissue from the pocket of her jeans.

"Was it . . . an accident?"

"No." She dabbed at her eyes. "Have you ever heard of Seasonal Affective Disorder?"

"SAD. Yes, I've read about it." He scrolled through his memory. "Isn't it a type of depression that occurs every year at the same time, usually in winter?"

"Yes. In hindsight, I think that was what Craig had—and moving to Hope Harbor made it a whole lot worse because a lot of days year-round are overcast or foggy. He'd get a little blue and moody in Phoenix on the rare occasions we had a few consecutive gray days, but since it was mostly sunny there it never occurred to me—or to him, I think—that he had a serious condition requiring medical attention."

A niggle of unease slithered up Michael's spine as he began to suspect where this might be heading.

"Once we moved out here, the blues became depression." Tracy hugged the cushion tighter against her chest and pulled her legs up into a protective tuck. "But I was busy with the farm, and he was traveling a lot, so I never realized how severe it was. Until the night I came home after a growers' meeting and found him in the garage with the door closed and the car engine r-running."

As her voice broke, Michael's suspicion morphed into shocking reality.

Tracy's husband had committed suicide.

Gut twisting, he forced himself to keep breathing. Tragic as his own loss had been, he couldn't begin to fathom the impact on a loved one from a desperate act like that.

He reached for her hand, but she shrank farther into the corner of the couch, the sadness in her eyes rending his heart. "Think about what I've told you, Michael. By convincing Craig to move here, I put him in the situation that caused his death. And if I'd paid more attention to him once we *were* here I would have realized he wasn't simply having difficulty adjusting to a new home and new territory. I would have done some research, urged him to get help, maybe been able to prevent him from taking that final, tragic step. So you're wrong about me having my priorities straight. I put the farm first." She swallowed, her chin quivering. "Bottom line, I was a terrible wife."

And I don't deserve a second chance to be one.

The words might be unspoken, but the message came through loud and clear.

She was wrong about that—but he couldn't just brush off her claims of culpability. Perhaps if she'd been more tuned in to her husband, she might have detected some warning signs. Might have realized the seriousness of the situation and convinced him to get help. Suggesting otherwise would be disingenuous—and could shut her down.

So how *should* he address all she'd told him?

As if reading his mind, she spoke. "You don't have to say anything. The truth is what it is—and Craig realized it too. On one of his really bad days not long before he . . . before he died . . . he accused me of loving the farm more than him. I thought he was being unreasonable—but in hindsight I guess he was right. I kept the farm alive better than I kept him alive." Her voice choked and she bowed her head, a world of pain in her defeated posture.

Time to make his move.

Scooting closer, he gently tugged the pillow from her grasp.

She lifted her chin. Tears brimmed on her lower lids, and her jade irises were seared with anguish. "W-what are you doing?"

He tossed the pillow aside and reached for her. "I think we could both use a hug."

"No." She pressed her hands against his chest, keeping him at arm's length, misery scoring her features. "Why would you want to hug me?"

"Because I'm sorry for everything you've gone through. Because I understand how easy it is to get distracted and neglect a spouse, and how the guilt can weigh on your soul. Because I appreciate your willingness to trust me with your story. Because I like you—a lot."

A quiver rippled through her. "Even after everything I told you?"

He retracted his arms. The hug would have to wait a few minutes. "We've both made mistakes we're not proud of, Tracy. That doesn't mean we're bad people; it means we're human. And humans are flawed. I wish I could change my life with Julie, and I know you wish the same about your husband—but we can't. Maybe the best way we can honor their memory is to learn from our mistakes and do better if we get a second chance."

She studied him. "That sounds like something Charley would say."

Yeah, it did. The philosophizing taco maker always had an interesting insight or two to pass along whenever Michael stopped for lunch after his beach walks—but this hadn't been one of them.

"To tell you the truth, I don't know where that came from. It's a new notion for me too—but it does make some sense."

"It's also scary." She fell silent as she traced the bold geometric pattern on the cushion in her lap. "You know, I thought I'd made peace with my life—and my choice to go it alone. But I've been confused . . . and unsettled . . . ever since you came to Hope Harbor."

He fought back an urge to smooth the worry lines from her forehead. "Why?"

After a moment, she lifted her gaze to meet his. "Because there's some pretty powerful chemistry between us. On my end, anyway."

So the attraction wasn't one way.

He exhaled, some of the tension in his shoulders evaporating. "It's on both ends."

A soft flush alleviated some of her pallor. "Even so, it's too soon for . . . that." She motioned toward the arms he'd extended. "We hardly know each other. Besides, there are obstacles. You're leaving in a few weeks, and . . . and you don't like cloudy weather."

Cloudy weather?

Ah.

Now he understood why she'd turned tail and run yesterday on the beach after his negative remark about Hope Harbor's climate. She was beginning to like a man who didn't care for gloomy days—and she'd already fallen for one of those with disastrous results.

"Let me address your concerns in reverse order. First, gray skies can be a downer when you're grieving—but I'm not prone to weather-related depression. Chicago and Kansas City can have long, cold winters without much sun, and I've never had an issue with that. So no worries there. Second, a lot can happen in a few weeks—including getting to know each other much better. Third, it's never too soon for simple signs of affection between friends . . . and those don't have to lead to anything else until we're ready."

She squinted at him in the dimness. "Are you always this logical and clear thinking?"

Logical? Clear thinking? With her sitting inches away, her breezy scent filling his nostrils and the golden-brown hair in her bedraggled ponytail itching for release?

"No." He hadn't even been certain his rebuttal was coherent. "But based on our histories, I agree that slow and cautious is a sound strategy."

He felt her relax slightly. "I can live with that."

"So what about that hug?"

She considered him. "A good-bye hug when you leave might be okay."

Without a word he stood and held out his hand.

Grooves appeared on her brow. "What are you doing?"

"Leaving. You have things to do tonight, and I don't want to cut into your beauty sleep too much. Besides, if leaving is the only way to get a hug, I'm out of here."

She hesitated, then took his hand and let him pull her to her feet. "We're going to keep this simple, right?"

"For now." It was the best he could promise.

She scrubbed her palms down her jeans and started for the kitchen. "I have something for you first."

He followed, slipping his arms into his windbreaker as she flipped on the light and picked up a loaf of cranberry nut cake.

"I sweet-talked Nancy out of this. After we shared that snack at the farm yesterday, I had a feeling you might not come around anymore. That if I wanted to see you again I'd have to take the first step. This was going to be my peace offering." She held it out.

He took the dense loaf but kept his focus on her. "Does that mean you would have come looking for me if I hadn't stopped by tonight?"

"I don't know." She smoothed her fingertips over the curved back of a kitchen chair. "I got the feeling yesterday you might be interested in me in a . . . romantic . . . sense, and I didn't think there was any future in that."

"What do you think now?"

She let out a shaky breath. "I think I might have been wrong."

"I'll take it." Not as definitive as he'd like—but great progress from an hour ago. "Walk me to the door?"

She eyed his outstretched hand. "I didn't think holding hands was part of the bargain."

"Consider it a prelude to the hug."

After another brief hesitation, she linked her fingers with his.

And her hand was nothing like he expected.

Tracy might radiate strength and sturdiness and self-sufficiency, and her palms might be callused from daily manual labor, but her fingers were small and delicate and fragile—and very, very feminine.

"Michael?"

Her uncertain query jerked him back to the moment.

With a gentle squeeze of those beguiling fingers, he walked her the dozen steps toward the door—wishing they were strolling hand in hand on the endless beach instead.

He'd have to work on that idea.

At the entry, he set the cranberry nut cake on a small table beside the door. "I'm not settling for a one-handed hug."

She shifted her weight as he faced her. "This feels a little . . . disloyal. You know?"

Yeah, he did. But he wasn't backing off. Wallowing in grief and guilt had gotten him nowhere.

"Maybe a hug will help clarify things."

"Or muddy the waters more."

"Let's be optimistic." He released her fingers and rested his hands at her waist. "Ready?"

"No."

"Set."

"Michael . . ."

"Go." He stepped closer, wrapped her in his arms—and discovered she was right.

The hug did muddy things up.

Not that there was anything sensuous in their embrace. It was simple, straightforward, friendly.

But she fit against him like she belonged there, filling the air with her fresh country scent, her soft hair tickling his chin, her heart beating close to his.

And he wanted more.

Tracy's arms crept around him, her touch tentative as she returned the hug. And once she emitted a soft sigh, so faint he'd wondered if he'd imagined it except for the puff of warmth against his neck, every doubt, every worry, every hesitation about taking this step evaporated.

Lifting one hand to the back of her head, he pressed her cheek to his shoulder.

Also a perfect fit.

The seconds ticked by . . . how many, he had no idea. Only the whistle of wind around the corner of the cottage, the faint rattle of a shutter, the distant crash of the surf, intruded to mark the passage of time.

And Tracy made no move to end the embrace.

At last, calling on every reserve of his willpower, he eased back, capturing her hands in his before she could step away.

She looked up at him, eyes wide. Then she inhaled sharply, as if she'd been forgetting to breathe and needed to fill her lungs with air.

He could relate.

So much for a simple, innocuous hug.

"I should go." He fumbled for the doorknob behind him. "But I'll be happy to come out to the farm tomorrow if you'd like some help."

She picked up the cranberry nut cake and held on tight with both hands, as if she needed some ballast to steady her. "You didn't travel all the way to Hope Harbor to work on a cranberry farm."

"True—but this trip hasn't turned out anything like I expected, anyway. At this point, I think going with the flow is the best plan. And I do swing a wicked weed eater."

She smiled, and his gaze dropped to her lips. *Don't go there, Hunter.*

He yanked his focus back up.

" . . . if that works for you."

"Sorry. I got distracted. What did you say?"

"I said you could help me with some fence repairs, if you're up for that."

"Oh. Sure. That's fine." He pulled the door open. He needed out of here *now,* or his whole slow and cautious plan would be history. "What time do you start?"

"First light these days—but come whenever you get up." She held out the loaf cake. "Don't forget this. The walk home might make you hungry."

He took the cake and stepped onto the porch. Fog had settled in, hiding the moon, and he zipped up his windbreaker. "I'll save it for tomorrow. I've already had my treat for the night." With a wink, he walked into the night, battling with each step the temptation to linger.

As he approached the road, he glanced back at the cottage. The scene was ghostly in the fog, but the warm light from the open cottage door glowed, silhouetting the slender woman who was fast laying claim to his heart.

How strange that his trek west in search of closure had led to romance.

But Tracy was right to be wary. In four short weeks he was scheduled to return to Chicago. It had been tough enough negotiating a two-month leave; there was no way he could extend it. Yet nurturing a budding relationship across two thousand miles would be a serious challenge.

On the other hand, walking away from his life in Chicago and starting over in Hope Harbor would be risky.

Blowing out a breath, Michael began to descend the hill that would take him back to town and his temporary home. Life could certainly be odd. He'd come out here seeking answers to one set of questions, only to end up with a batch of new ones. The whole thing was befuddling.

It wouldn't have been to Julie, though. His wife had gone through life believing everything happened for a reason. *God's* reason. Her implicit trust in the Almighty had been unshakable. Never once had she shown one iota of anger toward God, even when bad stuff happened.

The mist intensified, and he broke into a slow jog, tucking the cranberry nut cake inside his jacket as he passed the steepled church where Reverend Baker presided. His first visit there had been a bust . . . but should he follow Julie's example and lay his concerns before the Lord, trusting that his experience in Hope Harbor was part of a greater plan?

Perhaps.

He turned the corner to enter the homestretch toward Anna's—and as he pulled out his key to unlock the door to the annex, he made his decision.

Come Sunday, he'd reopen the lines of communication with the Almighty . . . and ask for help finding the elusive answers to his many questions.

16

"Is that sprinkler head still causing trouble? I thought I fixed it."

Tracy swiveled around, crossed her arms, and pinned her uncle with a stern look. "What are you doing out here?"

"Trying to preserve my sanity. I'm going stir-crazy in that house."

"Does Nancy know you escaped?"

"No." He stuck his hands in the pockets of jeans sitting too low on his hips. He'd lost weight during his siege with the flu. "She had to work at the café this afternoon. The second-Thursday-of-the-month bridge club was meeting, and they were shorthanded."

"You should go back to bed."

"I will, after I get some fresh air for a few minutes. Where's your helper today?" He scanned the beds around them from his perch on top of the dike. "Nancy says he's been a godsend."

True enough—but if her uncle didn't appear utterly drawn and worn out, Tracy would be tempted to accuse him of prolonging his recovery to create more opportunity for her and Michael to be together.

"He drove Anna to a physical therapy appointment in Coos Bay this afternoon."

"Is that right?" He gave an approving nod. "I like that boy. Helpful, considerate—and good-looking too." Uncle Bud grinned at her. "For the record, that last is Nancy's take. What do you think?"

"I think you should go back to the house and let me focus on work."

"I mean about what I said."

"I agree that Michael is very helpful and considerate." She angled away and fiddled with the sprinkler head.

"I meant the good-looking part."

Of course he did.

She busied herself with a wrench. "Depends on your taste, I guess."

"What does?"

As the man under discussion spoke, warmth flooded her face and she stifled a groan. He *would* have to show up now. How much had he heard?

Uncle Bud grinned. "We were talking about . . ."

"Your trip to Coos Bay." Tracy gave her uncle a warning glare as she cut him off. "How did it go?"

"Faster than expected. Anna isn't one to suffer fools gladly, and she wasted no time with the therapist. Show me the exercises, make certain I'm doing them right, and let me out of here."

"A woman after my own heart," Uncle Bud chimed in. "I don't take to those medical types, either."

"She more or less said the same thing—to the therapist herself. I thought Grace was going to sink through the floor in embarrassment."

"Nice of her to take the girl in. Tracy told me all about it. Nice of you to arrange it too."

Michael shrugged. "It was logical. You-scratch-my-back-I'll-scratch-yours deals are almost always a win-win." He gave the older man a once-over. "You're looking much better than you did when Tracy introduced us on Monday."

Folding her arms, Tracy shot her uncle the same dark look she'd directed his way three days ago after he'd traipsed out to the field on some lame excuse when all he really wanted to do was size up the guy who was offering them free labor.

Thank goodness Nancy had come after him, muttering about mule-headed patients as she dragged him back inside.

"Thanks. I'm improving."

"But you're not fully recovered yet. Go back in or I'll tell Nancy on you." Tracy arched an eyebrow at him.

"Are you trying to scare me?" He arched one right back at her.

"Yes."

"It worked. I'm leaving." He refocused on Michael. "A pleasure to see you again, young

265

man. And don't let Tracy work you too hard. She can be a slave driver when it comes to cran-berries. Bossy too."

"Uncle Bud . . ."

"But she has a wonderful heart—and a fun-loving side we don't see much of anymore." He ignored her exasperated sputter. "Now if you could get her to relax a little, maybe take a drive up to the gardens at Shore Acres State Park, you'd find out—"

"Uncle Bud." She fisted her hands on her hips, sharpening her tone. "I need to get back to work and you need to go to bed. Now."

"See what I mean? Bossy." Her uncle gave a long-suffering sigh, but there was a twinkle in his eyes.

He must be feeling better.

"She does know how to crack the whip." Michael grinned, playing along. "Even though I've been here sunup till sundown every day this week, I was afraid she'd dock me if I took a few hours off to drive Anna to Coos Bay. The only compensation for all my effort has been your wife's great cooking."

"The only compensation, huh?" Uncle Bud slid another glance her direction. "I might have to have a long talk with—"

"Michael . . ." Enough was enough. "I'm about done here. If you came out to work, you can help me spot-spray some weeds."

"I came out to work. Anna's settled at home and I have no other commitments for the day."

"Since three's a crowd, I'll leave you two to carry on." Eyes still twinkling, Uncle Bud strolled back toward the house, pausing only to pet the collies that raced up to greet him.

"I like him." Michael watched him mosey off.

"In case you couldn't tell, the feeling is mutual." She wiped her hands on her jeans. "Are you sure you aren't getting tired of working out here?"

He turned back to her. In spite of the long hours on the farm, he looked more relaxed every day. The intermittent sun was bronzing his skin, and the lines of strain around his mouth and eyes were diminishing. Outdoor work appeared to agree with him—in the short term, anyway.

"Not at all. And despite what I told your uncle, there have been other compensations besides Nancy's cooking."

Her sunglasses allowed her to scrutinize him without being too blatant. Did he mean fresh air and exercise—or her?

"I mean exactly what you think I mean." His blue eyes smiled down at her, warm and personal.

"Um, Michael . . ."

"I know, I know. Slow and cautious. But I'm a planner, and I like to think ahead. Lay the ground-work. See some progress. Any objections?" The question was lighthearted . . . but it had a serious undertone.

"It depends."

"On what?"

She bent down to pet Ziggy as he bounded up. Michael hadn't said what he planned to do after his leave from St. Joseph Center was up—and letting herself get carried away by a man who might be gone in three weeks wouldn't be wise.

Even if she was beginning to believe maybe, just maybe, she'd learned her lesson and would be a better wife the second time around.

Even if her heart urged her to take the plunge.

Even if Michael seemed like a man worthy of her trust and love.

Since they'd been candid with each other up until now, why not lay her concern on the table?

After a final adjustment to the sprinkler head, she crossed to the dike, scrambling up the steep grade. He reached out and gave her an assist with the last foot.

Once they were on the same level, she pushed up her sunglasses and met his gaze. "I'm worried about geography."

He considered her. "If that wasn't an issue, would you be okay with some groundwork?"

The moment of truth.

She swatted a bee away, focusing on the St. Joseph Center logo in the center of the snug T-shirt that covered his broad chest. "Are you saying you'd be willing to give up your job and relocate?"

"I wouldn't rule that out, depending on how things develop between us. But unless we *let* them develop, we'll never know what the potential is."

Hard to argue with that logic.

"Even if we . . . if we ratchet things up, I don't think we'll know each other well enough by the end of your stay to make that determination. And I'd never ask you to give up your job based on speculation. It would be too risky."

"I agree with you in theory—but you know what? Standing here with you right now, it doesn't feel risky at all."

He didn't touch her. Not with his hands. But his eyes . . . they were like a tender caress.

She could fall in love with this man.

Perhaps she already had.

And letting him walk away without exploring the electricity between them was no longer an option.

"Okay."

He cocked his head. "Okay what?"

"It's probably time to test the waters."

An endearing dimple appeared in his cheek.

Why had she never noticed it before?

But her fixation on his dimple dissolved when he stepped close. Very close.

"Is there any chance anyone could be watching us?" His low, husky question sent a delicious tingle up her spine.

"Not here." Had her voice actually *squeaked?* How adolescent!

"Good." He lifted his hand to play with a wisp of hair that had escaped her ponytail and gave her a slow smile. "Mmm. Mystery solved. It *is* as soft as it looks." He continued to toy with the strands as she fought the sudden urge to lean into him. "You never answered your uncle's question."

"What question?"

"About whether my looks are to your taste."

Drat her tendency to blush.

"So you did overhear our conversation."

"Only the last part. It was very interesting."

"Uncle Bud is a romantic."

"You're evading the question. So I'll go first." He released her hair and dropped his hand to her shoulder, the steady weight of it solid and reassuring. "My answer is yes . . . very much. Your eyes are the color of polished jade, and I've always been partial to jade. I like how the sun brings out the glints of gold in your hair. I like the shape of your mouth and the curve of your neck and your crazy-long eyelashes. You're a beautiful woman—and what I like best is that the inside matches the outside."

Oh.

My.

Word.

Michael had just taken a quantum leap from friendship to . . . *way* more than friendship.

Hope bubbled up and spilled over in her heart—and even though the sun was playing hide-and-seek with the clouds, her day got a whole lot brighter.

Also scarier.

"Too much?" Michael scrutinized her. He was still smiling, but there was a note of concern in his tone. As if he was afraid he'd gone too far and she might flee.

"Words like that could turn a girl's head."

"I'm more interested in touching her heart."

If this kept up, she was going to melt into a gooey little puddle at his feet.

"Mission accomplished." At least her voice wasn't squeaking anymore. "I guess it's my turn."

"No details necessary. I'm not fishing for compliments. A simple yes or no would be sufficient."

"Yes. I like your looks."

"Then we're done talking."

He lifted his hand again, his touch gentle as he cupped her face. His other hand moved to her back, urging her close. Then he dipped his head, until his mouth was inches from hers. "Nice and easy."

A reminder to himself—or a reassurance to her? Impossible to tell. And once his lips brushed hers, she didn't care.

Tracy let her eyelashes flutter down, blocking out everything but the kiss. It was slow and sweet—but by no means tentative. Her hands snuck around his neck as he molded her closer to him . . . tasting, touching, exploring. His arms were strong, his chest solid, his touch sure as he held her tight and told her in a language far more articulate than words his hopes for the future and how much he had come to care for her.

It was everything a first kiss should be.

And it ended far too soon.

He kept his arms around her after he broke contact, tucking her close against him, his breathing as uneven as hers. "I'd say we've officially moved beyond friendship."

"Yeah." It was all she could manage.

"Scary, isn't it?"

"Yeah." She pulled back slightly to examine his face. "So what do we do now?"

He shifted into position beside her, a touch of humor glinting in his eyes as he slung an arm across her shoulders. "Spot-spray weeds?"

"That's not what I meant."

"I know—but my answer stands. I propose we carry on as usual . . . with a few interludes like this thrown in. One kiss—one *great* kiss—is a beginning, not a conclusion. I think we should try for a slow build and see what happens."

"The voice of reason again." She exhaled. "I'm glad one of us has retained some left-brain function."

"Barely. Thinking straight with you beside me

is a challenge." He motioned toward the equipment shed. "Duty calls."

Right.

The weeds.

She started toward the shed, and he strolled along beside her, keeping his arm around her shoulders.

"How are you doing with your to-do list out here?" His fingers gently kneaded her overtaxed muscles.

"Better than I expected, thanks to you. In fact, I might be able to take off on Sunday. From the farm, anyway. I have some accounting work to catch up on."

"I thought you were going to do that last night?"

"Eleanor Cooper called. She needed a prescription picked up."

"You're stretched too thin, Tracy."

She didn't have to check out his expression to know he was frowning. She could hear it in his voice. "I didn't stay long. She asked about you, by the way. You made quite an impression."

He dismissed that notion with a wave of his free hand. "She was just glad someone fixed her gutter."

"It was more than that. You ooze empathy, and your manner has a way of instilling . . . I don't know. Confidence, maybe. That must be a great asset in your work. Growing cranberries is child's play compared to what you have to deal with every day."

"Cranberry growing has plenty of its own challenges, as I'm finding out—and I'm not talking about sore muscles." Shep bounded up to meet them as they approached the equipment shed, and Michael leaned down to pet him without breaking stride. "So what happens if you can't keep the farm running?"

The ever-present knot of worry in her stomach tightened. "I've tried not to dwell on that—but I do have a backup plan. I'll keep a small part of the land and live here, build my clientele in Hope Harbor and the surrounding towns, and go back to accounting full-time."

"I hope it doesn't come to that."

She swallowed. "I hope not, either—but I'm beginning to think it will take a miracle to save the place. Our reserves are . . ." She jolted to a stop as Uncle Bud exited the equipment shed. "What are you doing out here? I thought you were heading back to bed."

A guilty flush crept up his neck. "My next stop. I detoured in here for a minute to see how the insecticide supply was holding up. I don't want any weevil damage this year."

"It's fine. I'm on top of inventory."

"I expect you are." His gaze lingered on Michael's arm over her shoulder.

She slipped out from under it, doing her best to

hold back the blush fighting for release. "We're going to spot-spray weeds."

"Smart plan." He ambled past, still sizing her up. "You're losing your ponytail." He gave it a tug, smirking as he disappeared around the side of the structure.

She felt around. The whole thing was askew. Great.

Muttering a few choice words, she resecured it with a couple of quick twists of the elastic band.

"I think he suspects there was some hanky-panky going on out there." Michael motioned toward the beds.

"Then I'll have to do some damage control. I can come up with some explanation for why your arm was around my shoulders, and my ponytail often comes undone while I'm in the beds."

"Won't work."

"Why not?"

"You can't explain away how you look."

"What do you mean? How do I look?"

"Like a woman who's just been kissed."

She squinted at him. "You're kidding, right?"

"Nope."

"How does someone look like they've just been kissed?"

"It's hard to explain. I think it's an intuitive guy thing. But however it works, I guarantee your uncle figured it out."

She huffed out a breath. "That means he'll get

275

carried away, jump to conclusions—and be disappointed if things don't work out."

"He won't be alone." Michael leaned down for a quick kiss. "But for now, let's put this in God's hands and see where he leads us."

"I thought you were mad at God."

"I'm reopening the lines of communication. You want some company this week at Sunday services?"

Once more, a surge of hope swept over her. "You're going back to church?"

"Yep—but first we need to spray weeds."

He grabbed her hand and steered her into the equipment shed, the subject of God closed for now.

But his initiative on the faith front was a huge check mark in his plus column.

And one more reason why Uncle Bud and Michael wouldn't be the only ones disappointed if this budding romance fizzled.

17

"If there is one message we can take home from today's Scripture story, it's this: mistakes can be forgiven. Estrangements can be mended. Our heavenly Father is waiting to welcome us home if we but ask."

Reverend Baker scanned the congregation from

the pulpit. "So here's my challenge for you this week: follow that model. There are prodigal sons —and daughters—in many of our lives. Perhaps we've been one ourselves. Let us resolve today to reach out to those we've offended or those who have lost their way. As this story illustrates, it's never too late to begin again. Now let us go forth in joy."

As the minister concluded his sermon, Anna picked up her hymnal and assessed Grace out of the corner of her eye. The girl might have balked at coming to Sunday services, but she'd stuck to her promise to help with every chore—including driving her hostess to church. Not that Anna had *intended* to come . . . but the theme of the service, proclaimed on the church's front-lawn announcement board, had seemed tailor-made for Grace when Anna had spotted it on Tuesday.

It was hard to tell if the man's words had had any impact on the teen, though. Her expression was neutral, her crossed-arm posture less than receptive. Not a positive sign.

Yet strangely enough, Reverend Baker's words had managed to touch *her* heart.

She fingered the hymnal, the weight of it in her hands familiar, if long absent. After hearing and reading the prodigal son tale on dozens of occasions, she could recite it in her sleep. And she'd heard plenty of preaching on the topic too.

Reverend Baker's sermon, however, had offered

a different twist—the notion of reaching out instead of waiting for a black sheep to come home. That wasn't in the passage. The father in the Scripture story hadn't searched for his son. Perhaps, like her, he'd allowed anger to harden his heart . . . had let time pass . . . and given up any hope of a reconciliation. Yet the ending had been happy.

Her grip on the hymnal tightened.

John hadn't come back, like the prodigal son— but was there a chance her own story could end the same if she followed Reverend Baker's suggestion and took the initiative?

"Mrs. Williams, the service is over."

Anna blinked as Grace whispered in her ear. The last hymn had ended and the congregation was filing out.

"So it is." She replaced her unopened hymnal in the slot on the pew in front of her and stepped into the aisle, linking her arm with Grace's.

It was slow going, and as they shuffled along with the exiting throng, she could feel the surreptitious looks being aimed her way. There were a lot of new faces since she'd last occupied a pew here, but many were familiar. Yet no one spoke to her.

And why should they? She'd been rude and indifferent to everyone for years, lavishing her affection on critters who couldn't talk back—or talk *behind* her back. One by one her former friends had gotten the message and written her off as a bitter old woman, leaving her to the solitary, unencumbered, private life she preferred.

Or *had* preferred until Michael came along and flipped her quiet, peaceful, predictable world upside down. These days, every dawn seemed to bring a new challenge.

Yet truth be told, she was less lonely now. Being around people again might be more complicated, but it also made life more vibrant and interesting.

She searched the congregation. Her temporary tenant was here somewhere with the Sheldon girl. He'd told her yesterday he was coming. They must have slipped through a side door to escape the crush of people.

Not a bad plan.

On the opposite side of the aisle, Joyce Alexander exited a pew, studiously directing her gaze toward the back. Away from her old friend.

Spirits drooping, Anna absorbed the rebuff. They'd been close once, when their children were young. Same age, both with one son, active at church—and a host of other commonalities that had cemented their friendship.

But friends shared joys and hurts . . . and talking about John had been far too painful. It had been easier to build walls than open doors.

She watched Joyce squeeze through the crowd, the woman trying to get away as fast as possible. Who could blame her? In all these years, the only contact she'd initiated had been a sympathy note after Joyce's career-Army son had been killed in Iraq a decade ago. Her old friend hadn't responded—nor had Anna wanted her to. Renewing their friendship hadn't been her intent, and the message had been crafted to subtly communicate that.

But a lot of time had passed. Wounds healed and hearts could soften—couldn't they? Might the woman be receptive to an overture of friendship?

Before her courage failed, Anna pulled Grace through the crowd, leading with her uninjured shoulder until she was behind her old friend.

"Hello, Joyce." The greeting quavered, and she took a shaky breath.

Joyce angled slightly toward her, her manner wary as she bobbed her head. "Anna."

At least she hadn't ignored the greeting.

"Good sermon."

"Yes." The woman gave her a wary once-over. "I'm surprised to see you here."

"I have a houseguest, and I wanted her to attend." She jockeyed the girl forward. "This is Grace Lewis. Grace, this is Joyce Alexander, a . . . friend of mine."

"Nice to meet you." Grace mumbled the perfunctory sentiment.

Joyce returned it, but her focus wasn't on the young girl. "Are you . . . will you be coming back to church again?"

Anna continued to shuffle toward the door with the crowd. "I might."

"We have donuts afterward next Sunday." Joyce opened the top button of her sweater. Tugged down the hem. "They always . . . they still have the chocolate kind you used to like."

For some reason, Anna's eyes began to sting. She pulled her arm free from Grace's and groped in her pocket for a tissue. Must be the humidity.

You know what it is, Anna. You're touched because despite your snubs, Joyce is responding to your olive branch.

She sniffed and dabbed at her nose. "Damp day."

"I expect we may get some rain." The woman surveyed the gray sky as she stepped through the door and greeted the minister.

When it was her turn to do the same, the man gave her a big smile. "I thought I spotted you in the congregation today. I'm glad these aging eyes weren't playing tricks on me. And Grace . . . how nice to see you here." He shook hands with both of them. "How's your shoulder feeling?"

"Much better—and I have a great helper here." She gestured to the teen.

"Excellent. I must admit, from a selfish standpoint I hope you have a swift recovery. I'm missing your meat loaf. Thank the Lord Charley's is close by. Father Kevin and I have been wearing a path to his window—yet we both agreed during

281

our golf game on Thursday that while we love his fish tacos, you can get too much of a good thing. But please don't tell Charley I said that."

"Your secret is safe with me."

"Discretion is a great virtue . . . and speaking of virtues, I hope we'll see you here again soon."

"I might be back next week. I hear there will be donuts."

"I'll guarantee it if you promise to come."

She hesitated. "A week is a long way off."

"Well, you pray about it—and I'll do the same."

The crowd was backing up behind them, so with a quick good-bye to the minister, Anna took Grace's arm again and led her down the steps.

"What did you think of the service?" She handed over the keys as they walked toward the car.

"It was okay, I guess."

"Reverend Baker preached an outstanding sermon."

"I guess." Grace moved ahead and opened the door for her.

Cradling her arm, she slid into the passenger seat. "I can deal with the seat belt. I'm learning to cope with this one-handed business."

Grace closed the door without responding.

Apparently the minister's sermon hadn't transformed the girl's thinking. But perhaps it had softened the ground for the seed she wanted to plant.

As Grace took her place behind the wheel and

started the engine, Anna shifted toward her. "Let's take a drive to the bluff. I'm not up to climbing down the steps for a walk on the beach yet, but with this sky it will be stunning from above too."

Grace followed her directions, and in five minutes they were pulling into a parking space that offered a panoramic view of the sea stacks, cobalt blue ocean, and wide expanse of beach. A few people were on the sand, including . . . She peered down at the waterline. Was that Michael and Tracy? Walking hand in hand?

Hmm.

No wonder they'd wanted to make a fast escape from church.

"Mom and Dad and I brought a picnic lunch here once."

At Grace's wistful comment, Anna gave the girl her full attention. "That's the very subject I wanted to talk to you about."

Grace watched her, expression guarded, but remained silent.

"The two weeks we agreed you would stay with me are up on Friday."

"I know, but . . . I could stay longer if you need me. I wouldn't mind. There are a lot of things I could help you with until—"

"Grace." She gentled her tone. "You and your parents have to deal with this sooner or later. Putting it off isn't going to make it any easier. I've been talking to your mom every day, keeping her informed as I promised I would, and I think your parents are ready to have a calm, reasonable discussion."

The girl pulled a piece of lint off her sweater. "Is Dad over being mad?"

"Your mother said he's accepted the news." A hedge, but if she was lucky, Grace would let it pass.

"He hasn't checked my cell call record, has he?"

"He said he wouldn't. Has your father ever lied to you?"

Her lower lip quivered. "No."

"Then I think you can assume he's honored his word. So here's what I propose. Let's drive over to your house and talk this through."

"Now?" Panic flared in her eyes.

"Why not?"

"But . . . I don't even know if Mom and Dad are home."

"They are. I told them last night we might stop by—but I didn't make any promises. I wanted to leave the decision to you." For today. If this dragged on too long, though? Different story. Someone had to step in and take charge of this situation eventually. Talk some sense into these people.

Grace picked off the last vestiges of her iridescent purple nail polish.

Anna waited in silence.

At last the teen sighed. "I guess we can see what

they have to say. Maybe things will turn out like that story the minister talked about today."

So she *had* been listening to the sermon.

"I have great confidence God will work hard to bring that about—as long as we do our part too."

And should the meeting begin to deteriorate . . . she had a secret weapon in her arsenal.

If she could dredge up the courage to use it.

"This is so beautiful. I never get tired of the view." The wind lifted Tracy's hair, free for once from the constraints of her usual ponytail.

Michael stroked his thumb over the back of her hand as he watched her enjoy the gulls soaring like kites against the deep blue sky, the foamy surf crashing against the sea stacks, and the distant horizon that seemed to beckon with a promise of adventure.

"Me neither."

She transferred her attention to him. Smiled. "I'm talking about God's creation."

"So am I." He squeezed her hand as they strolled down the sand, his focus still on her.

Her shoulders drooped. "This particular piece of creation is very flawed."

"Not flawed. Just a work in progress—like every other human."

"That's a better spin, anyway."

"Truth, not spin."

A gull lifted his head from the mussel shell he

was picking at as they approached, and Tracy paused. "Well. Look who's here."

Michael glanced at the bird. "A friend of yours?"

"It's Floyd."

He gave the gull a dubious perusal. "How can you tell? They all look alike."

"Not close up. They have distinctive features, like humans. Floyd has a nick on the right side of his beak, and there's a black spot on the top of his head."

"If you say so." The bird still looked the same to him as all the others.

"Trust me, he and I have often gotten up close and personal when he comes banging on my back door. Which is almost every night. I think he's seeking companionship as much as food."

"Does he keep you awake?"

"No. He's always roosting before I go to . . ." She slid her hand into the pocket of her slacks and pulled out her cell. Frowned. "It's Uncle Bud. He rarely bothers me on Sunday mornings. Do you mind?" She held up the phone.

"Not at all. I'll commune with Floyd."

He released her hand and walked a few paces away—but the wind carried the conversation his direction.

"When did she start feeling bad? . . . Sounds like it. How can I help? . . . Don't worry about that. Just tell me what you need . . . No, of course not.

You need to stay there . . . Let me pull out a pen and paper."

While Tracy rummaged through her shoulder purse, Michael stifled his disappointment. The drive he'd been about to propose to Shore Acres State Park would have to wait.

"Got it. I'll be out within the hour." She ended the call, exhaled, and shoved the phone into her purse. "I'm going to have to cut our walk short. Nancy's got the flu."

"So I gathered."

She linked her fingers with his again. "Is it selfish to say I'd rather spend the day on the beach with you than deal with another crisis?"

"If it is, I'm guilty of the same sin. Maybe we can make up for it next Sunday." He turned them around, back toward the stairs leading to the bluff. "I'll walk you home."

She didn't talk much on the return trip, her mind no doubt busy itemizing the new chores that had suddenly landed on her plate.

Did this woman ever get a break?

Once they arrived at the drive that led back to the cottage, she wiggled her fingers free. "You don't need to come all the way to the door."

"Trying to get rid of me?"

"You know better." She rose on tiptoe and gave him a quick kiss—but backed off when he reached for her. "I need to get moving. Give me a rain check?"

He shoved his hands into his pockets to keep them out of trouble. "You don't need a rain check. That item will always be in stock."

"Nice to know." She flashed him a quick smile. "Is there anything I can do to help?"

"No. No sense both of us being exposed to germs—but thank you for offering." Lifting her hand in farewell, she hurried toward the cottage.

He waited until she disappeared through the door, then struck out for the annex. Maybe he'd use the empty hours stretching ahead to finish the mystery novel that had been languishing on his kitchen counter.

But first, he owed his dad a Father's Day call.

Twenty minutes later, after changing into jeans and a sweatshirt, he plugged in the coffeemaker, opened the plastic wrap containing the last piece of Nancy's cranberry nut cake, and pulled out his phone. Dad and Mom should be home from church by now.

He tapped in their speed dial number as the comforting aroma of coffee began to fill the annex.

His dad answered halfway through the first ring—as if he'd been hovering over the phone. "Michael? I've been looking forward to talking to you. How are you, son?"

At the anxious note shading his father's words, Michael's throat tightened. The frequent email exchanges with his family kept everyone up to date, but there was nothing like hearing the voice of someone you loved—and knowing they cared.

"I'm better, Dad. Really. Much more relaxed. How are you and Mom doing?"

"Fine. I was a little worried about this whole early retirement thing and moving out here to New Mexico, but I have to say it agrees with us. My golf game has improved too—and I'll be putting that gift certificate you sent to good use at the pro shop. But we miss seeing you and your sister and the grandkids."

"Beth sounds busy in her emails." He broke off a piece of the cranberry nut cake and took a bite. If anything, it tasted better now than when he'd opened the package on Tuesday.

"With three kids under the age of eight, I'd say that's a fair bet."

"Did you hear from her today?"

"Yes. She called earlier. I told her I'd already scarfed down half the fruitcake she sent."

"Fruitcake in June?"

"Fruitcake any month of the year suits me fine."

Michael shook his head. His dad was the only person he knew who actually relished fruitcake.

"I have a cake here I bet you'd like even better." He broke off another piece.

"I don't know. The fruitcake those monks bake is amazing. If you ask me, they're missing out on a great sales opportunity. They could sell those suckers year-round if they developed a marketing campaign to convince people it's not only for Christmas—though I understand they can hardly keep up with the holiday demand. They sell thousands of cakes all over the country . . . and at a pretty penny too. I think they're over thirty dollars a pop now."

Thousands of cakes?

Thirty dollars a pop?

Michael stopped chewing.

He might not agree with his dad about the year-round appeal of fruitcake—but why should the monks have the corner on a high-end holiday treat when cranberries were the real star of the season?

"Michael? You still there?"

"Yeah. Yeah, I'm here." The coffeemaker began to sputter, and he rose to pour himself a cup. "You just planted the seed of an idea."

"See? A payoff for calling your old man. Maybe you'll do it more often now—hint, hint."

Michael retook his seat, eyeing what was left of his cake. "The only payoff I need is hearing that you and Mom are doing well—but I'll try to get back into the habit of weekly calls. Things have just been . . . out of kilter for a while."

"I know. You've had a rough go of it. We understand. You finding what you need up there on the coast?"

"I think so. It's not turning out how I expected, but it's been . . . interesting."

"Well, we're a phone call away whenever you want to hear a friendly voice—though I hope you're hearing a few of those where you are too."

"I've met a lot of nice people."

One in particular.

"Glad to hear it. So tell me what you've been doing."

Michael complied, trying to gloss over his relationship with Tracy—but by the time he'd drained his mug and finished his recap, his father proved that while he'd retired from nine-to-five corporate strategizing, his analytical brain cells were still working fine.

"She sounds like a nice girl, this cranberry farmer. Can't be easy to be in that kind of business, with this tough economy."

"No. She works very hard."

"Is she pretty?"

Pretty?

More like drop-dead gorgeous.

But he tempered his response. "Yes."

"Nice?"

"Yes."

"Available?"

He hesitated. "Yes."

His diplomatic dad knew just when to back off. "Well, you take care of yourself—and if pitching in at that cranberry farm is helping you get back on track, keep doing it."

"That's my plan."

But as he and his father said their good-byes, he was already toying with an idea that might contribute a whole lot more to keeping Harbor Point Cranberries afloat than any amount of sweat equity he could offer.

18

The Lewis family reunion was not going well.

From her wing chair in the living room, Anna surveyed the players. Ellen Lewis's face was contorted, as if she was trying to hold back a sob. Her husband's complexion had taken on a florid hue. If Grace's posture got any more tense, she'd shatter at a mere touch.

And they were only five minutes into this family summit.

"I told you I couldn't stay here!" Grace directed the comment toward her while aiming a venomous look at her father. "He's already mapped out my life without consulting me."

"You're only sixteen." Ken started to rise, but when Ellen grasped his arm, he sank back onto the couch. "I think your mother and I know what's best."

"So what I want doesn't count?"

"What you want is what got you into trouble in the first place."

Grace shot to her feet, as if ready to bolt from

the house. "Every time you say stuff like that I want to puke!"

"Honey . . . please sit down." Ellen's words were shaky. "Ken . . . we agreed to talk about this calmly, remember? Let's all take a deep breath."

As tension quivered in the air, Anna stepped in. "Would you like me to wait on the porch while you discuss this?" Not her first choice, with this family's future hanging in the balance, but perhaps—with Ellen's intervention—they could come to a resolution on their own.

If not, she might have to pull out her secret weapon.

"No!" Grace darted her a panicked look. "You're the only one who listens to me. I want you to stay."

"Yes, please stay, Mrs. Williams." Ellen kneaded the twin creases above her nose. "We could use some calmer input, and it sounds like you and Grace have connected."

"Because she *listens!* Plus, she doesn't make me feel horrible about what I did. And you know what? She doesn't have to. I already feel horrible! I know it was wrong, okay? I made a bad mistake." Her voice hitched, and regret replaced some of the anger in her tone. "I can't blame you for being ashamed of m-me."

"Oh, honey, we aren't ashamed. We're worried and upset. Right, Ken? Ken." Ellen nudged her husband.

"Yeah."

A heavy silence fell as Grace and her father glared at each other.

Anna sighed. Someone needed to mediate this get-together—and it appeared she'd been elected.

"As long as I'm staying, may I suggest you let Grace tell you what she's been thinking? We've had some conversations about the situation, and I've found her to be quite articulate on the subject of her feelings and her options."

"Yes, by all means. We want to hear what you have to say, honey. Don't we, Ken?" Ellen sent a silent entreaty toward her husband.

He exhaled. Unclenched his fingers. Leaned back against the couch. "Yeah. You go first, Grace."

Grace looked over at her.

Anna gave her an encouraging nod. "Why don't you start at the beginning? With what you told me about how you felt after you moved here, and how hard it was to make friends."

Slowly the teen sank back into her chair, head bowed, tone muted now rather than defiant. "I don't think Dad wants to hear all that stuff."

Ellen took her husband's hand and met his gaze.

"Yes, I do." Ken sounded calmer and more in control now. "I knew relocating in the middle of your sophomore year would be hard, and your mom and I should have been more available to you after we got here. But we were busy settling in, and you've always been self-sufficient . . ." He exhaled. "Do you want to know part of the reason we're so upset? We feel some of this is our fault."

Grace lifted her chin and gave him a cautious look. "Seriously?"

"Yes."

Her shoulders lost a bit of their starch. "It isn't, though. I made the bad choice."

"Tell them about school, Grace." Anna rested her sling on the arm of the chair, reducing the weight. If she didn't ditch the thing soon, she'd have a pain in her neck as well as her shoulder.

To their credit, neither parent interrupted Grace as she haltingly relayed how difficult it had been to find friends among the established cliques, and how her boyfriend had filled the gap and eased the loneliness. She discussed the abortion issue, and her parents supported adoption as a better alternative—thank goodness. In the end, she revealed the name of the boy.

"Finally." Ken jumped to his feet. "I want to have a long talk with his parents."

Grace scrambled up too, once more on the defensive. "No! I don't want you going over there yelling and pointing fingers. I'm as much at fault for what happened as he is."

"I bet he pushed you."

"No, he didn't! We both just . . . got carried away. He's a really nice guy."

"Right." Sarcasm dripped off Ken's single word.

"He is!"

"Ken." Ellen stood and touched his arm. "Let's stay calm. It's more important to talk about what happens next than what happened before."

"That boy and his family need to take some responsibility."

"Didn't you hear a word I said?" A tear trailed down Grace's cheek, her pitch climbing toward hysterical. "And Mom's right. I don't want to keep focusing on the past—I want to decide what to do next."

"We can do that after we talk to the boy and . . ."

"Let's sit back down and try to . . ."

"Maybe I'll run away after all and . . ."

They were all talking at once—and no one was listening anymore.

This wasn't good.

Anna gripped the arm of her chair. Apparently it was up to her to try to salvage the situation—and she had only one tool at her disposal.

But could she share her deepest secret with these people who were almost strangers? And if she did, would it help them understand that the choices they made today could affect the rest of their lives?

As the shouting match continued, she squeezed the upholstery under her fingers. Years ago, she'd believed God put people in places where they could best serve their fellow travelers on life's journey. That belief had faded—but might this be a situation where it was true? Where she could help another family avoid the same mistake that had destroyed her relationship with her son?

Perhaps.

But God had better stick close as she took this leap, or she wouldn't have the fortitude to see it through.

Summoning up her courage, Anna plunged in. "If I could have a word . . ."

The melee continued.

"Excuse me."

Her raised voice got through to Ellen, who fell silent and shushed the other two members of her family. "I think our guest has something to say."

Ellen's emphasis on the word *guest* must have registered. Grace and her father stopped shouting . . . and all eyes focused on her.

"If you would all take your seats again, I have a few words to say."

For a moment she wasn't certain Grace or her father would cooperate, but once Ellen sat, they followed her example.

"We appreciate your perspective, Mrs. Williams. We want to do what's best for Grace, and if you have some wisdom to offer, we'd welcome it." Ellen directed a "muzzle it" look to her husband and daughter, and both remained silent.

Knotting her fingers on her lap, Anna forced her lungs to keep working. "I'm going to tell you a story no one in this town has ever heard—and I would ask that it stay in this room. It's a very sad chapter from my own life. One I'm not proud of, and which I regret to this day. I'm sharing it with you in the hope it might prevent you from going down the same unhappy path I did."

She groped for the glass of water they'd offered when she arrived. Took a sip.

"Twenty years ago, I lost my husband, George, very suddenly to a heart attack. After breakfast one Saturday morning, he got up to do the dishes like he always did on weekends. On his way to the sink, he collapsed. It was over that fast. One second he was joking about the weather, the next he was gone. I can still hear the sound of the china shattering on the kitchen floor—an omen, in some ways, of all that was to come."

Her voice rasped, and she took another sip of water.

"My son, John, was in college at the time. He was very close to his dad—not just because George was a great father but because my husband was a born mediator who understood the value of listening. John was more like me, quick-tempered and too fast on the draw. As a result, we often clashed. But thanks to my husband's intervention, none of our spats ever amounted to more than a here today/gone tomorrow squabble. Until the spring of John's sophomore year, a few months after George died."

Anna paused and fished in the pocket of her cardigan for a tissue.

"Are you okay, Mrs. Williams?" Grace leaned forward, face etched with concern.

"Yes, my dear. This is difficult to talk about—but I'll get through it." She wiped her nose and wadded the tissue in her fingers. "One weekend, John came home for a visit. I could tell he was agitated. I hadn't been sleeping well since George died, and I was constantly on edge myself. I should have given him some space, but instead I badgered him about what was wrong. Finally he told me." She moistened her dry lips and forced herself to say the hard words. "It turns out the son George and I had raised with the highest of moral standards had gotten another student pregnant."

Only her harsh, erratic breathing broke the silence in the room—but the attention of every member of the Lewis family was riveted on her.

"I was appalled—and I was even more shocked to learn there would be no marriage. The girl didn't want a husband at that stage of her life any more than John wanted a wife. I berated him, and he lashed back. Accusations were hurled. Harsh words were exchanged. I told him he was irresponsible, that I was disappointed in him, that his father would be ashamed . . . and a lot of other ugly, hurtful things. Within the hour he'd packed up as much stuff as he could cram into two suitcases and stormed out."

Her throat felt as parched as the tree in that Job citation Charley had given Michael, and she gulped more water.

"What happened next?" Grace was on the edge of her seat.

"I never saw or heard from him again."

The teen's jaw dropped. "You mean he . . . disappeared?"

"No. He went back to college, but he never came home again. I always thought he'd realize the error of his ways and marry the girl, or at the very least apologize for his disrespect the day he broke the news, but he didn't. Like I said, we were too much alike. Too fast to fly off the handle, too inclined to hold grudges. I didn't try to understand his perspective or cut him any slack for a poor choice that was no doubt driven by grief and the abject sense of loneliness only people who've lost a loved one can understand. I had zero compassion and passed judgment far too fast."

"But . . . surely in all these years you've considered getting in touch." Ellen seemed as stunned as her daughter by the shocking story.

"No. Both of us, I think, felt the other hadn't reacted appropriately. And the truth is, we didn't. We waited each other out, until the gap grew too long to bridge."

"So you don't know what happened to the girl or the baby . . . or where your son lives . . . or anything?" Grace stared at her.

"I have no idea what happened to the girl or the child. Thanks to the internet, I do know my son lives in Seattle, is married, and has one daughter." She released her tight grip on the tissue and flexed her fingers to restore circulation.

"You could contact him, couldn't you? I mean, that minister today said it's never too late to reconnect."

"Nineteen-plus years is a long time, Grace—and there's much to forgive on both sides. But I didn't tell you all this to burden you with my problems. I told you in the hope my story might soften your hearts and help you understand the importance of listening without judging. To realize that estrange-ments are sometimes never repaired. Please don't destroy your family as my son and I destroyed ours."

As silence once again fell in the room, Ellen swiped her fingers across her eyes. Grace sniffed. Ken's expression was thoughtful . . . and touched with remorse, if Anna was reading him correctly.

His next words confirmed that conclusion.

"First of all, thank you for sharing that painful story with us, Mrs. Williams. It was a wake-up call. My wife and my daughter are my world—and you've shown me how fragile that world can be if we forget that love has to be the first and most important emotion we bring to any prob-lem." He took his wife's hand and looked at

Grace, still sitting alone across the room. "When you were a little girl, we always called ourselves the Three Musketeers, remember?"

She nodded.

"I'd like us to be that way again. All for one, one for all. We'll get through this if we stick together." He rose and pulled Ellen to her feet. Moving toward his daughter, he extended his hand. "Can we try again?"

Anna gripped the arm of her chair as Grace hesitated.

God, please give this family a second chance!

Finally, the teen rose and took a tentative step forward. Then another. Once she put her hand in her father's, he pulled her into his arms. Ellen joined in the group hug.

Letting out a slow breath, Anna relaxed into the chair.

They were going to be okay.

And as she watched this family begin to bind its wounds, as she thought about Reverend Baker's sermon and the story of the prodigal son, a tiny flicker of hope ignited in her soul.

If the Lewises could mend their fences, was there a chance she and John could too?

Not likely, given the length and depth of their rift.

But now that Michael had managed to get her out of her self-imposed isolation, going back into it didn't hold a whole lot of appeal. And if she *was* going to rejoin life, she wanted her son—and his family—to be part of her world.

Yet reaching out to him would be risky. If he rejected her overture, that door would be closed forever.

And she wasn't certain she could survive such a final, crushing blow.

"We're really sorry to interrupt your Sunday, honey." Uncle Bud took the proffered prescription and led the way to the kitchen. "The good Lord knows you needed a day off."

"It's not a problem. This is what family does. How's Nancy?" Tracy opened the refrigerator and took a quick inventory.

"She's down for the count—and not at all happy about it. She says if she'd known the community property clause in our marriage included germs, she might have had a few second thoughts before saying I do."

Tracy chuckled as she removed some defrosting chicken breasts Nancy must have intended for Sunday dinner. "I don't think so. She grabbed the gold ring when she got you."

"Nope. I'm the lucky one." He filled a glass with water and pulled a teaspoon from the drawer for the cough medicine. "What are you doing?"

"Fixing dinner."

"Oh, sweetie, you don't have to do that. Why don't you go spend the afternoon with Michael?

You could take a walk on the beach or sit on the wharf or go for a drive."

No sense telling him she'd been daydreaming about those very possibilities until his call.

"I need to eat too. I might as well cook for all of us. Unless you were planning to prepare a gourmet meal?" She smiled at him over her shoulder. Even after years as a widower, he'd never learned to make more than an omelet and a grilled cheese sandwich.

He shrugged. "There's some soup in the pantry."

She gave him an appraising sweep. "You need more than soup. How much weight did you lose while you were sick?"

"A pound or two."

"Or five or six. We need to get some meat back on those bones, and soup won't cut it. Go ahead and take Nancy's medicine up. I'll get dinner going."

"You shouldn't be lingering in the house, with all the germs flying around."

"The windows are open, and I'll wash my hands a lot. Unless you don't want me to whip up my famous chicken in white wine sauce."

His eyes lit up. "You know that's my favorite."

"Yes . . . and Nancy has everything I need for the recipe. You still want me to leave?"

"Well . . ."

She grinned. "Go take care of your sick wife." She waved him off.

He left with no further argument.

By the time he returned, the meal preparations were well under way.

"How is she?"

"Crabby." Uncle Bud sat at the kitchen table. "I had no idea she'd be such a bad patient."

"What's sauce for the goose . . ."

"Very funny. So what plans did we interrupt for your day?"

She pulled out some green onions and began chopping. "I had some accounting work to do."

"I thought you told me yesterday you were going to take today off."

"From farm work."

"Hmph. Did you go to church?"

"Of course."

"Any news there? I feel like I've been out of the loop for a year instead of a couple of weeks."

"You'll never guess who attended—Anna Williams, with that teen she took in."

"Anna was at church?" His eyebrows rose. "Wait'll I tell Nancy. The old girl must be softening."

"Michael was surprised to see her there too." The instant the words left her mouth she cringed. Uncle Bud would be all over that slip.

"Michael was at church?"

If nothing else, Bud Sheldon was predictable.

"Yes. Do you want carrots or string beans with your chicken?"

"I like 'em both. Did you get a chance to talk to him long?"

So much for her feeble attempt at a diversion.

However, a sounding board might be helpful—and it wasn't as if she had any close girlfriends in town to confide in. Who had time to nurture those kinds of relationships?

"To tell you the truth, we sat together during the service—and we took a walk on the beach afterward. That's where I was when you called."

No response.

She peeked over her shoulder to find him frowning.

"What's wrong?"

"Now I'm doubly sorry I interrupted your day. You don't often have a chance to socialize, much less with an eligible man."

She turned the chicken in the sauté pan. Poked at the boiling potatoes. Got the vegetables started. Then she swiveled toward him.

He held up his hands. "I know, I know. Stop playing matchmaker."

Wiping her hands on a dish towel, she leaned back against the counter. "As a matter of fact, I could use some advice."

At her serious tone, he folded his hands on the table and gave her his full attention. Just as he used to do during her growing-up years when she came to him about a friend who'd hurt her feelings or a party she hadn't been invited to or a date that hadn't gone well. And he said the exact same thing now that he'd said in her youth.

"Tell me how I can help."

"I'm not sure you can. No one can predict the future, and that's kind of what I need."

"Should I assume this is about Michael?"

"Yes. We've gotten to be . . . friends."

"More than that, based on how you looked the other day out by the equipment shed."

A caution bell rang in her mind. "What do you mean?"

"You looked like you'd been kissed."

Chalk one up for the man from Chicago.

"No comment."

"None needed. Anyway, I'm guessing the distance is a problem." Her uncle scrutinized her.

"Yeah—and he's leaving in three weeks."

"How does he feel about Hope Harbor?"

"He seems to like it—and he enjoys being at the farm." She twisted the dish towel in her hands. "The thing is, it feels comforting to have him in the fields with me, even when we're working in different areas. Just knowing he's close by gives me this sense of . . . peace, I guess." Pressure built behind her eyes. "But he has a great career in Chicago. And a life there."

"Then why did he take a leave and come to Hope Harbor?" Uncle Bud held up a hand. "Rhetorical question. I'm not prying into the man's business. My point is, maybe that job and that life aren't what he wants anymore. Could be he's ready to think about a change."

"Even if that's true, I can't offer him any promises this early in our relationship—and what if things go south? What if he upends everything, moves here . . . and the romance fizzles? I don't need any more guilt in my life."

He tapped a finger on the table. "Did he ask for any kind of commitment?"

"No."

"Then if he decides to stay, it's his choice. Now, putting logic aside for the moment, what does your heart tell you?"

She played with a piece of the zesty green onion that was clinging to her hand. "That Michael Hunter could be my second chance."

"And how do you think he feels?"

"The same."

Her uncle refolded his hands. "I can't tell you what to do, honey. People have to make their own choices. But I can give you my two cents. Neither of you is a hormone-crazed teenager. Not that there aren't sparks, but they haven't short-circuited your brain cells. That's a plus. At the same time, while prudence is a virtue, don't let logic or fear or doubts or bad experiences deafen you to the voice of your heart. Feelings *do* count. And if the two of you feel half as much for each other as I suspect you do, it seems to me it would be worth giving this thing a shot."

She crossed her arms and studied him. "How do you always manage to get to the core of an issue so fast and come up with such sound advice?"

"Just call me Dr. Phil." He winked. "But when you get down to it, most things . . ." He sniffed. "What's burning?"

With a muttered exclamation, she spun around. The pan with the chicken was smoking—and a quick peek confirmed they'd be eating a slightly charred entree for Sunday dinner.

But burned chicken she could handle.

A burned heart—different story.

Yet as Uncle Bud offered a simple blessing over their food a few minutes later that included a request for guidance for his niece, Tracy felt more at peace than she had since Michael had entered her life.

Because her uncle was right.

Michael hadn't asked for any guarantees or promises. If he chose to stay, it would mean he believed—as she did—that they had great potential.

And if he didn't stay?

Well . . . long-distance courtships worked in books.

Maybe they could in real life too.

19

"I don't know about you, but I'm ready to call it a day."

Michael stopped refilling the fuel tank on the riding mower and turned. Tracy was silhouetted in the doorway of the equipment shed, the setting sun behind her outlining her slender figure and sparking the gold highlights in her hair.

Nice.

Even nicer?

The notion of spending a free evening with her.

"I like that plan."

"Good." She strolled into the shed, shoulders sagging, faint shadows beneath her lower lashes. "I need a hot bath and some shut-eye—after I take care of a few things on my non-cranberry to-do list."

Oh, well. A free evening together *would* have been nice if she wasn't so worn out, didn't have books to work on, wasn't running errands for her sick relatives, or didn't have a Helping Hands board meeting, church commitment, or one of a dozen other obligations that were always clamoring for her attention.

But he did have a topic to discuss with her, and laying off earlier than usual might give him the opportunity to broach it—if he could claim half an hour of her time.

And he knew the perfect bait to dangle.

"Before you do all that, would you like to grab some tacos at Charley's?"

She deposited her sprayer on a shelf. "I could be persuaded. I cooked ahead for Uncle Bud and Nancy when I came out after our interrupted walk yesterday afternoon, and tacos would save me having to fix dinner for myself. You want to clean up first?"

"Not unless you do." He recapped the fuel tank, wiped his hands on a rag, and brushed some dust off his jeans. "I'm hungry."

"The citizens of Hope Harbor have seen me dressed far worse than this. I say we go for it—if Charley is serving at this hour."

"We'll grab a bite somewhere else if he's not." He pulled out his car keys, grabbed her hand, and tugged her toward the door. "Let's go."

"I guess you weren't kidding about being hungry."

"I never kid about food."

Ten minutes later, as he claimed a parking spot on the wharf, Tracy grinned. "We're in luck. He's still open."

"Well, let's not push it. That window could crank closed any second."

She was already out of the car by the time he circled it. Taking her hand again, he picked up his pace until she had to break into a slow trot to keep up.

"Hey! This girl is tired. He won't shut the window in our faces." She waved at the proprietor.

He waved back.

"Sorry." Michael slowed. "With my advanced state of hunger, the aroma of those tacos is like a dandelion to a honeybee."

She chuckled. "A cranberry analogy, huh? I may make a grower out of you yet."

When they drew up at the window, Charley leaned his forearms on the counter and smiled. "I almost closed up ten minutes ago, but a little voice told me to stay open for a while. Now I see why. You two look hungry."

"Working in the cranberry beds all day will do that to you. We'll have two full orders of the taco du jour." Didn't matter what it was. After a dozen visits, Michael trusted Charley to give him a great meal.

"You're helping out at the farm?" Charley pulled some fish fillets from a cooler and set them on the grill, then began chopping up an avocado.

"Yes. Since last week," Tracy answered for him. "With Uncle Bud felled by the flu, I don't know what I would have done if he hadn't offered. It was providential."

"That's an apt word for it." Charley added some red onions to the mix. "How's the water situation at the farm? Been pretty dry lately."

"Yeah. We're irrigating a couple hours every other day. You'd think all this overcast weather would produce some rain, wouldn't you?" Tracy surveyed the cloud-studded sky. "But the cranberries don't care where the moisture comes from."

"No." Charley lined up some squares of paper on the counter and set a soft corn tortilla on each. "And it's amazing what a touch of water will do for a parched plant, isn't it?" The Mexican artist sent him a knowing look.

Michael reached into the pocket of his jeans and fingered the slip of paper with the citation from Job. Like the tree that had been cut down and left to wither and die, he, too, was sprouting tender new branches—thanks to the woman beside him.

Of course, Charley couldn't have had any idea how things would develop the day he'd sent over that complimentary order of tacos. He'd just sensed a stranger's sadness and passed on the quote to offer a generic touch of hope.

Hadn't he?

"Here you go." Charley added a dollop of some mystery sauce to each taco, wrapped them up, and put them in a bag.

Michael dug out his money clip.

"I can pay for my own." Tracy started to pull some bills from her jeans.

He stopped her with a touch. "This is on me.

Consider it a business expense. I have a cranberry-related topic to discuss with you."

"What kind of topic?"

"You want to get the waters?" He gestured to the two bottles Charley had set on the counter as he picked up the bag.

"What kind of topic?" She grabbed the bottles.

"We'll talk about it in the boardroom." He motioned toward the bench where he'd met Anna. "Thanks, Charley. These smell great."

"You're welcome. Enjoy."

Before they were halfway to the bench, the window on Charley's truck had been rolled closed.

"Whew. That was close." The aroma from the bag set off a rumble in Michael's stomach.

"Not really. He was waiting for us. You heard him."

He didn't try to hide his skepticism. "How could he know we were coming? *We* didn't know until twenty minutes ago."

"Maybe he wasn't certain it would be us, but like he said, his instincts told him *someone* was coming—and I've learned never to discount Charley's instincts." She sat and held out her hand for the bag. "I'll divvy those up while you tell me about this topic you want to discuss."

He claimed a spot on the bench and took the bundle of tacos she dug out for him. "I've been thinking a lot about your financial problems at the farm, and I had a conversation with my dad yesterday that spurred a revenue-generating idea I wanted to run by you."

"I'm all for revenue generation." She rounded up some wayward pieces of shredded cheese and tucked them back in the tortilla, but her attention was focused on him.

"Have you ever thought about selling your family's cranberry nut cake on a commercial scale?"

Some sauce dripped out of her taco, onto the napkin on her lap.

She didn't notice.

"You mean . . . start a bakery?"

"No. I'm talking about producing one item on a large scale. Like the monks do who bake this fruitcake my dad likes." He relayed his conversation with his father, along with some of the information he'd gleaned from a web search, ending with the prices they charged and the volume they sold.

She gulped. "They get that much for each cake?"

"Yes. I don't know what your cranberry production is, but I'm guessing a small portion of the crop would make a lot of cakes. The rest could be sold as usual. You could position it as a holiday offering in the beginning and expand if sales warrant."

"But . . . I don't know a thing about baking on

that scale. And we'd need to design packages and develop shipping procedures and create a marketing campaign . . ." Her voice trailed off.

"Don't forget sampling and publicity." Michael leaned closer. "But we can access some of that expertise without too much trouble. I have contacts with creative types, since we run all kinds of marketing campaigns for St. Joseph Center. My own background in nonprofit management would apply to marketing a product as well as an organization. And we both know someone who's an expert on cooking and baking in large batches."

"Who?" More sauce dripped out of her taco.

"You better eat that before any more of it lands on your lap."

She looked down. After wadding up the soiled napkin and replacing it with a clean one, she took a bite.

"Anna Williams. She cooked at the high school for years."

Tracy's eyes widened, and she fumbled for her water bottle to wash down the bite of taco. "Why on earth would she want to get involved in this?"

"I don't know that she would—but I do think she's beginning to rejoin the human race. Consider the evidence. She gave me a place to stay, took in Grace, went back to church . . . and yesterday I noticed she'd opened all the shades in her house for the first time since I've been there."

"Hmm." She took another bite of her taco.

Michael could almost hear the gears whirring in her brain. She hadn't jumped at the idea, but it *was* bold—and it would take her out of her comfort zone. Yet with her accounting and cranberry background and his management and marketing skills, he had no doubt they could pull this off.

If he decided to stick around long term.

Even if he didn't, though, he could help her launch this. Line up some people to assist.

"It's an interesting idea." A flicker of excitement began to glimmer in her eyes. "I wonder if it would fly? I mean, I guess the recipe could be adapted for large-scale baking . . . but would people buy it?"

"They buy fruitcake. And having sampled the monk's pride and joy as well as your family recipe, all I can say is . . . no contest. We just have to make certain we get lots of publicity—and there are a bunch of appealing angles, starting with berries grown on a three-generation family farm and cake made from an old family recipe. Consumers are hungry for that personal touch—pardon the pun—and so is the media."

"That's true." Yet all at once her glimmer dimmed. "But the initial capital investment is a huge stumbling block."

Of course money was a problem. That's why he'd already thought it through.

"It may not be as costly as you think."

"Whatever the cost, it will be too much." She poked at a dangling piece of red onion.

"Small business loans are available, and you might find some potential investors. In fact, I happen to know a nonprofit executive from Chicago who would be interested in a piece of a venture like this."

She stared at him. "I can't take your money."

"It's not a gift; it's an investment. One I suspect could return a lot more than the paltry rate CDs pay. Besides, I don't think it would take that much to get this business up and running. But let's not jump the gun. Why don't I ask Anna first if she'd be willing to look at the recipe and offer an opinion about how difficult it would be to both adapt it to large-batch baking and produce it in big volumes?"

Tracy nibbled on her taco. "I guess it wouldn't hurt to get her opinion—but let me run the idea by Uncle Bud first. He and I are in this together, and even though he keeps talking about retiring, for now we're full partners. I want to be sure he's comfortable talking about our financial situation with people outside the family. After we finish our dinner, I'll drive out and discuss it with him."

"I thought you had a long to-do list for this evening?"

"This is now top priority." She caught another glob of sauce before it hit the napkin. Sucked it off her finger.

His gaze dropped to her mouth. Amazing how such a simple gesture could make his pulse skyrocket and—

" . . . think it has potential?"

Only her last few words registered.

Becoming distracted by her lips was getting to be a habit—one he wasn't eager to break.

"I think it has great potential." He might not have heard her entire question, but the gist was clear. He hoped. "If your uncle's on board, why don't you email me the recipe? I can feel Anna out tomorrow when I drive her up to Coos Bay for an orthopedic appointment."

"Too long a trip for Grace to tackle at this stage of her driving career?"

"Probably—but that's a moot point. Grace has reunited with her parents. She's planning to come over a few hours a day to help Anna this week, but she went home yesterday."

"No kidding." Tracy finished off her second taco and moved on to the third, keeping pace with him. "I wonder if Reverend Baker's sermon had anything to do with her change of heart?"

"Could be . . . but I suspect Anna had even more influence."

"Why?"

"I think she and Grace bonded."

Tracy shook her head. "Life is full of surprises, isn't it?"

"Yeah."

And one of the biggest of all was sitting right next to him.

He left that unsaid as they finished their impromptu meal, but once he dropped her off at the cottage and was on his way back to the annex, her last comment replayed in his mind.

Life wasn't the only thing full of surprises.

Hope Harbor was overflowing with them.

And he had a feeling more were on the way.

Gripping the top of the flat bag, Anna shaded her eyes and scanned the parking lot for Michael's Focus. Congenial as he was, the man's patience was going to be taxed to the limit if she had to tap him for too many more trips to Coos Bay—not to mention extra stops like this. Fortunately she was mending well, according to the specialist who'd examined her shoulder.

A Focus backed out of a spot a few rows down, and less than sixty seconds later Michael pulled up in front of the store. Leaving the engine idling, he circled around to help her with the door and seat belt.

"Your mother taught you excellent manners."

He grinned. "I'll tell her you said that. There were times in my youth I think she despaired of me. I'll never forget the Sunday I snuck a frog into church in my pocket . . . which managed to get loose and hop up to the pulpit during the sermon. She never forgot it, either."

"I expect she didn't." Anna tried without much success to sound stern.

"And that was just one of the many scrapes I got into as a kid."

After taking his place behind the wheel again, he picked up the conversation as he maneuvered the car through the traffic, toward 101. "I think most little boys have a daredevil gene that can get them into trouble."

"I suppose so." Though truth be told, while John and she might have clashed on a multitude of issues, he'd never gotten into any real mischief.

Until after George died.

The car fell silent as they merged onto the highway and Michael accelerated toward Hope Harbor. She sensed him casting a few glances her direction, and an odd vibe wafted her way. Kind of like the one she'd felt the day he'd suggested she take Grace in.

Something was up.

Narrowing her eyes, she shifted toward him. No sense beating around the bush. "What's on your mind?"

He passed a slow-moving truck and sent her an amused glance. "I think you're beginning to know me too well."

"I used to be decent at reading moods."

"It seems you still are. I do want to ask a favor."

"You don't have another young woman who needs refuge, do you?"

"No. But I have a young woman who could benefit from your culinary expertise."

She arched an eyebrow. "I'm not a culinary expert."

"You ran the high school cafeteria for years. You cook for both of the clergymen in town. I'd say that qualifies you as an expert."

"I don't have any formal training."

"You have a better credential—experience. Interested?"

"I might be." Especially if this project made her feel alive again, like helping the Lewis family had. "Who's the woman and what kind of culinary assistance does she need?"

Michael pulled a folded piece of paper out of the pocket of his windbreaker and handed it over. "Tracy Campbell. Harbor Point Cranberries is having financial problems, and I came up with an idea that might help them generate some income. You're holding it."

She opened the slip of paper and skimmed it. "This is a recipe."

"I'm hoping it can be a profitable business."

As he filled her in on the background and fleshed out his idea, Anna gave the recipe a more thorough read . . . and tried to contain the sudden zip of excitement that raced through her veins.

A project like this would be a lot of hard work, but it could also be satisfying—and perhaps even fun.

Now there was a word that hadn't been in her vocabulary for a while.

"I know the cake is good." Michael flipped on his lights as they turned a corner and went from sun to fog. "I scarfed down a whole loaf of it last week. So I have no worries about whether it would sell. The question is whether the recipe can work on a commercial scale. That's where your expertise comes in."

"I don't see why not. It might need some fine-tuning, but I'm used to translating recipes for large-batch preparation. Those ginger cookies I gave you were a particular favorite at the high school, and they started with a family-sized recipe." She lowered the sheet to her lap. "Who's going to run this operation, and where do you intend to bake these cakes?"

"None of those details have been worked out. There's also an issue of funding. We're in the early stages."

"We?"

Michael's complexion reddened slightly. "I'm helping Tracy out."

Also walking hand in hand on the beach with her.

Romance appeared to be in the air along with the quest to save the cranberry farm.

"Well, if you need someone to coordinate the baking, I might be interested—and the high school kitchen would be ideal. I have connections there, and it's not used at night or on the weekends—or in the summer. That would give us plenty of time to bake cakes, at least in the early stages of this project. I suspect if the school was offered a small portion of the proceeds they'd be happy to cooperate. The sports programs are always underfunded."

Michael looked over at her. "Did you ever work in the business world?"

"No."

"You missed your calling. Those are all great ideas."

"I'm sure I can come up with more after I think through this for a day or two. In terms of funding . . ." She took a deep breath. There was more than enough in her portfolio to provide a comfortable living for the rest of her life, thanks to the wise investments she and George had made. Why not use a portion of the excess to give someone else a boost?

"I have one investor in mind already." Michael flashed her a grin. "Me."

The man was putting his own money behind this?

Definitely romance in the air.

"I might be interested in investing a little too. You seem to have a clear-thinking mind and a solid work ethic, and I know Tracy does. If you're both committed to this, I expect it will fly. The three of us should sit down and talk about it—if you want me to get involved, that is."

"I'll run it by Tracy later today, but I think you'd be a tremendous asset to the team."

Throat closing, Anna turned aside on the pretense of adjusting her seat belt. When was the last time anyone had viewed her as an asset? Or the member of a team? Oh, the clergymen missed her cooking . . . but anyone could make meat loaf. Besides, that was a solo occupation. This challenging project would involve a team effort—and she *could* contribute. George had always praised her head for business, and she knew her way around a commercial kitchen.

Wouldn't it be amazing if this was the beginning of a whole new chapter for her? All thanks to the man beside her—a stranger who'd walked into her life a month ago and ended up transforming it.

He might be paying her to live in the annex, but after all he'd done for her, she should be paying him.

Too bad he couldn't also help her resolve her deepest sorrow.

That, however, was hers alone to muddle through. And while hard work and an infusion of capital might solve the problem at Harbor Point Cranberries, neither of those would resolve her issues with John.

A recipe, however, might. One that contained

hefty portions of humility, remorse, understanding, empathy . . . and love.

But even if she could whip up all those ingredients, the finished product would be a whole lot harder sell than a tasty cranberry nut cake.

20

Michael was amazing.

As Tracy pedaled into town on autopilot, psyching herself up to whip through the errands she'd deferred from two days ago, she replayed their morning meeting with Anna.

He'd run the discussion like the executive he was. Efficient, on-topic, cutting to the chase on every issue. They'd reviewed some package-design quotes he'd already gotten from vendors he knew, listened to Anna's comments on the recipe and the positive response she'd received from the high school, and reviewed the very preliminary cost revenue analysis she herself had done based on limited information and a lot of guesswork.

As for the older woman's willingness to put money into the venture—mind-blowing.

Bottom line, it appeared Michael's idea had legs.

Who could ever have guessed that an old family recipe might—

"Tracy!"

At the summons, she braked, balancing herself with one foot on the pavement.

Father Kevin and Reverend Baker waved at her from across the street, each carrying a brown bag from Charley's. After dodging the cars on Dockside Drive, they joined her.

"Good morning." Or was it? She checked her watch. Sheesh. Twelve-fifteen already. "Sorry. Afternoon."

"That's okay. I often lose track of the days, let alone the mornings and afternoons." Father Kevin grinned at her. "Do you have a minute? Paul and I have an idea we wanted to run by you."

Another one? Her brain was already on overload from this morning.

Squelching a sigh, she shoved the baking project to a mental back burner. "Sure."

"We've reviewed Michael's report, and Paul and I believe that if we want Helping Hands to be as effective as possible, a paid director would be the best option."

"I agree—but there's no money for that. Not even seed money to fund the job for a few months until a director could get some fund-raising efforts rolling. Michael and I talked about it, and I don't think anyone would take a job like that on spec. People do have to eat."

"Of course." Reverend Baker transferred his bag from one hand to the other, sending a tantalizing aroma wafting her way. Somehow breakfast had slipped through the cracks in her busy schedule. "But we think perhaps this job could be a part-time position, at least in the beginning. In fact, if the person we hired was experienced, it might be able to remain part time . . ."

"Because a professional would be able to accomplish a lot more much faster than we do, with our well-meaning but amateur piecemeal efforts." Father Kevin finished his friend's thought.

"Yes, and if it was part time, this person could also work another job. That should tide them over until there was money in the till to begin paying a salary at Helping Hands."

Tracy pushed her sunglasses to the top of her head. "It won't be easy to find someone in this area with the kind of high-level skills you're talking about, and I can't think of any supplemental part-time work around Hope Harbor that would adequately compensate a person with that kind of background."

The two clergymen exchanged a look, and Reverend Baker spoke. "Unless we could find someone who might have the resources—and willingness—to do this for free until it's up and running. Like . . . Michael."

Tracy stared at them. "Michael?"

"He has the credentials, and he's already up to speed on the organization." Father Kevin rocked forward on his toes, radiating enthusiasm. "We were reluctant to put him on the spot, so since you two seem to have become good friends, we decided to get your take first. It wouldn't have to be a long-term arrangement. We just need someone to get the thing rolling and put us on the right track. Naturally, it all depends on how long he's planning to stay."

"Not long enough. He has to be back on the job in Chicago July 14."

Both of their faces fell.

"I guess our idea wasn't as inspired as we thought." Father Kevin exhaled and dropped back on his heels.

"I'm glad we talked with you before mentioning it at the next board meeting." Reverend Baker gave her a resigned smile. "Sorry to delay you, my dear. And please give Michael our best. Will the two of you be coming to services again on Sunday?"

"We haven't discussed it yet, but I think so."

"Good. Kevin and I sent him a thank-you note for all his work, but I'd like to express my gratitude in person."

"Or you could come to the ten-thirty Mass instead. We're always glad to have new parishioners." Father Kevin winked at her.

"Trying to steal my congregation again, I see." Reverend Baker pretended to bristle.

"Miracles do happen, you know."

"Ha! If I were you, I'd stick to working on my

golf game. Getting your score under par would be miracle enough."

Tracy smothered a grin. The two of them might indulge in verbal sparring and nurture a friendly rivalry, but Father Kevin's welcome gift of a box of Titleist high-end balls and an invitation to the links had been the beginning of a beautiful friendship.

"Well, if you two don't need anything else . . ."

"No. We've delayed you too long already. Besides, our lunch is getting cold." Father Kevin crinkled the bag in his fingers. "Have a blessed day."

Lifting their lunches in unison, the two men recrossed the street and strolled toward the pocket park tucked between the wharf and the river, next to Charley's.

Tracy continued to Sweet Dreams for one of the coffee cakes Nancy enjoyed—but her mind wasn't on her bakery visit. It was too busy pondering the idea broached by the clergymen.

Michael as the part-time director of Helping Hands.

Was it possible that idea, too, might have legs— *if* Michael decided to stay?

Even if he did, though, could he afford to take on a job that wouldn't offer any financial compensation for the first few months? He obviously had *some* money in reserve or he wouldn't be willing to invest in the Harbor Point baking venture—but that bout of generosity might have taxed his resources to the limit.

Besides, if he was thinking about making a big change in his life, nonprofit work might no longer hold any appeal. Based on his history, it was very possible he'd want to find a different kind of job.

Tracy handed the money for the coffee cake to the clerk with a distracted thank-you and returned to her bike. Stewing about those issues was useless. Why not ask him about his plans? After all, if they wanted to deepen their relationship, open, honest communication was important.

Even if honesty didn't always produce the hoped-for answer.

Anna filled the seed holder and slid it into position in the cage, leaning close to inspect the chickadee.

"Well, my friend, your stay with me is about up. And you'll be glad to leave, won't you, now that Thumper and your raccoon buddy are gone?"

After letting out a soft whistle, the bird went back to eating with gusto.

The phone rang, and Anna sent it an annoyed glance. Another charitable solicitation, no doubt. Or one of those calls about reducing credit card debt. She ought to get rid of the landline. Why waste the money? Her bare-bones cell was sufficient for the few calls she placed.

Except . . . John knew this number.

331

Huffing out a breath, Anna resealed the bag of seed and plunked it on a shelf as the machine rolled to voice mail. How pathetic was that? Like he'd actually pick up the phone one day out of the blue and . . .

"Anna? It's Joyce."

Her lungs froze, and she groped for the edge of the counter.

"I . . . I wasn't sure if this number was still good, but I . . . I guess it is. I wanted to let you know we're having a potluck at church on Saturday night. You might have seen the notice in the bulletin." The woman sounded as if she'd been running, her words choppy and breathless. "Anyway, your scalloped potatoes used to be a favorite, and if you want to come . . . well, I'll be there too. I could . . . I could save you a place." Silence for a moment. "Also . . . I didn't get a chance to ask about your sling on Sunday, but if you . . . if you need any help, let me know. Take care."

The line went dead.

For a full sixty seconds, Anna didn't move. When had she last gotten a personal call on her home phone?

Too many years to count.

Now this from Joyce—all because she'd made a simple, cordial overture.

Pressure built behind her eyes. Despite all the years that had passed, her old friend was willing to offer her a second chance—like the father in the prodigal son story.

Her gaze slid to the flat beige envelope lying on the kitchen counter, where it had rested since her trip to Coos Bay on Monday. A spur-of-the-moment purchase she'd almost thrown out the same night.

Slowly she crossed to it. Fingered the top. Pulled out the card and read the cover.

Happy 40th Birthday to a Special Son.

Hard to believe John would be forty on Saturday.

Card in hand, she moved into the living room, pausing beside the piano where he'd practiced with singular focus and determination to master the difficult, challenging pieces his teacher assigned.

She stroked a hand over the music stand, ran her fingers across the keys. The instrument was in perfect tune, as usual. Another unnecessary expense. The only one with any musical talent in the family had been John. Gracious, she hardly knew a treble from a bass clef.

Yet here the piano had sat, taking up space, for almost two decades—a part of John she'd never been able to let go.

Because he'd added such beautiful music to her life . . . in so many ways.

She returned to the kitchen, stopping as she passed to touch the outdated answering machine that held Joyce's message. Proof that reaching out could have positive results—even in the case of very old hurts.

Her fingers clenched around the card. Might a similar olive branch work with John?

Yet if it didn't . . . that door would be shut forever.

Lowering herself into the chair at the small built-in desk, Anna brushed a finger over the lettering for the word *son*. The embossed design gave the card dimension—the very thing missing from her life for almost two decades, after her world flattened the day John walked out.

Wouldn't it be amazing if they actually reconnected?

That would never happen, though, if she let fear paralyze her. Yes, it was possible he'd ignore her attempt at reconciliation. And yes, it would be difficult to bear a final rejection. Yet she'd be no more alone than she was now.

And alone wasn't working for her anymore.

Taking a deep breath, Anna opened the card, picked up a pen, and began to write.

"Ouch!"

At Tracy's exclamation, Michael shaded his eyes and squinted farther down the deer fence. "What's wrong?"

"Bee sting."

He dropped his shovel and strode toward her.

The spot on her forearm was already turning red beneath the stinger protruding from her skin. "How can I help?"

"You can't. Once you're stung, you're stung. I just need to get the stinger out ASAP." She tugged off her work gloves, then dragged her fingernail across the stinger, pulling it free. "She was a mean one."

"She?"

"Only female honeybees can sting—and this one packed quite a punch." She displayed the stinger on her fingertip.

"I thought they were supposed to be calm?"

"They are—unless you rest an arm right on them."

He winced, leaning closer to examine the stinger. "What's the thing on the end?"

"An efficient little pump that continues to push poison into the wound after you get stung. Very clever design." She flicked off the stinger and dug a small tube of toothpaste out of her pocket. After squeezing some on her finger, she spread it over the inflamed area.

"Home remedy?"

"It works."

"Shouldn't you wash the area first?"

She gave him a teasing look. "You *are* a city boy. Here in the country, we just carry on. I'm good to go unless this swells."

Michael frowned. When had he last been stung

by a bee? The school picnic in fifth grade, maybe? The date might be fuzzy, but he had no problem recalling how it had throbbed like the dickens.

"Doesn't it hurt?"

"Yep." She resettled her baseball cap and waved off another bee. "But bee stings are one of the hazards of cranberry growing. I've been stung too many times to count. The toothpaste will take care of the pain in a few minutes. If it swells, I'll ice it." She gestured to a shady spot beside the dike. "Why don't we take a break, though? I could use some water."

"Works for me."

He followed her to the tractor. She pulled two bottles from the small cooler she'd brought along and handed him one.

Michael twisted off the cap and took a long pull while she did the same.

"Let's take advantage of that shade." Without waiting for a reply, she led the way to the dappled patch of ground and dropped down, sitting cross-legged as she removed her baseball cap.

After joining her, he pulled his legs up and rested his forearms on his knees, letting the peace and quiet seep into his soul. The kinks that had knotted his neck and shoulders since Julie died loosened another notch—as they'd done each day he spent in the fresh air doing physical labor . . . with Tracy nearby.

He turned his head—and caught her watching

him. Her expression was . . . what? Nervous? Unsettled? Cautious? Whatever emotion it reflected, his antennas went up.

"You look like a lady who has something on her mind."

"A few things." She lifted the bottle and took a long sip, her slender throat working as she swallowed. "One of them concerns you—and your plans."

Ah. Now he could identify the emotion.

It was worry.

"I've been praying about that. Unfortunately, I haven't had any blinding flashes of insight."

"Does that mean a move out here is still a possibility?"

"I haven't ruled it out." He dangled the bottle from his fingers, between his knees. Should he mention his mixed feelings about relocating to a town his wife had cherished? Or his nagging feelings of guilt about moving on to a new love after failing Julie so badly? Or his fear that maybe he hadn't learned his lesson about priorities and could end up hurting a woman who'd already known more than her share of hurts?

No.

Those were issues he needed to work through on his own. Tracy had too much on her plate already.

When the silence lengthened, she spoke again. "In that case, I want to tell you about a conversation I had with our local clergy today."

He listened as she recounted her meeting with the priest and minister, along with their query about his interest.

"In the end, I told them you were scheduled to leave in less than three weeks. I didn't create any expectations on their end. But if you're leaning toward staying and have any interest in taking on the leadership role part-time, they'd be thrilled to have you. The whole board would—if you could handle being unpaid for the first few months." She lifted her bottle and finished off the water.

He did the same, buying himself a few moments to think. A ready-made job that played to his strengths was appealing—especially the part-time aspect. That should make it easier to keep work from dominating his life. And once he got Helping Hands organized and secured more consistent funding, he could cede the position to a qualified candidate if he chose.

It was ideal in many ways—though it would require him to accelerate his decision about his life in Chicago.

Tracy looked over at him in silence, waiting for his reaction.

"I could manage the finances." Best to start with the straightforward part. "Anna's rent is reasonable, and she might sweeten the deal for an extended stay. My day-to-day expenses are minimal, and even after investing in the cranberry project, I'll have some reserves. It's an appealing offer on a lot of levels. What do you think about it?"

She shifted her focus to the cranberry beds, the breeze playing with a few soft wisps of hair that had escaped her ponytail. Faint creases marred her forehead, and when she spoke, he had a feeling she was choosing her words with care. "This has to be your decision, Michael. I'd hate myself if I tried to influence you and you ended up having regrets."

Another bee buzzed her, and she lifted a hand to wave it away—giving him a front-and-center view of her forearm. Despite the application of toothpaste, it was clear the sting had swollen.

He reached over and captured her hand. "I think this needs ice." He laid a gentle finger beside the reddened skin.

She spared it no more than a cursory scan. "I'll give it another half hour." She tried to retract her hand, but he held fast.

"Can I tell you something?"

She searched his face. "Sure. I guess."

"If I followed my instincts, I'd resign from St. Joseph Center tomorrow, take the job with Helping Hands, pitch in at the farm—and focus on wooing you."

Her features softened, yet her gaze remained steady. "But . . . ?"

"But given our histories, I think it's prudent

not to rush a decision that could affect the rest of our lives."

"I gave the same answer to Uncle Bud not long ago when he asked me how things were going with us. He didn't diss prudence . . . but he did caution me not to let logic or fear or doubts or bad experiences deafen me to the voice of my heart. In his opinion, feelings *do* count."

"Smart man."

"Yes, he is—and his advice is generally sound. So I think you should take your time . . ."

"But also listen to my heart."

"That's what Uncle Bud would counsel."

He swiveled toward her and scooted closer, twining his fingers with hers. "Do you know what my heart is saying at this moment?"

"I think I can guess—and it's not very prudent."

No, it wasn't. Especially since he wasn't the only one with a lot at stake here. Until he got a better handle on how to proceed, it wasn't fair to Tracy to create an emotional connection that would leave her bruised and hurting if he ended up going back to Chicago for good.

Yet here, under a cloudless blue sky, with the tang of salt in the air and the lilting song of birds scoring the scene and her delicate hand in his, being with this woman seemed not only right, but meant to be.

For always.

And whether or not that came to pass, he wanted a kiss.

Now.

Lifting his hand, he leaned closer and cupped her nape, exerting gentle pressure to pull her toward him.

She came without resistance, her arms circling his neck as she took the lead with a depth of passion . . . with an urgency and need . . . that shot his pulse into the stratosphere.

This was not the simple melding of lips he'd intended.

This was her way of telling him, without ever uttering a word, how much he'd come to mean to her.

And it blew him away even as he pressed her close, returning as much as she gave, letting his heart have its say.

When the kiss ended, Tracy leaned her forehead against his, her breathing ragged.

Or was that *his* breathing?

Didn't matter. The next instant she wiggled free of his arms, grabbed her cap, and jumped to her feet.

"Race you back to the fence."

Before he could reply, she was off, a lithe figure on the run.

To the fence . . . or away from the tumultuous emotions the kiss had clearly stirred up in both of them?

He rose with far less haste, giving his blood pressure a chance to drop back somewhere in the vicinity of normal range. If he was a betting man, he'd lay money on the latter. She was running away—and running scared.

As any prudent woman would.

After grabbing the staple gun he'd been using to secure the wire fencing to the cedar posts they'd installed, he followed her back to the bed. He wasn't sorry about that kiss . . . but what it revealed was a wake-up call.

Tracy was falling fast—and so was he.

So to save them both another dose of heartache, he needed to make some decisions about his future.

And he needed to do it soon.

21

"Hey, Dad, check this out! A birthday card from someone in your hometown." Kelsey Williams bounded into the den, clutching a bunch of mail in one hand and waving a beige envelope in the other.

Frowning, John looked up from his laptop.

A card from Hope Harbor? How weird was that? He hadn't kept in touch with a single person from his youth.

Kelsey plopped beside him on the couch, as

usual a bottomless bundle of energy, and held out the envelope.

His heart stammered.

No need to read the return address or open the card to know who it was from. Even after a gap of nineteen-plus years, he knew his mother's handwriting.

Beside him, Kelsey went still. "Is this from my grandmother?"

For a fourteen-year-old, his daughter had an uncanny ability to tune in to moods.

He forced his lungs to reengage. "Yes."

"Epic!"

Not the word he would have chosen.

"What's epic?" His wife entered the room, carrying a huge bowl of popcorn along with the old movie he'd chosen as a lead-in to his birthday dinner.

Kelsey waved the beige envelope. "He got a birthday card from his mom."

As Denise set the bowl on the coffee table, her startled gaze connected with his—a more appropriate reaction than Kelsey's.

But Denise was the only one who knew the full story of the estrangement.

"You okay?" Her question was quiet, her touch on his arm gentle.

"Yeah."

Kelsey held out the card again. "Don't you want to open it?"

"Later." Maybe. "Put it on the table with the rest of the mail for now."

His daughter gave a theatrical sigh but complied. "I can't believe you don't want to see what it says."

"Whatever the message, it will keep." He powered down his laptop and closed the lid. "Right now I want to watch a movie with my two favorite people in the world."

"I'll get it going." Denise opened the DVD case. "Kelsey, why don't you fix our drinks?"

"I'm on it. The usual for everybody?"

"Yes." Denise sat beside him and took his hand as their daughter bounded out of the room. "What are you thinking?"

He forced a smile. "That I'm lucky to be married to an eminent psychologist—because I might need to engage your professional services if I decide to open that." He nodded to the card.

"I'm asking as your wife, not as a psychologist."

"Yeah. I know." He pulled her close and wrapped his arms around her, this woman who'd anchored his life and given it new meaning during some of his darkest hours. The woman he loved more than life itself. "I'm thinking it's surreal. She wrote me off long ago."

Denise pulled back slightly as the muffled sound of ice clinking into glasses filtered in from the kitchen. "I think you wrote each other off."

"True." Distance had given him perspective if

nothing else. There was fault on both sides for the estrangement—but more of it was on his mother's. On that point he'd never wavered. "I wonder why she'd contact me after all these years?"

Denise fingered the DVD, holding it by the edges, taking care not to damage the fragile disk. "Sometimes a life-changing event can prompt people to try to deal with unresolved issues in their past."

"Like a bad medical report." It was the first thing that had come to his mind. Maybe his mother had been diagnosed with some terminal condition.

Odd how that thought twisted his stomach when she hadn't been part of his life for almost two decades.

"That's one possibility—but I wouldn't jump to conclusions too fast." She tipped her head toward the card. "There's an easy way to find out."

"No. Not easy at all." No matter what the card said, he wasn't ready to read it.

"I thought you were going to start the movie?" Kelsey reappeared in the doorway, balancing a tray holding three glasses, and crossed to the sofa.

"Coming right up." With a final squeeze of his hand, Denise rose and slid the disk into the player.

A flash of lightning, followed by a window-rattling boom of thunder, raised the hair on his neck as the opening music for *North by Northwest* began to play. The turbulent weather was a perfect accompaniment for the classic Hitchcock suspense film.

And also for the turmoil roiling in his gut.

Denise nestled in beside him, and Kelsey dived into the popcorn on his other side. This was the best gift he could get for his fortieth birthday—a perfect afternoon and evening with the family that was the center of his world.

Yet as the movie began, as Cary Grant found himself pulled out of his quiet, predictable life and thrust into the midst of danger and intrigue, John felt his pain—thanks to the slim beige envelope resting on a table three feet away.

Because it might contain words that would change his world forever—*if* he found the courage to open it and read them.

And that was a big if.

"Are you certain I can't convince you to join me? There's always been plenty of food at the potlucks." Anna took the arm Michael offered and slid from his car.

He opened the back door and retrieved the casserole carrier from the seat. "No, thanks. I'm too tired from a full week at the farm to have the energy for socializing. Would you like me to carry this in for you?"

"Thanks, but I'm used to toting food around." She gripped the handle in her sling-free hand.

"Remember, I'll be happy to pick you up later if you like. All you have to do is call my cell."

"I may do that if I can't get a ride. But an old friend is planning to be here, and she may be willing to drop me off. What are your plans for the evening?"

"A quick stop at Charley's, followed by a walk on the beach."

"Sounds pleasant." She took a deep breath and nodded toward the church hall. "Let's hope everyone took Reverend Baker's sermon to heart last Sunday. I have some fences to mend."

"There might be a few holdouts, but I have a feeling you'll win them over."

"I hope you're right. And I do have one ally. She might help pave the way. Well . . ." Anna straightened her shoulders. "Here goes nothing."

With that she marched toward the door of the church hall . . . and into the fray.

The lady had pluck, he'd give her that. Walking into the unknown was always difficult, no matter your age . . . or circumstances.

Heaving a sigh, Michael circled back to the driver's seat and continued down Dockside Drive to join the queue at Charley's. A family group and two couples were ahead of him, but the wait would be worth it—though the time would go much faster if he had company. Too bad Tracy's backlog of accounting work had consigned him to a solo evening.

In fairness, however, it wasn't much of a Saturday night for her either.

He tuned out the couple ahead of him that was debating the merits of a movie versus some club in Coos Bay, focusing instead on the boats in the marina that had found a safe haven in Hope Harbor. Would the town offer the same to him if he stayed—or would its connection to Julie fuel the deep, aching regret he couldn't shake?

And was it even fair to his late wife to come at last to the place she'd held dear, only to find love with a different woman? The notion that he'd honor her memory by creating a new and better life built on the lessons he'd learned from his mistakes sounded nice—but was it more rationalization than truth?

Michael shoved his hands in his pockets, fisting them. He was no closer to finding those answers now than he'd been days ago—and in just over two weeks, he was scheduled to begin the long drive back to Chicago.

"You're up, Michael."

At the summons from Charley, he swiveled back to the taco truck. The other customers had wandered off, brown bags in hand, to claim benches or a picnic table in the pocket park.

He moved to the window. "One order."

"Tracy isn't joining you tonight?" Charley began assembling the tacos with his usual smooth efficiency.

"No. She's crunching numbers for some accounting clients."

"She works hard."

"Too hard."

"The cranberry business is tough. It's hard to make a living as a grower these days."

"So I've discovered."

Charley sprinkled what looked like shredded cabbage on three tortillas and added a dollop of . . . something. "You still helping out at Harbor Point?"

"Yes—and working on a new project that could give the farm a financial boost. The trouble is, I'm scheduled to leave soon."

"Schedules can change."

"But jobs don't stay in limbo forever. I pushed the limits to get two months off."

"You ready to go back?" He flipped the fish he'd placed on the grill.

"Not even close."

"Hope Harbor has a lot to offer." Charley dropped onto a stool behind the counter, giving him his full attention while the fillets finished cooking.

Michael swallowed. "It also has a lot of baggage."

The artist's eyebrows rose. "You've been here before?"

"No. But my late wife . . . her family used to vacation here when she was a child. She always wanted me to visit with her, but other things kept taking precedence." He raked his fingers through his hair. "I'm afraid the town might always be a reminder of my messed-up priorities."

As the admission hung in the air between them, he froze. Baring his soul even to friends and family wasn't his usual modus operandi, let alone spilling his guts to a casual acquaintance.

"I see your point. What was your wife's name?"

He was in too deep to get out. "Julie."

"And she would have been a summer visitor here . . . what? Twenty, twenty-five years ago?"

"That sounds about right."

"Can you describe her as a little girl?"

Michael tried to call up her image from the childhood photos she'd shown him, many of which had been taken on the Hope Harbor beach. "She was a skinny little thing. Long, wavy blonde hair and big blue eyes with the most amazing sparkle."

"Did she have a pink 'I love Hope Harbor' T-shirt? One of those with a heart instead of the word?"

Michael squinted at the man. "Yeah, she did." She'd been wearing it in one of the photos he'd found among her keepsakes when he'd gone through her things.

Charley rose, tossed a handful of chopped tomatoes on the tacos, gave the fish a final turn, and moved to the wall papered with children's artwork. He dug through the layers, pulled one drawing free, and set it on the counter.

"I think this was from her. She and her family were regulars, and she gave it to me her last day here on one of their trips."

While Charley assembled the tacos and wrapped them in parchment paper, Michael stared at the crude crayon drawing. A stick figure blonde-haired girl was in the center, standing on the beach with the sea stacks behind her, arms outstretched, a huge smile on her face. The artist had written the words "Be Happy!!!" in big letters across the cloudless blue sky at the top.

It could have been done by any child.

Except this girl was wearing a pink "I ♥ Hope Harbor" T-shirt.

And it was dated and signed at the bottom.

To Charley, the world's best taco maker. Love, Julie.

The signature might be childish, but it was his wife's. Same slant, same large caps, same curlicues on the end of her *e*'s.

She'd drawn this when she was ten.

"You think that's her?" Charley slid the tacos into a bag.

"I know it is. How did you . . . why do you . . . this is from twenty years ago."

"What can I say?" He shrugged. "I like art—especially children's art. And how do you throw away a gift from the heart like this?" He tapped the drawing that had yellowed through the decades and collected more than a few grease spots. "I don't display all the pictures my young customers have given me; some are in boxes at the studio. But my favorites are here."

Michael groped for his wallet and set a ten-dollar bill on the counter, struggling to come to grips with the latest curve Hope Harbor had thrown him.

"I like the message, don't you?" The man counted out his change and tapped the words "Be Happy." "It's timeless."

Yeah, it was—and it captured Julie's personality perfectly. The woman he'd loved had radiated joy, and she'd wanted all those she cared about to share it.

It seemed she'd always been that way.

Hand trembling, Michael ran his fingertips over the decades-old drawing.

"You can take that with you, if you like." Charley straightened out a bent corner. "I have a feeling I was only the caretaker."

"Thanks." The single word was all he could manage.

Julie's drawing in one hand, bag in the other, Michael returned to his car. When he looked back at the taco stand, a new batch of customers had descended.

Odd how no one had disturbed them while he'd been at the window on a busy Saturday night. It was like . . . fate.

Or some force even more powerful.

Michael fitted the key in the ignition, put the car in gear, and headed for the beach to eat his dinner, take a long walk . . . and do some serious thinking.

After hanging a left at the end of Dockside Drive, he began the ascent to the bluffs. But his previous thought keep strobing through his mind.

Some force even more powerful.

Like . . . God?

All these weeks, he'd wondered if the Almighty was hearing his desperate pleas for guidance and direction. There'd been no bolt from the blue, no writing in the sky . . . not so much as a subtle hint.

Yet in hindsight, it seemed God had been consistently nudging him along. Every single thing that had happened since his arrival in Hope Harbor had been transforming his life. Opening new doors. Taking him down paths he'd never expected to travel.

Now this.

He glanced over at the drawing on the seat beside him—a final gift from the woman he'd loved.

Be Happy!!!

That was about as close to writing in the sky as you could get.

Now all he had to do was define exactly what it would take for him to achieve the goal Julie had penned two decades ago.

• • •

The red "new message" light was blinking.

Heart pounding, Anna set the quilted casserole carrier on the counter, wiped her damp palm down her slacks, and edged toward the answering machine.

It wasn't John. It couldn't be. One card wouldn't wipe out nineteen years' worth of hurt. Not this fast, anyway.

Could it?

Please, God, let it be him!

She lifted her hand and pressed a shaky finger against the play button.

"Mrs. Williams, this is Ellen Lewis. We're planning to attend services tomorrow at the church you and Grace went to last week, and we wondered if you'd like us to pick you up. Just give me a call. And thank you again for all your help. Things here are so much better. Talk to you soon."

There were no more messages.

Swallowing past her foolish disappointment, Anna turned away from the machine.

Of course John wouldn't call this fast. Maybe, after thinking for a few days about what she'd written, he might consider getting in touch—assuming he'd opened the card. For all she knew, it had hit the trash seconds after it landed in his hands.

Trudging over to the sink, she unzipped the carrier—or tried to. It took three attempts, thanks to the tremors running through her fingers. Also foolish. She was too old, with too many hard miles on her odometer, to get carried away with impossible dreams. Those were for the young who hadn't yet been tainted by the harsh realities of life. She should be grateful Joyce had given her a second chance instead of wishing for the moon.

She put the casserole in the sink and twisted on the hot water tap to soften the potato residue that had hardened on the interior.

There were other things to be grateful for today too. The Lewises were back together, and the event tonight had gone far better than she'd expected, thanks to Joyce's intervention. The welcome she received might have been cautious, but no one had snubbed her. She could become part of this community again if she made the effort. Plus, there was a baking business to launch, giving her a new purpose and—

The phone jangled, and she jerked, her uninjured hand flying to her chest, hope swelling again despite her best effort to contain it.

Wiping her hand on a towel, she hurried across the room and snatched up the receiver with a breathless greeting.

"Anna? Joyce. You sound winded."

She closed her eyes and sagged against the counter. "I, uh, had to hustle to pick up before the call rolled to the machine."

"Oh. Well, I wanted to let you know I found your wallet on the passenger seat floor after I got home. It must have fallen out of your purse. Shall I run it back over?"

Her lungs kicked back in. "No need. I won't be going anywhere tonight."

"I'll give it to you when I stop by tomorrow to pick you up for church, then."

"That would be fine. And Joyce . . . it was really nice chatting with you tonight. It brought back a lot of happy memories."

"For me too." The woman's last word came out choked, and when she continued, her voice was shaky. "I'll see you tomorrow."

Once they said their good-byes, Anna placed a quick call to Ellen Lewis to decline her offer of a ride, then wandered back to the sink. The crusty potato remnants had loosened, and in short order she'd cleaned the dish until it was like new despite her one-handed scrubbing.

Perhaps her relationship with John could sparkle again—if he'd opened her card.

With a rueful shake of her head, she stowed the spotless dish. At this stage of her life, she should have learned that in general, happy endings were confined to books.

Yet try as she might, she couldn't quite snuff out the tiny flicker of hope that burned deep in her heart.

22

"Here you go, Eleanor." Tracy handed the older woman the small grocery bag containing baking powder and chocolate chips.

"Thank you, my dear. I'm sorry to bother you with this on a Sunday afternoon. I'd completely forgotten about signing up to make dessert for Reverend Baker this weekend until Margie from the food committee reminded me after the service." She leaned sideways and peered down the front walk. "Did you bring Michael with you again? You two made quite the handsome couple at church this morning."

With an effort, Tracy held on to her smile. Michael might have been with her in body, but his mind had been far away.

Something was up.

"No. He's out at the farm, helping Uncle Bud finish a fence repair that couldn't wait. Shep and Ziggy can't stand guard against the deer 24/7. I'm on my way to join them now."

"Pitching in at the farm, is he?" The older woman gave an approving nod. "I like a man who's not afraid to get his hands dirty."

That made two of them.

But Tracy wasn't about to discuss her preferences in men with Eleanor. Not after the unsettling vibes she'd gotten this morning from the very man she preferred.

She eased away from the door. "I better get moving. There's a lot of work to be done today."

"You fit in some fun too—preferably with that nice young man. I have a feeling he knows how to show a lady a memorable time."

She was out of here.

"Talk to you soon." With a wave, she jogged down the path, mounted her bike, and took off, pedaling at double speed—the sooner to see that nice young man and try to get a read on his earlier distraction.

But when she pulled into Harbor Point Cranberries less than fifteen minutes later, his Focus wasn't there.

"You got here fast." Uncle Bud strolled out of the equipment shed, staple gun in hand.

"Where's Michael?"

"He left ten minutes ago after he got a phone call. Said he had some urgent business to deal with. You want to help me finish up the corner post? I need another set of hands."

"Sure." She started toward the shed to get her gloves.

"Hey."

She stopped and turned back.

"Cheer up."

"I'm cheery."

"Could have fooled me."

Her uncle was way too observant.

She shrugged and toed a piece of gravel, shoving her fingers into the front pockets of her jeans. "Just wondering about Michael's call. It must have been important for him to renege on his commitment to help out here today."

"I expect it was." Uncle Bud weighed the staple gun in his hand. "You're worried he's going to leave, aren't you?"

Might as well admit the truth. "Yeah."

"You know, while we were working today, he talked a fair amount about the cranberry nut cake project—and he used the word *we* a lot. If he was thinking of cutting out, seems to me he wouldn't be doing that. Why don't you ask him about his plans if you're worried?"

"I did. Last time we talked about it, he was still trying to figure out what he should do."

"It's a big decision."

"I know." She brushed some stray strands of hair back from her forehead. "Let me grab my gloves."

It took her less than thirty seconds to retrieve them, and when she exited the shed, her uncle was waiting where she'd left him.

"You been bending the Lord's ear about this?"

"Some."

"Keep it up—and I'll join you. A man faced with a decision like that needs a lot of guidance. Best thing we can do is put it in God's hands and let him handle the hard work."

She pulled on one glove, shoulders slumping. "That sounds good in theory, anyway."

"Don't I know it." He bent down to pet Ziggy as the collie bounded up. "Worry is tough to shake, no matter how strong a person's faith is. Smart, capable, competent people like us"—he winked at her—"want to take charge and get answers now. Trouble is, our timeline isn't always God's. All we can do is pray Michael eventually makes the right decision—for everyone involved."

She tugged on the other glove, trying for a casual tone. "So if he decides to stay, how would you feel about that?"

"You want the truth?"

Her stomach bottomed out. Uncle Bud was a superb judge of character, and if he had any reservations about Michael she'd have to give them serious consideration.

Maybe she shouldn't have asked.

But burying your head in the sand didn't make storms go away, as he'd always taught her.

She swallowed. "Yes."

"From what I've seen, I think he's a fine man. And you didn't ask me about this, but I'll tell you anyway—I also think you suit each other. I liked Craig, but after watching you with Michael, I think he's a better match."

"How can you know that already? He's only been in town a month."

"Doesn't take me long to size up a person. I

knew Nancy was special the first day we met. Of course, we took our time about getting serious—but my instincts about people are usually spot-on." He hefted the staple gun. "You ready to fix fences?"

"Yes."

She followed him toward the beds, stopping to give Shep a pat that set the collie's tail wagging. Then the dog scampered off to join his buddy in another game of chase-the-bog-rats, yipping with enthusiasm.

If only human joy were that easy to find.

But her uncle was right about giving her worry to God. She'd already let Michael know in every way she could, short of actually saying the words, that she wanted him to stay. That her feelings for him ran deep.

Now it was up to him—and God.

"Thank you both for seeing me on such short notice." Michael shook hands with the two clergymen and took a seat at the table in Reverend Baker's office.

"No problem at all. Your request got me out of an altar committee meeting." Father Kevin grinned as he sat. "I don't know what our purpose here is, but a discussion about *anything* is better than listening to the ladies debate the pros and cons of flowers and liturgical banners and whether the altar linens need to be starched."

"I'm with Kevin." Reverend Baker claimed a

chair. "My Sunday afternoon would have included attending a monthly ministers' conclave in Coos Bay, where the most important thing on the agenda is usually the Ducks. Nice bunch of people . . . but not a vital meeting. So what can we do for you?"

Michael folded his hands on the polished walnut. "Tracy told me about the conversation you three had regarding Helping Hands—and your interest in having me take on the part-time director job."

After the two clerics exchanged a look, Father Kevin spoke. "I hope we didn't offend you by discussing this behind your back, but we didn't want to put you on the spot. It was an off-the-wall idea, after all—and Tracy explained you'll be leaving soon. I suppose it would have been a miracle to find someone with strong credentials who would do the job without pay, even for a few months."

Michael took a deep breath. This was where prayer had led him, but it was still a huge step. "Then you may be looking at one."

Reverend Baker cocked his head. "But I thought . . . aren't you planning to leave soon?"

"I was—but my plans changed."

"This is fantastic!" The priest leaned forward, excitement sparking in his eyes. "With your expertise and under your leadership, Helping Hands could become a powerhouse of charitable works. It would be everything—and more—we envisioned at its inception."

"My tenure with Helping Hands may be short-term, though." He needed to rein them in before they got too carried away. "Perhaps just long enough to get the new model up and running, put some funding in place. I'm in the process of evaluating whether I want to stay in nonprofit work. However, if I decide to step down, I'd work with you to find a replacement."

"However long you stayed, it would be a god-send—literally. Truly an answer to our prayers." Reverend Baker rested his elbows on the table and steepled his fingers, his demeanor growing more serious. "But we don't want the job to impose a financial hardship, either. As Tracy reminded us, people do have to eat. Are you certain you can manage this?"

"Yes." He might not be wealthy, but Julie's insurance money would tide him over for a while —and far better to use it to support a worth-while cause than for his own pleasure. Coupled with the reduced rent Anna had offered after he'd broached the subject of an extended stay, the stars were aligning to make this happen.

"Excellent. We'll call a special board meeting for this week to run it by the members, but I think we can assume it's a done deal. No one is going to turn down manna in the desert." Father Kevin grinned.

Reverend Baker rolled his eyes. "If you're going to use biblical metaphors, couldn't you come up with one a bit more flattering? Like the marriage at Cana. Saving the best wine till last."

"Manna is an excellent metaphor." The priest sniffed. "However, I could have used the pearl of great price too."

"No. Not a valid example. We're getting *our* pearl *free*. You need to beef up your Bible study."

Father Kevin harrumphed. "Don't get me started on another Bible study debate. Catholics read as much Scripture as—"

"Gentlemen." Michael tried to keep a straight face as he interrupted their exchange. The good-natured ribbing between the two clerics was a hoot. "Let me tie up a few loose ends before you schedule a board meeting. Now that I've confirmed your interest, I need to make certain there aren't any issues that could delay things. But once we move forward publicly, let me know the date of the board meeting and I'll wait outside while the members discuss this, in case there are any questions."

The pastor and priest both turned toward him, but it was Father Kevin who spoke. "I can't imagine anyone will have a single question."

"More likely, they'll want to kiss your feet."

Grinning, Michael pushed back from the table and stood. "Doesn't sound very sanitary. I'll settle for a few handshakes."

The two clerics rose too, and Father Kevin held out his hand. "I'll lead the brigade. We're very, very grateful."

Michael returned his firm grip.

"I expect Tracy is pleased by this development too." Reverend Baker's eyes twinkled as he gave him an enthusiastic hand pump.

"I haven't told her yet . . . but that's coming up very soon on my agenda. I have a couple more pieces of business to tie up first. So I'd appreciate it if you'd both keep this to yourselves for a day or two."

"I'll treat this as confidentially as the secrets entrusted to me in the confessional," Father Kevin promised.

"Confession may not be one of our traditions, but ministers know how to keep confidences too. I won't say a word." Reverend Baker smiled. "However, I have a feeling a certain cranberry grower is about to get some news that will make her very happy."

"From your mouth to God's ear."

"One of my favorite sayings." Father Kevin beamed at him.

"A Catholic priest favoring a Yiddish expression?" Reverend Baker hiked up an eyebrow.

"Hey, we're very ecumenical."

Michael stifled a chuckle. "On that note, I'll say good-bye."

But as he headed back to the annex to compose

a lengthy email and polish up the preliminary business plan he'd developed for the cranberry nut cake business, he hoped Reverend Baker was right about Tracy—and not just in the short term.

Because the decision he'd made after the events of last evening at Charley's—and after some heavy-duty mental debate and prayer that had gone on long past midnight—was going to change both their lives. Forever.

And while it felt right, there were no guarantees.

All he could do was go with his heart and trust that in the months to come, both he and Tracy would look back on this day with gratitude rather than regret.

"So are you ever going to open your mom's card?"

At Kelsey's question, John tightened his fingers on the wheel of the car. She might have given him a bye from this touchy subject on his birthday, but today it was fair game—as Denise had warned him it would be.

Especially now that his daughter had him alone in the car without her mother to run interference on his behalf.

"I don't know. Did you bring the extra balls?"

She toed the gym bag at her feet, beside the tennis racket. "A whole tube. So what about the card?"

Tell her the story, John. She's old enough to hear it.

Denise's quiet counsel from last night, after she'd gathered him close in the dark as he'd stared wide awake at the ceiling in the early morning hours, replayed in his mind.

But talking about this had never been easy. Even with the woman he loved.

"It's complicated, Kelsey."

His daughter gave an unladylike snort. "That's what you always say."

"It's true."

She swiveled toward him on the seat. "I'm not a kid anymore, you know. I can understand complicated issues. And I'm not naïve. I know bad stuff happens in the world. It's all over TV and the internet." She folded her arms, and he could feel the intensity of her gaze. "You act like what happened between you and your mom is a state secret. Besides, it's not like I'm going to Tweet it or text it or tell my friends. I know how to be discreet."

He couldn't argue with a thing she'd said.

So what *was* his reason for keeping the secret to himself at this point?

You know what it is, Williams. You don't want to lose face with your daughter by admitting you're less than perfect. This is more about your pride than her lack of maturity. Using her youth as an excuse doesn't cut it anymore.

Denise was right.

It was time to tell Kelsey his story.

After flicking a glance at the clock on the dash, he pulled into the next parking lot—for a furniture refinishing shop with a sign in the window that guaranteed to restore damaged heirlooms to a like-new state.

How ironic.

"What are you doing?" Kelsey scanned the lot, brow furrowed.

He angled into a spot, shut off the engine, and shifted toward her. It would be easier to watch the passing traffic while he told his story—but also cowardly. "We have a few minutes to spare before tennis practice. Long enough for me to tell you what happened between your grandmother and me. And if we need more time to talk, we can go out for a frappuccino. Missing one practice won't be the end of the world."

Her eyes widened. "Seriously?"

"Yes." He fumbled for the bottle of water he always kept in the car, took a long swig to lubricate his dry throat, then launched into the story.

Kelsey listened in silence instead of peppering him with questions in her usual style. Nor did she speak after he finished.

As the seconds ticked by, beads of sweat popped out on his forehead. Based on her expression, she was shocked . . . and disillusioned . . . and disappointed in him.

That hurt.

A lot.

But it was the reaction he'd expected—and the reason he'd held on to his secret for so long.

It was also what he deserved.

"Can I ask a question?" Kelsey played with a button on her sweater.

"Of course." He braced for her third degree. She wouldn't be satisfied with the halting, bare-bones confession that had skimmed over his sense of desolation and loneliness after his father died; his gratitude to the young woman who'd comforted him in his grief, and how that gratitude had led to inappropriate behavior; his panic when she'd shared the news about her pregnancy; her insistence on putting the baby up for adoption, and his ultimate capitulation; his confrontation with his unsympathetic mother; his decision to walk away from Hope Harbor and start a new life. Naturally Kelsey would want more details about . . . everything.

"Do I have a half sister or a half brother?"

"Brother."

"Do you know where he is?"

"No. It was a closed adoption. That's what my . . . his mother . . . wanted."

"Is there any chance we could ever connect?" Her face grew wistful. "I always wished I had a brother or sister."

"I doubt it."

Silence fell, and he braced for more questions.

But her next query wasn't what he expected.

"Why won't you open your mom's card?"

After everything he'd shared, she wanted to talk about the birthday card?

He frowned. "Don't you want to know more about what happened?"

She lifted one shoulder. "You explained it pretty well. I got the picture. I mean, it's kind of weird to find out I'm not your first kid . . . and I sort of wish there was a way to get in touch with my half brother . . . but most of the stuff you talked about happened way before I was born. The only bad thing left from those days is the split with your mom. Isn't that what's most important now?"

His daughter made it sound so simple.

And . . . maybe it was.

Maybe he needed to forget the past and focus on the present. Deal with today and go forward from here instead of looking back.

"I never thought of it like that—but yeah, I guess that's true."

"So if she sent you a card, she must feel bad about what happened too." Kelsey leaned closer and touched the fingers he'd clenched around the wheel. "This could be your chance to fix things, Dad. I mean, you go to church every Sunday. Shouldn't you follow what Pastor Bob always preaches about forgiveness and mercy and second chances and all that stuff? Like he said last week, you can't just listen to God's Word—you have to live it too."

Pressure built behind his eyes. When had his little girl grown up?

"You sound a lot like your mother."

"Does she think you should open the card too?"

"She hasn't said it as directly as you, but I'm guessing she does."

"So what are you going to do?"

"Think very hard about it."

Kelsey sighed. "Just do it, Dad. Don't overthink. That's what my coach always says about my serve —and you know what? It works." She checked the clock on the dash. "And speaking of tennis . . . I think we need to go."

"The offer of a frappuccino is still on the table if you want to talk some more."

"Can I take a rain check? I hate to miss practice."

"Sure." He started the engine—but as he put the car in gear, she touched his hand again.

"Thanks for telling me all that stuff. And just so you know, I love you more than ever."

John reached over and pulled her into a silent hug. No way could he manage to utter a single word.

They finished the drive to some tune Kelsey selected on the radio, but once he pulled into a parking spot next to the courts, she leaned over and gave him a quick peck. "Don't forget, I'm spending the night with Caitlin. Her mom will bring me home tomorrow morning."

"Got it."

She retrieved her overnight bag from the backseat, then grabbed her tennis gear off the floor of the front seat. "Open the card, okay?"

"I'm leaning that direction."

"Good." With a wave, she closed the door and jogged toward the courts.

Once she joined the group of students, he headed home—the conversation he'd been dreading since the day of Kelsey's birth at last behind him. And it hadn't been nearly as difficult to get through as he'd expected.

Might the same be true of the card his mother had sent?

John tapped a finger against the wheel. The only way to find out was to open it. If he didn't like what it said, he could toss it . . . or ignore it.

But as he rolled toward the house that was more home to him now than the small bungalow where he'd grown up, he had a feeling neither of those was going to be an option. That whatever the envelope contained was going to require some action on his part.

He could only pray that when the time came, he'd be up to the task.

23

Twenty-four hours with no Michael, and she was having withdrawal symptoms.

Expelling a breath, Tracy rose from her laptop, paced to the front of the cottage, and peered down the gravel drive, toward the dipping sun. As if wishing he'd appear at her door would make it happen.

How silly was that?

Combing her fingers through her hair, she returned to the table. She needed to finish this payroll report instead of wondering what was going on with a certain nonprofit executive from Chicago who'd left the farm unexpectedly yesterday afternoon and hadn't appeared at all today.

Hunker down and get the job done, Tracy. When Michael is ready to talk to you, he will. He sent you an email saying he'd be tied up most of the day; live with it.

Through sheer force of will, she managed to refocus on the project at hand . . . until a knock sounded on her door thirty minutes later.

Her fingers skittered on the keys, erasing a *couple of decimal points, and she forced herself to* fix them before responding to the summons.

It had to be Michael.

Who else could it be?

Bracing, she walked to the door and pulled it open.

It was him, all right. Dressed in those faded jeans that fit like they were designed for his lean hips and long legs, hair ruffled from the wind . . . and looking oh-so-appealing.

"Hi." His smile was warm.

A positive sign . . . right?

Or was he trying to soften the bad news he was about to deliver? Perhaps getting ready to tell her he'd made his decision and was going to return to Chicago.

"Hey." He touched her shoulder, faint grooves denting his brow. "You okay?"

"Yes." *Liar, liar.* "Come in." She stepped back and ushered him through the door.

He strolled past her, glancing at her glowing laptop on the kitchen table. "Were you in the middle of something?"

Yes. Thinking about you.

But she shook her head. "Nothing that can't wait. Just some number crunching." She motioned toward the couch. "Do you want to sit?"

"Yes." He grinned and grabbed her hand, tugging her along. "With you."

She let him lead her to the sofa but kept a discreet space between them after they sat.

Squinting, he studied her. "What's up?"

Go ahead and tell him what's on your mind, Tracy—but lead in slowly and be tactful about it.

"Are you leaving?"

Oh for crying out loud!

Could she have phrased the question with any *less* tact?

"Sorry." Warmth rose on her cheeks. "I didn't mean to be that blunt."

He lifted his hand and smoothed the furrows on her forehead with a gentle touch. "You've been worried."

"Yeah." No sense denying the obvious. "You seemed distracted at church yesterday, and you left the farm without much explanation. I had a feeling something big was up. That maybe you'd made your decision about whether to stay or go."

"I have."

Her breath hitched.

"I wanted to have all my ducks in a row before I said anything, but I see now I should have told you immediately. I'm staying."

She took a moment to let his words sink in. To savor the news.

Michael was moving to Hope Harbor.

Thank you, God!

"That's what I came to talk about tonight, in fact." He lifted a small attaché case she hadn't noticed till now, set it on the coffee table, and angled toward her. "It hasn't been an easy decision, but after a lot of prayer and soul-searching—plus a very bizarre experience on

Saturday night—I've decided Hope Harbor is where I belong."

She did her best to focus as he told her about his meeting with the local clerics; the email he'd written to the chairman of the board of St. Joseph Center and the phone calls they'd exchanged today; and the in-depth business plan he'd been working on for Harbor Point cranberry nut cake.

When he pulled the childish drawing out of his briefcase, she could only stare as he explained the history.

"That's . . . mind-blowing." She touched the edge of the yellowed paper. "Imagine Charley having this all these years."

"I know. Very strange. But it was the final push I needed to make my decision. I do have to go back to Chicago for a few weeks to close things down on the personal side and run the show at St. Joseph until they can find a replacement, but after that I'll be back here full time—working with Helping Hands and focusing on a special cranberry farm . . . and a very special cranberry farmer."

The tenderness in his tone—and his eyes—sent her heart soaring. This what she'd prayed for . . . yet he was giving up so much, making such a radical change. A niggle of worry dimmed her joy a few watts, and she forced herself to voice the concern she'd rather ignore.

"But what if things between us don't pan out? If

you leave Chicago, you'll be shutting the door on a whole way of life."

Based on his relaxed smile, he didn't share her apprehension. "I'm also opening the door to a lot of new possibilities. No matter what happens with us, I'm ready to find a new path. But you know what? I have a feeling things are going to work out fine here in every way. Wait till you see the plans I've been drawing up for the cake business. I've already sent out some media ticklers . . . and you won't believe all the places interested in hosting a tasting and carrying the product."

"You *have* been busy."

"Full speed ahead since yesterday afternoon. And things will get a lot busier. You and Anna and I need to meet this week and kick things into high gear. I'll stay involved long distance, and we can set up regular conference calls, but I'd like to be certain we have all our ducks in a row before I head east—including this one." He reached for her with a slow, intimate smile.

Adrenaline surging, she scooted closer, lifted her arms and—

Rap, rap, rap, rap, rap.

Groaning, she dropped her head.

"Let me guess. Floyd wants another handout."

"Yes. Talk about bad timing." She shot a disgruntled look toward the back door.

"We could ignore him."

Rap, rap, rap, rap, rap.

Michael chuckled. "Or not."

At least he was being a good sport about the interruption.

She rose and jogged into the kitchen, pulled some lunch scraps out of the fridge, and crossed to the back door. "He'll stop knocking if I feed him."

"You save stuff for him?"

"Not always." True . . . but barely. She kind of liked having Floyd around—most of the time. "Besides, he's a great garbage disposal. I never have to . . ." She flipped the lock on the back door and pulled it open. "Well, look at that. Floyd's found himself a new girlfriend."

Michael came up behind her to inspect the pair of gulls on her doorstep, his breath a delectable puff of warmth on her neck. "I thought you said they mated for life."

"They do." She set the food on the porch, then drew back as the two gulls dived in. "But after gulls finish grieving, they often find a new mate."

"Seems like there's a lesson to be learned there." Michael very deliberately shut the door and turned her to face him. "If Floyd can give love a second go, maybe we can too."

She put her arms around his neck. "I like the sound of that—but I still think the slow and easy plan is wise."

"Fine with me . . . as long as we keep moving forward."

She burrowed her fingers into the soft hair at the base of his neck and tried to keep the left side of her brain engaged. "You don't think we'll have any problems mixing business and pleasure, do you? I mean, you're putting money into this cranberry nut cake business. That makes us business partners."

"Oh, I think our partnership is going to be a whole lot more complex than that."

She raised an eyebrow.

"Down the road, of course." He slid his arms around her waist. "And my financial investment is small potatoes compared to the investment I plan to make on a much more important level. Starting now—unless you have any objections?"

Objections?

Was he kidding?

From within the circle of his arms, Tracy smiled up at him. "None at all. But don't we have cranberry business to discuss first?"

"The cranberries can wait. Because you, Tracy Campbell, are my top priority."

Without wasting any more words, he bent to claim her lips.

And as she gave thanks for this man who'd replaced the dark clouds in her world with an enduring sunshine no gray skies could ever chase away, Tracy did her best to make Hope Harbor's newest citizen feel very, very welcome.

• • •

"Could you use a cup of coffee?"

John shifted around in his seat as the patio door opened and Denise appeared on the threshold, hefting a mug.

"Yes. Thanks. It's cooling down out here."

She exited the house and joined him at the table, setting a basket and a pair of garden clippers on the ground beside her before handing him the steaming brew.

"Your roses are spectacular this year."

She surveyed the garden, one level down on the terraced property that led into the woods. "Yes, they are. It's such a joy to grow roses here after struggling with them in the Kansas heat while I was growing up."

"You ever miss your hometown?"

Her mouth curved up. "Home is more about being with the people you love than living in a certain place. When I think of home, two images come to mind—you beside me, and my parents in the Kansas farmhouse where I grew up." Her gaze flicked to the unopened card sitting in the middle of the table.

"I'm still thinking about it." She didn't need to ask her question for him to hear it. Not after sixteen years of marriage. "That's why I brought it out here." He took a sip of the coffee she'd doctored the way he liked it—a hint of sugar, a healthy splash of half-and-half, a couple shakes of vanilla powder.

Kind of like the way his mom had always known just how much brown sugar and milk to put in his oatmeal when he was a kid.

Denise leaned her head back to soak up the last rays of the setting sun. "It's peaceful here, isn't it?"

Usually.

"I'm not feeling it much at the moment."

She turned, the empathy in her expression warming him like the cups of hot chocolate his mom used to welcome him home from school with on rainy, blustery winter days.

"You know . . . putting it off won't make it any easier. Worry about the unknown is more stressful than dealing with facts."

"Thank you, Dr. Williams. Send me your bill in the morning." He tried for a teasing tone, but a sour note crept in.

Instead of taking offense, she leaned over and touched the back of the fist he'd rested on the table beside the card. "I work cheap—especially for people I love."

A surge of shame engulfed him. "I'm sorry. That didn't come out the way I intended. I do appreciate your input."

"And I appreciate your struggle. We all have our hot buttons. But here's the thing—you're in control no matter what's in that card. Your mother put the ball in your court, and my guess is she'll leave the next move to you. But you can't make that decision until you see what she has to say."

"Assuming I open the card."

"You will."

"How do you know?"

Winking, she stood and circled behind his chair to hug his neck. "Because I know you. You're not a man who backs away from the hard stuff. You might not open it tonight . . . but you will eventually. And in case you're interested in my professional opinion—if your mom is offering you the opportunity to heal the rift that's caused you a lot of pain for a lot of years, take it. Now I'm off to get a fresh bouquet for our table."

After picking up her basket and clippers, she started toward the stone steps that led to the terrace below.

John watched her descend toward the garden. His mom liked flowers too. Not roses so much, but the annual ones she grew along the edges of the fence. There had often been a vase of them on the kitchen table of his youth.

Denise and his mom would enjoy talking about gardening.

Slowly he shifted his focus to the beige envelope on the patio table. His wife was right. In the end, he'd open it. Why not save himself a lot of angst and do it now?

Pulse quickening, he took one more sip of coffee, set the mug down, and picked up the envelope.

It didn't weigh much more than the card itself. Nor was it bulked up, as if a long note had been tucked inside.

That would be like Mom. She never had been long-winded. More the don't-waste-words-and-get-to-the-point type.

The same type he was.

Only words that spilled out in anger had come easily—for both of them.

At least he'd conquered that curse in the past two decades. Learned to rein in his tongue until cooler thoughts prevailed. To be more like Dad.

Lord, how he missed that man, and his wise and gentle counsel. Even after twenty years.

Blinking to clear his vision, he slipped an unsteady finger under the flap of the envelope, pulled it open, and extracted a card.

The colorful impressionistic scene on the front of the card took him back to Hope Harbor in a heartbeat. The wharf pictured was very similar to the one that had been the playground of his childhood, flowering planters lining the edge, boats bobbing in the harbor, a bench in the foreground—like the one that used to be near Charley's.

He read the birthday greeting, tripping a little over the last two words. She still regarded him as a special son?

Hard to believe, after all the rancor and years of bitter estrangement.

Bracing himself, he opened the card.

The printed message was short and simple.

The day you were born, God blessed us with the greatest gift we ever received. May you be as happy in the years ahead as we were the day you first graced our lives.

Us. We. Our lives.

Interesting that she'd chosen a card meant to be from both father and mother.

Her handwritten note began on the opposite side, across from the printed message, and continued on the back.

Dear John,

No, I'm not at death's door.

I'm sure that was your first thought when you received this. What else could motivate your stubborn, self-righteous mother to get in touch after all these years?

As it turns out, a number of eye-opening things have happened recently that prompted me to reevaluate this long rift of ours—and to acknowledge how sorry I am it ever happened. If I could rewind the clock to that terrible day, I'd do and say things very differently. You needed understanding and empathy, not accusations and insults. I'm sorry I drove you away with my harsh judgment and even harsher words.

I chose this card because it expresses so

well what both your father and I always felt. What I still feel.

I know your hurt runs deep. I know your life has moved on, away from Hope Harbor. But age and experience bring perspective and some degree of wisdom—even for someone as old as me. I don't want to live the rest of my life with regrets. Perhaps you don't either. I know George would encourage us to mend our fences. That's what I want too—if you can find it in your heart to consider a reconciliation.

Whatever you decide, may your birthday be filled with love. I'm sending mine from here—as I always have.

Mom

A muscle in John's jaw twitched . . . and then he reread the words his mother had penned in a shaky hand. The writing was hers without question . . . but the contrite tone? Not her usual style—and certainly not the tone she'd used the day he'd walked out.

Apparently his mom had mellowed.

And she wanted him back in her life.

The words blurred, and he swiped his knuckles across his lashes. Never in a million years would he have expected Anna Williams to swallow her pride, admit her mistakes, and reach out to him.

Lifting his head, he found Denise sitting at the top of the stone steps, watching him.

"I didn't want to disturb you in the middle of that." She gestured toward the card.

"It packed quite a punch."

"I can tell."

"You want to read it?"

She rose, basket of roses in hand, and joined him. After setting the flowers on the table, she pulled a chair beside him, rested one hand on his knee, and took the card.

John watched her as she scanned the note, taking in every subtle nuance as the aroma of roses sweetened the air. The softening of her features, the slight quiver in her lips, the tremulous cadence of her breathing.

At last, eyes shimmering, she looked up. "It took a lot of courage to write this."

"Yeah."

She didn't press him about what he was going to do. That wasn't her way. She trusted him to take the high road and make the right choice.

And that choice was obvious. His mother was right. Age and experience did bring perspective . . . and a certain degree of wisdom. Not enough wisdom—or courage—on *his* part to take the leap his mother had by sending a note and initiating contact, but enough to recognize he'd been given a remarkable birthday gift.

He took the card from Denise, skimming the

words again as he spoke. "Do we have any set-in-stone plans for the Fourth of July weekend?"

"No. A picnic on the coast and fireworks in the evening, as usual."

"I'm thinking we might want to take a road trip." He tightened his grip on the card. "Hope Harbor is a seven, eight-hour drive. If we went down on the Fourth, I could pay my mom a visit on Saturday—and if that goes well, maybe the four of us could go to dinner."

Smiling, Denise leaned close and gave him a hug. "Sounds like a plan. And you know what? I have a feeling this is going to be the beginning of a whole new chapter in our lives."

He did too.

But as he held her in his arms, drawing strength from the love that had sustained him for more than sixteen years, he hoped his next chapter in Hope Harbor would be a lot happier than the last one.

24

"Since it's a holiday weekend—and I have a plane to catch—shall we wrap up this meeting?"

As he asked the question, Michael looked around Anna's patio table. Bud was eating his third piece of the cake Anna had baked from the high-volume recipe she'd been experimenting with in the high school kitchen. His landlady was inspecting a packaging comp from one of the three designers he'd contacted. Tracy was scrutinizing the legal profit-sharing agreement she'd insisted he and Anna sign in formal recognition of their investments.

"I'll second that." Bud polished off the cake. "Great job, Anna. Tastes just like the original—maybe better."

"It wasn't hard to adjust the recipe. I enjoyed tinkering with it."

"Bud's right. It's great." Michael gathered up the crumbs on his plate too.

"I appreciate the kind words—but I'll be interested to hear what your father has to say. He sounds like an expert on this sort of cake . . . from the consumer standpoint."

Michael nodded. "He is. And I saved the best news for last. He called me this morning to say the sample cake I sent arrived yesterday and it's already half gone. He wants to know when he can place an order. I think those monks he patronizes are about to get some serious competition."

"He really liked it?" Tracy shifted her attention from the legal documents to him.

"*Like* is too mild a word. To quote him, he's been devouring it." Michael flashed her a grin. "As far as I can see, we're good to go here. Bud, you're certain Nancy has enough frozen cranberries to get us through our public tasting sessions before this season's crop comes in?"

"She took an inventory last night. No problem. We've got a whole freezer full of them in the basement. I have no idea why she saved so many last season—but I'm glad she did."

"Okay." Michael picked up the package design they all liked best. "I'll notify this firm to proceed with bids for production."

Tracy combed her fingers through her hair, looking more than a little overwhelmed. "Now we just have a few small details to attend to . . . like selling and marketing and shipping and publicity and—"

"Hey." Michael laid his hand over hers. "We'll get there. We have a lot of brainpower behind this venture—and a boatload of enthusiasm. Remember, we all agreed this is a trial run. If we break even and get a positive response this season, we'll ramp up next year. Broaden the distribution, increase production, do some real advertising. Right?"

She let out a slow breath and managed a smile. "Right."

After a squeeze, he released her fingers. "I need to run, but I'll be in regular touch until I can wrap things up in Chicago and get back here. Anna, thanks for the samples and the great coffee."

"My pleasure." She lifted her left arm and wiggled her fingers. "All that stirring and mixing were more helpful than the exercises the physical therapist gave me. If I never see another sling again it will be too soon."

"Don't overdo it, though. We couldn't manage this without you." Tracy touched the woman's arm.

Anna patted her hand. "Don't you worry about me. I'm in for the duration. And don't worry about anything else, either. I have good feelings about this project. We're going to make this a grand success."

As the woman's eyes sparkled with excitement, Michael examined her animated face. What a change from his early days here, when dour and reclusive had better described his landlady.

"With all this positive energy buzzing around, I'm getting hungry again." Bud stood. "Think I'll mosey on home and see what Nancy's got in mind for lunch."

"It's only nine o'clock." Tracy arched an eyebrow.

"I'm playing catch-up from the weight I lost while I had the flu. You coming out to the farm later?"

"If I get back from the airport early enough."

"Don't rush on my account. With the extra help we've had these past few weeks, for once we're caught up." Bud held out his hand, and Michael stood to take it. "Thank you for everything, Michael—and come home soon."

Home.

What a beautiful . . . and apt . . . description.

Because while he might have come to Hope Harbor seeking answers, he'd also found home.

As Bud disappeared around the side of the house toward his car, Tracy rose and began to clear the table.

"Don't you bother with that. Now that I've ditched my sling, I'll have this cleaned up in a jiffy." Anna rose and waved her off. "You need to get Michael to the airport." She rubbed her palms down the fabric covering her hips and held out her hand to him. "We'll miss you."

He shook his head. "After all these weeks, I think we can do better than that." Stepping close, he pulled the older woman into a hearty hug.

When he released her, her hand fluttered to her chest. "My. Hugs from Grace and her mother and Joyce and you . . . I've been hugged more in the past few weeks than I have been in years."

"Can I give you one too?" Tracy circled the table. "If you and Michael weren't funding this project, our farm would be history. I'll be forever grateful."

"It's a pleasure, my dear. Having a project like this to work on has given new meaning to my days." Anna gave Tracy a squeeze and patted her back. "Now you two get a move on. Planes don't wait for latecomers."

Michael grabbed her hand. "That's our cue. Talk to you soon, Anna."

"Safe travels."

Tracy glanced at her watch as they crossed to the annex. "You're cutting this close, you know. It's a three-hour drive to Eugene."

"We'll make it. My luggage is already stowed in the trunk."

"We could take my car, if you'd rather."

And have her spend hard-earned money on gas? No way. Her finances were far too tight—but they wouldn't be for long if this project took off the way he expected.

"I'm already set." He pulled open the passenger door, waited while she slid in, and circled around to take his place behind the wheel. "You know, I could leave my car in long-term parking and save you the solitary drive back. You must be tired after all the Fourth of July festivities yesterday."

"I'm not a bit tired—and we've been through this already. Given all the weekend commuting I did during college, I could navigate this route in my sleep. Besides, it gives us three more hours together."

"Sold." He started the engine and pulled out of the driveway. "By the way, I enjoyed the fireworks last night."

Giving him a flirty smile, she wiggled her eyebrows. "Which ones?"

He tried to keep a straight face as he responded. "The ones that formed geometric shapes were pretty spectacular."

"Very funny." She gave him a playful jab on the shoulder.

"Actually . . . I think my favorite was . . ." He slowed to peer at the driver of the SUV that passed them.

"What's wrong?" Tracy checked the rearview mirror as the other vehicle receded.

"I think . . . I'm almost certain that was Anna's son."

"You're kidding!" Tracy twisted around, trying to keep the SUV in sight.

"I only got a quick glimpse, but he sure looked like an older version of the picture in her den—and a lot like me."

"Wow." Tracy settled back into her seat. "Wouldn't it be amazing if the two of them got back together?"

"Yeah. But you know what?" He smiled at the woman who was transforming his world, tugging her close for a stolen kiss while keeping one eye on the road. "I have a feeling that in Hope Harbor, anything is possible."

Anna stacked the plates in the sink, covered the one remaining piece of cranberry nut cake with plastic wrap, and finished off her cup of coffee.

How different—and better—today had been than her typical quiet Saturday morning with just her critters for company.

She surveyed the empty space at the far end of

the kitchen. All the cages and boxes had been stowed in the basement, with Michael's help. Not that she'd turn a blind eye to a creature in need if their paths happened to cross, but she wasn't going to seek them out anymore. She had too many other items on her agenda. Like a business to help launch—and a future filled with purpose instead of one where she simply marked the passage of days.

Only one thing was missing from her life now.

At the sudden downturn in her spirits, she clamped her jaw and shoved the stopper in the sink. After all the blessings God had showered on her these past weeks, she should be grateful instead of laboring over the one thing that hadn't gone her way. Expecting a simple birthday card to change John's heart overnight was foolish. Perhaps someday he might reconsider, but for now she'd have to leave it in the Lord's hands.

Squaring her shoulders, she turned on the tap and squirted some detergent into the sink. This was not a time to dwell on the past. There were plans to make for the new business and grocery shopping to do for her clergy clients and church to attend tomorrow . . .

The doorbell pealed, and she wiped her hands on the dish towel, a trill of anticipation zinging through her. Another recent—and positive— change. Not long ago, a caller would have rattled

—and annoyed—her. The few people who'd come to her door over the past two decades had been strangers soliciting donations for an organization she didn't support or proselytizing for a religion she didn't believe in or selling a product she didn't need.

Now?

Well, it could be someone from church or one of the neighbors or Joyce stopping by to see if she wanted to take a drive to Sweet Dreams for a Saturday cinnamon roll splurge, like they used to do.

And she just might indulge.

It was time to start living again.

Dish towel in hand, she hurried toward the front door, pulled it open—and froze.

For the tiniest instant, she thought Michael had come back. But in less than the millisecond that often marked the difference between Olympic medalists and those whose dreams had died, she realized it wasn't her tenant.

And once her visitor spoke, the timbre of his voice so long absent from this house—plus his greeting—confirmed his identity.

"Hi, Mom."

She lifted a hand to her chest.

Tried to speak.

Failed.

John shifted his weight from one foot to the other. "I considered calling ahead . . . but in the end I decided not to. I guess I should have. I didn't mean to shock you."

Shock?

That didn't begin to describe the kaleidoscope of emotions swirling through her.

She swallowed. Reached out a shaky hand. "John." His name came out a mere whisper.

He took it, his touch warming her cold fingers.

Once more she tried to find her voice. "Come in." Giving him a gentle tug, she backed into the house.

He followed—crossing the threshold he'd stormed out of more than nineteen long years ago.

When she made no move to shut the front door, he took the initiative. "I got your card. It . . . surprised me." As the lock clicked, he turned to her.

She squeezed the towel in her fingers. "Some . . . interesting . . . things happened this summer. They helped me realize I-I didn't want to spend the rest of my life with regrets."

"Your card did the same for me. That, and some nudges from my wife and daughter. I appreciate how hard it must have been for you to . . ." He stopped. Cocked his ear. "Is water running some-where?"

The sink!

With a startled exclamation, Anna hurried toward the kitchen. The basin was on the verge of overflowing, but she twisted off the tap in the nick of time.

"Close call—and my fault . . . again."

She swiveled toward him, gripping the edge of the counter behind her as the clock wound back several decades. "I'm surprised you remember that. You were only five."

"It's kind of hard to forget getting your head stuck behind the couch."

"Yes . . . I imagine it is." She set the towel on the counter, letting all the old, sweet memories swirl back. "You were always a curious child, wanting to see what was in every closet, behind every piece of furniture, and up every tree. You fell out of the apple tree in the backyard so often your father was on the verge of cutting it down. We were worried sick you were going to break your neck."

"Lucky thing I wasn't a cat, or I'd have used up my nine lives before I was ten."

A rush of pleasure swept over her. Despite all the curves life had surely thrown him, he'd retained his dry sense of humor.

He propped his shoulder against the wall. "As I recall from the day of the sofa incident, you and Dad were so busy trying to extricate me without crushing my skull you both forgot about the water running in the sink."

"Yes. I remember the lake on the kitchen floor."

"And I remember sitting on the infamous blue

detention chair for what felt like a lifetime."

"I still have that chair."

He grimaced. "I can't say I'm happy to hear that." He studied the empty space in the eating area and shoved his hands into his pockets. "But the table's gone."

"It was too big—and lonely." She motioned toward the living room. "Would you like to sit down?"

"Yeah. I would."

She followed as he led the way, drinking in every detail of his appearance. He'd filled out over the years, lost the skinniness of youth, but he was trim in his knife-creased khaki slacks and a knit sport shirt that drew attention to his broad shoulders. The crinkles around his eyes and faint grooves at the corners of his mouth were new, as were the sprinkles of silver in his dark brown hair . . . but oh my, he looked wonderful!

He came to an abrupt halt in the doorway to the living room. "You still have the piano."

"Yes."

After a moment, he walked over to it and ran his fingers lightly across the keys. "It's in tune."

"Always."

He turned back to her, his expression curious.

"It was a part of you I couldn't give up. Keeping it in tune . . ." She shrugged and twisted her hands together. "I know it sounds weird—and I often told myself it was a waste of money—but somehow keeping it ready to play gave me hope."

He didn't comment on that. Instead, he walked a circle around the blue chair and claimed the understated recliner George had always favored.

Once seated, he ran his hands over the arms. "This may sound weird too, but sitting here . . . I almost feel like Dad is with us."

"I feel the same. That's why I kept it."

She perched on the edge of the couch, as close to him as possible. Close enough to grab him if he tried to walk away. She was never, ever letting that happen again. "I'm glad you came, John. I was . . . I was afraid you'd throw my card away."

He met her gaze. "To be honest, I thought about it. But in the end, I couldn't. Because even though I went on with my life, even though I have a wonderful wife and daughter and a great career, there was always something missing. I could never put my finger on what it was . . . or maybe I didn't want to dig too deep. But after your card came, I had to admit the truth. The missing piece was you."

The cold, dark spot deep in her heart—the place that had always belonged only to John—was suddenly suffused with warmth and light.

Pressure built behind Anna's eyes, and she blinked to clear her vision. "That's how I felt. I said it in the card, but I'll say it again to your face. I'm sorry for how I acted the day you told me your news. I should have listened to what you had to say with love and empathy. I should have been understanding and compassionate. And I'm sorry I left you to deal with that traumatic situation on your own. I can't begin to imagine how difficult that was."

His Adam's apple bobbed. "There was fault on both sides. I said some terrible things that day too. Things that can still make me cringe. I didn't think you'd ever be able to forgive me."

"I couldn't. Not for a long while. But time has a way of softening harsh memories. And there were extenuating circumstances. Each of us was grieving and distraught, trying to come to grips with your father's death in our own way—and our short fuses were shorter than usual."

"Still—I deserved a lot of the things you said. What I did was wrong. You and Dad raised me to be better than that, to hold to higher moral standards. I felt guilty and ashamed. I knew you'd be disappointed in me . . . as you had every right to be. I guess I was hoping you'd understand—but I should have cut you some slack. Reined in my own temper."

Anna sighed. "Should haves won't change the past for either of us—but I do understand now how people can make bad mistakes, especially if they're distraught. The good Lord knows I've made plenty of my own."

He leaned forward and clasped his hands, resting his forearms on his thighs. "I'd like to start fresh, if we can. Clear the air between us. Bring you up to speed on my life and hear about yours."

She waved a hand in dismissal. "The story of my life since you left could fit on one page. I shut down, became the town recluse. All I did was go to work and tend to this house. That changed this summer, however . . . for a lot of reasons."

"Will you tell me about them?"

"Yes. But we don't have to catch up all in one day."

"We can cover a lot of ground, though. I'd like to tell you about what happened after I left that day—then introduce you to my wife and daughter. They're chomping at the bit to meet you."

"Are they here?" Her lungs locked.

"We're staying at a hotel in Coos Bay. We'll be driving back to Seattle tomorrow. That's where I live."

"I know." She smoothed out a crease in her slacks. "Google is . . . it's a wonderful thing."

His eyebrows rose. "You kept up with me?"

"As much as I could. There was never a lot on the internet." She swallowed. "I have to admit, I've often wondered what happened to the girl and that baby—my first grandchild." Her voice caught, and she clasped her hands in her lap.

For the next half hour, she listened as he told her how the girl had wanted to arrange a closed adoption for the baby . . . how he'd initially argued against that in case the child someday wanted to locate his or her birth parents . . . and how he'd yielded to her wishes in the end. He talked of the jobs he got on nights and weekends to pay expenses not covered by his scholarship; about finishing at the top of his engineering class and receiving multiple job offers; of launching a successful career and meeting the woman who became his wife.

As he spoke, Anna's heart swelled with pride. Despite his mistakes and setbacks, despite her rejection, despite his struggle to survive on his own, her son had taken responsibility for his actions and become a fine man with a capacity for kindness big enough to forgive his mother's terrible mistakes.

"You did well, John. I'm proud of the man you've become."

"Well, I've paid a lot of tuition in the school of experience, that's for sure. Now tell me about your life here—and the events that persuaded you to contact me."

"How long do you have?"

"My time is yours—until tonight, when I'd like to introduce you to Denise and Kelsey and take you all to dinner."

Joy bubbled up inside her. Could there be any nicer way to spend a Saturday?

They talked for hours . . . through several pots of coffee, through a thrown-together lunch of soup and sandwiches on the patio, into the midafternoon, until finally he stood to collect his wife and daughter from their day exploring Hope Harbor and to get ready for dinner.

Anna followed him back into the house, through the den, past the living room—where he paused.

"I wonder how many hours I spent on that piano bench?"

"Quite a lot—and on occasion under duress if your buddies were playing baseball. Do you still play?"

"Yes. In fact, I fill in at church whenever our music director has a conflict."

Her spirits soared at that news. "I'm glad. You had an amazing talent."

"But you and Dad were smart to steer me to a more stable career. The unpredictable life of a musician wouldn't have suited me." He looked from the piano to her. "Would you like me to play a piece before I leave?"

Oh, sweet mercy! Could this day get any better?

"I'd love it."

He crossed the room and slid onto the bench, once more running his fingers over keys that had been silent too long. Then he launched into the opening strains of "Amazing Grace."

As the beautiful melody filled the house . . . and her heart . . . with music and hope, Anna closed her eyes and let the words of the hymn scroll through her mind.

I once was lost but now am found, was blind, but now I see.

How appropriate that her son had chosen this song. For despite the many dangers, toils, and snares they'd both faced, God had indeed led them home.

And as she watched him play, back at this piano where he belonged, Anna gave thanks for the unexpected blessings of this amazing summer.

Epilogue

Five Months Later

"From Hope Harbor, the home of Harbor Point Cranberry Nut Cake, I'm Lisa Nesbitt with this week's edition of *Made in Oregon*."

As the TV personality from Portland lowered her mike and instructed the cameraman to get a final close-up of one of the cakes, Michael smiled. The national-network-affiliate program had statewide viewership—and potential coast-to-coast pickup from sister stations.

He leaned a shoulder against the wall of the high school kitchen where they'd filmed the last scene of the in-depth interview. Cranberry nut cake sales might already be solid, but this kind of exposure was worth its weight in gold.

Tracy and Anna shook the reporter's hand, and he gave them a thumbs-up as they walked over to join him. "You two did great."

Anna dismissed his praise with a flip of her hand. "Tracy's the one with the stage presence and silver tongue. But I have to admit it was epic—as Kelsey would say—to be in the spotlight for a few minutes. I felt like a real celebrity. Wait till I tell her about this!"

"It *was* a lot of fun, wasn't it?" Tracy's eyes were dancing with the same enthusiasm and excitement she'd radiated in every interview and tasting gig she'd done over the past four months. "But I don't know if they get this program in Seattle."

"That's okay. I'll record a copy of it for them and we'll have a private showing when I go up for Christmas." Anna slipped off the pristine Harbor Point Cranberry Nut Cake apron she saved for photos and retrieved the flour-dusted version from a nearby counter. "Now it's back to baking for me. We have lots of orders to fill in the next two weeks."

As she hustled away to supervise the part-time crew they'd hired to help during the crunch, the reporter said her good-byes and exited the building, the cameraman on her heels.

"You really did do a great job." Michael touched Tracy's shoulder, redirecting her attention to him.

"Thank you." She covered his hand with her own, her features softening, then scanned the bustling operation that had occupied the cafeteria kitchen every weekend since harvest began—and during the frequent late-night baking sessions they'd scheduled during the week. "It's hard to believe how this thing has taken off."

"Thanks in large part to you. You've done a terrific job telling your story to the public and the media. You win new cranberry nut cake fans with every appearance—as the backlog of orders proves."

"It's easy to be enthusiastic about a product you believe in—and when the fate of your family farm hangs in the balance."

"I don't think it's hanging anymore."

"No." If she glowed any brighter, they could turn off the lights in the kitchen. "I brought the books up to date last night. Despite the start-up expenses, we're going to generate enough profit this year to keep us in the black and also let you and Anna recoup a significant part of your investment."

"And next year will be even better."

"Seems that way." She shook her head. "I still can't believe people are paying twenty-five dollars a pop for these cakes."

"I told you they would—as long as we positioned them as a high-quality, high-end treat. That 'handcrafted in small batches . . . from our home to yours' tagline you came up with is a winner."

"But you're the one who got the word out with your great sales and marketing skills. You deserve a huge chunk of the credit for our success—and also for the success of Helping Hands. I reviewed those numbers last night too. There's sufficient donor and grant money coming in now to not only fund the program but pay a part-time director."

"Things have gone well."

"Better than well." She twined her fingers with his. "It's about time you got some compensation for all the hours you've put into building our humble little let's-help-our-neighbors program into an organized effort that will benefit hundreds of people. Maybe thousands."

He gave her hand a squeeze. Helping Hands was on his list of topics to discuss with her today—but it wasn't the most important one. Nor was this the place for that conversation.

"Can you get away for a quick lunch?"

"Yes. Anna has everything under control here. That woman is a dynamo—and she has amazing organizational skills. Besides, I need to swing by the cottage and change. This outfit might look nice on camera"—she swept a hand over the gray slacks that hugged her trim hips and the soft wool sweater that matched her green irises—"but jeans are much better for real work. Give me a sec while I tell her I'm cutting out."

Michael waited as the two women held a quick conference. Anna glanced his way during the exchange, her eyes twinkling, then waved Tracy toward the door. He couldn't hear their conversation, but whatever the older woman said brought a becoming flush to Tracy's cheeks.

Sixty seconds later, she'd ditched her apron, grabbed her jacket, and joined him. He held it while she slipped her arms inside.

"Where do you want to get lunch?" She zipped up the front.

Taking her arm, he guided her toward the door. "Why don't we see if Charley's is open today?"

She examined the blue sky as they walked toward his car. "He might be. It must be close to sixty."

"Yeah. I'll take this over a Chicago December any day."

"I'm glad you like it here, Michael."

At her soft, earnest comment, he pulled her close for a reassuring squeeze, then opened the car door. "I don't just like it. I love it. In fact, I . . ."

No.

He needed to save those words until the right moment—and the right place.

And the high school parking lot wasn't it.

He kept the conversation light during the short drive, slipping into a parking spot a few doors down from Sweet Dreams.

Tracy hopped out before he could get her door, grinning at him across the roof. "This is about where we met, you know."

"Not the best beginning."

"But the ending was happy."

And it was about to get happier.

He hoped.

"True. Now let's get those tacos. Any minute now, Charley could decide to shut down and go play artist for the rest of the day." Grabbing her hand, he tugged her across the street and gave her a nudge toward the bench where he'd met Anna. "Why don't you claim that for us while I place the order?"

She surveyed the deserted wharf. "I don't think we have to worry about beating off a crowd."

"You never know. There could be a sudden rush."

"Ya think?" She gave him her teasing smile. The one that lit up her face and never failed to inspire a soul-deep gratitude for the gift he'd received the day she'd cycled into his life. "Of course, Charley does have a legion of fans. A hungry horde could show up at any minute. No worries—I'll throw myself across the bench and fend off any inter-lopers while you go get our food."

He watched as she moved down the sidewalk with her characteristic lithe grace, head held high, focus trained on the distant horizon. She was a beautiful woman—inside and out. Despite all the sorrow and challenges that had been her lot, her smile was ready, her heart warm, her foundation of faith and values solid.

She was the kind of woman any man would treasure as a partner for life.

And if he was lucky, that was exactly the role she would play in his.

Very, very soon.

Tracy claimed the bench Michael had asked her to secure, then checked out the taco stand. No one else was in line on this December Saturday, despite the pleasant weather. Their food would be up fast.

And that was fine. With the orders for cranberry nut cake pouring in, she'd been running at warp speed and burning up calories for weeks. At this rate, they'd be busy up to the last shipping date before Christmas.

Thanks, in large part, to Michael.

She watched him as he spoke with Charley. She might have discovered a latent talent for PR, but he was phenomenal at business. He'd made contacts, lined up publicity, tracked down suppliers and negotiated favorable terms, over-seen the development of an amazing website—the list was endless.

Not to mention the fact that the original idea was his too.

The conversation between the two men was

410

too quiet to hear from this far away, but both appeared relaxed and happy. Especially Michael.

What a change from the tense, troubled man who'd sent her bicycle—and her life—veering off course almost seven months ago.

But she loved her new direction . . . and the man who'd steered her toward it.

Resting one arm along the back of the bench, she savored her new, soul-deep contentment that was as constant and dependable as the tide. Day by day, with his kindness and compassion and strength and intelligence and humor and tenderness and so many other things, Michael had buoyed her spirits and filled her heart with love and hope.

And one of these days—soon, she hoped—perhaps he'd realize it was time to move past the slow and cautious course they'd plotted and take a leap of faith.

He turned toward her, as if sensing her perusal, and she lifted her hand.

Instead of waiting for their order, he picked up the two bottles of water Charley had set on the counter and joined her.

"Charley said he'd bring the order over when it's ready. Slow day, apparently."

She scooted closer to him as he sat. "A little on the cool side too. Mind if I steal some of your body heat?"

"Is that a come-on, Ms. Campbell?" He handed

her a bottle of water, draped his arm over her shoulders, and drew her close.

"Maybe." She snuggled into him, resting her cheek against his shoulder. "Too bad we don't have a little more privacy."

Chuckling, he uncapped his bottle and took a swig. "Hold that thought for later. In the meantime . . . I met with Father Kevin and Reverend Baker this morning."

She watched a fishing boat cross the harbor toward the wharf, gulls circling in its wake. "Some new crisis with Helping Hands?" With the organization in his capable hands, no need to worry like she used to.

"I wouldn't call it a crisis. More like a change."

Some nuance in his inflection put her on alert, and she straightened up to look at him. "What kind of change?"

"Making me permanent part-time instead of temporary part-time. After running the show for the past few months, I think the job can be done on that basis indefinitely—which will leave me plenty of time to work on farm business. What do you think?"

"I think it's great! I bet they did too."

One side of his mouth slanted up. "Father Kevin said he felt as if a yoke had been lifted from around his neck . . . and Reverend Baker promptly told him their yoke might be easier, but getting rid of it wasn't an option. They were still debating a verse from Matthew when they left to play golf."

She snickered. "That sounds like them."

"Two orders of fish tacos coming up." Charley stopped beside them, a brown bag in each hand.

"We could have come over for these." Tracy inhaled the savory aroma as the man handed her a bag.

"Not a problem. It's been quiet today—so far." Charley winked and strolled back toward the taco stand.

Tracy watched him over her shoulder. "What was that all about? And why did he give us separate bags?"

Michael shrugged. "Charley marches to the beat of his own drummer. Dig in."

She didn't need any prodding. Not with the appetizing aroma activating her salivary glands.

Letting Michael carry the bulk of the conversation, Tracy focused on her food, mumbling brief answers when necessary while she chewed. Only after she dug to the bottom of the bag to pull out her third taco did she come up for air—and discover he was still on his first.

"Aren't you hungry?" She gestured to his bag as she started to peel back the paper.

"I had a big breakfast."

"That's never stopped you in the past. You usually beat me to the finish."

"I'll get there. Go ahead, eat up. You don't want

that to get cold." He motioned toward her half-unwrapped taco.

She studied him. Some . . . odd . . . vibes were wafting her way. "You okay?"

"Yeah." He picked up his taco and took a big bite as if to prove it.

Hmm.

What wasn't he telling her?

She finished unwrapping her taco, folded back the white paper . . . and froze.

A diamond solitaire in a gold band, encased in plastic wrap, sparkled at her from the top of her taco.

"Remember when I said a few months back that I thought our partnership was going to go way beyond business?"

At the husky question, she lifted her chin and searched Michael's blue eyes. "Yes." Her response came out in a croak.

"I'd like to make that official. So I had Charley add some extra spice to your order."

She glanced over Michael's shoulder to find the taco man watching them, elbows propped on the counter, smile splitting his face. He gave her a thumbs-up.

"I figured since everything that's happened in Hope Harbor began on this bench, it was a fitting place to propose."

Tracy jerked her focus back to the man beside her.

Apparently he was as anxious as she was to leave slow and cautious behind.

Hallelujah!

Heart soaring, she unwrapped the ring with shaking fingers. "Yes."

A couple of beats of silence ticked by.

"You're making this too easy."

Her fingers stilled, and she caught her lower lip between her teeth. "Oh. I bet you had a speech prepared."

A teasing light glinted in his eyes. "That . . . plus some backup arguments and action plans in case you balked."

"Yeah?" She fingered the ring. The sun caught the facets and sent off sparks that put last summer's Fourth of July fireworks to shame. "What kind of action plans?"

"Very persuasive ones. But I guess I don't have to use them." He plucked the ring from her. "Shall I slip it on?"

She shoved her hands under her thighs. "Uh-uh. I want you to give me your speech and tell me more about those action plans."

Closing his fingers around the ring, he set his food aside and took her hand, all humor vanishing from his demeanor. "Should I get down on one knee?"

He was serious.

Her throat tightened, and she shook her head. "No. Side by side is fine for proposing—and for life."

"I like how you think, Tracy Campbell." He stroked the back of her hand with his thumb. "The truth is, I like everything about you. Your warmth and kindness and sense of humor and courage and strength and faith and so much more. All the qualities that led me to this moment. To knowing I want to spend the rest of my life beside you, making you my priority, giving you all the love that's in my heart." His last word rasped, and he paused.

She wasn't feeling any too steady herself.

"I had no idea what I would find in Hope Harbor after I made that long trek west." Michael locked gazes with her. "All I knew was that my soul was parched. Dying. Then I met you . . . and everything changed. You refreshed my life. And for as long as I live, I'll give thanks every single day for the gifts of love and healing God had waiting for me here. So even though you've already given me your answer, I'll make the proposal official. Will you marry me and let me spend the rest of my life filling yours with joy and love?"

Her vision misted, and she groped for the fingers he'd clenched around the ring. Peeled them back. Held out her left hand. "Yes—because God blessed me too the day you sent me tumbling into the street. At the time, I thought it was an accident. Now I realize it was a blessing in disguise."

He slid the ring onto her finger, leaned close, and—

Squawk, squawk, squawk, squawk.

At the rude interruption, Tracy peeked to her left. Two seagulls stood on the rocks leading down to the water.

One of them was very familiar.

"Don't tell me . . . Floyd is stalking you." Michael kept his forehead pressed against hers.

"With his girlfriend in tow. I can't believe . . ."

"Floyd! Get over here!" Charley called out the command in a stern tone she'd never heard him use. "And bring Gladys."

"Gladys?" Mirth threaded through Michael's voice.

"Don't ask me. Floyd never introduced us." She sighed. "It's nice of Charley to try, but seagulls don't . . ."

She stopped speaking as the two birds flapped into the air and coasted over to the taco stand, where Charley tossed them a few scraps.

Michael turned to watch the scene too. "That man has a magic touch with everything. But how does he know Floyd's name?"

"I guess I must have mentioned it to him once." Not that she recalled—but what other explanation could there be? "Besides, who cares? The important thing is they're out of our hair."

"Right." He scooted closer. "Where were we?"

"I think you were about to implement an action plan." She put her arms around his neck.

"How are you with public displays of affection?"

She did a quick sweep of the waterfront. "Floyd and Gladys and Charley are the only ones around. The birds are busy eating—and not much gets past Charley, anyway."

"Good point." He pulled her close. "But first . . . any thoughts on a wedding date?"

"Soon. During the slower season on the farm. I want to have lots of time to devote to us."

"An excellent strategy. As for the slow season . . ." He gave her a roguish grin. "I think this year's might be a bit livelier than usual. Ready for a preview?"

A tingle of excitement zipped through her. "More than."

They leaned toward each other, meeting halfway. And in the moment before their lips met, in the instant before she lost herself in his kiss, gratitude overflowed in her heart.

For while Michael might have been the one who'd set out on a cross-country trek seeking answers, she too had finished a journey. She too had found a new beginning. She too had come home.

Right here in Hope Harbor.

Author's Note

Welcome to Hope Harbor, a charming fictional town on the spectacular Oregon coast.

For many years, I've wanted to set a book . . . or two . . . or more in this beautiful part of the country. So in the fall of 2013, I booked a flight, sought out some charming B&Bs, and set off to explore. I was convinced this scenic area would provide the perfect locale for the town I'd already named Hope Harbor.

I'm happy to report that the trip exceeded all my expectations. In Florence, I found charming storefronts and to-die-for cinnamon rolls. In Bandon, I learned about seagull romance. In Cape Perpetua, I got up close and personal with amazing starfish. In Brookings, I watched the sun set in a secluded cove with a silver-white harbor seal for company. And everywhere I went, I savored the endless sandy beaches and sea stacks.

When I got home, I took all those bits and pieces of real-life coastal Oregon and created Hope Harbor. I hope you enjoy visiting this delightful town as much as I enjoyed writing about it.

As always, many people played a role in the creation of this book. My special thanks to:

Oregon cranberry grower Daryl Robison

(owner of family-farm Pacific Bogs for many years), who helped me fine-tune all the details about my fictional Harbor Point Cranberries operation. Thank you, Daryl, for answering my numerous questions so thoroughly and promptly.

The amazing team at Revell. In this crazy world called publishing, I couldn't ask for a better partner.

All the readers who make it possible for me to bring to life the characters who ask me to tell their stories. I give thanks for you every day.

My parents, James and Dorothy Hannon, who have always been—and continue to be—an enthusiastic cheering section.

And finally, my husband Tom. Thank you for your encouragement and understanding—and for all you do to create an environment that allows me to meet my page count day after day.

About the Author

Irene Hannon is a bestselling, award-winning author who took the publishing world by storm at the tender age of ten with a sparkling piece of fiction that received national attention.

Okay . . . maybe that's a slight exaggeration. But she *was* one of the honorees in a complete-the-story contest conducted by a national children's magazine. And she likes to think of that as her "official" fiction-writing debut!

Since then, she has written more than forty-five contemporary romance and romantic suspense novels. Irene has twice won the RITA award—the "Oscar" of romantic fiction—from Romance Writers of America, and her books have also been honored with a National Readers' Choice award, three HOLT medallions, a Daphne du Maurier award, a Retailers' Choice award, a Booksellers' Best award, and two Reviewers' Choice awards from *RT Book Reviews* magazine. In addition, she is a two-time Christy award finalist.

Irene, who holds a BA in psychology and an MA in journalism, juggled two careers for many years until she gave up her executive corporate communications position with a Fortune 500 company to write full-time. She is happy to say she has no regrets! As she points out, leaving behind the rush-hour commute, corporate politics, and a relentless BlackBerry that never slept was no sacrifice.

A trained vocalist, Irene has sung the leading role in numerous community theater productions and is also a soloist at her church.

When not otherwise occupied, she and her husband enjoy traveling, Saturday mornings at their favorite coffee shop, and spending time with family. They make their home in Missouri.

To learn more about Irene and her books, visit www.irenehannon.com. She is also active on Facebook and Twitter.

Center Point Large Print
600 Brooks Road / PO Box 1
Thorndike, ME 04986-0001 USA

(207) 568-3717

US & Canada:
1 800 929-9108
www.centerpointlargeprint.com